So you thought airlines were dynamic multi-million pound concerns . . . you thought pilots were randy handlers of knobs and levers . . . you thought air stewardesses were happy to oblige. . . . You were DEAD RIGHT!

There's no in-flight tedium with Glamour Airlines. It's up, up and away the sexiest way to fly . . .

Also by Stanley Morgan
in Mayflower Books

THE SEWING MACHINE MAN
THE DEBT COLLECTOR
THE COURIER
COME AGAIN COURIER
TOBIN TAKES OFF
TOBIN ON SAFARI
TOBIN IN PARADISE
TOBIN IN TROUBLE
TOBIN FOR HIRE

MISSION TO KATUMA
OCTOPUS HILL

The Fly Boys

Stanley Morgan

Mayflower

Granada Publishing Limited
Published in 1975 by Mayflower Books Ltd
Frogmore, St Albans, Herts AL2 2NF

First published in Great Britain by
Hart-Davis, MacGibbon Ltd 1974
Copyright © Stanley Morgan 1974
Made and printed in Great Britain by
Richard Clay (The Chaucer Press) Ltd
Bungay, Suffolk
Set in Linotype Plantin

For Linda

With love and deep appreciation for her incalculable contribution to this and many other stories. From a very fortunate author.

One of the most gratifying aspects of writing is, in my experience, the heart-warming alacrity, with which an author's plea for help is invariably received. Indeed I cannot recall a single occasion when the response to a request for technical or other assistance was less than immediate and whole-heartedly enthusiastic.

So acknowledging, I offer my appreciation to all, and in particular to the gentlemen listed alphabetically below, who so generously gave of their time, patience and professional guidance towards the making of this book.

Sqn. Ldr. Alec Bristow, D.F.C., A.F.C., M.T.A.I., R.A.F. (Retd.)
Captain Gordon Cochran, B.O.A.C.
First Officer Mario Coutsoftides, Cyprus Airways
Captain Barry Hesketh, Cyprus Airways
First Officer Christopher Males, Cyprus Airways
Captain Trevor Marsden, B.O.A.C.
Captain Sam Melling, Cyprus Airways
First Officer Tony West-Padgett, Cyprus Airways

And finally, a special acknowledgment to DESMOND ELLIOTT, my special agent, who not only provided the seed for this story but, by encouragement, nurtured it to fruition.

I

'PEABODY...!'

Colonel Godfrey Berskin's barked remonstration cracked like a bull-whip across his palatial penthouse lounge, jerking Joshua Aloyisius Peabody from the brink of slumber into upright, heart-thumping alertness.

'Sir!' he barked in response, befuddled by exhaustion, for the merest moment believing himself to be back in the officers' mess, Aldershot – then quickly realizing he, most unfortunately, was not.

'Goddam it, Peabody, you were asleep on duty!' rapped Berskin. 'Get your fat ass over here and pour us some bourbon – then hit the extractor fan and get rid of this goddam fog! I can't tell an inside straight from a hot flush in this murk.'

Peabody's nose rose four indignant degrees and his thin lips compressed with disdain. With a scornful tug at the lapels of his crumpled morning coat, he braced his shoulders, imperiously thrust forward the proud mound of his belly and proceeded across the room in arrogant butler's gait, heartily regretting for the umpteenth time that night that he had allowed himself to be seduced from that hot-bed of ancient breeding, D'Arbly Towers, by mere money.

How, he questioned himself yet again as he dispensed the amber liquor from a crystal decanter into the Colonel's glass. could he ever have been foolish enough to exchange the proud old grandeur of the Towers for this ... this *philistine* goldfish bowl perched fourteen floors above Central Park in the heart of dreadful New York City ... swop dear, dignified London for the monster of violence and corruption that lay below ... and, above all (and here the real anguish took him), how could he have exchanged the frail, noble gentility of old Lord Gascoigne D'Arbly for the loud-mouthed, *nouveau-riche* vulgarity of the creature now seated beneath him, his teeth clamped aggressively around an indecently large cigar, his wolf-grey eyes peering with ferocious cunning at the five cards clutched in his grasping fingers.

Money, Peabody answered himself dispiritedly, as he circuited the vulgar little green-baize gaming table to refill the glass of Clarence F. Dewey, the Colonel's most detested poker opponent and all-round rich fink. One thousand dollars a month money and all found – including his own apartment on the floor below.

One thousand dollars a month! Ten times more than that stingy old berk D'Arbly had ever coughed up – plus a luxury apartment in the Berskin Building in place of that rat-infested box-room in the east wing of the Towers! An offer no human being could be expected to refuse.

But, oh, the ignominy of it – butlering for a creature of such crudity and vulgar ostentation as Berskin. Granted, His Lordship had had his faults, had not been averse to fetching him a crack with his riding crop and calling him a silly old fart from time to time ... and yet always with such *breeding* ... oh, *how* he missed the Towers ...

'O.K. – get the fan, Peabody, I'm chokin' ta death,' growled Berskin.

8

'Sir,' sniffed Peabody, trembling with chagrin.

'An' yuh can get that goddam look of disapproval offa your mug, Peabody – you ain't goin' to bed until we've finished this goddam game – even if it lasts *another* two days!'

'As you say, sir,' sneered Peabody.

'Yes, sir – as *I* say, sir – an' don't you forget it. Dewey, you deal the shittiest bunch of cards imaginable. Gimme two. And, Peabody . . .'

'Sir?'

'Rustle up some chow, I'm starved.'

'Certainly, sir.'

'O.K., Dewey, your bet.'

Seething with indignation, Peabody stiff-backed it down the long, sumptuously appointed room to where a cold buffet, arrayed in silver servers along the marble top of a Louis Quinze dresser, awaited Berskin's pleasure, and there, while he arranged slices of turkey, pork and rib of beef on Dresden platters and smothered them with a mountain of assorted pickles (the rising aroma offending his sensitive English nostrils in the extreme), Peabody cast surreptitious glances towards the distant card-table and reflected yet again upon the ignominy of his current employ, detesting anew the man responsible for it.

Oh, would that he had not pursued the advertisement that had appeared in *The Times* six months before. 'English butler required by retired American military gentleman' it had read. 'Excellent salary and own apartment overlooking sylvan setting. Duties light and of most pleasant nature. One year minimum contract on acceptance.'

Stunned by the salary mentioned at the interview in London, he had readily accepted, and with all haste had been flown out first-class 747, arriving in a state of sedate excitement at the prospect of meeting his new master – a gentleman, he imagined, of quiet, dignified bearing and kindly disposition.

Instead he had met Berskin and was still suffering from the shock.

The man was a lunatic – a five-foot-four, iron-haired tornado, an eruption of volcanic energy and bewildering impulsiveness, patriarch of a mammoth business empire which he controlled from this very penthouse, Berskin's penthouse, in Berskin's Building . . . in Berskin's entire city block.

Colonel Godrey Berskin, it appeared, owned half of America – from oil wells in Texas to gold mines in Alaska and a multitude of interests in between. He owned shipyards, newspapers, supermarkets and TV stations right across the country. He owned bowling-alleys and restaurants, hot-dog stands and used-car lots, distilleries and bunny-clubs in a hundred major cities. And not the least of his more recent acquisitions was a totally controlling interest in three of the top money-earners in the world of pop music – Jimmy Silver, Marc Dart and Wensley Pocket – fifty per cent of whose annual earnings alone poured more than twenty million dollars into the Berskin coffers.

But, Peabody reflected despairingly, Colonel Godfrey Berskin was certainly no gentleman. The description that *did* apply to this gauche, rude, loud, rumbumptious little squirt could, he felt, more accurately be described in American terms than in English. Hustler, carpetbagger, roustabout, promoter. For Berskin was a compulsive showman and his manifold deals were, without exception, always conceived with theatrical flair and executed with an abundance of fairground razzamatazz. Everything he did had to be big, bold, brash and eight times larger than life – even his poker playing.

The games Peabody had witnessed and the amounts of money won and lost in this very room had, at first, been quite incomprehensible to him. Not hundreds, not thousands, but millions of dollars had changed hands between these two men during their two-, three- and even four-day orgies at the cards. Once every month Berskin and Dewey would face each other across the baize. The furniture would be cleared from the centre of the room, jackets removed and shirt-sleeves hoisted, bourbon, food and cigars placed ready – and then the action would begin.

And *what* action. Tense, terrible and endless. Hour after tension-filled hour Peabody would be required to dance attendance to their slightest whim, not only providing for their physical needs but also keeping an accurate mental account of money lost and won. At this very moment he had been on his feet for thirty-seven hours and was likely to remain so for another thirty-seven unless the existing impasse between the two men was dispersed by a major win for one or the other –

until one of them finally threw down his cards and cried 'enough!'

Of Clarence F. Dewey Peabody knew little – except that if Berskin owned one half of the United States then Dewey most certainly owned the other half. Like Berskin, Dewey, a pale, middle-aged, flabby creature of ice-cool disposition and a calm, persuasive, almost hypnotic voice, was into everything – iron and steel, property, entertainment and food, in addition to owning his own airline, an interest, Peabody knew, that Berskin eyed with considerable envy.

Peabody transferred the laden plates to a serving trolley and as he propelled it across the lush, pale-green Chinese carpet he further studied the two men, half-hidden from him in the mist of eye-watering cigar smoke. Lit dramatically by the stark triangle of white light issuing from a low-hanging overhead lamp, they presented a tableau of wily greed yet presented it in markedly contrasting styles – Berskin, small, wiry, jaw-juttingly aggressive, hunched forward attackingly; Dewey composed, expansive, filling his chair with fat, peering through half-closed, sinisterly half-smiling, pebble-black eyes at the cards held in plump, white, spatulate fingers, occasionally passing a languid hand through his sparse black hair and shifting his cigar from one side of his loose, rubbery mouth to the other.

A spider, reflected Peabody. A lecherous, lethal tarantula, lurking in the shadows, waiting to strike.

'Your bid,' Dewey said pleasantly, his voice a velvet caress, complementing the permanent, pristine half-smile.

'I know, I know,' growled Berskin, gnashing his cigar and showering the baize with a thumb of ash. 'Aw, god*dam* it ... Peabody, get rid of this!'

'A ... herm,' Peabody coughed discreetly for attention.

Berskin looked up. 'Yeah, what is it?'

'The, er, food, sir.'

'What about it?'

'It's here, sir.'

'Well, I can see it's here, Peabody – yuh damn-near touched down in our laps! Back off a piece an' give me some air – an' get rid of this goddam ash. Ten thousand, Dewey – an' screw yuh!'

11

'Your ten and ten more,' Dewey answered coolly.

'Then ten more an' up yours!'

'And yet another ten, Berskin – with the compliment returned.'

'Then I'll make it twenty an' damn all pikers!'

'Your twenty and thirty more.' Dewey's smirk deepened. 'I've got you this time, Berskin.'

Berskin uttered an oath that caused Peabody to wince. 'Oh yeah – well, your thirty and *fifty* more! You gettin' all this, Peabody?'

Peabody sniffed, affronted. 'Certainly, sir.'

'O.K. – gimme the tally.'

'The pot now stands at one hundred and forty thousand dollars, sir.'

'Chicken shit. Dewey ... let's get some meat in there. A quarter of a million says you're bluffin' with a lousy pair.'

'My quarter of a million says you're a terrible judge of character, Berskin ... and *another* quarter of a million is going to prove it.'

'Horse balls,' rapped Berskin, who was sitting with a handsome full-house – aces and kings. 'Dewey, I'm gonna bury you. O.K. – half a million!'

'Seen.'

Berskin slammed his cards down. 'House full, baby – aces and royals!'

'Mmm,' mused Dewey, casting an appreciative eye over the cards, and then languidly laid down his own. 'Top flush, I fear, Berskin. Terribly sorry.'

'Shite!' Berskin smote the table with his fist and rounded on Peabody who was whisking away the cigar ash into a silver crumb-tray. 'Peabody, what's the goddam tally?'

Peabody straightened and cleared his throat. 'The extent of your commitment to Mr. Dewey is now two million four hundred and fifty three thousand dollars, sir.'

'Jesus Christ. O.K., Peabody, serve the food.'

Berskin ate quickly, hunched over his plate, his eyes flicking furtively in tempo with a scurrying brain. Clarence F. Dewey, by extreme comparison, ate leisurely and with quiet dignity, a snow-white linen napkin tucked into the neck of his soiled white shirt, a superior, victor's smile upon his lips.

'Think you're good, don't yuh?' Berskin growled peevishly, shovelling a mountain of pork and mustard pickle into his mouth. 'Think you're one red-hot poker player, don't you, Dewey?'

'Well, certainly the best here, Berskin,' Dewey responded, with an ease befitting a man two and a half million dollars ahead.

Berskin looked up, eyes flaring, his voice tremulous and low. 'Well, now, I'm gonna tell you something, Dewey ... I am up to *here* ...' he slashed the knife across his throat, 'playin' penny-ante pat-a-cake with you. An' I am sick to *death* of sitting across here lookin' at that goddam smug, self-satisfied mug o' yours ...'

'Really,' smirked Dewey, deliberately slicing into his chicken breast.

'Yeah, really. An' what's more I'm gonna wipe that damned superior, supercilious grin off once an' for all. I'm gonna *take* you, Dewey – big an' hard. I'm gonna *blast* you! We are gonna play a game that's really gonna *hurt* – a sky-high, men-from-the-boys gut-jolter ... !'

'Now, Berskin,' smiled Dewey, 'don't get carried away.'

'I don't *intend* gettin' carried away, Dewey,' Berskin breathed passionately, stabbing the fork at Dewey's midriff. '*You're* the one who's gonna get carried away – straight down to Skid Row ... busted!'

'Mmmm,' Dewey demurred insolently, delicately removing a chicken bone from his lips. 'So it's sky's the limit, hm?'

Berskin laughed scathingly, shaking his head. 'Oh no, Dewey ... it's "outer space" is the limit. This time I'm really gonna *hit* you!'

'Talk,' Dewey replied airily, 'is an expensive commodity, Berskin. Instead of sitting there beating your gums I would suggest you replace the mouth with money and get on with it.'

'You're damned right I'm gonna get on with it! Peabody ... !'

'Sir?'

Peabody emerged from the gloom, his heart quickened by the conversation he had just overheard. Many times he had witnessed explosions of temperament between these two men,

13

caused as much by physical exhaustion as just plain hatred of each other, but never had Berskin's outbursts appeared so manifestly virulent, so brutally determined. Something huge, Peabody sensed, was imminent – a contest of such outlandish magnitude that all previous wagers would seem puny by comparison.

Just look at him, Peabody reflected as he approached his master – a Dobermann quivering on the leash, desperate for release to fly at the throat of the ice-cold foe. God help us all tonight; Armageddon is surely upon us.

'Sir?' Peabody repeated, drawing close.

'Get this crap off the table!' snapped Berskin. 'Break open a fresh deck of cards! Fill the glasses! Get more cigars! And sharpen that computer mind of yours, Peabody – the money's gonna flow thick an' fast!'

'C . . . certainly, sir.'

Peabody performed his duties with all speed, nervously exhilarated by the imminence of a momentous occasion. Then, with glasses filled and a supply of cigars placed to hand, he retired a short distance from the table and waited, tremblingly, as Berskin tore the cellophane wrapping from a virgin deck.

A silence as taut as a full-drawn long-bow gripped the room as Berskin, a fresh cigar clamped between determined teeth, shuffled the cards, the rip of the boards sounding unnaturally loud in the tense, vibrant silence.

'Cut!' He slammed the pack down.

Dewey, seemingly cool as ever, leaned languidly forward and delivered the coup and relaxed again into his chair, raising coal-hard eyes at Berskin.

'Nervous, Berskin?'

'Just puzzled, Dewey – about how I'm gonna spend your money.'

Dewey laughed quietly. 'There is an ancient adage, Berskin – about counting your chickens before they're hatched.'

'Sure,' growled Berskin, beginning to deal. 'And there's another one about screwin' yourself. Make no mistake, Dewey, this time I'm gonna get you. You're as good as dead.' His head snapped round. 'You ready, Peabody?'

Peabody coughed nervously. 'At . . . your pleasure, sir.'

'And it's certainly gonna be that, Peabody,' he grinned, fan-

14

ning his five cards. 'O.K., Dewey – how's about a hundred thousand for openers?'

Dewey affected a bored yawn. 'Very much on the low side, Berskin. I'd personally prefer two hundred thousand.'

Berskin nodded. 'Then we'll make it five. Cards?'

'None. I'll play these.'

Berskin froze ... and for a long, electric moment he gazed fiercely, unblinkingly into the lazy-lidded insolence of Dewey's smirk until, finally, his own cynical sneer disrupted the harsh lines of his iron countenance.

'*Sure* you'll play those,' he grunted contemptuously. 'And I'm gonna play these. One million!'

The outrageous bid cracked across the table, startling Peabody and visibly shaking Dewey with its vehemence – though only for a moment. Stirred now from his languor, Dewey's counter-bid came rapping back, flung like a gauntlet into Berskin's aggressive face.

'Two million!'

This time Berskin gasped, faltered, recovered, and with renewed vehemence barked, 'Three million!'

Dewey came upright, black eyes flaring, 'Four million!'

Peabody gasped aloud.

'Five million!' bellowed Berskin.

'*Six* million!' roared Dewey.

Berskin's eyes narrowed murderously. 'You ... *bastard!* seven million!'

'Damn you, Berskin!' seethed Dewey. '*Eight* million!'

'Gentlemen ... gentlemen!' cried Peabody in despair, wringing his hands helplessly.

'Shut up, Peabody!' roared Berskin. '*Nine* million!'

Dewey's furious fist crashed into the table. '*Ten* million!'

'Yuh lousy Wop crud ... *eleven* million!'

'You pumped-up, pint-sized peacock ... *twelve* million!'

'*Thirteen* million and half of Jimmy Silver, yuh bloated Boston *bum!*'

'*Fourteen* million and my *Big Dick Frankfurter factory*, you ... you senile old knicker-groper!'

Silence! Tense, terrible, eyeball-to-eyeball hatred fizzed across the table.

Berskin gasped, gaped, glared, his puny body trembling

with passion, and then, 'Right ... RIGHT! you cold-eyed callous-assed, pussy-kisser ... ! MY INTEREST IN JIMMY SILVER ... MARC DART ... AND WENSLEY POCKET – TWENTY MILLION THE LOT ... AGAINST DEWEY AIRLINES TAKE IT OR LEAVE IT!'

Dewey leapt out of his chair, thrust his jutting chin into Berskin's glaring face. 'I'LL *TAKE* IT!'

'RIGHT!'

Berskin jumped up, sent his chair flying. 'Peabody! Check the cards!'

Both men slammed their hands face-down on the table and whirled away, trembling with emotion, grinding their cigars to shreds, almost staggering from fatigue.

Peabody, utterly shocked, walked falteringly to the table, stared for a bewildered moment at the two face-down fans of cards, then slowly reached out and turned them over.

Berskin, visibly shaking, grabbed the cigar from his mouth. 'Well?'

Peabody cleared his throat. 'It ... herm ... it would appear, sir, that you ... that you ...'

'That I *what*, you blithering idiot?'

'That you ... now possess an airline, sir.'

Berskin stared, frozen in an attitude of disbelief, then slowly his gaping countenance crumpled in a grin of beaming glee and he let rip a 'YAAAAHHHHOOOO!' that rattled the chandelier.

Clarence F. Dewey slumped and walked with staggering steps towards the door, head bowed, spirit broken, sent on his way by Berskin's ruthless chuckle.

2

Friday: four days later.

In the sumptuously appointed recording studio fifteen floors below the penthouse in the basement of the Berskin Building, Colonel Godfrey sat slumped in a chrome-and-leather armchair, one puny leg cocked over the armrest, a twelve-inch cigar clamped between his teeth.

Up on the stage, surrounded by a plethora of microphones, amplifiers and instruments, a group of four hideous youths dressed in pirate gear and calling themselves Skull and Crossbones were drumming, plucking and twanging themselves into a froth, attempting to convince the Colonel they were worthy of his patronage. For this was audition morning, a twice-monthly occurrence at which the best of the pop groups and solo artists, previously culled by Berskin's army of talent scouts from a multitude of applicants, were presented to God himself.

Out front, clutching a hand-mike on a nine-thousand foot cable, a pale, pimply stick of a kid with waist-length orange hair on top of which perched a live green parrot wearing an eye-patch, was screaming a self-composed, hieroglyphic inanity about hereness and nowness entitled 'Haecceity' – sentiments based upon Duns Scotus's term for that element of existence on which individuality depends and who gives a stuff?

God certainly didn't. He wasn't listening; but he *was* watching. Watching the creature's movement, the blatant sexuality of his wild pelvic gyrations, the twitch and thrust of his skin-tight black-leather trousers.

Suddenly Berskin came to his feet and bellowed, 'O.K. – cut the crap ... CUT IT!'

The group came to silence like a run-down gramophone. Berskin leapt on to the stage, yelling into the wings for his producer. 'Flynn!'

A gnome appeared, peering apprehensively at Berskin through spectacle lenses thicker than jam-jar bottoms.

'Yes, Colonel?' he enquired, wringing his hands obsequiously, a manner Berskin heartily approved.

'This one's got somethin', Flynn,' said Berskin, jabbing his cigar at Parrothead. 'Got the movement that counts, yuh know ... ?'

'Certainly, Colonel, that's just what I figure mys ...'

'Shut up, Flynn – and get me four handkerchiefs.'

'H ... handkerchiefs, Colonel ... ?'

'That's the word I used, Flynn. You havin' trouble understanding it?'

'Er, no, sir ...'

'Then go get them, Flynn – fast!'

Flynn scuttled away, his twisted gait reminding Berskin of the Hunchback's progress through the Notre Dame belfry.

Berskin turned to the youth who was now feeding the parrot with peanuts from his pocket.

'Great gimmick ya got there, kid,' he said, stabbing his cigar at the parrot. 'How d'ya stop it crappin' on your head?'

In answer the youth turned round.

Berskin grimaced and stepped back. 'I see.'

'They say it's lucky,' muttered the youth.

Berskin nodded. 'Could be. I like what I see, kid – at least from the front. The sound's godawful but I reckon the bottom half of you is promotable.'

At that moment Flynn came lurching up, holding out the handkerchiefs. 'You have a cold, Colonel?' he enquired solicitously.

'Flynn, you're an idiot.'

Berskin took the handkerchiefs and turned to the youth. 'Here, kid, stuff these down ya trousers – gotta build up your image, you're a bit on the puny side down there. Gotta give the women somethin' to drool over.'

The youth accepted the padding with a look of perplexity.

'Get 'em in,' commanded Berskin, turning to leave the stage.

By the time he had resumed his seat the handkerchiefs were in place, creating a phallic bulge the size of a fist.

'Great!' Berskin called up. 'Now make with the noise and let's see it all hang out!'

'An' a one ... two ... three,' called the youth, bashing his nine-inch heel on the floor.

The studio exploded. The kid went into paroxysms, jerking his all into the face of an imaginary audience, the spotlights following every thrust.

' 'KAY ... OKAY!' yelled Berskin, waving his arms for hush.

The cacophony died.

'Great!' called Berskin. 'Flynn! Give 'em a six months contract an' get a tour lined up ...'

While he was talking to Flynn, the studio door opened and a pretty brunette entered and walked across the floor towards Berskin, walked with a sexy lilt, conscious of her excellent legs and a plentiful bosom hugely revealed in a low-cut white cotton blouse.

She drew close to Berskin. 'Excuse me, sir ...'

He turned, his frown of irritation dispersing instantly as his eyes fell upon her enormous knockers. 'Well, hello ...'

'May I have a word with you, sir?'

'Eh?' He winced.

19

'May I...'

'Come closer, child, these monkeys have deafened me.'

She came closer, bent towards him. 'That better, sir?'

'Much,' he gulped. By God, they were beauties. 'What's your name? You work for me? How long have you been here?'

'My name's Amanda Allgood, Colonel...'

'By golly, that's no lie.'

'And I've been here a month. I'm the studio secretary.'

'Is that a fact. Well, what can I do for you, Amanda?'

'There's an urgent call from the penthouse, sir – from your accountants. They would like you to go up as soon as possible.'

Berskin nodded. 'I'll come up right now. Ride the elevator with me, child, I wish to discuss your future with the company.'

Five minutes later, at the penthouse floor, the elevator doors opened and Berskin stepped out. 'That's settled then – and another fifty a month – O.K.?'

'Wonderful,' smiled Amanda, buttoning her blouse.

She gave a little wave as the elevator doors closed and with a grin Berskin turned and walked into his outer office. Six grey-suited men sat there looking disturbingly woebegone. As Berskin entered they rose as one and followed him into the conference room in Indian file.

'Well?' he demanded, slipping into his throne-ornate chair at the head of a vast rose-wood table.

Silently the men took their seats, three on either side of Berskin, and in unison opened their brief-cases and extracted papers.

Their spokesman, Berskin's chief accountant and general dogsbody, a crew-cut, bespectacled manipulator named Heinrich Himmler, shuffled his papers nervously before finally speaking.

'Colonel... you will appreciate, of course, that four days has been quite insufficient for a detailed analysis...'

'Himmler,' snapped Berskin. 'Cut the goddam jazz and get on with it!'

'C... certainly, sir... well, in round terms... and taking all things into consideration... b... bearing in mind the invisible contingencies and the extraordinary conditions inherent in the c... conglomerate vicissitudes of running an airline ... the cross-coordinates of a delicate profit-to-loss ratio based on the equilateral conversion of ...'

Berskin slammed the palm of his horny hand on to the table, making all the ink-pots jump. 'In round terms, Himmler, an' cuttin' out all this bullshit – what in hell have I *inherited*?'

'A pup, sir – a real dog. In less vernacular idiom – a company which is currently losing one million dollars a week and which is on the verge of bankruptcy ...'

Berskin gaped. 'Bank ... CCHHRRIISSTT AALL BBLLOOODDYYMMIIGGHHTTYY ... ! ! I'LL KILL HIM! !' This time he slammed his balled fist into the rose-wood and ink leapt out of forty-two pots down the line.

'That misbegotten ... Wop ... CRUD! Bet me a bum company! I'll SUE him! MURDER HIM!'

'Y ... yes, sir ...' stuttered Himmler, wincing at the on-slaught and wishing he was somewhere else.

Thrusting back his chair, Berskin leapt up and began a hunched pace around the room, hands behind his back, trailing smoke from a furiously burning cigar. Then, after five full circuits of desperate, angry computation, he swung in again and sat down, hunched forward over the table, now outwardly calmer but inwardly blazing, his voice low and mean.

'All right ... all right ... so tell me just what I *have* copped, Himmler.'

Himmler cleared his constricted throat nervously and began reading from the papers held in his shaking hands.

'Well, sir ... Dewey Airlines is a charter company possessing International licences which permit them to fly to most countries in the world. At the present moment the fleet comprises six Boeing 707 airliners and several small light aircraft ...'

For twenty minutes Berskin listened without interruption to the list of holdings he had won from Clarence F. Dewey, his expression unchanged throughout the entire recitation, and when at last Himmler came to the end, Berskin slumped back into his chair and fixed the accountant with a preoccupied stare, his mind elsewhere.

'Why, Himmler ... WHY is this company losing one million dollars a week?'

'W ... with respect, sir, there has been little enough time to

21

assemble a comprehensive list of holdings...' Berskin's eyes sliced through him and he continued hurriedly, 'but if I may be permitted a personal ... though unsupported ... opinion...'

Berskin nodded brusquely. 'Go ahead.'

'Competition, sir ... and promotion – or rather lack of it. Dewey Airlines would appear to have lagged far behind in the matter of self-promotion. Other companies, being aware of the vast extent of competition, are spending hundreds of thousands ... *millions* of dollars in advertising. They employ top P.R. and advertising agencies to project eye-catching – and hence fare-catching – images of themselves. Take National Airlines as an example with their appeal to the public through a pretty air stewardess, inviting them to "fly her". Or TWA's campaign...'

'Sure, sure,' Berskin snapped irritably. 'I get the message, Himmler. And what have Dewey Airlines been doing?'

Himmler shrugged. 'Nothing, sir. If you will permit the observation, my colleagues and I have come to the conclusion that Dewey Airlines has been run in a way that would almost indicate a ... well, a policy of intended loss...'

Berskin's frown deepened. 'A *what*?'

'An ... intended loss, sir – for tax purposes.'

Berskin glared at him. 'You mean ... you mean Dewey let me bet the cream of my pop menagerie against a bum, tax-loss company...?'

'Well, so it would seem...'

'God ... DAMN, the...' Berskin's jaw snapped shut, reason now beginning to prevail over anger. 'All right, Himmler ... now you just find out what sort of an image Dewey Airlines *has* got! What do the *public* think of Dewey Airlines? What are the *crews* like? What is the food ... service ... and every goddam thing *else* like? I want facts, Himmler. I wanna know just what kind of a bum airline it *is* I've picked up! Is there any hope for it ... can we pick up the pieces – or do we throw the whole cock-rotting heap into the trash-can and cut our losses!'

Alive now with the prospect of new, exciting action, he yanked a fresh cigar from his breast pocket, bit off the end and spat it across the table.

'Get some crew in here, Himmler – on the double. I want to hear what *they* think of Dewey Airlines. Make it . . .' he glanced at his watch, 'make it three o'clock. I'm gonna get some lunch. Dismissed.'

He pushed back his chair and strode from the room, cursing the fatherless Clarence F. Dewey for the cunning, conniving viper he was, yet stirred to bubbling excitement by the one element more necessary for his survival than air itself – challenge!

A bum, down-at-heel tax-loss, eh? Well now, he'd just see about that. But first – a spot of lunch.

He burst through the door of his private suite and made for the desk intercom.

'Sir?' his secretary answered.

'Lunch.'

'Yes, sir – Peabody's right here with the trolley.'

'Screw Peabody, Miss Destry. I want the new maid.'

'Certainly, sir.'

Moments later Amanda entered.

3

At three o'clock sharp the meeting reconvened in the Board-room, Colonel Godfrey Berskin now looking somewhat more relaxed and wearing a tight, secretive smirk.

'Well, Himmler, whatya come up with?' he demanded, taking his seat.

'A stroke of good fortune, sir ...' beamed Himmler.

'About goddam time. O.K. – overwhelm me.'

'The Chief Pilot, sir – a Captain Rossiter. We found him off duty. He's in the waiting-room now.'

'Good man – get him in.'

Himmler gave the nod to one of his deputies who went out of the room, returning a moment later with a man who, from his appearance, might have been a hot-dog stand attendant or a fairground barker on a coconut shy. By no stretch of the imagination might he have been an airline pilot.

He was short, stocky and, since he was only in his late thirties, prematurely grey-haired. His face was that of an alley cat, handsome but battered, good-humoured but scarred by casual cynicism. As he came to a halt just inside the room, a figure of slovenly devil-may-care, one hand thrust into the pocket of his crumpled grey slacks, the other reaching for a cheroot in the breast pocket of a hideously coloured Hawaiian shirt, bare toes exposed in open beach sandals, he lazy-eyed the assembly one by one and then, as though none of them existed, took all the time he needed to light his cigar.

Godfrey Berskin, having risen half out of his chair in anticipation of greeting a man of some distinction, stared disbelievingly, then shot a bewildered gape at Himmler, gasping, 'Himmler ... this is some kind of *joke*?'

'N ... no, sir ... this is Captain Rossiter, sir.'

'My chief *pilot*?'

'Your chief pilot, sir. He ... he was cleaning out his rabbits when we called, sir.'

Berskin sniffed. 'I *believe* you.'

Rossiter, having ignited his foul-smelling cheroot, now decided to move. He approached the table, nodding congenially to everyone. 'Hi, how are yuh?'

Himmler rose. 'Er, Captain Rossiter ... may I introduce the new owner of Dewey Airlines – Colonel Godfrey Berskin.'

Rossiter nodded. 'Hi – how are yuh?' and offered his hand.

Diffidently Berskin raised his own hand but suddenly changed his mind and, pointed with it. 'Captain Rossiter, please be seated – down there.'

Rossiter nodded. 'Sure thing, glad to. This heat's a killer.' He ambled down the line, slumped into the fourth seat from Berskin, stretched out his legs and let go one hell of a yawn. 'Yoweee...' He grinned, shaking his head. 'Must be ninety-five out there and the humidity a touch higher.'

'Captain Rossiter...' growled Berskin, still staring in amazement, 'we are assembled here to discuss a matter of grave importance, not only to us but certainly to *you* ... and I would be grateful for your alert and undivided attention.'

Rossiter nodded, blowing out a huge pall of smoke. 'You got it. Shoot.'

25

Berskin's mouth worked in silent exasperation. How *dare* this man ... !

'Captain Rossiter ...' he choked, 'could it be that you did not properly hear Himmler's introduction ... that you do not fully appreciate who I *am* ... ?'

'No, I heard him fine. You're Colonel Godfrey Berskin – the new owner of Dewey Airlines.' He turned to Himmler. 'Ain't that what you said, sir – verbatim?'

Himmler nodded uncertainly.

'So ...' Rossiter continued amiably, 'what can I do for you, Colonel?'

'You can get some dadblasted respect in your manner for a start, Rossiter! Berskin exploded. 'You come slouchin' into a top-level board meeting that's trying to decide the fate and future of *your* source of employment as though you'd come to clean out *my* rabbits!'

'Oh, you've got rabbits, Colonel? Now, that's nice. I always say a fella who likes rabbits can't be *all* rotten ...'

'No, I have *not* got rabbits!' fumed Berskin.

'Guinea pigs maybe?'

'No! And I ain't got a turtle or a jumping frog either! What I *have* got is a half-assed airline that is losing one million dollars a week – and the moment you walked through that door, Rossiter, I suddenly realized *why* it is losing one million dollars a week!'

Rossiter raised a benign brow. 'Is that a fact? *I* did that for you, huh? Well, I'm sure glad to have been of some help.' He slid upright in his seat and got to his feet. 'Well, sir, if that's all I can do for you ...'

'Siddown!' choked Berskin, chomping his cigar clean in two.

'Oh, there's more?'

Berskin lunged forward, elbows on the table, and shook the butt of his cigar at Rossiter. 'Now, look here, Rossiter ... !'

Rossiter *was* looking – at his fingernails. 'Colonel ... let's get one thing straight before we go any further, shall we? If you want my respect – and my help – you would do well to reflect on the fact that I am not a professional rabbit breeder, I'm the chief pilot of an airline. Don't let the shirt fool you, I don't wear it in the cockpit. Now ... what can I do for you?'

He looked up at Berskin, finding him with his mouth open.

'I ... I ...' Berskin faltered, nonplussed, then, with a determined straightening of the shoulders, resumed his briskness. 'The company's in a goddam mess, Rossiter, and we're here to find out if it's salvable. I want to know *why* it's losing one million bucks a week. Himmler here has come up with the notion that Dewey ran it as a deliberate tax-loss, refusing to compete with the other airlines ...'

'Himmler's right,' nodded Rossiter sagely.

'Refusing to advertise ...' Berskin stopped. 'He *is*?'

Rossiter shrugged. 'Sure he is. Dewey didn't *want* passengers. Half the time the crews are hanging around the Ops room playin' pinocle an' running up a nice fat wage bill.'

Himmler sat back in his chair, smirking smugly. 'Just as I thought.'

'Shut up, Himmler,' snapped Berskin. 'Go on, Rossiter.'

Rossiter shrugged. 'What's to go on about? We don't get business because we don't go after it, it's as simple as that.'

Silence gripped the room. Berskin, breathing heavily, was deep in thought, his eyes darting hither and thither, seeing nothing.

'Indeed,' he uttered at last. 'Well, by God ...' More heavy breathing, and then: 'Well, I'm gonna tell you something, Rossiter, things are gonna change around here – and change radically! You reckon with the right kind of promotion that Dewey Airlines could compete – make money?'

'Why not? You've got the planes ... the crews.'

'Good men?' rapped Berskin.

Rossiter smiled. 'Good enough. They take 'em up and bring 'em down – more or less in the right places. What more do you want?'

'*Much* more!' Berskin exploded, making everybody jump. 'Godfrey Berskin has never yet been associated with any business enterprise that was just "good enough", Rossiter! It has to be excellent ... superlative! A thoroughgoin', rip-roarin' success through and through – yuh got that!?'

'Sure,' shrugged Rossiter.

'All right!' Berskin smashed his dead cigar butt into an ashtray with a determination that could well have symbolized the destruction of all that had pertained in the past, then lit a new one as though kindling a new, exciting future. Now, leaning forward, he levelled this symbolic future at Rossiter and addressed him in a low, determined tone.

'You, Rossiter, are about to see a transformation of Dewey Airlines that will take your *breath* away. We are gonna compete! We are gonna advertise! We are gonna produce a brand-new conception in air travel the like of which neither the industry nor the public have ever before witnessed or thought possible! The public will be desertin' the PanAm's and the TWA's and the National's in *droves* before I'm through! They're gonna be fightin', beggin' and pleadin' to get seats on our planes by the time I'm finished with 'em...'

'Mighty glad to hear it, Colonel,' Rossiter replied casually. 'And how do you intend goin' about it? Most of the gimmicks have been tried before – double-feature movies ... stereo music ... more leg room...'

'Crap!' thundered Berskin. 'Half-assed ideas thought up by small-thinkin' men! Men without vision -- without flair!' Now his voice took on a hushed, vibrant intensity. 'No, Rossiter ... we are going to produce something quite revolutionary – a gimmick so devastatingly appealing to every man and woman there'll be mile-long line-ups at *our* ticket counters every day of the year ... people in their thousands *begging* to be allowed to fly on our planes ... people taking trips to places they don't want to go to – just to get on board. Because *we* will have something to sell that none of the other airlines has ever dreamed of – not double-feature films or stereo music, not wider seats or more leg room, not ten-course meals or any *other* mundane, crappy idea. We, gentlemen ... will have – GLAMOUR!'

The strange, unexpected word hung in the air like a spectre ... mystifying, bewildering, and for many moments after its triumphant proclamation all those at the table continued to stare at Berskin, their minds trying to encompass its full meaning, its application in this particular instance, until finally Himmler, as though representing their capitulation, at last broke the silence and gulped, '*Glamour*, sir?'

Berskin released a slow, taunting smile and nodded. 'Glamour, Himmler – the one commodity *all* of us crave to lighten our dreary, workaday lives.' His eyes flashed to Rossiter who was looking at him with a sort of reserved scepticism, intrigued yet cynical, as though trying to decide whether Berskin was a genius or a nut.

'Rossiter ... I have a job for you. Within one week from today I want you to produce for me one entire crew of outstanding glamour. The men must be young, tall, handsome and personable – in short – a *wow* with the ladies. Got it? And the stewardesses ...' he permitted himself a wry, man-to-man smile, 'well, I think you know.'

Rossiter half returned the smile. 'Yes, sir. I think I do.'

'O.K. Now, I envisage an inaugural flight three weeks from tomorrow – Saturday – so get cracking on that – top priority, got it?'

'Yes, sir. You'll have them within one week.'

'Good.' Berskin turned to Himmler. 'Get this, Himmler – I want you to effect a change of company name immediately. As from *now* we will no longer be known as Dewey Airlines. Three weeks from tomorrow the first 707 will take off from Kennedy bearing our new colours and a totally new image. It will be a *free* inaugural flight for fifty select passengers – including top-ranking and highly influential people from a wide strata of public life – politics, business, theatre, TV, radio, press, et cetera, et cetera – I'll get out a list later.' Now he addressed the table, his voice rising with fervour as the ideas began tumbling from his excited, fertile mind.

'Gentlemen, that 707 will take off to the biggest fanfare of publicity the world of civil aviation has ever known. We'll hit world headlines overnight – because this inaugural flight will be no quick five-dollar flip around New York – this one is going to last an entire *week* ... !' (A gasp from the table.) 'One week, gentlemen – covering not only the United States of America ... not only *Europe* ... but the whole world! Think of it! – TV, radio and press coverage every step of the way! By the end of that week every cotton-pickin' chicken farmer from Kansas to Karachi will have heard about us – *and* the sort of treatment we give our passengers. It's gonna be fun and games all the way, gentlemen – a riot of fun ... an orgy of luxurious self-indulgence – with no expense spared! By God, I'll have PanAm and TWA down on their bended knees *begging* for handouts before I'm through. O.K. – well, that's the plan in principle, the details will be worked out as we go along. But in the meantime we've all got enough to do, so let's get cracking. Meeting adjourned.'

He stood up briskly and was striding towards the door when Himmler, still in shock, stammered, 'Er, Colonel, sir ... there's just one thing ...'

Berskin came to a halt and turned. 'What is it, Himmler?'

'There, er, name, sir ... the new name for the company?'

Berskin smiled, teasing and yet triumphant. 'It's GLAMOUR, Himmler ... GLAMOUR AIRLINES ...' then added devilishly, 'Incorporated, of course,' and left the room.

4

For Alfred B. Rossiter (known more familiarly throughout Dewey Airlines as 'Cock-up' Rossiter ever since that fateful night three years earlier when he had somehow landed at the wrong Miami airport in fog and, while attempting to park his 707 in unfamiliar surroundings, had sheared off the entire tail section of a slumbering DC8), the assignment to assemble within one week a crew of outstanding glamour was as simple as shearing the entire tail section off a slumbering DC8, and even before he'd reached street level he had already made his choice.

Settling into the rear seat of the Dewey Airline limousine waiting at the kerb to return him to his rabbits on the roof of his apartment block in Queens, three miles from the J.F.K. airport, he lit a fresh cheroot, slid on to his spine and began to review the personnel he had chosen, knowing full well that the choice could not be bettered. A more handsome, personable and lecherous bunch of idle layabouts was not to be found, either in Dewey Airlines or any other airline flying international from the U.S.A. – old tax-loss Dewey himself had seen to that. It had all been part of the diabolical tax-loss plan.

'Go!' Dewey had commanded Rossiter, his Chief Pilot and Personnel Selection Officer. 'Find me men who *enjoy* doing nothing ... who prefer long, stagnant lay-overs to flying ... who regard dedication to duty as a dirty word.'

And Rossiter had gone. He had scoured the world's airlines for air-competent miscreants and jovial layabouts and had returned with a right old bunch, the choicest of whom he now had in mind for the inaugural flight of Glamour Airlines.

For First Officer and co-pilot, he reflected, the All-American air-screw himself, Ramjet Rogers, was an absolute must. Paul 'Ramjet' Rogers – with more paternity suits behind him than miles of runway – would have the dames crawling up the aisle in their hundreds and hammering on the cockpit door. Ramjet Rogers, whose chief preoccupation was with his own dark-haired, broad-shouldered beauty and striking likeness to a young Victor Mature (whose sultry, heavy-lidded image he never ceased trying to perfect) would alone, Rossiter reflected, supply all the glamour Berskin desired and more, and coupled with the next guy he had in mind might well prove altogether too much.

For Second Officer and Navigator it had to be, of course, 'Lord' James Crighton-Padgett – six feet two of top-drawer English charm and a bounder through-and-through. A splendidly decadent young fellow he'd discovered quite by accident in the bar at Ascot on the very day Lord Jim had been drummed out of BOAC for appearing on duty out of uniform – a misdemeanour, Rossiter had thought, hardly worthy of such severe punishment – until Crighton-Padgett had confided that he'd been caught *completely* out of uniform, humping the wife of a top BOAC exec in the luggage bay of a grounded VC10.

Curious young fellow in many ways, thought Rossiter – a man to whom seduction came so easy he found it necessary to devise devious means and complex plans in order to extract from its accomplishment any worthwhile merit, but nevertheless an easy guy to have around.

So far, so good, then – Rogers and Crighton-Padgett. Enough cool, aesthetic sophistication alone to glamour PanAm and TWA clean out of the skies. But of course he would need an engineer – and it had to be Bush McKenzie.

For the female passengers who eshewed aestheticism and went a bundle on muscle, Morton 'Bush' McKenzie would fit the bill down to the last bulging bicep and pullulating pectoral.

Rossiter had encountered the flaxen-haired Australian Adonis, most gentle of giants, in a dive on the Sydney waterfront, defending his side-kick (a mild-mannered English cabin steward by the name of Michael 'Sugar' Sweetman) from the taunts of six brutal Aussie dockers, the moment of introduction taking place with Bush's apology for demolishing Rossiter's table with three hundred pounds of inert Aussie docker. Bush McKenzie – lovable guy and a perfect choice, provided he could be kept out of trouble, for if McKenzie had one failing it was that he didn't give a stuff for anyone's authority, was totally irrelevant in the face of opposition, and was inclined to call everyone 'cock', no matter who, a habit that might conceivably cause him to fall foul of Berskin, but who gave a damn? Bush McKenzie it had to be, regardless.

So much for the cockpit crew.

And in the cabin – who else but Michael 'Sugar' Sweetman as steward? – as bent as a salmon gaff but a wizard at placating irate passengers, comforting old ladies and getting maximum effort from idle stews. He looked so helpless, poor lamb, everyone fell over themselves to help him. Nice little guy with the cheeky gaiety that would be absolutely right for the sort of launch flight Berskin had in mind. So – Sugar it was.

And the girls . . . ?

Rossiter grinned lecherously. One hundred and twenty airstews were employed by Dewey Airlines and every one of them a belter. Hadn't he chosen them himself? No, not strictly true. There had to be some goddam perks to being the Chief Pilot, so for a certain monetary consideration he had leased to each 707 captain the privilege of selecting his own stews from a line-up of applicants that had more resembled a parade of

33

potential Miss America's than birds simply wanting to fly.

The result had been most gratifying. The captains, hand-picked by Rossiter and therefore a hornier-than-average bunch of free-loaders, had of course picked the little chickens who not only *were* most likely to but who also *looked* most likely to – and Dewey Airlines had wound up with a galaxy of short-skirted, long-legged, big breasted beauties that were the envy of all the other airlines.

So, schemed Rossiter, re-lighting his cigar and relishing the thought – why shouldn't he make a little *more* bread on this jaunt in the same way? Why not allow Ramjet, Lord Jim and Bush McKenzie – and even Sugar Sweetman, who had to work with the girls – choice of air-stews on this inaugural flight? It had to be worth a C-note at least. Yeah, why not? He'd call them up and put the proposition to them as soon as he reached his apartment.

With the crew now mentally assembled he abandoned that project and turned his thoughts to Berskin and the entire Glamour plan. Berskin – a screw-ball and no mistake, and yet he had to admire the guy's push. Glamour Airlines, yet! Well, maybe it was all to the good. He was getting tired sitting on his ass in Ops playing pinocle, he needed some action. A seven-day, round-the-world junket, hm? Maybe if he pushed Berskin he could have some say in where they dropped down, Singapore and a wild little Chinese stripper chick by the name of U Kum Tu popping into his mind. He would pursue the possibility in the very near future.

He came out of his seat and tapped the driver on the shoulder. 'On the left, right here, mac.'

The limousine slid into the kerb and as he climbed out on to the pavement, a monster 747, fresh off the Kennedy runway thundered overhead, making him wince and shaking the decrepit ten-storey building.

'Goddam PanAm,' he muttered, winking at the driver.

As the car sped away, he entered the cool, flaking hallway and crossed the broken-tiled floor to the ancient elevator. Flinging open the trellis gate, he stepped in and was about to slam the gate shut when Mrs. Wesolowski's bellow arrested him.

'Hey, there ... Kepitain Rossiter!'

Now he did slam the trellis, placing protective steel between him and the tyrannical old baggage who came trundling up to assail him.

'What is it, Mrs. Wesolowski, I'm in a hurry.'

'You always in a hurry. Hey – who d'you think owns zis building, huh?'

Rossiter sighed as his fingers crept surreptitiously up the panel to the tenth button. 'Why, you do, Mrs. Wes ...'

'You damn right I own it! An' when I let apartment to you, I say "no pets" – right!'

'By golly, that's right, Mrs. Wesolowski, that's just what you said ...'

'So why you got pets up there, Kepitain Rossiter? Why you got goddam rebbits all over my roof ... ?'

Rossiter's mouth dropped open. 'Pets? You think those are *pets*? Y ... you think I'd keep them nasty, stinkin', lettuce-nibblin' *vermin* as *pets*, Mrs. Wesolowski ... ?'

She blinked, uncomprehendingly. 'Vell ... vat else ... ?'

Rossiter moved closer to the bars, peered left, then right, continuing in a guarded whisper. 'Mrs. Wesolowski ... may I tell you something in the strictest confidence? Well, let me put it this way – are *you* a woman who can keep a secret of the *gravest* importance to our nation's security ... ?'

Her mouth opened. 'Vell ... sure ting I can keep a secret. Vat you take me for – a gossip or somesink?'

He shook his head. 'No, of course not. I take you for a woman of superior intelligence, Mrs. Wesolowski – quick on the up-take, quick to realize the importance of any given situation.'

She regarded him suspiciously. 'You *do*?'

'Of course. We are trained in lightning-fast character analysis in the ...' he lowered his voice still further, '... the Department.'

Her eyes widened. 'The De*part*ment?'

He nodded stiffly.

'You mean ... ?'

He nodded again. 'Mrs. Wesolowski, I think you have a right to know – since it *is* your roof – those rabbits up there are *not* pets. They are taking part in a highly secret experiment of great national importance.'

'Experiment?' she whispered, catching his tone.

'Of *great* national importance. Top, *top* secret!'

'Mein Gott!' she gasped. 'But ... vat are zey doink exekly?'

'I ... don't think I can tell you that, Mrs. Wesolowski ... and yet ...'

'Ja?' she breathed, hopefully.

'Well, it *is* your roof.'

'Certainly, it's my roof.'

'O.K. Well, the Department is conducting an experiment ...' At that moment another 747 thundered overhead, obliterating speech for a full half minute. As the noise subsided, Rossiter continued, '... in the field of Sexual Disenchantment by Sonar Distraction, do you understand?'

'Hm?'

He affected a glimmer of a superior smile. 'In layman's terms, Mrs. Wesolowski, the deterrent effect on breeding habits by excessive noise.'

'Ah!' Her eyes lit up.

'You understand now?'

'Sure, I unerstend. How can ya do it wid some dumkopf next door shakin' the walls wid his hi-fi!'

'Exactly. Well, the Department has selected *your* rooftop because it lies directly in the flight path of the eastbound 747s – as we've just heard ...'

'Mein Gott, don't I know it! One day the whole building is gonna fall down!'

'Precisely. Well, the Department figures that if the noise of those jets stops those danged rabbits breeding, we could be on to one of the greatest Commie deterrents of all time! Think of it – the total wipe-out of all Commie populations in one generation without a single shot being fired! All we have to do is build bigger, noisier jets and fly over their houses! No breeding – no kids!' He pressed the tenth button and the rickety elevator gave a cough and jerked into creeping ascent. 'Think of the honour, Mrs. Wesolowski!' he called down as she slowly disappeared from sight. '*Your* rooftop!'

'I'm tinking, Kepitain Rossiter, I'm tinking!'

'Must see how the little blighters are doin'. I'll report later!'

'But, Kepitain Rossiter ...'

'Yes, Mrs. Wesolowski?'

'Zese big, new jets vould hef to fly over *American* houses to get to Russia! Von't zey wipe out America, too!?'

Rossiter pretended he hadn't heard. Fancy the old bag thinking of that.

He let himself into the apartment and was immediately overwhelmed by disenchantment. The place stank of cabbage and ammonia fumes seeping from the prehistoric fridge. Last week's dishes filled the sink and the bed hadn't been made. The living-room was like an oven, the bedroom hotter than a furnace which meant the air-conditioner had packed up again. He crossed the room to it, twiddled the knobs, cursed, then stepped back and booted it one with the sole of his sandal. It gave a grunt and started.

He entered the kitchen, opened the fridge and through stinging, tear-filled eyes located a warm Budweiser, wondering why in hell he put up with the ammonia stench when the fridge didn't even work.

Unzipping the Bud, he tipped the can to his mouth and returned to the living-room, flopped down in the lumpy armchair and reached for the phone. Now ... which one first?

He decided to take them in order of seniority, and so, smilingly conjuring up a vision of what he might well be interrupting, began to dial the Manhattan number of Paul 'Ramjet' Rogers. And although he was never to know it, his vision was right on the button – down to the last licentious detail.

5

'Paul ... ?' she groaned, wonderingly.

'Yes, honey?'

'My *God*, you're huge in there ...'

He smiled down at her, delighted. 'You complaining, Anastasia.'

'Heavens, *no*! It's wonderful ... wonderful.'

'I'm very glad.'

'Is it ... wonderful for you, Paul?'

'Sublime, honey ... ecstatically ... fantastic.'

'Paul ...'

'Yes, angel?'

'This may seem a funny time to mention this ... but do you know who you look like from down here?'

'No,' he lied, relieved that at last she'd noticed. They usually didn't take so long.

'You're the image of Vic ... tor Mature ... a *young* Victor ... oh baby, that's *crazy* ... Mature, of course.'

He laughed. 'Oh, really?'

'Yes ... you've got his dark, languorous eyes ... and his *Jeezus*, that's beautiful ... his full, sensual mouth ...'

He chuckled his deep, throaty Victor Mature chuckle. 'Really? Anything else?'

'I wouldn't know,' she giggled. 'But I hope for Mrs. Mature's sake he's got your ... oh my God, Paul, it's happening ... !'

'Go, baby, go!'

'Oh ... ohhh ... oh, Paul, I'm *coming* ... !'

'Come ... come!'

'My God ... Paul ... darling!'

'Say it, baby, say it!'

'You're wonderful ... wonderful!'

'I know ... I know!'

'Big as a house ... strong as an ox ... !'

'For you, angel, all for you.'

She grabbed his shoulders, pulled him hard against her, drove up into him, gasping, crying, 'Paul ... PAUL! Fill me ... FILL ME!! Ohh, that's beautiful ... BEAUTIFUL!'

She collapsed beneath him, thighs akimbo, gasping for air. 'Oh, that was ... too fantastic ... crazy ... unbelievable.'

'All ... you imagined?' he gasped.

'Oh, more ... much more, my Captain. Come ... lie beside me ... hold me tight.'

Cradling his handsome, curly head on her breast she stroked the perspiration from his noble brow and traced a finger along his patrician nose, gazing as she did across the room, its curtains drawn against the fierce afternoon sun, to where his Dewey Airlines uniform hung on the wardrobe door for all to see.

'A captain ... and still so young,' she sighed admiringly, smiling wistfully at the four gold sleeve rings that so proudly reflected the room's meagre light. 'You must be very brilliant.'

'I've had the breaks, Anastasia,' he admitted modestly.

She shook her golden head. 'Oh no ... you forget that Daddy's a senior executive with National. I know what it takes to become a captain.' She turned to him, smiling proudly.

'You know, even though you weren't in uniform at the party last night, I knew you were a captain even before you told me. How could you possibly be anything else?'

'You're very sweet, Anastasia,' he smiled, kissing her right nipple. 'Tell me ... had I not been a captain – would you have still come here today?'

He knew damn well she wouldn't. He'd been tipped by Ronnie Duffle of TWA that for the amorous Anastasia it was definitely skippers or nothing. A terrible snob, Anastasia, but, he reflected, a wonderful piece of ass and one he proposed enjoying for many a steamy afternoon to come.

'Well ...' she demurred, replacing a recalcitrant curl from his forehead, 'one *does* have a position to maintain ...'

'And you maintained it magnificently,' he teased, tweeking the nipple between thumb and finger and making her jump.

'Oh, but I have many other positions, too, my Captain,' she smiled, squirming against him and kissing his ear.

'You have, Anastasia?'

'Hm hm,' she nodded. 'Some old ... some new ... some borrowed ... and some very blue ...'

'You know, I think I'd like to try some of those blue ones.'

'You would ... ?' She stopped biting his chest and cocked her ear towards the lounge. 'Isn't that your phone?'

'Yes ... ignore it.'

She chuckled. 'How I admire a man of quick decision – true captain material.'

'About those other positions ...' he grinned, drawing her over him and biting her ear. 'What are you doing tomorrow afternoon?'

'Probably ... you,' she growled, squirming between his open legs. 'Paul, darling, they're not giving up – I think you'd better answer it. I can't concentrate while it's ringing.'

'All right ... but stay right here, I haven't finished with you yet.'

'You haven't? In that case, *you* stay and rest up – *I'll* answer it.'

'No ... no, I'll get it ...'

'Aha! You said that too quickly, Captain Rogers. Are you hiding something ... is it a girl?'

'No ... no, I haven't ...'

40

'Ha! Well, we'll just see!'

She shot off the bed and sprinted for the lounge. Ramjet shot after her but got his foot caught in the trailing sheet, tripped and fell to his knees. And by now Anastasia was at the phone, announcing breathlessly, 'Captain Rogers' residence.'

A puzzled silence ... then an ear-blasting guffaw. '*Who* Rogers?' Cock-up laughed scathingly.

'Er ... *Captain* Rogers,' she replied indignantly. 'Who is this?'

'Well, honey, I'm not too sure. But since Rogers has promoted himself, so will I. Tell him it's General Rossiter calling.'

'What ... do you mean "promoted himself"?' she demanded.

Ramjet came through the door fast, sensing disaster. 'Who is it?'

'Oh ho, I get it,' chuckled Rossiter. 'O.K., honey, put "Captain" Rogers on.'

Frowning at Ramjet she held out the phone. 'It's a General Rossiter. What's going on, Paul? He says you've promoted yourself.'

'Eh? Who says?' He snatched the phone. 'Hello!'

'Naughty, naughty, "Captain" Rogers,' wheedled Rossiter. 'Hey, what sort of a goddam pitch have you been givin' the poor dame?'

'Oh Christ ... you!'

Anastasia was prodding his shoulder. 'What did he mean – "promoting yourself"?'

Ramjet slapped his hand over the mouthpiece. 'A joke, baby – he's a nut! Always joking ... fellow-captain ... always taking a rise ...'

She frowned, suspiciously.

'Truly!'

'Rogers! Are you there?!' bawled Rossiter.

'Yes, dammit ... !'

With a toss of her head Anastasia turned her pretty tail and disappeared into the bedroom.

'Now you've done it!' Ramjet whispered hoarsely down the phone. 'Jeezus, Cock-up, your sense of timing is *atrocious*! What d'you want?'

'Just the merest moment of your precious time, Number One, to discuss something as flippant as flying. But if it's not convenient...'

'No, it is not convenient! I am standing here bollock-naked and she...'

'All right ... all right! The image offends my sensibilities, call me back when you get your shorts on. But make it snappy!'

Ramjet slammed down the phone and rushed to the doorway, arriving in time to see Anastasia peeling away the fourth stripe, flimsily attached to his uniform sleeve with cellotape.

She rounded on him, eyes flaring. 'You ... *crum*bum! You're only a bloody *First*!'

'Now, Anastasia ... honey...'

'Don't you honey me, you ... lecher!' she cried, hurling the detached stripe at him and snatching up her knickers. 'God, the *shame* of it ... seduced by a bloody First!'

'Baby ... please...'

'Don't come near me! Don't touch me! Oh, the ignominy! Rogers, if this ever gets out...' She slid on her dress, stepped into her shoes and ran for the door. 'One word of this, you ... you four-flusher – and I'll get you busted down to *Second*!'

He winced as the door slammed and slumped dejectedly on to the bed. All for the sake of one lousy stripe ... such a wonderful piece of grumble...

The phone bell jerked him out of his brown study.

'Right, now hear this,' gruffed Rossiter. 'As from fifteen hours today we no longer work for Dewey Airlines. Some nut by the name of Berskin won us in a poker game four days ago and has it in mind to launch us with a brand-new image three weeks from tomorrow. In three weeks, Rogers, we take off on a seven-day, round-the-world inaugural flight the like of which has never been seen – one 707 tellin' the world we're the greatest, the classiest, the most romantic, the *most* in every dimension, in short, Rogers, that we are GLAMOUR AIRLINES! Yes, kiddo, that's our new name and our new vocation – GLAMOUR! G for Gorgeous, L for Libido, A for Amorous, M for Muscular, O for Orifice, U for Undress and R for ready when you are, Mrs. Robinson.'

Ramjet was making strangled noises, down the mouthpiece. 'You m ... mean ...'

'Sure, I mean – the old tax-loss days are over, Rogers. This is money-makin' time.'

'No more *pinocle*, Cock-up?'

'No more anythin' that doesn't make a buck. This guy Berskin is out to pan PanAm and transcend Trans World – and *I* got the job of gettin' together a crew for this round-the-world inaugural flight. You interested?'

Despite shock, Ramjet's devious mind was working furiously, had now locked on to a guide beam of self-interest and was quickly homing on to what could be in this for him. A seven-day, round-the-world flight ... publicity ... fame ... women! His picture in every newspaper ... civic receptions wherever they landed ... women!

'I'll take it!' he blurted. 'And thanks, pal '

'It'll cost you a hundred,' Rossiter heard himself saying, his own devious mind reacting automatically to Ramjet's overt enthusiasm, his innate love of money working independently of conscious thought.

'Eh?' gasped Ramjet.

'Take it or leave it, Rogers – there ain't another First in the company who wouldn't pay double for this opportunity.'

'O.K. ... O.K. I'll take it.'

'Good – you're in.'

'Who else is going?'

'In the cockpit – Lord Jim as Navigator ...'

Rogers emitted a groan.

'And Bush McKenzie is Engineer. Sugar Sweetman heads up the cabin crew.'

'How about the girls?'

Rossiter grinned. 'Yeah, how about them? You got any preference, Ramjet?'

'Sure I got a preference.'

'O.K. – for another C-note she's in.'

'What!'

'Rogers, we've got one hundred and twenty stews in Dewey – and every last one of 'em willin' to give their *all* to get on this flight but I just ain't got time to negotiate. Now, that's gotta be worth *some* compensation ...'

'Fifty bucks, Cock-up, an' not a cent more!'

'Seventy-five!'

'Sixty!'

'O.K., you got a deal. What's your choice?'

'Wilma Fluck.'

Rossiter chuckled obscenely. 'O.K. Stand-by for further orders – an' get rested up, you're sure as heck gonna need it.'

He put down the phone, delighted with the way things were going. A hundred and sixty bucks *and* Wilma Fluck – one of the cutest lay-overs in the company, dumb as a rug but the spitting image of Marilyn Monroe – was not a bad start, but maybe, now that his mind was fully attuned to the possibilities, it would get even better.

He picked up the receiver, paused for a moment to consolidate his approach, then began to dial, knowing that another two hundred bucks was as good as in the bank.

Dammit, he was beginning to like this Glamour idea, danged if he wasn't.

6

A few miles south-east of Queens across the East River in Greenwich Village, James DeCourcey Crighton-Padgett, comfortably esconced in a well-appointed top-floor studio-apartment overlooking Washington Square, put down his luridly illustrated girlie magazine and rose from the voluptuous depths of a leather armchair to answer the doorbell, pausing at the long hall wall-mirror for a final check on his appearance. Perfect, he judged – the artiste epitomized. Black beret at a suitably jaunty angle, white silk kerchief knotted at the throat, complementing the sensual black silk shirt open to the third button, fleetingly exposing his deeply tanned torso; white, snugly fitting flared slacks encompassed by a wide, black-leather belt sporting a huge silver buckle; and, finally, black, high-heeled gaucho boots with squared toes to complete the ensemble. Really quite breathtaking, he modestly allowed.

Setting a long ebony cigarette-holder between snow-white teeth, he slipped his image a collusive wink, continued to the door and opened it.

She was as stunning as her portrait in *Artists' and Photographers' Models Directory* had promised and more – a tall, lithe, red-headed creature of outstanding facial beauty and belting figure, most of which he could see due to the plunging, rising characteristics of her tiny, pale-green summer dress which might more accurately have been described as a widish belt for the little it covered.

James took a step back, the sight of her naked thighs setting his heart a-hammer and for the briefest moment almost destroying his cool. Almost. Breeding and experience count hugely at such moments and with scarcely more than a clearing of the throat to cover his confusion, he arched the Crichton-Padgett brow a devastating millimetre higher and bathed her in his suavest smile.

'My dear, how terribly nice of you to come. Won't you come in?'

'Uh?' she went, raking him with a head-to-toe appraisal not only of blatant disbelief but also of intense suspicion, then commenced to chew, cow-like and open mouthed, on what must have been a full half-pound of gum, her diagonal jaw action completely shattering her regal pose and simultaneously wounding James's sensitive soul.

'You English or somethin'?' she enquired, her vernacular immediately placing her origins just across the Brooklyn Bridge and not, as James had envisaged from her photograph, sixty blocks north of Greenwich in the swank area of Central Park West.

Still, his nature compelled him to reason, there *was* the body. All must surely not be lost.

'Er ... yes – English.' He smiled, conquering disappointment with another flash at her incredible gams. 'Won't you come in, Miss ... er ... Vanderbilt – or may I call you Sabrina?'

She crossed the threshold, shrugged carelessly. 'I don't care watcha call me so long as ya pay union rate. Hey ... this is some swell joint – not like summa the joints I get called to.'

46

'I'm delighted you approve,' remarked James, closing the door and following her into the lounge.

She came to a halt, transfixed by the display of nude paintings adorning the walls, her ruminating momentarily abandoned. 'Say ... did you do all these?'

'Who else?' James smiled pleasantly, studying her incredible bottom.

'Hey, they're terrific!'

She approached a study of a Junoesque blonde strewn in wild abandon across a fur-covered bed and whistled at the price-tag stuck in the bottom right-hand corner.

'Two thousand bucks! Gee, no wonder you can afford a swell pad like this.'

'I'm so glad you like, it makes for a happier relationship ... er, *working* relationship straight off. May I show you the studio?'

'Sure, why not?'

He led her from the lounge into the adjoining room, a room almost completely filled by the decadently huge, fur-covered double-bed that appeared in all the paintings. The only other furniture comprised a well-stocked liquor cabinet and an artist's easel, complete with virgin canvas.

Moving no further than the door, she eyed the bed and then James with what can only be regarded as growing suspicion, then ducked back through the door and took another squint at the paintings.

'You ... always paint the same things – naked dames on this bed?'

'Invariably,' he replied coolly. 'One has discovered that in this highly competitive field specialization, as well as talent, is necessary in order to achieve a modicum of commercial success ... er, you may remove your clothes any time you wish, Sabrina ... take Shepherd, for instance – he sticks to elephants and railway engines and therefore ... is ... anything the matter, Sabrina?'

She screw-eyed him, chewing reflectively. 'I dunno ... sumpn don't quite gel around here. You *sure* you painted all them dames out there?'

'My dear girl,' he half laughed, 'why shouldn't I?'

'I dunno ... maybe it's you. Maybe your hands ... your

47

clothes are too clean or sumpn. Most of the painters I pose for live like pigs – splash paint everywhere.'

James released a pained laugh. 'But is that any reason why *I* should live like a pig?'

'No ...' she said, uncertainly. 'But, I'll tell yuh, I've had some quaint experiences posin' for you guys. Some of youse ain't what yuh make yourselves out ta be.'

James gasped, affronted. 'Good heavens, you mean ... ?'

'Sure, I mean. I mean they ain't no painters at all. They're just doity old fakes who wanna see a dame naked is all ... an' get their doity hands on her – an' a heck of a sight woise!'

'And *worse*!' gasped Jim. 'But ... my dear Sabrina ... you're not seriously suggesting that *I* have got you up here merely to ogle your naked body and ... and touch your naked flesh and ... well, now, look – if you feel unsafe with me I would rather you left right now ... !'

'Now, hold on, mister, I wasn't sayin' ...'

'Well, what *were* you saying? First you insult me by implying I haven't painted those studies out there ... then you criticize me for preferring clean hands and clothes ... and *now* you're suggesting I've got you up here for ulterior motives ...'

'No, I ain't suggestin' that ...'

'Well, what *are* you suggesting? Really, I would rather you left this instant than continue under this painful cloud of suspicion. I'm sorry about your fee ... and of course I shall feel obliged to report the incident to your Directory ...'

'Now, hold on ...'

'No, really – I'm quite hurt by your cruel insinuations. I would have thought that with your experience you could have spotted the dedicated artist from the wanton playboy ... would have learned to distinguish the fire of zeal in the eye of the creator from the light of lust in the leer of the lecher. Really, I ...'

He turned away, quite overcome.

'Look, I'm sorry ...' she said earnestly, thinking about her fee.

James turned. 'You are?'

She nodded. 'It's just ... well, a girl can't be too careful.'

'Of course ... I quite understand. Are we ... friends, then?'

She shrugged. 'Sure.'

'Yes ... yes!'

'In a gown of rich green silk, your flame-red hair bedecked with diamonds, sapphires and emeralds you are the envy of every woman and the earnest desire of every man in that vast ballroom – and yet you have eyes for no one but your Charles. Resplendent in a suit of lush black satin, he approached ... takes you in his arms, tenderly ... like this – no, don't open your eyes – you must *feel* the part! You *are* Nell Gwyn and I *am* King Charles. We begin to dance ... round and round and round ...'

James now held her very close, his pulse erupting at the warm, spongy press of her near-naked breasts, the perfume of her hair which rose into his nostrils causing a shiver of delight to ripple down his spine.

'You're ... *very* lovely, Nell,' he croaked, 'so very beautiful. How my courtiers stare. Such beauty as yours must be captured for all time – must be set down on canvas for all to see. I want to paint you, Nell ... would you like to be painted?'

'Oh yes ... yes!' she whispered.

'Then ... come! Finish your champagne ... drain your glass and we shall start!'

She did so.

He took her hand, led her towards the bed. 'Good ... that's excellent, Sabrina. You really feel the part!'

She opened her eyes and squinted at him. 'I feel squiffed.'

'No matter – you're doing marvellously. You even *look* like Nell Gwyn. The champagne has given you a radiance ... an iridescence! Quickly – I must get it down on canvas. Slip off your clothes while I prepare the pallet.'

Abandoning her, he slid behind the easel and pretended to mix paints while surreptitiously watching her disrobe.

In a romantic, champagne trance, weaving nicely, she slipped the zip of the tiny green dress and shook it from her shoulders to the floor; then, before Jim could recover from this bra-less half-naked sight of her, she hooked her thumbs into her minuscule knicks and pushed them to her toes. Kicking them aside, she turned towards him and stretched up her arms, gloriously naked, unashamedly nudified and far more inviting than Crighton-Padgett could stand.

'Oh my God!' he gasped, sticking his thumb in the yellow

51

ochre, 'Oh, how wonderful ... !' and, abandoning the pallet, rushed towards her, wiping his thumb down his black shirt. 'Nell ... Nell – quickly ... on the bed! Let me pose you!'

He caught her by the shoulders, her hot flesh scorching his trembling hands, and drew her backwards to the bed. 'There ... up a bit ... lie back against the pillows ... stretch out your legs ... oh ... wonderful ... now, recline ... *languish* ... you are the arch-temptress, the King's mistress, a right royal sexpot ... perhaps one knee raised ... oh, that's fantastic ... perhaps the thighs *slightly* further apart? ... Oh my God ... here – the champagne ... take the full glass ... sip from it ... look at me over the rim ... there – hold that! Hold it!'

He rushed back to the easel, grabbed up a charcoal stick, looked at Sabrina and the stick shattered between his fingers.

'Wonderful ... hold it ... take a sip!'

She swallowed the lot.

Jim raced over to the bottle, refilled the glass, ran back to the easel, picked up the charcoal stick. Her eyes were closing, the glass drooping in her limp hand.

'Sabrina!'

'Hi, out there!' she grinned. 'That you, Kingy?'

Crighton-Padgett's heart leapt. The time had come! 'Yes, Nell, it is I!'

He ran to the bed, sat on it, his hand on her thigh. 'Nell ... Nell, you're so beautiful ...'

She hiccuped. 'I'm shickered.'

'A mere illusion. Nell, I can no longer resist you! I must have you or die ...'

'Die-tiddley-ie-tie ...'

'I would sacrifice my *kingdom* for one moment in your arms. I worship you ... *all* of you! I kiss your feet ...'

He did so. She giggled.

'... your knee ... your thigh ...'

'Hey, watch it, Charlie.'

'Nell, I am desolate for your arms ...'

'You wan' my arms, Charlie – here y'are ...'

She flung them wide, tossing the champagne over the wall. He gasped. 'You *mean* it? Oh, Nell ...'

He shot off the bed, frantically ripped away his shirt, kicked away his trousers, flung himself naked at her side and show-

52

ered her with kisses. 'Nell ... Nell, this is ... awfully good of you ... oh, what wonderful breasts ... what perfect flesh...' kiss, kiss, kiss.

'Charlie ... I feel awful dizzy ...' The hand clutching the glass flopped on to the bed. '*Awful* dizzy ...'

'Nell, I yearn for you ... *burn* for you ...' kiss ... kiss ... kiss.

'Charlie, whadya doin' down there ... ?'

'Oh, flesh of satin ... heart-shaped hair of golden flame ...'

'Charlie, the room's goin' round ...'

'Teeth of pearl and eyes of emerald hue ...'

'*Charlie* ... !' A plaintive wail.

'Forgive me, Nell, I must have you ... now! Oh, that's incredible! Ohh ... oooh! Aaawww!'

'Charlie, will ya get outta there ... ?'

'A thousand pardons, Nell ... but this is heaven ... *heaven*! OHHH! OOOOHH!'

'Charlie ... I feel sick ...'

'Ohh, this is incr ...' He stopped. 'Eh!?'

'I'm gonna be *sick*, Charlie!'

'Oh ...'

'Right now!'

'Oh my God! Quick – the bathroom – that door!'

She slid from beneath him and staggered round the bed to it, uttering a crescendo groan of imminent disaster, and slammed the door.

'Oh ... buggerit!'

James swung his legs over the side of the bed and heaved a long, despondent sigh – and at that moment the telephone in the living-room rang.

Groaning anew, he heaved himself off the bed and went to answer it.

'Crighton-Padgett,' he announced spiritlessly.

'Well, well, if it isn't old Down-in-the-mouth himself. What's the matter, C-P – another diabolical seduction gone awry?'

James uttered yet a third groan. 'Rossiter – your facility for accurate deduction is exceeded only by your aptitude for telephoning at the worst possible time. I do not wish to speak with you. Goodbye.'

'James! This is your *captain* speaking! Now, get her tongue out of your ear and lissen good – because I have a proposition to put to you that you cannot possibly refuse! Are you listening?'

'Cock-up, you have my undivided indifference ... continue if you must.'

'O.K., here it comes. James, I find myself in the position to let you in on the deal of a decade, the opportunity of a lifetime, the adventure of ...'

'Cock-up ...'

'Yeah?'

'How much?'

'A measly C-note ... the adventure of ...'

'Goodbye, Cock-up.'

'James! You will live to regret it, I *promise* you!'

'Good*bye*, Cock-up.'

'Lissen to me! It's a seven-day ...'

'Goodbye ...'

'... round-the-world ...'

'... Cock-up.'

'... cock-up!'

'Mm?'

'I mean it! James – there'll be broads, dolls, birds, pigeons, female lady girls by the thousand – do I have your attention?'

'Mmm ... momentarily. Carry on.'

'Jim, we've been taken over. We are no longer Dewey Airlines ... everything's changed! Ever heard of Colonel Godfrey Berskin?'

'The dynamic promoter chappie who ...'

'The same! Well, *we* are about to be promoted dynamically. The old tax-loss image has gone for ever – from now on it's GLAMOUR all the way – beginning three weeks hence with a seven-day, round-the-world inaugural wing-ding for *one* Glamour Airlines 707!'

'Glamour Airlines?'

'Our new name.'

'I don't believe it ...'

'Believe it, James, it's true.'

'My God. And ... round-the-world, huh?'

'Right round.'

'For *one* 707?'

'*One* . . . which means *one* captain . . . *one* First . . . *one* Engineer . . . and, of course, *one* Navigator.' A reflective sigh. 'My, my, that crew is sure in for one heck of a time . . . parties, publicity, fame . . . fortune. As I was remarking to Ramjet just a short while ago . . .'

'Rogers! Is he in on this?'

'Well, naturally – he saw the potential straight away. Said it was worth every *cent* of two hundred bucks . . .'

'*Two* hundred!'

'Jim . . . I like you. I know there shouldn't be favouritism in the cockpit but, hell, I'm only human. Give the guy a break, I said to myself – keep the overheads down, he'll repay the thought a thousand-fold. One hundred, Jim, and you're in – do we have a deal?'

'Cock-up . . .'

'Jim . . . I'd hate to have to remind a nice Nav like you that we have another thirty-nine other Navs on the Dewey books . . .'

'. . . we have a deal.'

'Splendid. Now . . . about the cabin crew. Ramjet said to me, "Cock-up, I would give *anything* to have that cute little goose-ball Wilma Fluck along on this venture . . . tending our every need . . . pandering to each erstwhile whim . . .'

'How much, Cock-up?'

'Another C, dear boy – not a cent more.'

' "Boobs" Buchanan?'

'A perspicacious choice. Cash, of course.'

'But, of . . .'

A movement behind Jim caused him to turn.

SSPPLLAATTT!!

A handful of Samurai Blue caught him plumb in the mush. 'You lousy . . . crummy . . . lecherous . . . connivin' . . . FAKE!'

SSPPLLOODDGGEE!! Burnt Orange closed one eye. 'You dirty . . . randy . . . philanderin' . . . fornicatin' . . . BUM!'

SSPPLLOOTT!! Verdant Green obliterated his navel. 'You sex-crazed . . . mealy-mouthed . . . finger-happy . . . busy-dicked . . . CRUM!'

CCRRUUMMPP!!

The painting of the reclining blonde descended with the

force of a butcher's cleaver upon his head, the canvas bursting about his ears and the frame coming to rest upon his naked shoulders like an ornate horse-collar.

'Whe ... wha ... glub!' he gulped.

SSLLAAMM!!

The building shook and she was gone.

Throwing down the phone, he staggered, one-eyed to the nearest wall, perceiving instantly the root of his discovery. The paintings were hanging awry, their price tags removed, the identity of their real author, one Boris Shakachaski, James's downstairs neighbour, revealed.

'Crighton-Padgett!!' the swinging mouthpiece was shrieking.

James stumbled to it, scooping Verdant Green, Burnt Orange and Samurai Blue from his naked person.

'Glob?' he answered.

'What in hell's goin' *on* over there?'

'Blip ... glab ... blut ...'

'Oh, you eatin', Jim? O.K. – call me back when you're finished.'

7

'Pete Pulver's Palaestra.'

'Hi, Pete – is Bush McKenzie there?'

'Who's this ... Cock-up? Sure, he's woikin' out now. Hold on, I'll take it to him.'

Pete trailed the phone wire across the gymnasium floor to where the sweating blond giant was burnishing his bulging biceps bending four million pounds of pig-iron. 'Bush, it's fer you!'

'Seventy-six ... phhew! ... seventy-seven ... phhew! ... who is it, Pete? ... seventy eight ... phhew!'

'It's Cock-up.'

'Oh Christ. 'Ere, hold it up, will yuh? 'Ello! ... seventy-nine ... phhew!'

'Bush! ... my antipodean amigo ...'

'Cut the crap, Skip – I already told you eight times. I don't *want* any bleedin' rabbits ... eighty-two ... phhew!'

'Bush!' wheedled Rossiter. 'You mistake my intentions. I am the bearer of glad tidings!'

'Oh, you transferrin' to PanAm? ... eighty-six phhew!'

'Don't be a smart-ass, McKenzie – an' put those goddam weights down, I've got somethin' to tell you!'

'I can't – I'm on a hundred ... eighty-eight ... phhew! ... but go ahead with the con, I'm listenin'.'

'*What* con! So help me, McKenzie, I've gotta mind to leave you out of the whole beautiful deal for insolence...'

'O.K., g'bye, Skip ... ninety-two ... phhew!'

'McKenzie, it ain't *rabbits*! It's a seven-day, round-the-world luxury junket to launch our new glamorous image because as of fifteen hundred hours today we are no longer Dewey Airlines we are GLAMOUR AIRLINES an' too goddam bad you ain't got the sense to listen because as a good an' loyal buddy I had you in as Engineer on the *one* 707 scheduled to launch the whole beautiful campaign an' too bad you're gonna miss all the fun an' the fame an' the females an' the fornication' an' goodBYE!!'

CCRRUUMMPP!!

Four million pounds of pig-iron hit the floor.

'SKIP ... !'

'Goodbye, McKenzie, you ... you *ingrate*!'

'Now, Cock-up ... how the heck was *I* to know?'

'Well ... say you're sorry.'

'Get stuffed.'

'McKenzie, do you appreciate the full import of what I've just bin sayin' – because if *you* don't, the others certainly do. They saw it immediately as bein' worth every lousy penny of two hundred bucks and...'

'Others? What others? What two hundred b...'

'Why – Ramjet and Lord Jim.'

'They're in on this?'

'Sure they're in – couldn't keep them out! Men of perception, of course ... saw the potential straight away – the fame, the adulation. As Ramjet astutely observed – what's two hundred lousy bucks when you're gettin' your picture on the front page of the World's Press. Quite, Lord Jim agreed – just think of the civic receptions, the TV appearances, the parties ... the women ... !'

'Two ... hundred?' McKenzie repeated reflectively.

'Merely to cover expenses.'

'Who's expenses?'

'Just leave that to me, Bush, baby – I'll cover all the angles. You don't have to worry your head about anythin'. I, er, take it you agree, then ... ?'

'Well ...'

'Good man. Welcome aboard. Now, get back to those push-ups, I want you in A1 shape. We'll be gettin' a preliminary briefing in two or three days – I'll pick up the cash then – O.K.?'

'Er ...'

'Fine.'

Rossiter put down the phone and let out a whoop. This was easier than breeding rabbits and there wasn't much to that.

Getting another warm beer from the fridge, he settled again in the armchair, lit a new cheroot in way of celebration, and reached once again for the phone, assured of yet another hundred at least before he commenced dialling.

Sweetman. The kid was a push-over.

'Hello,' the voice answered. 'Mrs. Sweetman speaking.'

Rossiter could barely contain a chuckle of triumph. A double push-over. Sweetman lived with his mother!

'Well, hello, Mrs. Sweetman, how are you? This is Captain Rossiter speaking – Michael's captain. Is the dear boy in?'

'Why, yes, he is, Captain – he's right here, putting up a shelf for me.'

'Now, isn't that just like him – he's always so helpful. You must be very proud of him as we are in Dewey Airlines, Mrs. Sweetman. We consider him one of our most efficient, kind, thoughtful and helpful stewards and that's the reason I'm calling right now. May I have a word with him – if it's not too much trouble?'

'Why, certainly, Captain. It's been a pleasure talking to you.'

'And to you, Mrs. Sweetman.'

Rossiter grimaced at his own excruciating sickliness and rinsed his mouth with beer to kill the taste. Some things were not worth doing even for money. Almost.

'Hellooo!' Sugar yodelled down the phone.

'Well, hello, Michael. Captain Rossiter here – how are yuh, my boy?'

'In absolute *agony*, Captain mine – I've just hit me thumb with the hammer.'

'Gee, that's too bad.'

'Not to worry, I'll give it a suck. And how are you, Captain?'

'Well, Sugar, I'll tell yuh, I am just cock-a-hoop ...'

'Oooh ...'

'I have just heard some mighty exciting news about old Dewey Airlines that you are gonna *love*! Sugar, we have just been taken over by a fella named Berskin who is going to turn the old tax-loss company upside down. As from today we are no longer Dewey Airlines, we are GLAMOUR AIRLINES, and three weeks tomorrow we take off on an inaugural flight, backed by a million-dollar promotion campaign, to launch the new image.'

'Really!'

'Think of it, Sugar – a seven-day, round-the-world giggle for *one* 707 – me in charge, naturally ... Paul Rogers is First Officer, Jim Crighton-Padgett is Nav, and your old pal Bush McKenzie is the Engineer ...'

'How ... *super*!'

'Quite a team, heh? – and quite a proposition, wouldn't you say?'

'Oh, I would, I would! It sounds absolutely *terrific*, Captain!'

'It *is* terrific, Sugar – the flight of a lifetime. Now ... how do *you* feel about headin' up the cabin crew?'

A gasp. 'Me! Ohh, Skip, that would be *gorgeous*!'

'No need to thank me, my boy. You're the best there is and I only want the best. The way you handle those old dames is a lesson for all aspiring stews in tact, diplomacy and pure heart.'

'Well, that's *fright*fully nice of you to say so, Cap ...'

'Forget it. This is going to be a mighty important trip for us, Sugar – we're gonna have celebrities on board – politicians, TV personalities, you name it, and I want to be sure every-

thing back there in the cabin is in the best possible hands –
now, whadya say?'

'Ohh yes . . . yes, count me in and thank you ve . . .'

'Think nothin' of it, it's my pleasure. There's . . . just one
teeny matter that's hardly worth the mentionin' in the light of
so much opportunity and excitement . . . but you'll appreciate,
I'm sure, that to get this kinda thing off the ground one has to
do a fair amount of behind-the-scenes wheelin' and dealin',
know what I mean . . . ?'

'Er . . . no.'

'And I'm sure you apprec . . . huh?'

'I'm *ever* so sorry, Skip, but I don't know what you . . .'

Rossiter laughed. 'Kid . . . we got eight 707s – right? And five
crews to every ship – right? That makes forty Firsts, forty
Navs, forty Engineers . . . *and* forty Chief Stews all willin' to
sell their grandmas for a crack at this inaugural hoe-down –
right? An' that means one *heck* of a lot of work for yours truly
– sortin' things out . . . fightin' them off . . . workin' all the
hours that God sends gettin' this thing together. Why, only an
hour ago Ramjet Rogers said to me: "Skip, I can see your
overheads are gonna be piling up on this deal – and if you're
not careful you're gonna be way outa pocket!" At which point
Jim Crighton-Padgett came up with an offer that really
touched me. "Skip," he said, "I don't know about the others,
but I'll be only too glad to help cover your expenses for a crack
at this smasheroo, chance-in-a-lifetime deal," and, so help me,
Sugar, he thrust a coupla C-notes into my hand. Wouldn't take
no for an answer. Now, whadya think of that, don't that just
grab yuh?'

'Captain, that's unbe*liev*able! Mind you, that's Jim Crighton-Padgett all over – generous as the day is long. So . . . as I
understand it, Ramjet, James and Bush have *paid* you money
for the privilege of crewing this inaugural flight, is that
right . . . ?'

Rossiter released a guffaw. 'Heck, no – not *paid*, Sugar,
good heavens, no. Look upon it more as a . . . as a gesture of
appreciation for all the . . .'

Something was going wrong. The kid was not reacting as he
should!

'. . . for the . . . Sugar, baby, do you understand the *implica-*

tions of this smash-hit, wizz-bang, bifferoo flight ... the publicity, the fame, the ...'

'Oh, *certainly*, Captain. I can see a right old knees-up for all concerned ...'

'*Well*, then ...' laughed Rossiter, with a glimmer of relief.

'But I can also see a *great* deal of extremely hard work for the cabin crew – which, as you say, is why you've chosen me out of forty potential candidates.'

'Oh, indeed, Sugar! No one better suited – a fine, reliable head on very young shoulders ...'

'Well, then, my Captain, I *do* feel that my professional skill and dedication to duty should in itself sufficiently warrant my inclusion in this special crew – *and* – since the glory of a successful flight will undoubtedly reflect on your *own* goodself – should constitute sufficient reward for all your extra-curricula pre-flight efforts ...'

'Well ... yes ... that is ... I ...'

'In other words, dear Captain, since *you* are calling *me* and not I you, I must presume you *need* whatever talent I possess in order to fulfil your own immediate ambitions.'

'Well ... yes ... but ...'

'And although Ramjet, James and Bush McKenzie may feel it necessary to ensure their places on this smash-hit, wizz-bang, bifferoo flight with a contribution towards your expenses, I'm *terribly* afraid I must decline for the reasons stated. *If*, however, you feel *strongly* about my financial participation ...'

'I do ... I do!' bellowed Rossiter. Goddam it, he must have been out of his *mind* choosing this smart-assed, mealy-mouthed ... I mean, who'd have *thought Sweetman* coulda come out with a mouthful like that!

'Now, you listen to me, Sweetman ... !'

'... then I have only one recourse ... oh, excuse me, Captain, the tape's run out. Just a sec while I turn it over ...'

'Huh? Tape? *What* tape, Sweetman?'

'Er, my cassette recorder tape, Captain. As shop-steward for our local union chapter I make a point of recording all calls, you never know when you'll need to refer to something. There, that's all right now ... you were saying, Captain ...?'

Rossiter gagged. 'Y ... you mean ... this conversation is on tape, Sweetman?'

'Oh yes, every word. As I was saying – if you feel *strongly* about my financial participation in this venture, my only recourse would be to put the proposal to my union by way of this tape and let them decide for me. Should they, of course, decide in *favour* of my paying you two hundred dollars ...'

'*Sweetman*, my dear *fellow* ... whoever said anything about you paying me two hundred *dollars* ... ?'

'Oh, I'm sorry. I somehow felt the implication since you said James Cright ...'

'Good heavens, *no*, Sweetman! My dear chap, you've got it all wrong ... perhaps I expressed myself badly. Sugar, baby ... you don't honestly believe your captain would expect the cabin crew to chip in the same amount as the cockpit crew, do you ... ?'

'Well, just how much did you have in mind, Captain?'

'Why ... nothing at *all*, Sugar! Bless you, don't you know your old Skip yet? Do you honestly think I'd take a plug nickel from a sweet, hard-workin' guy like you? No, Michael, I must decline your most generous offer. I know it comes from the heart – but no thanks. Your talents back there in the cabin are reward enough for me. Well, I'm mighty glad to have you aboard, Sugar. I'll be in touch in the next coupla days for a prelim briefing. Take care of yourself, now ... don't want to lose you, do we? So long, old buddy.'

'Toodle-oo, Captain.'

Rossiter slammed down the phone and booted a beer can across the room. God*dam* the sneaky, smart-assed, motherlovin' punk! Why ... *why* – out of forty weak-kneed, subservient, forelock-pluckin' stewards, all blessed with a finely honed respect for the Chief Captain, did he have to pick the one punk kid who wasn't and didn't!

Cock-up, he thought, savagely chomping his cigar to shreds and spitting it out with vehemence, you've cocked it up again! Two hundred semolians down the drain because you didn't vet the little squirt.

A union steward yet!

The thought brought him out in a cold sweat. One word of this to the union and ... the consequences were so terrifying he abandoned the thought with a shudder and turned his mind to pleasanter matters – to Wilma Fluck and Babs 'Boobs' Buchanan to be precise – two of the sweetest pieces of grumble he'd ever come across. Well, he hadn't personally, but he knew plenty who had and the reports had been most encouraging.

The prospect of phoning them quite cheered him up, and so, with a lighter heart and a fresh cheroot going, he began to dial.

8

Wilma's line was engaged, so he tried Boobs Buchanan and got through. She sounded out of breath.

'Hello!'

Rossiter jerked the receiver from his ear, his inner-drum twanging like a tuning fork. Geez, she had a lousy voice.

'Hello, Boobs – guess who this is?'

'Henry Fonda?'

Godalmighty, how did a screech like that ever get through stew-school.

'Right in one,' he laughed. 'Only I've changed my name – it's now Rossiter.'

'Cock-up!' she squealed delightedly.

Deciding to overlook the familiarity in deference to immediate self-interest, he continued, 'The one an' only. Say, have you got a moment to listen to the offer of a lifetime, baby?'

'Gee, Cock-up, I didn't know you cared. You know, you're the only guy in Dewey that never tried anythin' at thirty thousand feet?' She gave a giggle. 'Made me wonder how you earned that nickname!'

'Yeah, well, that's another story, Boobs, involvin' quite a different kind of tail. You just come in, you sound kinda breathless.'

'No, I was in the shower when the phone rang. This weather I take ten showers a day. Hardly get time to get my clothes on.'

'You got 'em on now?'

'No. I'm standing here dripping all over the carpet – naked as sin.'

Rossiter gulped. 'That's quite a thought. Remind me to put in a TV phone some day.'

'Hey, you're *naughty* ...'

'We'll talk about that some other time. Listen, baby, I gotta surprise for you – Dewey Airlines ain't Dewey Airlines any more. A coupla days ago a big wheel by the name of Berskin won us in a poker game and is hell-bent on changin' our image, can you believe it?'

'Berskin?'

'Yeah, a Colonel Godfrey Berskin ...'

'Him!'

'Why – you know him?'

'*Every*one knows him. He made Jimmy Silver, Marc Dart and Wensley Pocket what they are today!'

'Yeah? Well, what *are* they?'

She tutted. '*Cock*-up ... you mean you haven't *heard* of them? They're three of the biggest pop-stars in the world!'

'Is that right? Well, rabbits is more my game. Anyway, to get to the point – we're launching our new name – GLAMOUR AIRLINES – in three weeks time with a seven-day, round-the-world promotion flight backed by a promotion campaign like you'd never believe ... OWW!'

Her shriek of delight blasted down the earpiece, scrambling his brains.

'Round the *world* ... !'

'Sure,' he winced. 'And ...'

'Seven days!'

'Yep ... and ...'

'Oh, Cock-up, Cock-up – take me, *take* me! I'll work for nothing ... scrub floors ... anything...!'

'Anything?'

'ANYTHING!' He almost dropped the phone.

'Well, now ...' he smirked, changing ears, 'there's kind of a problem here, Boobs, as you might well imagine. I've got no fewer than one hundred and twenty screamin' air-stews on my tail...'

'Oh, I know ... I know...'

'Believe me, the pressure is tre*men*dous.'

'Of course, of *course* ...'

He released a chuckle. 'Boobs, you have no *idea* what some of those naughty girls have been offerin' to get on that flight ...'

'Oh, Cock-up, I do ... I do! And *whatever* they're offering, I'll *double* it!'

'Y ... you will?'

'*Treble* it!'

'Oh, I don't think *that* will be necessary ...'

'Then *what*? Name it and it's yours.'

'Well, now, Boobs, I will admit there have been one or two items of expense ...'

'Of *course* there have. For gosh-sakes, you must be *in*undated with expenses. Just ... how much ... precisely ...?'

He sighed a troubled sigh. 'Well ...'

'A hundred?'

'Well...'

'A hundred and fifty?'

'Er ...'

'Two hundred!'

'Boobs, how on earth did you know? That happens to be exactly the figu'...'

'Done!'

'It's a deal. You're in.'

'Oh, Cock-up, I love you!'

'Call you in a coupla days, honey. Go back to the shower, you'll catch your death.'

He threw down the receiver, leapt out of his chair and let

rip a yiippee. It was easier than stealin' carrots from a rabbit!

And now . . . for Wilma!

Humming 'I've Got Plenty Of Money' and feeling ace-high to a busted flush, he dropped back into the chair and fingered her number.

This time she answered, 'Hello . . . Marilyn speaking,' her cool, breathy, little-girl-lost caress oozing into his ear and patching up the damage Boobs' shriek had wrought.

Rossiter grinned. The kid was a kook. Knowing she looked like Marilyn Monroe she'd really gone overboard for the image and now walked and talked like her – even called herself Marilyn and who could blame her with a name like Wilma Fluck?

'Wilma?' said Rossiter.

'Who . . . who is this?'

'Jack Lemmon. You're wanted on set, baby. It's our big scene in the sleeping compartment.'

'Look, who *is* this?' Under pressure, Marilyn wavered in favour of Wilma, a Bronx edge beginning to assassinate the Monroe cool. 'You some kinda nut, maybe?'

'The opinion *has* been expressed from time to time,' said Rossiter with rare good humour. 'Relax, baby, this is your Captain – Al Rossiter – and keep makin' with the pianissimo, I need it.'

'Cock-up!' she breathed, now fully restored to the role. 'Gee, it's nice to hear your voice.'

'Likewise, honey, I'm sure. Say, that's a great impersonation you do.'

'Impersonation? Of who, Cock-up? I'm not impersonatin' anybody.'

'No? Well, blow me if you don't sound exactly like Marilyn Monroe.'

'I *do*? Gee, it's nice of you to say that. *Lots* of people tell me I look and sound just like her, isn't that great?'

'Terrific.'

'Don't you think she had the loveliest voice in the whole wide world?'

'The best, baby – gave me goose-bumps even when she was screamin'. Now, listen, Wilma . . .'

'I just think she was the greatest star ever, don't you, Cock-up . . . ?'

'The absolute most. Now, honey . . .'

'The way she walked . . . and moved. Did you ever see "The Seven Year Itch"?'

'Forty-seven times. Now, kid . . .'

'Well now, didn't you think that scene where she stands over the subway grating and lets the draught blow up her clothes just the sexiest . . . loveliest thing you ever saw . . . ?'

'Never quite got over that, Wilma. Now, honey . . .'

'I do that all the time, you know. When it's hot and sticky like right now I go down to the subway grating and . . .'

'WIL – MA! Will you cool it just a minute, honey, I got somethin' important to tell you . . .'

'Gee, I'm sorry, Cock-up – I get kinda carried away . . .'

'Baby, one day that could well happen – but before they come for you, hear this. Wilma, I could well be about to give you the break you've been waitin' for all your life. Dewey Airlines is finished – kaput! As from today we are GLAMOUR AIRLINES! You hear that, baby – GLAMOUR! G for Gertrude Lawrence, L for Lana Turner, A for Arlene Dahl, M for Guess who!. O for Olivia DeHavilland, U for Ursula Andress and R for Rin Tin Tin . . .'

'Ohhh . . . Cock-up!' she gasped.

'Well now, I thought it might just appeal to you. But that's not all. Wilma, I could make you famous! Three weeks today I am taking off on a seven-day, round-the-world promotion flight that will attract TV, radio, press . . . and *film* attention in every country on this globe!'

'Films!' She was almost in tears.

'Sure, why not? And naturally anyone in my crew is gonna hit the headlines every time. Don't you see it, Wilma . . . ? Lights . . . cameras . . . action! And here, folks, we have one of the two super-glamorous air-stews serving aboard the GLAMOUR AIRLINES inaugural special . . . how about a big hand for . . . Miss Wilma Fl . . .'

'No! Cock up . . . make it Marilyn,' she pleaded.

'O.K. . . . for Miss Marilyn Fl . . .'

'No! Could you make it . . . Mungo?'

'Eh?'

'Oh, *please*, Cock-up!'

'O.K., kid – Miss Marilyn Mungo. Marilyn – say a few

words to the ten billion people watching out there ...'

'Hi, everybody ...'

'That's enough. Well, what do you think, Wilma?'

'Oh, Cock-up, please ... *please* take me!'

'Heck, I want to, honey – it's just that ... well, I'm bein' *besieged* with all kinds of temptation from the other girls, you know how it is. Bóobs Buchanan, of course, has kinda *assured* her place on board by helpin' out with the expenses – you know, the unavoidable overheads concomitant with such a tricky operation ... drinks for the TV boys ... some small financial inducement for the lads at M.G.M., I'm sure you understand ...'

'Oh, I do, I do! Cock-up ... is there any way in which I can help? I don't have much put by, but ...'

'Er, how ... much *do* you have put by ... ?'

'About a thousand dollars.'

Rossiter gulped. 'Oh, now, honey, that wouldn't be necessary ...'

Damn it! Why didn't he get through to her first! He couldn't very well go back to Boobs now and up the ante ... *could* he? No – cast the thought aside, Rossiter. Greed goes before a fall. You're still doin' all right.

'No, two hundred would be plenty, baby ...'

'It's yours! I'll bring it round right now ... !'

'Woah ... woah!' he laughed. 'No need for that. I'll be seein' you in a coupla days for a prelim briefing, it'll do fine then. O.K., honey, the job's yours.'

'Oh, Cock-up – how can I ever thank you?'

'Just don't go fallin' down any subway grating, that's all.' Fat chance with an ass like hers! 'So long, Gorgeous.'

He replaced the receiver and stood up, stretched extravagantly, crossed the room with a magnanimous air and fetched the dozing air-conditioner another smart kick up the tochas.

'Well, you slovenly slob, how about *that* for an afternoon's work! One ultra-glamorous crew assembled – so I'm in the big with Berskin ... two of the greatest air-screws in the business on board to help while away the time – *and* – nearly a thousand of America's finest in the bank to slow down the overheads!'

He strolled to the cracked wall mirror and regarded himself with unabashed admiration.

'Cock-up, you old tiger ... with all due modesty you're the greatest. Cunning as a fox, tenacious as a whippet, sneaky as a snake in the grass. Yeah ... snea ... ky!'

He laughed out loud, brought his teeth together with a clang and was inspecting them closely when the telephone rang. He crossed to it with a merry little skip.

'The Rossiter residence!'

'Hello, Captain Rossiter?'

'Sure, speaking – how are yuh?'

'Not too well, Captain – not since I heard a tape recording a while back between you and one of our shop-stewards, Mr. Michael Sweetman ...'

Rossiter's ebullience fell away like a cast-off skin. 'Wh ... who is this?'

'My name is Callaghan of the Transport Workers' Union, Captain,' the voice said easily. 'And we just wanna hear from you that the conversation between you and Sweetman was just one big joke – y'know – a leg-pull.'

'A *leg*-pull!' laughed Rossiter. 'Well, of course it was a leg-pull ... a joke ... it was just one big laugh, for heaven's sake!' He gave another laugh to prove it. 'Good heavens, you don't think a man in my position ... an *airline* captain ... a Chief Pilot, for Petesake, would go around ...'

'No, of course not, Captain. It's unthinkable, isn't it?'

'Unthinkable! – exactly.'

'Well, thanks for putting our minds at rest, Captain. We knew there was nothing more than that to it, but we just wanted to ...'

'To make sure! Of course ... and quite right, too. You have a duty to protect your stewards ...'

'And stewardesses, Captain ...'

'And ... stewardesses, of course ...'

'Yes, that's true, we do – and of course the penalties for any attempted bribery or *extortion* are extremely ...'

'Severe – yes, I'm ... fully aware of that, Callaghan.'

'Naturally, *cockpit* crew are out of our jurisdiction ... yet I sure would hate for that tape to fall into the wrong hands – say the hands of the Airline Pilots' Association, for instance, hey,

Captain – joking though it was intended to be . . .'

'J . . . joking!' nodded Rossiter, sweat cascading down his face. 'A leg-pull through and through. Good heavens, Callaghan, you don't think for one moment . . .'

'No, of course not, Captain – though as I said to Sweetman, I sure would hate that tape to fall into the wrong hands. It could put your captain in a mighty embarrassing . . .'

'Position. You know you are so right. I guess I just never thought of that . . . when I was pulling Sweetman's . . .'

'Leg. Sure, who would? We all enjoy a good joke – and, ha! that sure was a good one. Fancy – a captain selling seats to his own crew! Ha . . . !'

'Ridiculous, isn't it, Callaghan?'

'Crazy. Well, so long, Captain.'

'Goodbye, Callaghan . . . oh, Callaghan, just a thought in passing . . . does Sweetman still . . . have those tapes?'

'No, he handed them over to me – for sort of safe keeping. You know – so they don't accidentally fall into the wrong hands, know what I mean?'

'Oh well, that's . . . very gratifying.'

Callaghan chuckled unnervingly. 'Sure hope none of your crew owes you any money, Captain. Sure would be a hoot after this if someone saw them handing over a fistful of bills to you and thought you . . .'

'My God, wouldn't that be . . . a . . .' gulp 'hoot!'

'Well, so long again, Captain. Have a happy inaugural!'

Rossiter smashed down the phone and flung his cheroot at the wall.

'GGOODDAAMMMM YYOOUU, SSWWEETT-MMAANN!'

He would kill the little runt! *Murder* him! Nail his balls to the runway and fly off with his scrawny body! *Right*, Sweetman, you are gonna get *yours*! Somewhere . . . somehow . . . some*time* during that one-week, round-the-world flight . . . !

A furious thumping on his door shocked him out of his murderous plotting.

'WHO IS IT!' he bellowed.

'It's me – Mrs. Wesolowski! Kepitain, you kom out an' do somesink aboud zese rebbits! – zey all eskape-ed from zeir

hatches and are krapping all over my roof! Everyver I look –
krep ... krep ... krep!'

'OHHHHH ... SHITE!' roared Rossiter.

'Call it vat you like – but get ze stinkin' things offa my roof
– NOW!'

9

One week later, on a sultry Friday afternoon with thunder in the heavens, the first official meeting between Berskin and crew convened in the board-room atop Berskin Building.

Those in attendance (and at this moment lined up at the door awaiting His arrival) were, in order of seniority: Captain Alfred Rossiter, First Officer Paul Rogers, Engineer Officer Morton McKenzie, Second Officer James DeCourcey Crighton-Padgett, Steward Michael Sweetman, Stewardess Babs Buchanan and Stewardess Wilma Fluck.

Accountant Heinrich Himmler was also present; and Peabody was there, aloofing around in the background, detesting everybody and suffering a particularly piquant attack of nostalgia for Lord Gascoigne D'Arbly and the Towers.

'Boy, I could sure use a drink,' remarked Ramjet, address-

74

ing Lord Jim who was cleaning Samurai Blue out of his fingernails with a toothpick. 'Really hung one on last night. Met this Russian chick in...'

'Sssh!' went Rossiter, taking the opportunity to glare yet again at Sweetman down the line.

Ramjet turned slowly and regarded Cock-up with his hooded, Victor Mature glower. 'You shushing me?'

'Yes. The moment calls for a certain circumspection, Rogers – we do not want to hear about your disgusting dalliance with any Red rooster.'

Ramjet frowned, askance. 'Y'know something, Cock-up – I think you've flipped.'

'And don't call me that in here! Here you call me "captain"!'

'I think you flipped when Sweetman slipped us copies of that tape and...'

'That's enough, Rogers! We won't mention that tape ever again!'

'It's gonna cost you, Cock-up...' Rogers taunted smilingly.

'Captain!'

'Captain Cock-up.'

'Rogers...' seethed Rossiter, 'you are on the inaugural flight *and* you've got Wilma aboard, what more do you want?'

'Nothing ... yet,' Ramjet grinned devilishly. 'But no doubt I'll think of something.'

'Bah!' went Rossiter who had been in the foulest mood imaginable ever since the Day of the Tape when, in addition to losing the entire nine hundred and sixty dollars extracted from the crew, he had, at Mrs. Wesolowski's insistence, gone up to the roof and come upon a scene of unbridled and horrifying fornication, discovering the Angoras screwing the daylights out of the Argentines, the Beverens bashing bulldust out of the Himalayans and the Flemish Giants fucking hell out of the Harlequins. Realizing instantly that in twenty-eight days time there was going to be such a goddawful explosion of rainbow-hued, weirdly proportioned, slant-eyed, Dutch-speaking, Angente-Bevalayan-Flemquins, he decided immediately to chuck the whole bleedin' issue off the roof and take up tropical fish.

No, it was not Al Rossiter's week.

Suddenly the board-room door bust open and in marched a parade.

In the lead – two young office boys bearing between them a huge blackboard mounted on an easel.

Behind them came Miss Destry, bosoms thrusting, carrying under his arms several long rolls of paper.

Next, to everybody's amazement, an outrageous, effeminate creature with shoulder-length, dark brown wavy hair streaked in front with white, dressed in a purple silk shirt with billowing sleeves, navy-blue neckerchief and tight, *tight* white trousers.

In he flounced, smiling archly and making lips at all the chaps down the line, and came to a halt at the head of the long rose-wood table where the blackboard had now come to rest.

Peabody, at the door, cleared his throat. 'Ladies and gentlemen – the Chairman, Managing Director and Sole Stock Owner of Glamour Airlines ... Colonel Godfrey Berskin!'

In swept Berskin, nattily dressed in a para-military suit of lovatt green, cigar clamped between his teeth, trailing more smoke than a VC10 at take-off.

'All here, Peabody?'

'All present and correct, sir.'

'O.K. – make with the introductions.'

'Certainly, sir ... may I present your Chief Pilot – Captain Alfred Ross ...'

'I know Rossiter, Peabody. Hi, how are you, Rossiter?'

'Lousy.'

'Fine ... fine.'

'And this is First Officer Paul Rogers ...' continued Peabody.

Berskin stepped back to take in the whole of Rogers, then regarded him with a puzzled squint. 'Ain't I seen you before somewhere, Rogers?'

Rogers rendered his slow, lop-sided Victor Mature grin. 'Quite possibly I remind you of someone, sir?'

'Huh huh,' nodded Berskin, 'sure you do ... it's ...' he snapped his fingers recollectively. '... oh ... what's his name?'

'Someone in the ... *movies*, perhaps, sir?' lop-sided Rogers even more.

'Yes ... yes ... same eyes ... same mouth ... oh ...'

76

'Someone whose name begins with . . .'

'No! Don't tell me . . . I'll get this one by myself.' Berskin once again looked Rogers up and down, nodding appreciatively. 'Yep, you'll do nicely.'

He moved on, craning his head even higher to accommodate the towering McKenzie.

'This is Engineer Officer Morton McKenzie,' announced Peabody.

'Well, you're a big 'un,' Berskin commented admiringly.

McKenzie grinned. ' 'Ello, mate, how y'goin'?'

Berskin frowned, perplexed. 'And what in hell accent is *that*?'

'Er, Engineer McKenzie is one of our . . . hm . . . antipodean cousins, sir,' interposed Peabody.

'He means I'm a flamin' Aussie,' grinned Bush. 'Sydney.'

Berskin grimaced. 'Sydney? I thought you said his name was Morton, Peabody . . .'

Peabody winced. 'And this, sir . . . is Second Officer James DeCourcey Crighton-Padgett . . .'

'The *hell* it is,' gasped Berskin.

'Har d'you do,' drawled James, putting it on a bit.

'English,' confided Peabody with undisguised relish.

'Splendid . . . splendid!' nodded Berskin, raking Lord Jim's tall, slender, elegance with approbation. 'An international crew – couldn't be better.'

He moved on, taking in Sweetman's youthful, clean-cut radiance, his pristine cleanliness and cherubic, dimpled smile.

'And you, my boy?'

'Steward Sug . . . Michael Sweetman, Colonel,' Sugar announced effusively. 'At your service, yes, indeed. Rest assured, Colonel, the cabin will be in good hands while *I'm* in charge. Not a problem will arise that will not be promptly and diligently overcome to the satisfaction of all.'

'Crud,' muttered Rossiter.

'Well, I'm mighty glad to hear it, Sweetman,' said Berskin, quickly losing interest as his eyes fell . . . boooiinngg! . . . upon Boobs Buchanan's balloons and plunged headlong down her chasmic cleavage. 'Well now . . . and whom do we have here . . . ?'

'Stewardess Barbara Buchanan,' Peabody announced stiffly.

'My dear ...' ogled Berskin, 'words fail me.'

'Hi, Colonel,' she squeaked. 'I, too, am at your service.'

'A promise I shall assiduously bear in mind, Miss Buchanan, danged if I won't, yes, sireee ...'

He hadn't even noticed her voice.

Peabody leaned closer. 'And this, sir ... herm, sir ... !'

'Mm?' With reluctance Berskin hauled up his eyes.

'And this is Stewardess Wilma F ... Fluck.'

'Wilma who?'

Marilyn, suitably prepared with pre-moistened ruby lips, peeped at Berskin through a curtain of short, blonde hair and breathed, 'Hi, Colonel. Gee, I'm so *thrilled* to meet you.'

Berskin stepped back, agog, fingers snapping recollectively again. 'Don't tell me ... ! I got this one ... it's ... Monica Vitti! Stap me if you don't look the spitting image of Monica V ... hey, did I say somethin'?'

Wilma had dissolved into tears.

'She's ... just a bit upset, Colonel,' Boobs Buchanan interjected quickly, passing a comforting arm around Wilma's shoulders. 'It's all the excitement, I guess ... we're all tremendously excited.'

'And with good cause!' enthused Berskin, reverting to his old dynamic self and striding away to the head of the table. 'Right – please be seated! Er, Miss Buchanan – here on my left!'

When they had settled themselves, Berskin leaned forward on the table, hands clasped together, one eye closed against the rising cigar smoke and regarded them one by one, his gaze finally lingering on Bab's boobs for a full ten seconds.

At last, with obvious effort, he dragged them away and looked across at Rossiter, nodding approvingly.

'Captain Rossiter ... I wanna tell you you have done one fine job of selecting the crew for the inaugural flight of Glamour Airlines, yes, siree. In fact, I doubt that you could have come up with a crew that pleased me more. Every one of these fellas here is handsome enough to weaken the knees of a Nantucket nun ... and the ladies ...' another sneaky peek at the Buchanan boobs ... 'well, a lovelier pair I never have seen in my goldarned life.

'So – O.K. – we got a heck of a crew. But just what is old

God Berskin gonna *do* with 'em? Well, I'll tell yuh...' He leaned even further forward, eyes narrowed, fervently afire. 'I am gonna make you the best-known goldarned air-crew in the entire world!'

Now he sat erect, his voice rising with passion. 'I am gonna spread you over the front page of every newspaper ... every magazine ... every printed pulp and periodical on this entire globe! You will hit TV in every metropolis from New York to Nanking and every radio station this side of the moon! You will ... what's the matter with her *now*!'

Marilyn had dissolved into tears again.

'She's just so *excited*!' explained Boobs, once more consoling Marilyn with an arm.

'O.K.,' scowled Berskin. 'Appreciate that – but try an' keep the noise down. All right ... so that's what old God Berskin is gonna do for his Glamour crew. But how, you might be askin' yourselves, is he goin' to achieve all this? Well, no new project ever made a goddam column-inch by hidin' its light under a bushel. My boys Jimmy Silver, Marc Dart and Wensley Pocket are where they are today because I sold 'em big! – dressed 'em up ... made 'em shine! – hit the public with an image they couldn't ignore! My boys don't wallow in obscurity – they *scintillate*! And that's just what *you're* gonna do! And that's what your *jet-plane* is gonna do! Anywhere and everywhere in the whole wide world that you fly folks are gonna look up and say – "There goes GLAMOUR!"'

He turned quickly to the two young lads at the blackboard. 'That thing ready? O.K. – Miss Destry ... pin up the first illustration!'

Miss Destry, a cool efficient creature with short dark hair and spectacles, released a single sheet of paper from the roll she was carrying and deftly pinned it by its four corners to the blackboard – then stepped away.

The table gasped.

Rossiter came to his feet, mouth gaping. Ramjet winced and shut his eyes. Bush McKenzie murmured, 'Holy ... *cow*!' and Lord Jim uttered a long, wry groan.

'What ... is *that*!' gasped Rossiter.

Berskin smiled archly. 'That, Captain ... is your aero-plane.'

'But ... it's PINK!'

'Nipple pink, to be precise. You will also perceive that the tail-section is done in candy-stripes, the doors and windows have been re-styled in heart-shape design ... and the four Rolls-Royce engine cowlings have been sprayed with mother-of-pearl sequins.'

'Jeezuschrist,' gasped Rossiter.

'Mighty eye-catching, wouldn't you say?' suggested Berskin. 'Like I said, the whole world is gonna know when one of *my* planes flies overhead. And just to make absolutely sure ... Miss Destry – next illustration, please.'

Again Miss Destry approached the board and pinned up a second sheet. As she moved to one side, revealing the picture, Rossiter fell forward on the table, visibly shaking.

'Now, this, as you can see,' continued Berskin, quite undeterred by Rossiter's histrionics, 'is an underneath shot of the plane – as seen from the ground when in flight. Again we have candy-stripes on all four wing surfaces ... the mother-of-pearl sequins on the engine cowlings ... but, in *addition* – our new slogan "GLAMOUR AIRLINES LOVE YOU!" emblazened right along the bottom of the fuselage in brilliant day-glo puce! Man, is *that* ever gonna make them look up! Next picture, Miss Destry ...'

And one more time Miss Destry stepped to the board ... and stepped away again.

'I ... think I'm gonna be sick,' murmured Rossiter.

'And here, folks – the *interior* décor of this incredible plane which, I can now reveal, will from now on be known by the name "Glamour Puss" ...'

'Yerk!' went Rossiter.

'Note the candy-striped walls ... the hearts-and-flowers curtains ... the specially designed, armchair-comfortable, white-fur-covered, two-by-two seats with the cupid motif on the seat-belts ...'

Rossiter was now shaking his head and looked on the verge of tears.

'And note also ...' Berskin was saying excitedly, 'that the first five rows of seats, those directly behind the starboard galley, have been replaced by a low stage, the purpose of which is for in-flight, live entertainment. On the port side, the seats have been removed to accommodate a bar, the purpose of which, ha ha, I needn't go into ... BUT NOW! – an even greater surprise for you all ...'

'I can't stand it ... I can't *stand* it!' Rossiter was groaning, holding his head.

'And to present it to you – Monsieur Binky Everard!'

The wavy-haired fruit in the purple shirt came to his feet, moved slightly away from the table and clapped his hands loudly three times.

The doors flew open and into the room strode three tall, snake-hipped male models attired in outrageous, breathtaking silver lamé uniforms, complete with nipple-pink lapels, nipple-pink buttons and ditto sleeve-stripes, their airline caps also in silver lamé with peaks of nipple pink.

Around the table they strode, like three Gene Kellys in an airline musical, then one by one mounted a vacant chair and stepped on to the table, posing butchly, hands on hips, legs astride.

'Ladies and gentlemen...' announced Binky. 'I proudly present ... the new GLAMOUR AIRLINES uniform for men! Aren't they absolutely *divine*?'

Rossiter, his bulging eyes ping-pong balls of disbelief, stared up at the uniforms and gulped like a beached grouper, a tinge of green spreading upwards from his gills.

The others gaped, stricken to silence, most by horror, Sugar by delight.

'Di ... *vine*!' he at last managed, receiving a nose-wrinkle of appreciation from Binky.

'Note, if you will, the snug, figure-fitting battledress design of the jacket,' Binky enthused, prancing to the table, '...the flowing flare of the divine trousers ... and the sequin-encrusted shoes with silver buckles – cleverly complementing the engine cowlings. Quite, quite stunning! Well, so much for you chaps ... and now – for the *ladies* ... !'

Once again he clapped his hands. Once again the door flew open and in strode Amanda, stealing the breath of everyone in the room in a pale pink see-through plastic skirt and jacket, under which a candy-striped bikini of the minutest dimensions barely covered her essentials.

'Eeeeeeekkk!' screeched Boobs, screwing up her nose with delight.

'Oh my *Gosh*!' breathed Marilyn. 'Isn't that just ... *super*!'

Rossiter stopped gulping.

McKenzie gasped, 'Holy ... cow!' again.

Lord Jim remarked, 'Good God.'

And Ramjet smirked.

In came Amanda, everything wiggling, bouncing and twitching. Striding to the table, she mounted the chair and joined the male models, assuming the same pose – hands on hips and thighs akimbo.

'The new ... GLAMOUR AIRLINES uniform ... for *ladies*!' announced Binky – and was received with stunned, staring silence.

Berskin's eyes snapped round the table. 'Well...!' he barked. 'What d'you think of them?'

'Glub ...' contributed Rossiter.

'Hee hee ... bleedin' marvellous!' chuckled McKenzie, flexing his great fingers.

'I concur – absolutely,' grinned Jim, peering up Amanda's skirt.

'Oh man, oh man,' muttered Ramjet. 'Boobs Buchanan in *that*!'

At that moment Cock-up Rossiter exploded. 'O.K. – I will *tell* you what I think, Colonel ... I am *not* wearin' any goddam poncy silver-lamé drag outfit with nipple-pink stripes – *that's* what I think!'

Berskin's eyes flared angrily. 'Oh yeah ...?'

'Yeah!'

'Oh, I don't know, Cock-up,' interjected Lord Jim. 'I do think it has a certain refreshing *je ne sais quoi* ...'

'Yes, you would, you great Limey pouff! Well, if you wanna ponce around lookin' like a fairy on a peppermint stick, go ahead ... but include me *out*!'

'Rossiter ...' seethed Berskin, shaking his finger, 'you are gonna wear that uniform whether you like it or *not*!'

'I am ... *not*!'

'Oh yes you ... *are*!'

Rossiter came out of his chair. '*Nothing* ... in this goddam *world* ... would induce me to put one *foot* inside that hideous

concoction of preposterous bad taste! It is flashy . . . theatrical
. . . absurd . . . and demeaning!'

'Nothing, hey?' smirked Berskin.

'Nothing!'

'O.K. . . . well, here's somethin' that's gonna change your
mind, Rossiter – just only little word . . . how about – "tape"?'

Rossiter stopped, the rebuttal on his lips, and gaped, eyes
bulging. 'T . . . tape?'

'T . . . a . . . p . . . e – tape, Rossiter – as in . . . cassette
recorder?'

Rossiter's bulging gaze swept to Sweetman who was innocently inspecting the uniform on the model in front of him.
'Why . . . you . . .' seethed Cock-up.

'How now, Rossiter?' enquired Berskin.

Rossiter slumped, crestfallen. 'O.K.,' he muttered bitterly,
'looks like you've got me over a barrel . . .'

'Indeed it does,' allowed Berskin pleasantly. 'Well, shall we
get on?' He turned to Binky Everard with a congratulatory
nod. 'Well done, Binky – off you go . . . take the lads with you.
Er, Amanda, honey – you come and sit here beside me, I may
need you for reference purposes.'

Binky clapped his hands and the models leapt from the
table and strode from the room, followed by Binky.

'O.K.,' said Berskin, 'and now to the schedule. We haven't
had time to work out all the fine details, but broadly speakin'
this is how it will go, Startin' tomorrow and continuing for the
next two weeks, we are gonna hit the nation's papers with a
massive advertising campaign promoting the slogan "GLAM-
OUR AIRLINES LOVE YOU!" . . . and this will culminate
in a party – to be held in the Glamour maintenance hangar at
Kennedy Airport two weeks tonight – that will be the most
glittering social occasion of the year. *Everyone* will be there –
maybe even the President himself – I'm workin' on that now.

'This wing-ding, covered by every press, radio and TV out-
let in New York State and a few more besides, will be at-
tended by *one thousand* guests and will last about four hours.
During the course of the evening a Grand Draw will be held –
in fact *two* grand draws – one for the Press and one for members of the public. A total of *fifty* free seats will be available for
the super-luxurious, seven-day, round-the-world junket aboard

"Glamour Puss". Ten of those seats will be allocated automatically to well-known personalities of stage, screen and politics – as yet we don't know who, but they'll be people with the power to attract publicity. Twenty seats will go to the winners of the Press draw ... and twenty to the winners of the public draw, the names being selected from applications requested in our newspaper ads.

'The other high spot of the evening will be the unveiling and public inspection of the transformed "Glamour Puss" which, until that moment, will be hidden behind a huge drape. Quite a moment, that – I'm looking forward to it myself.

'Then ... the following evening, Saturday, the winning guests will assemble in the VIP Lounge at Kennedy and at nine o'clock will take off on the first leg of their round-the-world flight ... but here's the kicker, Rossiter – no one, not even *you*, will know where you're going!'

Startled gasps all round. Rossiter jerked forward. 'Eh?'

'No, sir ...' grinned Berskin. 'This is gonna be the GRAND MYSTERY TOUR to cap *all* mystery tours! No one in that plane will know where they're heading until just before you land. You will be given an initial compass heading and altitude when you take off from Kennedy and from then on you'll be passed from area control to area control until you're given instructions to land ...'

'CRAP!' roared Rossiter.

'Everything will be taken care of, Rossiter,' Berskin insisted. 'The entire operation is being planned by your own associates in Glamour and every step of the way will be monitored by men as professional as yourselves. The only difference between this and a regular flight will be that you won't have a specific final destination.'

'And what happens if our *radios* fail?' Rossiter enquired scathingly.

'You will be carrying maps covering all routes in case of such an emergency,' replied Berskin smugly. 'It's all being covered, Rossiter.'

'Well, I don't like it – not one little bit – an' I'm damn sure my crew don't like it, either!'

'Oh, I don't know ...' drawled Lord Jim. 'Rather fun, really ...'

'Ha! The way you navigate, Crighton-Padgett, this trip will be no different from all the others! You *never* know where the hell you are until we land!'

'Naughty, naughty,' grinned Jim, wagging his finger.

'McKenzie ... *say* something!' pleaded Rossiter.

'Well, mate, on second thoughts – now we know it's all bein' covered by the lads at base, I can't see any 'arm in it. No, I'm inclined to agree with Jim – could be a right old giggle.'

'Rogers ... ! Back me up, for Chrissake ... !'

'I remember a film once ... Victor Mat ...'

'Screw the film, Rogers! – this is life-an'-death reality! How the hell would you like bein' suddenly dumped down in Sioux City when you think you're headin' for San Francisco?'

'I'd like that fine, Skip – there's a dame in Sioux City who ...'

'*Screw* the dame in Sioux City ... I mean ...'

'Precisely,' grinned Ramjet.

'Aw ... *knickers*!'

'You appear to be out-voted, Captain,' smirked Berskin. 'And though it might be a trifle ... un*ethical* ... of me to repeat that *nasty* little word again ...'

'All right ... all right!' snapped Rossiter. 'Have it your way! Get this cockamamie show on the road and just see what happens – but ten bucks to a bent Boeing we end up in the Atlantic when we should down in Pensicola! But who am *I* to complain – I'm only the goddam *captain*!'

'Splendid,' beamed Berskin. 'I felt you'd see it my way. Well, meeting adjourned, folks. Happy landings!'

'Yeah ... wher*ever* you are,' scowled Rossiter, his mind working feverishly on avenues of revenge.

10

As Berskin had promised, the massive press promotion campaign broke the next day.

In the morning editions of no fewer than eighty-seven major dailies covering the entire country, full-page teaser ads in stunning nipple-pink and day-glo puce startled the nation at its breakfast, arresting the appetite of even its most ad-apathetic citizenry with the eye-searing savagery of their brilliant colour.

Typifying, perhaps, the nation's reaction – that of Mr. Stanley Orbach, an out-of-work Bronx taxi-driver of 97 Heavensent Buildings, junction of Webster and Tremont.

'KER ... IST ORL ... MIGHTY ... !'

'Stanley Orbach – watch yuh language in fronta the kid!'

'Bella, I'm blind ... I'M BLIND!'

'Will yuh quit foolin' around, Stanley? Ain't it enough I got you un'er my feet all day . . . ?'

'Bella, yuh gotta see this *ad*.!'

'No, I don't gotta, Stanley, on account of I'm cookin' these lousy eggs right now . . .'

'Honey, but dis is important! All dese years you've bin livin' under the misapprehenshun . . . the un'ers*tandable* misapprehenshun . . . that nobody in the whole wide world loves you – an' all dis time you've bin *wrong*! 'Cos Glamour Airlines love you! Says so right here . . . look.'

He turned the page towards her.

She flinched. 'Stanley . . . that was a damnfool thing ta do. I gone an' bust your eggs . . .'

'Kinda hits yuh, don't it?'

'Like typhoid. So – who're Glamour Airlines already?'

'Search me – just says here they love yuh.'

'An' I wonder what fink thought *that* one up?'

'Beautiful . . . beautiful!' exclaimed Colonel Berskin, tossing the *Washington Post* on to a mountain of eighty-six other dailies piled before him. 'Let 'em chew on *that* with their Post Toasties, Peabody! Think of it – an entire nation agog with just one ad! Two hundred and sixty million souls askin' themselves but one question at this very moment – who *are* Glamour Airlines and why do they love *me*?

'Well, Peabody, they're going to have to wait another three days to find out. Tomorrow they get the same ad. as today – and again the day after . . . and three days from now there won't be a priest, politician, prostitute or pig-farmer from Portland to Puget not burstin' blood vessels with curiosity. *Then*, Peabody – we hit 'em with the answer!'

'Indeed, sir . . . er, shall I serve the devilled kidneys now, sir?'

'Peabody . . . ! I don't give a tiger's tit if you stick your dick in the rice pudding. How can you think of food at a time like this. Get Rossiter on the phone and let's hear what the miserable bastard thinks now.'

'Begging the Colonel's pardon, but Captain Rossiter and the other members of the crew are downstairs – being fitted for their new uniforms.'

'So they are ... so they are – O.K., Peabody, hit me with the kidneys, I'll talk to him later.'

And in the fitting-room:

'Everard ... !' barked Rossiter. 'You touch me there just one more time an' I'll take a handful of these sequins and sew them to your SCROTUM!'

'Ooh, Captain, you're so *masterful*! Now, stand still, for heaven's sake ... how can I *possibly* get this crotch right when you're jiggling around so much.'

'*Screw* the crotch, Everard! An' screw every *other* part of this sicky outfit!'

'Tut tut tut,' tutted Lord Jim, fastening his flies. 'Such lack of appreciation for so sensitive a talent. You really look quite divine, Cock-up. The silver lamé matches the greyness of your complexion to perfection – and the nipple pink could not more closely compliment the ruptured blood vessels in your eyes. What do you say, Ramjet?'

'Mm?'

First Officer Rogers had his own ruptured eye glued to a crack in a door leading into the adjoining office, also temporarily serving as a fitting-room, and had had it so glued for the best part of five minutes.

'I was remarking on our beloved captain's appearance,' frowned Lord Jim. 'Er, Ramjet ... what are you looking at in there?'

'Nothing.'

Ramjet broke away from the crack and glanced dutifully at Rossiter who was perched enraged on a low plinth in the centre of the room. 'Yeah, terrific, Cock-up. And when you quit flying you're a dead cert for principle boy in a fag pantomime.'

He couldn't wait to get back to the crack in the door.

'Ramjet ... what *are* you looking at in there?' insisted Crighton-Padgett, crossing the floor.

'I found it first, shove off.'

'My *dear* fellow ...'

'Well, kneel down, then – there's plenty of crack below.'

James knelt, a chancy move with Binky not six feet away, but well worth the risk, he was soon to discover.

'I ... say!' he exclaimed gleefully.

'Ain't they somethin'?' chuckled Ramjet.

'Ramjet, how *could* you? You might have let on a bit sooner.'

'Does Ford tell General Motors everything?'

'Hey, what you blokes got there?' enquired Bush McKenzie, attired in jockey shorts, socks and sequined shoes, pausing, prone, on his tenth set of twenty push-ups.

'Never you mind,' murmured Lord Jim. 'You carry on pushing – much healthier for you.'

'Nah, come on – let's have a decko,' said McKenzie, getting to his feet.

'No room,' muttered Ramjet. 'Wowee, just look at *them*, Jim!'

'I'm looking . . . I'm looking!'

'I . . . I can get a chair?' offered McKenzie.

Ramjet shrugged. 'O.K. – get a chair.'

Bush got one, climbed on it, leaned at a perilously sharp angle and got his eye to the crack.

'H . . . holy . . .'

'Ain't they magnificent?' grinned Ramjet.

'Fan . . . tastic!' gasped McKenzie.

'Here . . . what you fellas peerin' at?' demanded Sugar, hoving up in his lace-trimmed underpants and sequined shoes.

'Hee hee, nothin' that would interest you, Sugar, me old sweetheart,' laughed McKenzie. 'Wrong door for you, old love.'

'Whatever d'you mean? Come on, let's have a gander.'

'You'll have to lie on the floor,' said Ramjet, sucking in breath. 'By the . . . wow! just get a load of . . .'

Sugar dropped to the floor, brought his eye to the crack – and let out a yelp. 'Oh my God, how disgustin'! Ooh, you dirty pigs!'

'What in hell is goin' on over there!' demanded Rossiter.

'Ssssshhhh!' They all shushed him.

'Captain!' scolded Binky. 'Will you *please* . . .'

'Aw, shut it, Everard!' cried Rossiter, leaping off the plinth, the unsewn legs of his trousers flapping about his skinny limbs like silver tarpaulins. 'Lemme in there! Move it, you guys! Rogers . . . !'

'Get knotted, Skip . . .'

'Crighton-Padgett . . . !'

'My *dear* fellow, you must be joking.'

'McKenzie . . . !'

'Up yours, Skip . . .'

'SWEETMAN!'

'With the greatest of pleasure, I must say.'

Sweetman wriggled backwards and down went Rossiter.

'Captain!' wailed Binky. 'My uniform . . . !'

'Go play with yuhself, Everard!' rapped Rossiter, getting his eye to the crack. 'My *God,* just look what we got here . . .'

What they had there, in fact, was a splendid, unobstructed view of both Boobs Buchanan and Wilma Fluck standing absolutely mother-starkers before a full-length mirror.

'You know, honey,' breathed Marilyn, caressing her own satin hips, 'my measurements are *exactly* hers – to the absolute quarter inch.'

'I think you have a *fabulous* body, Wilma,' squeaked Babs, squeezing her own enormous boobs together and regarding the effect in the mirror. 'I blame my mother for lettin' these get out of hand. You know, she wouldn't let me wear a bra until I was *seven*. Imagine that – seven yea . . .'

At that moment Bush McKenzie fell off the chair, the door burst open and all four voyeurs cascaded into the room.

'Gee,' breathed Marilyn, turning towards them. 'Don't you guys *ever* knock?'

*   *   *

'Yes?' grunted Colonel Berskin, fingering the intercom switch.

'Mr. Himmler is here to see you, sir.'

'Send him in, Miss Destry.'

Himmler entered.

Berskin nodded. 'Siddown, Himmler, whada we got so far?'

The accountant settled himself, opened a brief-case, extracted a note-pad and began.

'First – politics. Senator Sam Chortle has definitely accepted – and with alacrity.'

Berskin snorted. 'Chortle would. Had no doubts about him from the start. An appetite for publicity exceeded only by his voracious greed for cunt and country cookin' – in that order – but can he pull air-time! O.K. – next ...'

'Theatre and movies. Miss Gloriana Fullbrush – yes!'

Berskin's eyes flew wide. 'Good *man*! My God, that dame's worth a million column inches minimum! I can see the headlines, Himmler – "GLORIANA FLYS GLAMOUR"! Well done, Himmler ...'

'Er, there *is* a list of conditions, though, sir ...'

'Yeah, naturally,' grimaced Berskin, sobering a bit. 'O.K. – shoot.'

'She wants seating accommodation for *three* of her young bulls ... "bodyguards", she calls them.'

Berskin smirked. 'Three, huh? Well, we're gettin' off lightly – she's got a stable of twenty!'

'She says she needs at least three to protect the jewellery she'll be carrying – up to two million dollars worth – including the big stone that hit the headlines last year ...'

'The Madonna Moonstone! She's willin' to bring that along?'

'She insists on it, sir – says it pulls more publicity than all her rave-ups and orgies put together.'

'Hot ... damn!' gasped Berskin, smiting his hand with a fist. 'If this ain't gettin' more beautiful by the minute. O.K. – she's got seats for three studs. Anything – give her anything!'

'In ... cluding a hundred thousand dollars, sir?' Himmler asked hesitantly.

'What!'

'That's what she's asking – a hundred thousand dollars for ... one moment, sir, I have the transcript of her exact words ... yes, here we are ... "for the honour, prestige and immeasurable profit to be gained by Glamour Airlines by virtue of my presence. And if that old tart Berskin thinks he's gettin' me for nothin' he can roll up his old flack-jacket and shove it up his ..."'

'O.K., Himmler, O.K. – give the bitch her money – we'll get every cent of it back in publicity and more. Anything else?'

'Minor concessions regarding her personal comfort but nothing of great import, sir.'

'O.K. – look into the insurance angle for the jewellery, will yuh?'

'I already have, sir.'

'Good man. Right – next?'

Himmler now hesitated, a sly, self-congratulatory smile twisting his thin lips. 'This, I think, might please you, sir ... Delicious O'Hara – yes!'

Berskin gaped. 'Delicious ... O'Hara! You *did* it! How, man, how?'

Himmler's smirk became more pronounced. 'Here, sir, I must admit to a small subterfuge. A few months ago an ... "acquaintance" of mine – a porter in a hotel down in Tampico, Mexico, happened to inadvertently stumble into a bedroom and inadvertently discovered Miss Delicious O'Hara coupled in a somewhat ignominious sexual pose with the gentleman firmly tipped to be vice-president of the United States in the next administration ...'

Berskin's eyes popped. 'Good God, man, not ...'

Himmler nodded. 'The same, sir – married with eight children.'

'But what ... how ... I mean, we've only your "acquaintance's" word for ...'

'Ah, I forgot to mention, sir – my acquaintance also happened, quite inadvertently, to be carrying on his person a miniature lapel camera and in the excitement of the moment ... inadvertently pressed the shutter mechanism and ...'

'Himmler!' gasped Berskin. 'But that's ... blackmail!'

'Indeed it is, sir,' Himmler admitted contritely.

'Dirty, low-down, filthy, stinkin' blackmail!'

'As you rightly say, sir.'

'Hee hee,' chuckled Berskin, rubbing his hands together. 'Delicious O'Hara ... the sexiest stripper of 'em all! ... *queen* of bump and grind brigade – and we've got her! Himmler, there's a big fat bonus in this for you, so help me. I didn't think there was a chance of getting her on board.'

'Nor would there have been without ... a little gentle persuasion, sir. I *did* try a normal approach at first, of course ...'

'Of course – and what was her reaction?'

'I, er, have the transcript of *her* conversation with me also, sir ...' He flipped through the note-pad and found it. 'Ah, yes

... the relevant part reads: "... wouldn't give Godalmighty Berskin the sweat from one of my old G-strings, never mind a week of my time, the trumped-up, pushy little four-eyed crumb..."

'That's enough, Himmler! But ... well done, well done. So – she wouldn't give me a week of her time, eh, the big-boobed bag? Well, now, we'll just have to see what *else* we can think up for that sweet-ass to generously donate. O.K., Himmler, let's move on – what other goodies have you got?'

'Trouble by the crate-load with this next one, sir – but he's never out of the news. Mr. Lush Life himself – Vincent Martino!'

'Lush Martino! Hell, that's *great*, Himmler. Any trouble with him?'

'Not during the negotiations, sir – all he wanted to know was how much bourbon we can carry in a 707 and when I told him there'd only be fifty passengers so the balance of the luggage space was all his, he said he couldn't wait to get on board. At least I *think* that's what he said – he was a trifle incoherent at the time.'

'Yeah, you had me worried for a minute there, Himmler – sounded like he'd gone dry. Splendid. That guy makes the front pages so often, the news guys must follow him around waitin' for him to fall down...'

At that moment the telephone rang. Berskin snatched it up. 'Yeh?'

'Sir, there's a Mister Craven Snipe on the line for you, do you wish to speak with him?'

'Yeh, I sure do, put him on.'

Berskin covered the mouthpiece and said excitedly to Himmler, 'It's Snipe! Did you speak to him?'

'No, sir, not yet. He was out of town when I called – digging dirt in California. But I left a message for him to call...'

'Hell ... o?'

The snide, sinister Snipe drawl, sweet as cyanide, slithered out of the mouthpiece into Berskin's earhole. Berskin detested Snipe as everybody detested Snipe, the dirtiest dirt-digger in the business – detested his pseudo-English aristocratic posturing, his withering cynicism and his towering success as a gossip columnist. But, perhaps above all, Berskin detested Snipe because he needed him.

'Well, hel*lo*, Craven, how are you?' he gushed sickeningly.

'Er, who *is* this, pray?'

'Wh ... it's me! – God Berskin!'

'Oh, it's *that* call. I had one in to the White House simultaneously. Well, all right, Berskin, now you're on – what have you got for me?'

Berskin's mouth worked silently, nonplussed with the anger Snipe invariably evoked. 'Wh ... what have I *got* for you! Craven, you mean you haven't seen the *ads*?'

'Ads? What ads, old boy ... ?'

'Now, come *on*, Craven – you must have picked up the scam! This morning I launched Glamour Airlines in eighty-seven major dailies ...'

'Oh, *those* ads.'

'Craven, are you tellin' me you haven't heard about the gigantic boffo launch two weeks from now ... the huge socko party we're holdin' in the Glamour hangar at Kennedy ... the draw for fifty places on the seven-day, round-the-world mystery flight ...'

'No, old boy, I'm not telling you that. I have heard whispers in that vein ... but what about it?'

'Wh ... what *about* it! Craven, there's gonna be enough juice flyin' on that flight to fill your column for a month! We've got Senator Sam Chortle aboard ... Gloriana Fullbrush ... Delicious O'Hara ... Lush Martino ... !'

'Berskin – is this your somewhat perissological method of inviting *me* to attend this quaint function ... ?'

'Er ... no! ... yes!' He slapped his hand over the mouthpiece. 'Himmler – what the hell's "perissological"?'

Himmler gaped ... then shrugged.

'Having trouble with "perissological", Berskin?' Snipe taunted. 'It means excessively verbose, old sport – so get to the point.'

'I knew what it meant, Sn ... Craven,' spat Berskin. 'I was lighting a cigar. And yes, I *am* inviting you aboard.'

'Mmm,' Snipe mused indolently. 'Well now, I *really* don't think I could possibly devote one entire week of my eminently valuable time to the inane philanderings of those two prick-happy nymphs Fullbrush and O'Hara ... nor to the liquor-swish and gut-rumblings erroneously mistaken for conversation from Lush Martino ...'

'Well ... no ... I didn't think you'd be able to manage an entire *week*, Craven ... perhaps five days ...? Three ...?' wheedled Berskin.

'I, er, take it you plan to invite – or have already invited – a host of lesser journalistic talent?'

'Well, sure, Craven ... one or two top-liners. The bulk of the Press will have to take their chances in the Grand Draw, but to protect ourselves we're gonna make *sure* that one or two big names win ...'

'Including gossip columnists, I presume?'

'Well, sure ...'

'Tell you what I'll do, Berskin – throw out the competition and I'll do the entire week.'

'What ... you mean ...?'

'I *mean*, Berskin – throw out the competition and I'll do the entire week! Need I remind you that my column is syndicated in no fewer than three hundred and forty publications around the world and that there aren't another *five* dirt-diggers put together who can get you the coverage that I can?'

'No ...' choked Berskin, raging inwardly, 'there is no need to remind me, Craven. But what about the draw ...? What if one of the other dirt-diggers wins a *place* ...?'

Snipe's chuckle was entirely humourless. 'If he wins, Berskin, you lose. It's up to you to see no other dirt-digger gets on that plane – right?'

'But ... that means rigging the draw!' protested Berskin.

'Yes, doesn't it,' smiled Snipe. 'Oh, I *know* how thoughts of such recourse must offend your innate integrity, your unswerving insistence on total honesty in *all* your business dealings, Berskin, but in this instance I'm afraid that, if you want me, you'll just have to force yourself ...'

'O.K.!' seethed Berskin. 'You've got a deal!'

'Ho ho, hold on, it's not as easy as that, old boy. I shall of course require written assurance that *all* my travel facilities – hotels, meals, whatever – will be provided to my customary standard of excellence. I shall require foresight of certified copies of the entire week's menus. I shall require ...'

'O.K., O.K. – get it down on paper and let me have it,' snapped Berskin.

'Splendid. You really are the most congenial fellow with whom to transact business, Berskin.'

'The pleasure's all mine!' rapped Godfrey and slammed down the phone. 'The bastard! The mealy-mouthed ... muckraking ... multi-moronic ... pig! But, by heaven, we got him, Himmler ... we got him!'

'I ... thought you handled him rather well, sir.'

Berskin's eyes flashed, then, seeing (though scarcely believing) that Himmler was not being funny, he continued, 'Er, yes ... well, let's get on, shall we ...'

But they did not get on. The telephone then rang again ... then again and again and again. The storm had broken; the deluge had begun. By mid-morning the Berskin switchboard had accepted four hundred and thirty-six calls from newspapers, journals, magazines, trade papers, radio- and TV-stations, airline caterers, plastic component suppliers and a large assortment of nuts and cranks.

At twelve noon Berskin dropped the receiver on to his desk, slumped exhaustedly back into his chair and blinded Himmler with a radiant grin.

'Himmler, baby ... we've done it! Glamour is on its way! Hold the fort – I'm goin' out to lunch.'

II

Monday, two days later, and the Glamour uniforms were ready, the effect of this fact on the lives of the crew being instantaneous and, with one exception (Cock-up Rossiter) decidedly gratifying.

At ten o'clock that morning an edict went out from Berskin in an emphatically worded directive delivered at a specially convened 'Crew participation in the Glamour Launch – its obligations and requirements' meeting, during which Berskin's attitude was fervently totalitarian – to say nothing of plain bloody adamant.

'Now, listen, you guys and gals an' listen good – the eyes of the world will soon be upon you. The success or failure of this entire venture could well rest upon your own well-padded shoulders. The theme of the project is GLAMOUR – an' by God, GLAMOUR is what the customers will expect to find the moment they step aboard that plane.

'Now, I can only do so much. I have planned the décor ... the food, the entertainment – both in-flight and during hotel stop-overs. I have selected as guest passengers the most glamorous celebrities possible – big names like...' he paused theatrically, cocked an expectant brow, ensuring their full attention, '...like ... Gloriana Fullbrush, for instance!'

Ramjet, Lord Jim and Buch McKenzie sat up, paying attention for the first time.

'Gloriana Fullbrush!' exclaimed Ramjet. '*She'll* be on board?'

'Sure, she'll be on board, Rogers,' smirked Berskin. 'What d'you think God Berskin's organized here – a two-bit outing for tired teachers? This is the big-time – *all* of you get that inta your heads right now. This is the launch of a multi-million-dollar business – not some crack-pot practical joke I've personally taken a fancy to! O.K. – so Gloriana Fullbrush shocked yuh – now get a load of this one! We will also have on board none other than that queen of sophisticated sexuality herself – Delicious O'Hara!'

Stunned silence – quickly broken by awed gasps.

'Delicious ... O'*Hara*!' gulped Ramjet.

'How utterly amusing,' commented Lord Jim.

'Right there ... in our plane!' gaped Bush.

Cock-up Rossiter uttered a disdainful 'Huh!' and continued scowling, an expression that had not deserted his countenance since the uniform-fitting session two days before.

'*And ...*' continued Berskin, delighted with their awed reactions, 'a name, now, to impress our *female* cabin staff! Girls, we will have aboard none other than ... wait for it ... none other than ... Vincent Mar*tino*!'

Boobs Buchanan emitted a squeal like a rusty hinge and Marilyn gasped, 'F'gosh *sakes* ... Lush Mar*tino* ... !'

'Well, I'm glad to see you're all impressed,' Berskin went on smirkily. 'Now maybe you can all see just how big and important the league is that you're all playin' in. Once "Glamour Puss" takes off a week next Saturday night, it'll be over to *you*! I'll have done all *I* can. But ... before that time comes, don't think you're all just gonna sit around takin' it easy. From today, when you take delivery of your new Glamour uniforms, you're going to be the centre of a heck of a lot of attention!

Every fashion editor, every features editor an' every *other* kind of editor of every newspaper, trade paper, magazine – especially the *women's* magazines – is gonna want a piece of you. They'll want to know who is *flying* "Glamour Puss" – you, your*selves*, personally.

'Now, I don't expect you to give personal interviews to *every* tabloid that hankers for them – for one thing there wouldn't be time ... and, anyway, the Publicity Department has already covered that angle by issuing a general biographical release on all of you, together with photographs. But there'll undoubtedly be one or two additional interviews you'll have to give – and when you do, I will expect you to conduct the interviews with good heart and an appropriate degree of circumspection, you all got that? Now ... I know some of these journalists can get pushy. They may ask some personal and impertinent questions that you may well find annoying – but I want you to hold the thought *at all times* that you represent GLAMOUR AIRLINES! From the moment you take possession of that uniform you are GLAMOUR! – an' never forget it.'

'Oh yeah,' muttered Rossiter.

'Apart from enjoying an adventure of a lifetime,' Berskin continued, 'you will also receive more column inches for your scrapbooks than the first guys on the moon – so bear your responsibilities in mind. Any questions?'

'Yeah,' scowled Rossiter. 'Have you finished? – I need the can real bad.'

*   *   *

The general biographical release issued about the crew by the Glamour Publicity Department did not, of course, suffice the requirements of the Press. Indeed they served only to whet, rather than staunch, the voracious appetite of the newshounds (a reaction not only anticipated, but cunningly engineered by the wily Berskin, who had personally composed and cleverly under-worded the release in a manner designed to bring the Press hammering on the door for more).

And hammer they did.

By noon that same day Berskin was so heavily under pressure from the howling pack that he was forced to make a premature and 'unexpected' appeal to the crew while they were still downstairs trying on their uniforms for a final check.

'Folks,' he announced, bursting in upon them, 'my *God*, it looks as though this thing has taken off bigger than I ever dreamed possible. I've got a hundred journalists breakin' down my doors an' it looks like I've got to let them in. I'm sorry about this. We had plans for an orderly, full-blooded Press conference just prior to the fight, but these guys obviously don't want to wait that long. So – prepare yourselves for the onslaught. Get into your uniforms and line up in the outer office as you lined up before – Captain Rossiter on the left ... then you, Rogers ... then McKenzie ... then Clifton-Puget ...'

'Crighton-Padgett,' drawled Jim.

'Yeah, sure ... then Sweetman ... then the girls. And, girls – go to it, huh? Knock 'em cold. O.K. – I'll be back in fifteen minutes.'

'Goddam ... bullcrud!' bellowed Rossiter, hopping around on one foot getting his trousers on. 'What in hell does he expect us to say to one hundred scribblers?'

'Tell 'em about your rabbits, old boy,' suggested Jim, smoothing the creases out of his Savile Row pinstripe jacket and running it through with a hanger.

'I haven't *got* any rabbits!' growled Rossiter, crashing into the wall. 'My landlady sic-ed the law onta me – claimed they were "abrogating her lawful environmental perquisites and desecrating her rightful expiations"!'

Lord Jim winced. 'Sounds awfully sore.'

'What were they doin'?' asked Bush McKenzie.

'Crappin' on her roof,' grunted Rossiter.

In ten minutes they were dressed and examining the result in mirrors.

'Well, now ...' smiled Ramjet, tilting his outlandishly peaked silver-lamé-and-nipple-pink cap to an even more rakish angle. 'Damned if that don't look something.'

Good God, he was thinking – I look more like Mature in this outfit than even Mature would look in this outfit, the realization prompting him to give his already Mature-drooping eyelids another five degrees of flap. Then he had to reduce it because he couldn't see anything. Sen*sat*ional, he decided.

'Well,' sighed Lord Jim, tightening the battledress jacket around his slender, athletic waist. 'Hardly Savile Row but not bad – though I do expect to hear of my London tailor's suicide the moment these colours hit *The Times*.'

'There – how do I look, Sugar?' asked Bush McKenzie.

'Oh, absolutely devas*tato*! The lights simply *zings* off the silver lamé every time you ripple a muscle. Those biceps bear a striking resemblance to a python that's just eaten lunch.'

'And Sugar, of course, looks positively angelic,' observed Jim. 'I do believe, old son, you stand in grave danger of being raped before this trip is through.'

'*I* should be so lucky,' sighed Sugar.

'Goddam ponsy nonsense,' growled Rossiter, struggling red-faced with the buckle on his sequined shoe. 'YOW!' he yelled, snapping his fingers and sticking one in his mouth. 'Broken my goddam nail!'

'Count ten and think of the glory,' consoled Jim, and Rossiter replied with a very naughty word.

And in the adjoining room:

'Marilyn ... you just *gotta* help me,' wailed Boobs.

'Sure, honey, whadya want me to do?'

'Wait till I breathe way ... way out – then catch this bra hook for me, will you?'

'Of course. O.K. ... I got it.'

Whhhooossshhh!

'Right!' croaked Boobs, turning pink and buckling at the knees.

Snick!

'Wow! You did it! Oh my God, just *look* at them! Aw, Marilyn ... don't you think they're *awfully* big?'

'Honey, I think you've got a *terrific* figure, honest I do. I think you're gonna knock the customers sideways in that bikini.'

'That's what I'm afraid of. If I turn round too quickly I could *blind* somebody!'

'You're gonna blind them *all*, baby. Here, put the see-through skirt an' jacket on and let me look at you.'

Boobs did so, then regarded her image in the mirror. 'Gee, I

101

dunno, Marilyn – don't I look kinda top heavy?'

'*Non*sense, honey, you look terrific.'

'I wish I had your hips to balance things up. You've got a real scrummy figure, Marilyn.'

'Thanks, Babs. Did I ever mention I've got *her* measurements – right down to the last quarter inch?'

'You've got *her* everythin', Marilyn, so help me. If I walked inta this room right now an' saw you for the first time, I would *swear* it was her standin' there.'

'Gee, you really think so?'

'God's honour ... even to the way you wiggle your lips like that.'

'Oh – was I wiggling my lips? I had no idea. It just comes natural to me.'

A rap on the door interrupted her performance.

'You ready, girls, Everybody's waiting!'

'Sure thing, Colonel Berskin.'

They assembled in the outer office, in line as Berskin had ordained.

Up and down the line he strode, nodding, peering, narrow-eyeing them for imperfections.

'Sweetman, straighten your tie ... McKenzie – fasten your flies ... Miss Buchanan ... Miss Buchanan, I hate to mention this ... but your right nipple is showin' – BACK IN LINE, YOU RANDY BASTARDS! ... tuck it in, there's a good girl – save it for the customers up aloft. O.K....'

He stepped away, braced his shoulders, addressed them all.

'Well, you look just great ... glamorous and eye-catching, which, of course, is the object of the exercise, an' I'm mighty proud of you. Now – show me that you can be proud of yourselves! I'm gonna open those doors now and I want you to strike a pose that'll shock those rampagin' journalists to a standstill! Right ... heads up ... eyes bright ... shoulders back! Watch it, Miss Buchanan...! Too late, you popped out again. Maybe we oughta get you a size bigger at that. O.K., honey...? Right, then ... here we go!'

He strode to the door and slipped through, pulling it to behind him.

'Ladies and gentlemen of the Press...' the crew heard him

announce, quieting the clamour outside. 'I present to you . . . the very first public appearance . . . of the new GLAMOUR AIRLINES uniform . . . as will be worn . . . for the inaugural round-the-world flight . . . by the very first . . . GLAMOUR AIRLINES CREW! Ladies and gentlemen . . . THE CREW!'

The doors flew open. In surged a tidal wave of humanity, peering about them, the front line now espying the dazzling spectacle arrayed before them, peering, gaping, wincing, astounded, now coming to a stiff-legged halt, unable to believe what they were seeing. And those behind surged on, pushing into the forward line; craning to see what had caused the forward line to halt – and finding it.

In a sea of speechless faces, Manny Schmutter of *Flight and Times* was the first to voice an utterance, his remarks, judging by the expressions of those around him, entirely representative of the mass.

'My mother's life – vass *is* this – a joke or somesink! We hit the wrong *room*, maybe? You people rehoisin' for a Gilbert and Sullivan operetta perhaps?'

That did it for Rossiter. This, the final insult after so much aggravation, finally and irrevocably snapped his elastic. Levelling a trembling finger at Schmutter he bellowed, 'How'd you like to collect a mouthful of sequins from the toe of my boot, mister!'

'LADIES and gentlemen . . . !' Berskin rushed in, glaring furiously at Rossiter, '. . . how very gratified I am to witness your astonishment! This, of course, is *precisely* what we hoped to achieve. I have no need to remind you of the *enormous* competition facing a newly emergent airline. With the long-established giants like PanAm and TWA constantly engaged in multi-million-dollar publicity campaigns, how *else* could we hope to make any impact in the aviation world – if not by a policy of deliberate shock? We *need* the nation . . . the whole *world* to sit up and take notice . . . and if your . . .' a wry smile, 'your somewhat *riveted* attention is anything to go by, I'm sure we can anticipate no less a degree of interest from the general public.'

Pop!

A flash-bulb exploded. Berskin stepped back, startled, but

quickly and eagerly recovered. 'Yes – by all means! Fire away!'

Pop! Pop! Pop-titty-pop! Pop! Pop! For two or three minutes the room exploded with white light.

'Splendid ... wonderful!' gushed Berskin, wringing his hands with delight. 'Everybody got enough?'

Pop!

'Thank you. And now ... it is my very great pleasure to introduce the crew. On your left – the gentleman with the four pink stripes on his sleeves – our Chief Pilot – Captain Alfred Rossiter!'

'How about a salute, Skipper?'

'No!' snapped Rossiter.

'Aw, c'mon, Captain...'

'Just ... Captain Rossiter's little joke, ladies and gentlemen,' Berskin laughed coldly, glaring at Cock-up. 'But we in Glamour have got him well and truly ... "taped", eh, Captain? Now how about a salute ... there, that's better.'

Pop! Pop! Pop!

I ... will ... get ... even ... with ... you, you ... smarmy ... crumb! seethed Rossiter – and suddenly ... suddenly! – the inspiration came to him, quickening his heart, lifting his spirits. And now he couldn't *wait* to be interviewed!

'And next in line...' Berskin was saying, 'First Officer Paul Rogers, our co-pilot on this trip.'

Ramjet collected himself, arched his right brow, pouted his bottom lip and fetched them a magnificent Mature glower.

Pop! Pop! Pip!

'And next ... the Australian member of our crew – Engineer Officer Morton McKenzie!'

'Mm, what a big fella,' someone muttered.

'Build us a salute there, McKenzie!'

Pop! Pop! Poop!

'Thanks a bunch!'

'And next ... adding a touch of *English* charm to Glamour – Navigator James DeCourcey, er, Crighton-Padgett!'

An outbreak of whistles brought from Jim a lazy, boyish grin that induced, to Ramjet's chagrin, a positive flurry of flashes.

Pop! Pop! Poopity-pip!

'And now ... to our cabin staff. I'd like you to meet ...
Steward Michael Sweetman...'

Pop! Pop! Plop!

'... and two of the *loveliest* little fliers in the business
... Stewardesses Boo ... Barbara Buchanan and Wilma
Fluck!'

'YYOOWWEEEE!!'

'Smile, girls...!'

'How about a profile shot, Barbara!'

'Mamma *mia*, getta load of those boobs!'

'Cheeky one – over the shoulder, Wilma!'

'Geez, wouldya look at them *boobs*!'

'Deep breath, now, Barbara! Christalmighty – quick,
George, get it!'

Pop! Tiddly-pop-pop! Pop! Pop!

'All right, folks!' shouted Berskin. 'They're all ... yours!'

His words were drowned in the ensuing rush. The front line
split up, scattered – the male members of the Press making a
bee-line for Babs and Wilma, the ladies crowding Ramjet,
Lord Jim, Bush and Sweetman.

Rossiter, gratefully, managed but one source of interest – a
pugnacious, cigar-chewing half-pint who bore a passing likeness to Edward G. Robinson.

'Say, Captain, could I have a word with you?'

'With great pleasure.'

'How long you bin in this racket?'

'Er, three days ... are you gonna take this down?'

'I'm takin' it down – in here.' The little guy tapped his
head, knocking the ash off his cigar all over Rossiter's sequined
shoes. 'Whadya mean – three days ... you a wise guy or
sumpn?'

'No, sir, I am not a wise guy – and neither am I a pilot.'

'Y ... you're not a *pilot*!'

'No, I'm not. I'm an ice-cream manufacturer – Rossiter's
Raspberry Ruffles, you may have heard of them. I gave Berskin an excellent price on the Glamour ice-cream concession
and he's letting me play captain on the inaugural flight. Don't
you think that's peachy of him?'

Edward G. gaped and slowly removed the cigar from the
corner of his mouth.

Rossiter turned and nodded to the line-up of crew. 'In fact, none of these men can fly a plane – this is all top-show for the photographers. Take Rogers, for instance – he's a bit-player in the movies – stand-in for Victor Mature. Looks like Mature, doesn't he . . .?'

'Yeah . . .' nodded E.G., staring open-mouthed at Rossiter.

'And Crighton-Padgett . . . well, Berskin happens to owe his father quite a bundle, so old man Crighton-Padgett leaned on Berskin a little to get his son outta town for a while. The boy's hot.'

'Hot?'

'Compulsive arsonist. He's wanted in London under the name of ffitch-ffrench – his *real* name.'

'Crighton-Padgett ain't his real name?'

Rossiter gave a laugh. 'Are you kiddin'? Does it *sound* like a real name?'

'No . . . I guess it don't,' E.G. said weakly. 'Well . . . what about that McKenzie character?'

'Now, be honest, does he *look* like a flyer? Get a load of the muscles . . .'

'Yeah, I have . . .'

'Well, don't let 'em fool you. Our Janice is as queer as a two-toed boot!'

'J . . . Janice?'

'Sssh! You want him over here?'

'Well . . . whose gonna *fly* the goddam plane?'

Rossiter winked. 'Boobs Buchanan – who else?'

'The . . . the *dame*?'

'What dame?' laughed Rossiter. 'That ain't no dame. You ever see a dame with boobs that big? They're plastic blow-ups! Buchanan's a transvestite, mister . . .'

'My God . . . lissen, buddy, can I quote you on all this?'

Rossiter shrugged. 'Sure, quote me, it's the truth, ain't it?'

E.G. shook his head. 'I dunno . . . but, by Jiminy, it makes beautiful headlines . . . so long, Rossiter.'

'Oh, you goin' so soon?'

Rossiter, his face wreathed in a grim smile, watched the little guy scurrying from the room, then turned, only to be intercepted by a tall, lanky character who looked nothing like Jimmy Stewart.

'Say, Captain, could I possibly have a word with you.'

'Sure thing,' nodded Rossiter. 'What would you like to know?'

'Well, first off – how long you been in this business?'

Rossiter glanced at his watch. 'Almost . . . four hours, sir.'

'F . . . four *hours*!'

Cock-up caught him by the elbow, looked left and right, 'Listen . . . could I interest you in an absolute *exclusive* . . . ?'

Meanwhile:

Al Coles of the *Daytona Daily* was putting it – or doing his damnedest to put it – to Wilma Fluck whom he had fancied like mad on sight.

'Er, Miss Fluck . . . or may I call you Wilma . . . ?'

'Gee, I'd be grateful if you'd call me Marilyn, Mr. Coles,' she sighed.

'Marilyn? But I thought your name was Wilma . . . ?'

'Yes, it is?'

'But . . . you prefer . . . Marilyn?'

'Gee, the way you *say* it!'

'And how about Fluck – you keen on that?'

'I hate it. I'm gonna change it.'

'What to?'

'To Mungo.'

'Huh huh . . .'

Marilyn Mungo, he mused. So that's the angle – she's a nut.

'Marilyn . . . Mungo . . .' he muttered, scribbling 'nut' on his pad. 'Marilyn . . . did anyone ever tell you you looked just like . . .' his eyes swept up to hers.

'Like . . . ?' she whispered expectantly, wiggling her lips.

'So help me, you do – the spitting image of . . .'

'Of . . . ?'

'She . . . was your idol, wasn't she? Your heroine . . . ?'

'Oh yes . . . yes!'

'Mine, too. I've got her photographs plastered all over my pad.'

'You *have*?'

'All over. Maybe you'd like to come up an' see them?'

'Oh, I'd just *adore* to, Mr. Coles.'

107

'O.K. Well, how about this evenin' – say about ... seven o'clock?'

'Seven. That would be just *adorable*!'

'O.K. – let me have your address, I'll pick you up. An' don't bother to eat dinner, I've got a little something up there. And, er, wear that uniform, why don't you ... I'll take some ... "stills", hm?'

'Gee, that would be wonderful!'

Coles wrote down her address and pulled out of the crowd to find a telephone. Two minutes later he was on to his brother-in-law in the Stills Department, Paramount Studios.

'Frank, I need fifty eight-by-tens of Monroe – fast!'

While meanwhile:

'Miss B ... Buchanan ... what was your r ... reaction the first time you saw the G ... Glamour uniform?'

This was Herbie Kax of the *Baltimore Bugle* who had broken out in a cold sweat the moment he'd clapped eyes on Bab's boobs and was still freezing to death.

'This uniform ... ?' she squeaked.

Herbie winced. Geez, she had a lousy voice – but who cared!

'... I loved it!'

'You did? Didn't you think it was k ... kinda ... daring?'

'Sure, it's daring,' she giggled. 'It's real sexy!'

'And that doesn't worry you?'

'Why should it worry me?'

'Well ...' Herbie fingered his collar, 'it sure as heck worries me ... an' I figured it might worry some of your male p ... p ... passengers. I mean ... when your bendin' over them ... servin' coffee and ...'

'All part of the Glamour service,' she answered brightly.

'Is that right? An' just how f ... far does the Glamour service go, Miss Buchanan?'

She raised her chin, straightened her shoulders and parroted, 'It is our bounden duty to attend to our customers' every need.'

'But ... ain't you afraid that somebody ... might ... m ... might ...'

'Might *what*, Mr. Kax?'

'W ... well ... make a *grab* for you ... I mean ... there's only so much a man can *stand* ... and if I was sittin' in that seat an' you were bendin' over me in that uniform ... I mean, bendin' real *close* ... and those ... bosoms ... those gorgeous ... beautiful ... swollen ... damn-near naked ... I couldn't ... I don't think I'd be able to ... oh Jesus, I just *got* to ... !'

'OUCCHH!'

'See! I just *had* to!'

'Mister ... *KAX*!'

While also meanwhile:

Delores Delores, blonde, lush-bodied reporter of *Tomorrow's Woman*, was giving F/O Paul Rogers the five-star, no-holes-barred, come on. With sly, secret smiles and taunting green eyes, she had cleverly drawn him away from the group and was now esconced with him at extremely close quarters in a corner of the room, plying him with questions in husky, intimate tones that had long since reduced him to trembling jelly.

F/O Rogers was, of course, adoring every quiver.

And the reason for this zealous application to duty on her part was not so much his personal attraction for her (which undoubtedly existed since she was inclined to find most things in trousers personally attractive to her) as the promise from her magazine of a thousand-dollar bonus *and* departmental promotion should she acquire a seat on the seven-day, round-the-world inaugural flight – an inducement she regarded as worthy of any sacrifice, come what may.

And so with cunning, determination and all sexual stops out, she continued.

'Mr. Rogers ...' she pleaded, husking beautifully, 'I ...'

He smiled easily. 'Ramjet.'

'I ... hm?'

'Call me Ramjet, everybody does.'

'*Ramjet?*'

'It's ... a type of aero-engine – extremely powerful.'

'And how *well* it suits you.'

'Thank you.'

The scene, he thought, was going rather well. He'd never sounded *more* like Victor Mature – exactly the right gravelly edge. The dame was a push-over. He began working on an approach.

'Miss Delores . . .'

'Oh, please call me Delores,' she implored.

'Call you by your surname?' he frowned, raising a superb Mature brow.

'It's also my first name – Delores Delores.'

'How did that happen?'

'My father stuttered.'

'I see . . .'

'Ramjet . . . gee, I think that's cute – Ramjet Rogers. It sounds so . . .' she shivered, '. . . wow!'

'Delores . . .'

'So . . . *strong* . . . so powerful! You are powerful, aren't you – those shoulders . . .'

'Well,' he smiled modestly.

'Ramjet, there're so many questions I want to ask you . . .'

'Well, ask away – I'm all yours.'

She shivered again. 'Don't *say* that – it's not fair. You have no right to . . . huh! but what would a man like you care about a girl's feelings?'

'Oh, I care a great deal about *your* feelings, Delores.'

'You do? You – a suave, sophisticated hero of the skies? I'll bet you have a *horde* of glamorous, beautiful women dogging your every footstep wherever you land.'

'Well . . .' he demurred.

'Oh, Ramjet . . . there just isn't *time* today to ask you all the questions I want to ask. I want to know about the essential *you* – about your childhood . . . how you began flying . . . the women in your life . . .'

So help him, she was helping him!

'Then . . . how about tonight?' he asked casually. 'We could have dinner . . .'

'Oh yes!' she cried eagerly. 'But wouldn't you mind . . . working after hours?'

'For you, Delores – anything.'

'I . . . really think you mean that,' she said, almost in awe.

'Well, of course I mean it.'

She slumped. 'Oh . . . but that still wouldn't be enough. Ramjet . . . you don't understand – I want to do an *in-depth*

110

piece about you – *you* – the Captain's right-hand man! Don't you realize how *important* you are to this venture ... ?'

'Well ...' Of course he knew.

'Ramjet ... I'm going to level with you. I'm not just going to do a *piece* on you – I want to do a series! I *know* the readers of *Tomorrow's Woman* will want to follow what Ramjet Rogers is doing *every step* of that seven-day tour. I want to be *there*, Ramjet – right there in the plane, sending back daily reports, building this thing into something big! And I want photographs! Ramjet Rogers at the controls ... Ramjet Rogers making decisions ... and, oh, Ramjet, you would photograph magnificently!'

'You ... think so, Delores?' he asked, suddenly looking to his right so she could catch his profile.

'*Think* so? I *know* so. Look at you – that careless shock of hair ... the soulful, naughty eyes ... Ramjet, you should be in the movies.'

'Aw, come on ...'

'I mean it!' She half closed her eyes and peered at him. 'You know ... you remind me of someone in the movies ...'

'Oh, really?' Quickly he lifted his brow and gave his eyelids a drop more droop. 'Whoever could that be?'

She shook her head. 'I just can't think ... anyway, what d'you think of the proposition? Would you like your own series in *Tomorrow's Woman*?'

'Well, sure I'd like it. Thanks a lot ...'

'Well ...' she said glumly, 'I'm afraid it's not as easy as that. Sure, my magazine would go a bundle on it. You'd get the series all right, but ...'

'But what?' he asked, lowering the brow a notch because it was beginning to give him a headache.

'Well, there's no guarantee I'll get on board, is there? I mean, there'll be *hundreds* of journalists willing to give their front teeth to get on that trip ... and with only twenty places allocated for Press ...'

'Hmmm,' Ramjet said thoughtfully.

'Look, Ramjet ...' she moved in closer, all but touching him, her perfume scrambling his senses. 'You want this – right?'

'Hm ... ? Oh, the series – yes, of course.'

'And *I* sure want it. Isn't there something you can do to help? I mean, you're a very important person. Couldn't you have a word with Colonel Berskin ... ?'

'Berskin?'

'Well, why not? I'm sure if you told him how important it was to your career ... Ramjet ... ?'

He gulped – because now she *was* touching him. 'Yes, Delores ...'

'We ... could make a start tonight ... have a quiet, intimate dinner somewhere and then get right on it. I can't wait to get your details down.'

'Same here,' he choked.

'We could put in a real ... heavy night, huh – sort of get the initial groundwork done, know what I mean?'

'S ... sure.'

'Then just think of it – with me on board, every time we landed there'd be another session to look forward to. I could come to your room or you could come to mine and we'd get right down to it. How's that sound?'

'Sounds ... fantastic.'

'O.K., then – how about it? Colonel Berskin's right over there ... why not ask him now?'

'N ... now?'

'Sure, why not?'

'But, Delores, what if he says no – is it still on for tonight?'

'Well, of course – you think I'd miss dinner with you? There's a cute little Italian place down on Lafayette and Canal – the Il Pirata – nice and intimate. I'll meet you there, say ... eight o'clock?'

He nodded. 'Eight o'clock ...'

'Now, off you go and talk with Berskin.'

'O.K. Wait right here.'

He was back inside a minute, crestfallen in the extreme, shaking his head. 'No dice, Delores, he won't go for it. Says if it ever leaked out that he'd favoured any one journalist it could blow the whole thing.'

'Oh,' she sighed, slumping dejectedly. 'Well, you tried.'

'Is the ... dinner still on?'

She raised her eyes, smiling bravely. 'Sure, it's on. Eight o'clock ... the Il Pirata ... Lafayette ...'

'...and Canal. You think I'd forget?'

'See you then. Excuse me, I must have a word with the others.'

In the meantime:

'Captain ... I can hardly believe my *ears*!' another man who also didn't look like Jimmy Stewart was saying.

'I know it's difficult,' Rossiter agreed, 'but you know Berskin.'

'Well, sure, I know him...'

Rossiter shrugged. 'Well, then...'

'But ... to organize his own hijacking!'

'Sssh, keep it down. This is strictly between you an' me, pal – and worth a lot to you, I'll bet.'

'Well, sure! Captain, this is one hell of a scoop!'

'Of course. It ain't every day a reporter gets his hands on a hijacking before it happens. Er, listen, pal ... I don't wish to sound mercenary, but...'

'Hm?'

'Well, we fly boys have gotta eat, too, y'know. I mean, I could be slippin' this scoop to every newshound in the room, but I'm not – I'm givin' it to you ... for practically nothin'!'

'Oh sure, pardon me. It's ... well, it's just so un*usual* for the skipper of an airline to...'

'I quite understand. Shall we say ... fifty? – and the phone's right through there.'

And while this was going on:

'No, madam – P-A-*D*-G-E *double* T – of the Berkshire Crighton-Padgetts,' Lord Jim was explaining, not loftily yet with a certain superiority.

'For gosh*sakes*,' exclaimed Elsa Hardacre of the trade journal *There and Back*. 'And how long's your family been going, sir?'

'Going where, Miss Hardcastle?'

'Acre, sir...'

'Acre? To my knowledge none of the family has ever been to Israel. Nothing anti-semitic, you understand – it's just that they've always preferred something a little more westerly – Menton, Antibes, Juan-les-Pins...'

'No, no . . .' fluttered Elsa. 'I meant . . . you said "castle" and it should have been "acre".'

'Castle?' frowned James. 'Have my family ever been to which castle, Miss . . . er . . . well, hello there.'

'Hi,' she smiled.

Delores Delores had appeared from nowhere, though of course he'd spotted her ages ago across the room. She came close, ignoring Miss H., smiling her entrancing smile.

'May I have a word in your ear, Mr. Crighton-Padgett?'

'Certainly,' he grinned. 'Which one? Er, would you please excuse me, Miss Hardcastle . . . ?'

'Acre, sir – certainly.'

He moved away, taking Delores' comely arm. 'Strangest woman. Kept insisting my family had been to Israel. And what, my dear, is your lovely name?'

'Delores Delores.'

'How infinitely unique.'

'May we . . . find a quiet spot?'

'The quieter the better. How about my place?'

Her eyes crinkled. 'The far corner is what I had in mind.'

He sighed despondently.

'. . . at least . . . for now.'

He brightened visibly.

They reached the corner and she turned to him. 'Mr. Crighton-Padgett . . .'

'James.'

'Really? How wonderful.'

'Oh?' he laughed.

'I mean the whole thing . . . James Crighton-Padgett. It sounds so very English.'

'That's probably because it is.'

'James . . . listen to me . . .'

'Anything – as long as I can look at you.'

'I have . . . a proposal . . .'

'The answer's yes, of course I'll marry you.'

'Will you be *serious*!' she laughed. 'James . . . my readers are women – and every last one of them would fall flat on their backs . . . I mean, would give their *hair* for a big piece of you . . .'

'Any particular piece?' he grinned.

'Oh dear, I appear to be saying all the wrong things. Do you usually get women in this state – no, don't answer, it's obvious you do . . .'

'Delores, will you have dinner with me tonight?'

'What I meant was . . . hm?'

'I said – will you have dinner with me tonight?'

'Well . . . look – I'll have dinner with you on one condition – that you allow me to continue working. I want to do a piece . . . heck, no, I don't – I want to do a whole *series* on you, James Crighton-Padgett. James, do you know how *important* you are to the success of this project? You are the *navigator* – the Captain's right-hand . . . ! James, I want to be *there* – on board with you – sending back daily reports to my women readers . . .'

And simultaneously:

'Pssst!'

'Mmmm . . . ? Oh, hello there, Captain! Say, I was hop-in' . . .'

'Sssh! Listen . . . what paper d'you represent?'

'Why, the, er, *Fort Worth F . . .*'

'Splendid! Just the man I've been lookin' for. Come over here now, what would you say . . . to a confidential *exclusive*?'

'Well, what kind of . . .'

'A scoop, man! A thoroughgoin', double-dyed piece of dirt that'll shake the foundations of all we hold near-and-dear and also put *you* right on top of the pile with your editor!'

'Well, I . . . I mean . . . for land*sakes* . . . !'

'Precisely.'

'But . . . what kind o' dirt . . .'

Rossiter glanced furtively left and right and drew closer. 'Smuggling?'

'Smug . . . !'

'Ssssh! You want the room to know? Now . . . get this down . . .'

Some moments later:

Colonel Godfrey Berskin, standing momentarily alone, peering at the lively assembly through a veil of cigar smoke, was an extremely happy man. Things, he could see, were going

115

magnificently. The Press were showing, if anything, even more interest than he had hoped, and the indications were that tomorrow's newspapers would bring a wealth of publicity to supplement the second teaser ad.

The crew, too, he perceived, were responding most gratifyingly – chattering freely and with good grace, posing for photographs whenever required, smiling abundantly. Even Rossiter (about whom he had had grave initial doubts) appeared to have overcome his earlier fit of pique and was entering into the spirit of the occasion with creditable enthusiasm.

Yes, things were indeed going swimmingly ...

At that moment up suaved Lord Jim, picking his ear with studied nonchalance, a pose designed to wrong-foot Berskin as to the importance of his imminent request.

'Colonel,' he nodded and proceeded past, then, as though the thought had just struck him, turned back. 'Oh, Colonel ...'

'Yeah, what is it, Crighton-Padgett?'

James smiled disarmingly. 'A small personal favour, sir, if you'd be so *very* kind. By the *purest* coincidence I have just discovered that a certain young lady present here today is a distant cousin – fourth cousin twice removed on mater's side. Naturally I would like to assist a member of the family if I *could* ... and I was wondering if you couldn't possibly ... sort of ... *waive* the rules regarding the selection of Press representatives in her case. I can assure you ...'

'Who's the dame, Crighton-Padgett?'

James sniffed. 'The, er, young lady in question ... is standing over there ... the most attractive one with blonde hair and ...'

'Tits yuh could stand cakes on ...'

James gasped. 'I *beg* your pardon, Colonel. I'm sure mater would ...'

'Mater schmater, Crighton-Padgett – she's no more your fourth cousin twice removed than Peabody's grandmother. She's a dame who wants on that tour so bad her teeth are achin'. Favour denied!'

'But, Colonel, she promised me ...'

'The moon, I know. Buzz off, C-P – an' get circulatin'.'

116

And, of course, anon:

'Hello there.'

Bush McKenzie turned, thrilling to the low-pitched huski-
ness of the velvet voice, the unmistakable invitation inherent
in its timbre. Oh boy ... she was a corker, a cracker, a slender
blonde knock-out – and with fancy-at-first-sight suddenness
the reception, for Bush, took on a new meaning. Verily, he
thought, I would have the greatest difficulty saying no to *anything* she asked me.

'Well, well,' he grinned down at her. 'And where've you
been hidin' your little self?'

'You're ... Morton McKenzie, aren't you?' she soughed
sexily.

'At your lovely service, darlin' – but make it "Bush" Mc-
Kenzie – Morton has a tendency to send me plummeting into
the depths of black depression.'

'All right,' she laughed. 'Bush ... may I have a quiet word
with you?'

'Well, you're not exactly shoutin' right now, are you, angel.
That's a real lovely voice you've got there ... soothes a fella
down like a massage with a mink mitten.'

'Thank you. Shall we ... head for the corner over there?'

They headed.

'Would you mind tellin' me your name – just so's I know
who I'm fallin tail-over-wing-tip in love with?'

'Not at all,' she laughed. 'It's Delores Delores – of *Tomorrow's Woman.*'

'Delores Delores,' he repeated. 'I once knew a bird named
Nellie Nelly – came from Wagga Wagga. Also knew a girl
named Alice who came from Sydney and a fella named Sydney who came from Alice. Names are mighty interestin'
things, aren't they? Imagine carryin' a name like Annie Seed-
balls around all your life ...'

'Bush ...' she laughed.

'Oh, sorry, love – now, what can I do for you, I wish?'

'I ... think it's more – what can we do for each *other*.'

'Well,' he grinned, 'I will if you will – whatever it is.'

'Bush ...' her green eyes flickered with transparent yearning
over his muscular form, her desire unashamedly obvious in the

gnawing of her lower lip, '... have you any idea what you do to a girl – and what a biographical series about you in my magazine could do to an entire *nation* of girls ... ?'

'Mm?'

'Bush, I've been watching you. You stand head and *shoulders* above all the rest of them. There isn't another man in that crew that matters a damn when you're around – they simply melt into insignificance. Just ... look at you! Those shoulders ... those arms! Bush ... you are almost inhumanly beautiful ... god-like ... !'

'Eh, steady on ...'

'There, you see – and modest to boot! Bush ... at first I wanted to do a piece on you for the magazine but now I've changed my mind – I want to do a whole *series*! I want to be right there with you – on that plane – day and night ... !'

'And ... night?'

'And night – following your every move, reporting your every command ...'

'Well, I don't actually ...'

'Bush McKenzie, don't underestimate yourself! Rossiter may be captain in name – but where would he be without his engineer?'

'Right up it love, granted ...'

'Then let us get our priorities right, for heaven's sake. There's only one series worth doing and you know it – and that's the Bush McKenzie Story.'

'Well, that's very nice of you, darlin' – thanks a ...'

'But, Bush ...' she clutched his mighty arm imploringly, 'I need your help ...'

'Anythin' – just name it.'

'As you know, only twenty places have been allocated on the plane for Press and I may not get on, Unless ...'

'Unless?' he gulped, quaking at her touch.

'Unless someone intercedes for me ... unless someone with *your* kind of influence has a word with Berskin. Oh, Bush ...' she looked up at him, her misty, soulful eyes melting his big cobber's heart, '... I would be *terribly* grateful, you have no idea. I'd do ... *anything* ... to ...'

'Anythin'?' he gulped again.

'All you have to do is name it?'

'Well, for starters ... would you have dinner with me to-night?'

She smiled wanly. 'Of course I'll have dinner with you. But ... may I name the restaurant? It's a particular favourite of mine...'

'Of course...'

'The Il Pirata – Lafayette and Canal – say about eight o'clock?'

'You're wonderful, Delores...'

'Oh, look, there's Berskin now. Do you think you could ... ?'

Bush glanced across the room, took a determined breath, and nodded. 'Leave it to me – you'll be on that plane. Wait right here.'

'Watcha, cock...'

Berskin turned, pricked by annoyance at the familiarity of McKenzie's form of address yet allowing his ruffled feathers to be smoothed by the fact that everything was going swimmingly.

'Hello, McKenzie, how's it going?'

'Smooth as a copper knob, mate. Look, I've got a kind of a little favour to ask. I want you to pull a few strings an' make certain a certain little lady gets on that inaugural flight – now, hang on ... don't get your knickers in a knot – this is no cert skirt I'm stickin' in me duffel bag for an overnight roly-poly – she's a legit journalist. That's her over there – the one with the blonde hair and...'

'O.K., what's your angle, McKenzie?'

'Angle, mate? I don't know what you mean...'

'Like hell you don't. What did she promise you – a two-page bedspread if you get her on the tour?'

'Colonel, you have a sleazy mind...'

'Sure, it's sleazy. The answer's no, McKenzie. Tell her to get in line with the other eight million journalists who're gonna be clammerin' for a free trip round the world. Favour denied.'

'But...'

'No buts! There's enough corruption in this septic world, McKenzie – and I refuse to contribute to it. So long!'

Bush departed, muttering obscenities.

119

Well, well, well, mused Berskin, taking another, this time *harder*, look at Delores Delores and finding his juices a-surge. A swell-looking dame ... just achin' to get on that tour. Maybe he'd have a little chat ...

He sauntered over, smiling with his teeth.

'Hello, there. I'm God Berskin ...'

'Yes, I know,' she sighed, surrendering her hand. 'I'm Delores Delores ... of *Tomorrow's Woman*. I'm *awfully* glad to meet you.'

'I ... hear you're kind keen to fly with us?'

'Colonel ... I would give *anything*,' she pleaded desperately.

He grinned fiendishly. Dammit – why hadn't he thought of it before!

The reception wound down about two o'clock, Berskin winding up with a speech of such sickening unction he cleared the room fast. Nothing, however, could dampen his ebullient high spirits.

'Well done ... well done!' he gushered, shaking Rossiter by the hand and hugging the girls to his breast. 'Marvellous ... ! Wonderful ... ! Just wait till we see those papers tomorrow!'

Yeah, thought Rossiter – just wait!

Ramjet was also doing some heavy thinking – about dinner with Delores Delores in the Il Pirata at eight o'clock.

And James Crighton-Padgett was also doing some thinking – along patently similar lines.

And as for Bush McKenzie – he was counting the minutes to eight o'clock and a fabulous dinner with Delores Delores at the Il Pirata – Lafayette and Canal.

'I'm proud of you ... proud of you *all*!' Berskin was going on, most of his mind locked in sexual fantasy as to how the evening would proceed *after* his intimate little dinner with Delores Delores in the Americana Hotel – 7th and 52nd. 'God Bless you all – now take off and enjoy yourselves! You certainly deserve it!'

Energetically he strode from the room, then rode the elevator to his penthouse suite, wondering now how many *other* dame journalists, built like Delores Delores, would be willing to give just *anything* to get on that inaugural flight.

12

At five minutes to eight that evening, Ramjet Rogers entered
the foyer of the Il Pirata trattoria, Lafayette and Canal, and
came to an astounded halt, unable to believe his eyes. For
there, standing at one of the ornate wall mirrors, inspecting his
elegant reflection with narcissistic approbation, was none other
than – Lord Jim!

Unbelieveable!

Eight million nine hundred and forty-two restaurants in the
city of New York and Crighton-Padgett had to chose this one!

Quickly, Ramjet ducked behind a huge potted aspidistra
and began working on a plan to avoid the suave swine. He
could take no chances. Women had a nasty habit of buckling at
the knees when introduced to Crighton-Padgett, and Delores
Delores, he determined, would not buckle tonight! At least
not for Dandy Jim!

Yes, he would remain right there, hidden in the foliage, until Delores Delores arrived and then he would quickly intercept her and suggest another restaurant – explaining that the chef had just been carted away suffering from smallpox or something.

And so, cursing the odds that had led Lord Jim to the Il Pirata, he pressed further into the fronds and settled down to wait.

But ... our Jim, known besides other names as 'Hawkeye' at Eton, had, to his utter dismay, already spotted Ramjet in the mirror and was now frozen with horror, his normally amiable features caught in a bare-fanged snarl.

Confound it! he cursed. Seven million New York restaurants to choose from and Rogers had to plump for this one! It was nothing short of uncanny.

Noting with some relief that Rogers had now disappeared from view behind a dense aspidistra, he cautiously sidled sideways and slipped into the 'gents' – and from there continued to hold the foyer under surveillance through a crack in the door.

Delores Delores would not, he conjectured, be long, and at first sight of her he would nip out, intercept her, and hustle her off to another restaurant, explaining that the *maître d'* had just gone off his rocker and poisoned the *soup de jour* or something.

The question of self-confidence did not, of course, arise – he could hold his own with the best. But in the case of Ramjet Rogers it was best to take no chances. Women had a nasty habit of getting strangely short of breath when confronted by Rogers' heavy lidded ogle and Victor Mature pucker, and he could take no chances. If Delores Delores was going to get short of breath he'd damn-well see he, himself, was responsible.

So, cursing his luck anew, he lit a fag and settled down to wait.

At this very moment, whistling happily to himself at the prospect of din-dins with Delores Delores, Bush McKenzie, resplendent in his Sydney Athletic Club blazer and pink-flowered shirt, turned into the doorway of the Il Pirata and entered the foyer – and there, to his utter despondency, spotted none other than Ramjet Rogers hiding in the aspidistra and

122

peering through the fronds in the most furtive and suspicious manner as though hiding from someone.

How bleedin' unbelievable! Bush gasped. Four billion restaurants in this blinkin' city and Rogers had to chose the Il Pirata!

Hardly pausing in his stride, he continued across the foyer, face averted from Rogers and his handkerchief to his nose, and headed for the dining-room, there concealing himself behind a curtain while keeping an eye on Rogers through the gap between curtain and wall.

Of course Delores Delores was *his* date, all right – but with Ramjet Rogers it was best to take no chances. He'd seen birds go all a-tremble with first sight of Victor bleedin' Mature out there, and if Delores Delores was going to do any trembling, he was damned if Rogers would be the cause.

Shaking his head at the outrageous bad luck that had brought Rogers to this very restaurant, he collected his scattered wits and began laying down a plan of campaign.

From here he could see the street door, and the moment Delores appeared in the threshold he would make a bee-line for her, hustle her back into the street and leap in the first available cab – telling her the Health Department had just discovered the spaghetti was made with cat-mince or something.

Well, muck his luck, fancy Rogers turning up here. But what was he doing hiding in the aspidistra!

'A-herm!' A polite clearing of the throat immediately behind Bush brought him away from the gap. Standing there, immaculate in evening dress, a menu tucked under one arm, his black hair shining like a polished boot, was Senore Giovanni Meduso, head waiter of the establishment.

Bush winked. 'Hello, cock, how're yuh goin'?' he enquired, and returned his eye to the gap.

Meduso coughed again. 'Er ... the Senore wishes a table?'

'Mm...? No, thanks, mate, not just now ... got a little problem out in the foyer.'

Gingerly Meduso peered round the curtain, his eyes popping as he espied Ramjet skulking in the aspidistra, his old heart erupting at the unmistakable signs of imminent violence.

Trouble was no stranger down on Lafayette and Canal.

123

Situated as it was on the borders of both Chinatown and The Bowery, scarcely a day went by devoid of some kind of trouble – muggings, rape, robbery or a little inter-gang mayhem. Only a month ago Joe Fucknuts Fordello had filled the gutter right outside the restaurant with his gushing blood, shot to ribbons by Gentle Jesus Jones.

And now – here it was again – right *inside* the restaurant this time! Meduso's weary old legs began shaking with terror.

'Senore ... *please* ... I wanta no trouble ... !'

'Eh ... ?' Bush turned his head and grinned. 'Nar, there's no trouble, mate. I'm just waitin' for that bloke hidin' in the aspidistra to shoot an' then I'll ...'

Sweat loomed on Meduso's brow. 'No, *please*, Senore ... no shooting, I a-beg you ... !'

Bush laughed. 'Nar, you don't underst ...'

At that moment, Peg-leg Charlie Beaver, toothless white-uniformed attendant of the Gents' Washroom, came clumping round the curtain in something of a hurry, searching for someone in authority and finding Meduso.

'Pssst! Hey, Meduso ... come here!'

The quaking Meduso, casting terrified glances between Bush and Ramjet, sidled over, walking backwards.

'Peg-leg ... we ...'

'Listen! – there's somethin' mighty queer goin' on in my washroom! There's a weird kinda English fella bin standin' in there for five minutes peerin' through the door casin' the foyer ... !'

'Peg-leg ... !' wailed Meduso, 'we gotta plenty trouble! Look ... ! – the guy hidin' ina the aspidistra ... an' this one behinda the curtain! They're gonna have a shoot-out, Peg-leg ... I gotta call the cops!'

The cops arrived in exactly fifty-seven seconds.

Unheralded by the usual ear-splitting cacophony of whooping sirens, ten of New York's biggest and finest burst suddenly into the foyer, crouching low, revolvers pointing everywhere in the most threatening and determined manner.

Two raced across the foyer to the dining-room, flung back the curtain and flattened Bush McKenzie's face against the wall, their hands clawing for his gun.

Two more went at Ramjet so hard he shot backwards very rapidly and sat down with a thump in the aspidistra pot, snapping off all the fronds.

While a third pair galloped across the foyer and slammed into the Gents' Washroom, smacking Lord Jim hard on the nose and pinning him like a Spam sandwich between door and wall.

'OUT!' rapped Sergeant Weiskopf.

Frightfully shocked and bleeding profusely from his battered snoot, Lord Jim staggered out into the foyer, blinking with dismay at the sight of Ramjet Rogers crawling out of the aspidistra pot, his arse covered in wet soil.

'UP!' demanded Patrolman Hennesey, dragging Rogers to his feet and throwing him against the wall for a quick frisk.

And then...

'OUT!' yelped Patrolman Pelham, shoving Bush McKenzie through the curtain.

And now Lord Jim's bewilderment was complete.

'You!' he gaped.

'You!' gasped Bush.

Ramjet whirled round to Bush. 'You!'

And through the ring of uniformed cops came a huge plain-clothed detective with a face like a burst sofa, sighing wearily as he eyed the three dishevelled miscreants.

'Well, now, ain't that somethin' – none of you know the other two wus here...'

'Doe, dat's dot strictly true,' Jim muttered miserably through his bloody hanky. 'I dew dis mad was here bud I didn't doe dis mad was here...'

'And I knew *he* was here but I didn't know *he* was here,' contributed Rogers.

'And I...' Bush began.

The detective held up his hand. 'No, don't tell me – I think I got it ... you knew *he* was here but you didn't know *he* was here – right?'

'No, wrong, mate. I knew *he* was here but I didn't know *he* was here.'

The detective, whose name was Sergeant Bellamey Haimaiker, frowned. 'Are you English?'

'No, cock – Australian.'

'Ain't that the same?'

'No – it bloody is not!'

'O.K. ... O.K. – you with the nose – you English?'

Lord Jim sniffed. 'Daturally.'

'And you – with the Minnie-Ha-Ha headdress ... ?'

'You have to ask?' drawled Ramjet, removing the aspidistra frond from his hair.

'Well now, what we got here – a Mafia rub-out?' enquired Haimaiker. 'You were gonna shoot him ... and you were gonna shoot him – right?'

'Sergeant ...' interjected Patrolman Pelham.

'Shoot *him*!' gasped Bush, nodding at Ramjet. 'Are you *nuts*!'

'That's the kinda question destined to bring you a lotta grief,'· Haimaiker drawled threateningly. 'Well, if yuh weren't gonna shoot *him* – how could you be gonna shoot *him* if yuh didn't know he was hidin' in the washroom?'

'Look, mate – I wasn't goin' to shoot *anybody*!' Bush insisted.

'Well, you were certainly gonna shoot *somebody* ... or *somebody* was certainly gonna shoot somebody – 'cos the guy that phoned us said so!'

'That'sa right!' cut in Meduso, pointing at Bush. 'He saida to me, "I'ma just waitin' for datta guy hidin' ina the aspidistra to shoot!" I-a heard him wid my owna ears, Sergeant!'

'Nar, I didn't mean shoot "shoot", mate – I meant ... you know – blow ... skidaddle ... hop it!'

'Sergeant ...' Patrolman Pelham tried again.

'O.K.,' sighed Haimaiker, 'so nobody was gonna shoot anybody. So what were *you* doin' playin' Little Bo Peep in the aspidistra, mister? And what were *you* doin' lurkin' in the lavatory, English?'

'I ... I ...' began Lord Jim.

But Haimaiker held up his hand. 'O.K. – now before you guys utter another word I've gotta tell you somethin'. As I am about to book you on charges rangin' from bein' in possession of offensive weapons to ...'

'*Sergeant* ...' pleaded Patrolman Pelham.

'Just a minute, Pelham – I gotta advise these guys of their legal rights ... From bein' in possession of offensive weapons to creatin' a disturbance in a public place, I have gotta advise you guys of your legal right – right?'

He regarded them each in turn and heaved a weary sigh like he'd done this a few times before.

'Now – do you fellas know what Miranda-Escobeda is?'

'A ... Mexican fan-dancer?' offered McKenzie.

'Sort of ... Peruvian hotpot?' suggested Lord Jim.

Ramjet winced.

Haimaiker glanced at Patrolman Weiskopf. 'Weiskopf, we have a coupla clowns. No, gentlemen, Miranda-Escobeda is no dish – either Mexican *or* Peruvian ... it is kinda cops' code language for a Supreme Court decision which embodies the rights you have and of which I'm about to appraise you – dig?'

'Sergeant ...'

'Hold it, Pelham. First – you have the right to remain silent if you so choose, you understand that?'

'Yes,' the three villains chorused.

'Do you also understand that you needn't answer any of my questions?'

Silence.

'Well, *do* you?' demanded Haimaiker.

'But, Sergeant ...' said Lord Jim airily, 'that in itself is surely a question – and therefore something we need not necessarily answer?'

Haimaiker opened his mouth but changed his mind and jerked a look at Patrolman Weiskopf.

Weiskopf shrugged. 'I reckon he's right, Sergeant.'

'The *hell* he is! Well, I'll be damned ... nobody ever came up with that one before.' He shot a suspicious glower at Crighton-Padgett and continued more hesitantly, the rug of confidence now less secure beneath his big, flat feet.

'And ... do you un'erstand that if you *do* answer my questions, your answers may be used in evidence against you?'

'I do believe,' Lord Jim began facetiously, slipping McKenzie a wink, 'that that is ...'

'Another question,' Haimaiker finished, nodding in bewildered accord. 'Weiskopf, what's goin' *wrong* here? Why ain't City Hall seen this before?'

Weiskopf shook his head, equally perplexed.

Haimaiker heaved a pained sigh and tried again, his attitude one of defeat even before he began. 'I must inform you . . .' he said quickly, racing through it now in a kind of cornered desperation, as though hoping that sheer speed would do the trick, '. . . that you have the right to consult with an attorney before or during questioning, do you underst . . . damn it to hell, Weiskopf, that's another *question*!'

'Yes, Serg . . .'

'But, *hell*, man . . . !'

'Sergeant *Haim*aiker . . . !' Patrolman Pelham was now almost in tears.

'Pelham, you are not *helpin'* matters! I have gotta get these three gun-totin' punks inta the Precinct but I cannot do it until they have answered the goddamn *questions* . . . !'

'But, Sergeant . . .' wailed Pelham, 'that's what I've bin tryin' to *tell* you! They ain't *totin'* any guns!'

'Pelham, I don't care if . . . they . . . were . . .' Haimaiker slowed, came to a halt, his eyes beginning to bulge terrifyingly. Livid purple patches of rage swelled into his russet cheeks and tiny spittal bubbles loomed at the corners of his mouth. 'P . . . Pelham . . .'

'Y . . . yes, Serg . . .'

'. . . you mean you have allowed me to process a Miranda-Escubedo on these three guys on the understandin' that they were caught in possession of offensive weapons without endeavouring to inform me to the *contrary* . . . !'

'S . . . Sergeant, hell, I've bin *tryin'* to tell you . . .'

'Yes, now, fair's fair, Serg . . .' Bush McKenzie cut in. 'He's been tryin' to get a word in edgewise for the last ten minutes – hasn't he, fellas?'

'Indeed he has,' agreed Lord Jim.

'Sure he has,' concurred Ramjet. 'At least four times . . .'

'Thanks, fellas,' said Pelham.

'SHUT UP!' bellowed Haimaiker. 'Y . . . you three punks . . .' He shook a furious fist in their faces. 'I am gonna *get* you . . . I am gonna . . .'

'Ah ah, Sergeant,' said Lord Jim, 'Remember Miranda-Escobeda . . .'

'FUCK Miranda-Escobeda! Weiskopf – get 'em in the

waggon! I'm gonna book you for disturbin' the peace if noth-in' else ... MY PEACE!'

'Now ... just a minute, Sergeant,' said Lord Jim with superior ease, in the tone of a supremely confident Q.C. about to destroy a dithering witness. '*We* have not disturbed any-body's peace. If anybody's peace *has* been disturbed, I would venture to suggest it is you yourself who has done the disturb-ing – barging in here with these men ... waving guns around and generally terrifying everyone...'

'Oh, you'd venture to suggest *that*, would you?' nodded Haimaiker. 'Well now, let me tell you somethin', Lord Snooty ... what the hell's your name anyway? Weiskopf – why haven't you taken these men's names? Do I have to do every-thing around here?'

Weiskopf leaped forward, hoisting a pad from his trouser pocket. 'Name?'

James grinned amiably and wagged a finger. 'Uh uh, Weis-kopf – that's another question.'

'GIVE HIM YUH GODDAM NAME!' thundered Hai-maiker. 'AND THAT AIN'T A QUESTION – IT'S AN ORDER!'

'James DeCourcey Crighton-Padgett,' rattled Jim.

Weiskopf winced as though his ears hurt and turned to ap-peal to Haimaiker.

'Listen, English...' warned Haimaiker.

'James DeCourcey Crighton-Padgett,' insisted Jim, adding, 'Hyphenated, of course.'

'Which part?' rapped Haimaiker.

'Between the Crighton and the Padgett, naturally.'

'Oh, please forgive us,' Haimaiker smiled facetiously. 'It ain't too often we get hyphens down on The Bowery. Don't suppose we've had more than ... ooh – five or six this week. You got that down, Weiskopf?'

'It'll do for now,' sighed Weiskopf. 'O.K. – what's yours?'

'Morton McKenzie – with a small "c" and no "a".'

'Any hyphens?' sneered Weiskopf. 'Next?'

'Paul Rogers – with a capital "R" and no "d".'

'As I was saying,' continued James, who was feeling much more cheerful now his nose had stopped bleeding. 'Not for one moment could the behaviour of any one of us be interpreted as

129

disturbing the peace – and it would seem to me, Sergeant, not only a blatant abrogation of our civil rights but a flagrant denunciation of the entire democratic process – which the whole world *knows* you hold so dear in this country – to even contemplate running us in for what we *were* doing.'

Haimaiker gaped. 'What *are* you, English – a smart-ass lawyer or sumthin'? O.K., wise guy, then just what *were* you three doin' skulkin' around behind curtains and aspidistras and peekin' through cracks ... ?'

Lord Jim cast a hesitant glance at Bush and Ramjet. 'Well, *personally*, Sergeant ... I was waiting for a young lady, we are going to have dinner here. Then, suddenly, I spotted ...'

'What time were you supposed to meet her?' growled Haimaiker, his innate relief that the three men weren't armed hoodlums overshadowed by the creeping realization that the way things were shaping he wasn't going to be able to book them for *anything*. Dammit, there had to be *something*!

'Er ...' Lord Jim swept a look at his watch, his frown puckering concernedly. 'Eight ... o'clock,' he murmured, almost to himself, suddenly remembering why he *had* been lurking in the loo.

'Eight o'clock, hey?' scoffed Haimaiker. 'Well, it looks like the little lady ain't gonna make it, don't it ... or maybe there *was* no dame, heh, Clifton ... er ...'

'Crighton-Padgett,' prompted Weiskopf.

'Yeah ...' said Haimaiker, turning his attention to Bush. 'An' what about you, McKenzie with no "a" an' a small "c"? What's your story?'

Bush was grimacing at Jim, his mind tumbling at the incredible coincidence of their mutual circumstances. 'Well ... that goes for me, too, Sarge. *I* was *also* waitin' here for a young lady ... and I was goin' to have dinner here ...'

'Ha!' Haimaiker exploded, cheered anew by the rushing instinct that at last he was getting his teeth into something. 'Now, ain't *that* a coincidence. An' I suppose *your* dame was gonna meet you here at eight o'clock, too!'

'Well, as a matter of fact ...' McKenzie swallowed hard, '... she was.'

'Now, ain't that just peachy. O.K., Rogers – just fuh laughs – let's have yours.'

'Sergeant...' gulped Ramjet, whose expression, as he gaped at Lord Jim and Bush, was a *compote* of horror, bewilderment and shrieking disbelief, '... you are not gonna believe this ... but I was also waiting for a young lady ... and *we* were gonna have dinner here...'

'HA!' thundered Haimaiker, throwing his arms in the air. 'Weiskopf, did ya ever meet three hoods this dumb in all yuh *life*?'

Weiskopf shook his head wonderingly. 'Never, Sarge. I've met some dumb hoods ... some *real* dumb hoods in my life ... but never hoods this dumb – not ever.'

'O.K., you dumb hoods.' laughed Haimaiker, 'just for the record ... hee hee, this is gonna be good ... what were the names of the dames you were all waitin' for?'

'Delores Delores,' they all chorused.

Haimaiker stared ... then exploded with laughter.

Lord Jim glared at Bush; Bush glared at Ramjet; Ramjet glared at Lord Jim ... then Lord Jim glared at Ramjet; Ramjet glared at Bush ... and so on until everybody had glared at everyone else.

'Im ... possible!' gasped Lord Jim. 'She promised *me* ...!'

'Ha!' scoffed Ramjet. '*I* spoke to her first! She came right over and...'

'Are you blokes *nuts*!' exclaimed Bush. 'She told *me* to meet her here...'

'Bollocks!' roared Ramjet. 'She's gonna do series on me for her magazine and...'

'On *you*!' Jim laughed scathingly. 'My dear fellow...'

'What a lot of bleedin' cock!' bellowed Bush. 'She's gonna do a series on *me*!'

'On *you*!' shouted Ramjet. 'Man, you're out of your skull ...!'

'QQUUIIEETTTTTT!!' bellowed Haimaiker.

And in the hush that ensued the only sound to be heard was Haimaiker's own deep-throated, sinisterly victorious chuckle. 'Gentlemen ... without fear of abrogatin' *anyone's* civil rights ... or denouncin' our *dearly* held democratic process, I deem the furore you've just been makin' – conducted in a public place – to have constituted a flagrant disturbance of the peace. Officer Weiskopf ... would you be so very kind as to show these gentlemen to the limousine?'

Exit our heroes muttering – linked by handcuffs *and* a common bewilderment, each man's miserable mind occupied by the same puzzling question.

Whatever happened to Delores Delores?

13

What happened to Delores Delores was that she was having a thoroughly lousy, boring time with a lecherous old berk who had, at the very last moment, craftily switched the venue for dinner from the glamorous Americana Hotel to his penthouse suite on the pretext of expecting a very important telephone call which he simply *had* to take.

And with only that other doddering old twit, Peabody, in attendance to serve the meal, Delores Delores was regretting more and more that she hadn't worked this out differently.

Her attendance on the inaugural flight was, of course, her prime mover. With the promise of a thousand dollars bonus *and* departmental promotion she simply *had* to get on that flight, and in this regard was prepared to sacrifice a great deal; yet somehow she now felt that with more astute planning she might have been able to accomplish her objective and also avoid the battle she was about to have with Dirty Berskin.

What a dilemma this was for a career girl to face. Why was it that men in Berskin's authoritative position always looked and behaved like Berskin? Why *couldn't* the chairman of a big corporation look like that delicious Paul Rogers ... that suave, sophisticated James Crighton-Padgett ... or the husky, lovable McKenzie? Why *did* the chance of career advancement and immediate bonus always depend on a flip in the hay with filthy old men like Berskin.

As she sat there, across the table from him she turned her agile, scheming female mind to a plan that would not only ensure her position on the flight but keep her this side of the Berskin blankets – knowing a Herculean task confronted her from the way he was ogling her cleavage at that moment.

'A little more wine, my dear?' he enquired smarmily. 'Peabody – hit the ... I mean – a trifle more of the '59 for Miss Delores. Wonderful year – '59,' he leered. 'Excellent vintage year for Burgundy, Rhine and Moselle and Champagne ...'

Pretentious twot, thought Peabody as he poured the wine. Doesn't know a Sancerre from a Seven-Up.

'How very knowledgable you are, Colonel,' Delores sighed, fluttering her long, dark lashes, a ploy she knew worked devastatingly in candlelight. 'How I admire mature men of the world – they're so much more ... *interesting* than young, empty-headed gadabouts.'

She raised her glass and gave him the eyes over the rim – another ploy she knew worked devastatingly in candlelight. 'Well, here's to you, Colonel ... *and* to a successful series.'

'Thank you, my dear, how very charming ...'

By God, this is going well, thought Berskin, draining his glass. A few more drinkies with dinner ... then a little music and a few more drinkies – and if she's not tucked between the sheets by midnight my name's not God Berskin. The very thought of it started his hand shaking, and a fleeting vision of the build-up to actual penetration got his heart a-throb. A little close dancing ... her head on his shoulder ... a caress or two ... getting bolder ... the pulling of her zip ... the dropping of her gown ... that fabulous body standing before him in bra and panties ... pop! the bra is unhooked ... peeled away

134

... her huge, velvet breasts burst from their confines ... "Take me, Colonel, take me!" ... off with the panties and on to the bed ... her thighs part ... stretch wide ... wide ... !'

'Colonel ... !'

'Um?'

'A little more wine, sir?'

'Oh ... certainly, Peabody ...'

'A penny for them,' laughed Delores Delores, knowing damn well what the randy old bastard had been thinking.

'Oh, nothing ...' he laughed nonchalantly. 'Just preoccupied for a moment with a ... little project I have in mind.'

'Of course. I understand how readily a man of your stature can become preoccupied with ... projects. That's what makes this series such an exciting prospect. I'm so glad you approve ...'

'Well, of course, I ... um? What ... series was this precisely?'

She smiled demurely. 'Why Colonel ... you haven't been listening to a word I've said.'

'Um? Nonsense, my dear, heard every ... but, just to refresh my memory ... got so much to think of, you know.'

'Of *course* I know. Colonel ... the series is about *you*!' She leaned closer, offering him more cleavage. 'Colonel ... or may I call you Godfrey?'

'Please ... call me God,' he gulped, the shakes starting again.

'How very fitting,' she said earnestly. 'God ... you know, of course, that I find every aspect of your personality *utterly* fascinating – your strength ... your wisdom ... your exciting flair for extravagant promotion ... your, dare I say it ... "sex-appeal" ... ?'

'Sex ... appeal? You think I'm ...'

'Oh ... eminently!' she gushed, closing her eyes. 'And I just *know* that every one of my women readers is going to feel the same about the series – *your* series. God – The Godfrey Berskin Story! But, God, I want to do this properly ... *fully*. I want to delve deep! That's why it's so important I get on that inaugural flight. I don't just want the outer shell of Godfrey Berskin – the cold biographical details – I want to capture the *soul* of this great man! I want my readers to know the *real*

135

Godfrey Berskin – as portrayed through his achievements! ... through his most recent achievement – the launching of Glamour Airlines!'

'Of course, of course,' he agreed, wishing like hell she'd get on with her dinner so he could clear Peabody out of the way. 'My dear ... your meal is getting cold.'

She gave a start, looked down at her plate. 'Oh, I'm sorry. God, forgive me ... the excitement of the series has spoilt my appetite ...'

'Don't give it a thought. Peabody, clear the table ... then clear o ... I mean, you may retire for the evening.'

'Er, would the young lady desire some fruit ... ?' enquired Peabody, gleefully getting the boot in. 'I would gladly prepare some delicious *peches a la Cardinal* if she so desired ...'

'No, I don't think so, Peabody, thanks all the same,' insisted Berskin, slipping Peabody a glare. 'Just clear the ...'

'Or perhaps a delicate *compote de poires* ... ? A great favourite with my former master, Lord ...'

'Peabody, no thanks. Just c ...'

'Ah, I have it!' exclaimed Peabody, smiling down benignly at Delores Delores. 'The dessert of the gods – a delicate, angel-kissed *crêpe suzette* – done in the classic method ...'

'PEABODY! Clear the goddam table ... !' bellowed Berskin.

Peabody inclined his head deferentially. 'As you wish, sir. I presume you will be taking coffee ... ?'

'Then you presume wrong, Peabody! – just open that bottle of bubbly and shove off!' Berskin's expression changed to one of fawning coquetry as he said to Delores Delores. 'My dear, shall we retire to the living-room? There's something I'm dying to show you.'

I'll bet, she thought.

Berskin took her arm and propelled her from the room to the huge floor-to-ceiling picture windows which overlooked Central Park. Drawing back one section of the window, he guided her out on to the balcony and exposed her to the evening view of the twinkling city, a view that never failed to transport his female victims into a mood of romantic susceptibility.

'Oh ... how wonderful,' she gasped.

'Thought you'd like it, my dear.' He moved closer, slipped an arm about her waist on pretext of aligning her eye with his pointing finger. 'That's the Empire State ... and that's the PanAm building...'

He was shaking again, trembling all through at the contact of her warm, supple body against his thigh. Her hair touched his cheek, its fragrance wafting over him like a heady breeze and suddenly he could stand it no longer ... he had to have her! He turned her roughly into him, startling her with the brutal suddenness of the move, gasping hoarsely, 'Delores, I must have you! You are driving me insane!'

'Colon ... el!' she gasped, pushing hard against his chest. 'Please ... be*have* yourself!'

'I can't! I'm wild about you! I must have you! You want a seat on the inaugural flight don't you ... ?'

'Yes, of course I do!' she panted still pushing.

'It's yours ... it's yours! But I must have you ... now!'

'Do I get that in ... *writing* ... Colonel?'

'Of course ... anything!'

'Er ... herm.' A cough from the doorway. Berskin and Delores whirled round, still locked in combat. 'Er ... will that be all, sir? I've opened the champagne ...'

'Yes, Peabody, that will be *all* – good*night*!'

'Goodnight to you, sir ... goodnight, miss ...'

'Good ... *night*, Peabody ...' gasped Delores, straining to contain Berskin's groping fingers.

'Er ... just one small additional point, sir – will it be an omelette or scrambled eggs for breakfast tomorrow ...?'

'Peabody ... ! Omelette, damn you ... !'

'And, er, tea or coffee, sir?'

'COFFEE! ... NOW – GET OUT! GO HOME! DROP DEAD!'

'Certainly, sir. Goodnight again, sir ... goodnight again, miss ...'

'AND SHUT THAT BLOODY WINDOW!' bellowed Berskin, wincing as Delores Delores bit him on the wrist. 'Ouch! You little vixen!' he cried, thrilling to the pain. 'My ... *God*, but you're a wild-cat!'

Kinky, thought Delores Delores. Likes a bit of rough stuff. O.K., buster, you'll get it!

Bam! She kicked him in the knee.

'YYOOWW!'

But still he clung on.

Thud! She booted him in the shin.

'HIIPPE!'

Crunch! She sank her molars into his thumb.

'YAARROO!!'

Then he let go.

Quickly she sprang to the window and, flinging it back, raced inside, Berskin hobbling hard behind her, sucking his thumb.

'Iss o ood – oo an't eshcape!'

Lithe as a whippet, she raced across the living-room, flung open a door and leapt through.

'Tee hee!' chuckled Berskin. She'd run into his bedroom!

Delores Delores came to a stricken halt, mortified by the sight of the double bed.

Bang! The door slammed behind her. She spun round. Berskin was crouched there, about to attack.

'Now, Colonel...!'

'At last I have you in my power...!' he chuckled, making claws of his fingers. 'Come here, me beauty...'

'Colonel...! Now, no...!'

Desperately she glanced around, searching for a weapon.

'There's no escape, my dear...' he chuckled, whipping off his jacket, ripping away his tie ... shirt ... shoes ... socks ... trousers ... standing now in a pair of ridiculous striped boxer-shorts, his skinny legs protruding from them like knotted pipe-cleaners.

Oh no ... no! she thought, not even for a place on the inaugural flight!

Suddenly ... he pounced!

Moving with bewildering speed (sexual motivation inducing long-forgotten agility) she stood no chance. Pinned by his grasping arms she fought like a tigress but to no avail. Zzzzzziiippp! went her zipper and rrrriiipppp!! went her dress. With a scream she wrenched herself away, abandoning the rendered garment to his clawing hands.

Berskin's eyes became saucers. She was naked! No bra ... no panties! Just delicious Delores Delores!

With a cry of exultation he hurled the ragged remnants into the air, shot his shorts down to his ankles and booted them across the room.

'OHHH!' gasped Delores Delores. 'You rude man!'

'I WANT YOOOUUU!' he wailed and leapt upon her.

With a shriek of terror she ducked beneath his brutal outstretched hands and raced to the dressing-table. Snatching up a bottle of after-shave lotion she turned and let him have it. But wily Berskin saw the move and ducked.

CRASH! It hit the wall and shattered in a thousand fragments. Desperately now she began hurling everything she could lay her hands on ... a bottle of cologne ... a hair brush ... a flask of talc! Zonk! The flask caught him mid-chest and burst asunder, spraying him with powder.

Then he was on her, pinning her arms, panting into her face, 'You are mine, Delores ... MINE!'

'STOP ... STOP!' she cried.

'Not until I have had my way with you! Do you want that flight or don't you?'

'Yes ... YES!'

'Then – to bed!'

'No ... NO! Not until you put it in writing!'

'Eh ... ? You mean ... now?'

'Yes – this minute!'

Berskin stopped struggling. 'Stay here!'

He ran to the dressing-table, pulled open a drawer, took out paper and pen. 'This ... is ... to certify,' he panted, scribbling furiously, 'that ... the ... bearer is ... entitled ... to ... you still there?'

'Yes.'

'Don't move! ... a seat ... on ... the inaugural ... flight ... of Glamour ... Airlines ... there!' He slammed down the pen and came rushing back to her. 'It's there ... !'

'Have you signed it?'

'Of course I've signed it! What d'you take God Berskin for – a piker? Now, where were we ... ah, yes ... *got* you!'

'EEEEK!'

'To the bed!'

'No ... not that!'

'Yes, that ... this! Come ... on!'

Her valiant resistance was futile against his sex-crazed strength. Dragging, pulling, half-lifting her, he got her to the bed and threw her brutally upon it, then hurled himself on top, pinning her helplessly, forcing her thighs apart and wriggling inside.

'Oh, that's wonderful . . . ! Delores, you are mine . . . !'

'You brute . . . you *brute*!' she cried, thinking to herself, oh well, now I'm here I may as well get it over with. At least I'm on that tour! A thousand dollars *and* promotion to look forward to – not bad for a boring meal and a quick stick. Better play it up, though, in case he changes his mind.

'Let me in . . . let me *in*!' he was gasping, poking it in her leg.

'Never! You black-hearted rapist!'

'Keep . . . still, damn you, woman!'

'Ho no. You want it – you find it!'

'Aaah! . . . Ooohhh! . . . Oooohhh! Oooouucchh!'

And then . . .

'Er . . . herm!'

Delores Delores glanced round Berskin's pounding shoulder and gave him a slap. 'Colonel . . .'

'Huh?' He stopped thrusting and looked down at her.

'I . . . think somebody wants you.'

Berskin shot round. 'PEABODY . . . !'

'Begging your pardon, sir . . . but we appear to be out of eggs. Would a poached finnan haddock . . . ?'

'PEA . . . BODY . . . you blithering . . . idiot . . . !'

'I'm terribly sorry, sir . . . it was always my understanding that you liked finnan haddock. Perhaps a mixed grill, then . . . a little steak . . . a slice of liver . . . a sausage or two . . .'

'G . . . G . . . GET THE HELL *OUTTA* HERE!' choked Berskin.

'Just as you say, sir. Goodnight again, sir . . . goodnight again, miss . . .'

As the door closed, Berskin collapsed on to Delores and began to moan, beating the pillow with his fist and shaking his head in distress. 'What am I gonna *do* with him!'

'Now, never mind – he's only doing his job. He's looking after you . . .'

140

'I'll *kill* him!' wailed Berskin. 'He *hates* me! My own butler *hates* me!'

'No, he doesn't ... he's just got a terrible sense of timing, that's all,' she said consolingly, seeing her place on the flight disappearing until she cheered him up again. 'Now, come on, you were having so much fun ...'

'I can't ... I can't!' he cried.

'Of course, you can ...'

'I *can't*!' He raised himself up and peered down. 'Look what he's done!'

'Oh,' said Delores Delores sympathetically, having to peer hard to see anything at all. 'Well, never mind, we'll soon get him big and strong again. *I* know! – a glass of champagne will do the trick.'

'You think so?'

'I know so. Quick – go and pour two glasses, I'll have one myself.'

'You will?' said Berskin, brightening.

He got off the bed and ran into the living-room, returning instantly with two glasses and the bottle – held modestly in front of him.

'Come and sit down here,' she smiled, patting the bed.

With trembling hands he poured two glasses, gave her one, sank his own and poured another.

'You're very nice to me,' he smiled wanly, guzzling half the second glass, eyeing her beautiful boobs with a surge of awakening sexuality.

'Well, why shouldn't I be? – you've been very nice to me, letting me go on the tour and everything ...'

'Delores ... may I kiss your breasts?'

'Now, now – let's keep it nice and friendly.'

'But that would be friendly. I can't think of anything friendlier than kissing your breasts.'

'Colonel ... you are coming to the boil again, I can tell!'

He gave a cavalier laugh and tossed off the remainder of the second glass, quickly poured a third. 'It's this stuff ... you're absolutely right about it. The desire is coming back real fast ... !'

'Colonel ... now, no ... !'

'The heck no!' he laughed, flinging the third drink down his throat and bashing down the glass. 'Come here, my dear . . . !'

'Ooh, you naughty man . . . here, take my glass.'

He swept it from her hand and launched himself at her. Delores Delores spun away from him . . . came to her knees . . . but with a whoop he was on her . . . behind her . . . grabbing her hips and hauling her on to his throbbing protrusion.

'OHH!' she gasped. 'Oh, you filthy beast . . . !'

'TALLY . . . HOOOOO!' he laughed exultantly. 'GOT YOU AT LAST!' and in he plunged.

'OOOHH!! . . . OOOWWW!! . . . OOOOH!!' she cried.

'Ho . . . ho! me beauty! Feel the thrust of that . . . and that!'

'I can . . . I can! You unmitigated beast . . . !'

'Ha ha!' he laughed. 'By God, you're a wonderful screw, Delores Delores . . . ha ha! . . . ho ho! . . . hee hee!'

'You beast . . . you swine! You filthy lecher!' Delores pretended to cry. Actually she was quite enjoying it. The old boy wasn't at all bad for his age, though his skinny hips were banging her a bit. I wonder what I should wear for the launch party, she pondered – the long black silk or the orange and brown abstract?

'Oooh! . . . Aaaah! . . . Eeeeh!' the Colonel was gasping, performing with commendable vitality.

Assured that he was quite happy for the time being, she left him to it and turned her mind to thoughts of the flight. Seven days away on a mystery tour. Where would they *land*, for heavens sake? And how could she plan her wardrobe when she didn't know what climate to dress for?

'Eeeeh! . . . Aaaah! . . . Ooooh!' Berskin was raging.

'You filthy-hearted rapist!' she threw in to keep him sweet.

What if she packed her furs and they landed in the desert? Or, conversely, took her bikinis and they downed in Alaska! Well, some of each was the answer. Perhaps she ought to ask Berskin what her baggage allowance was going to be – to give her some idea of how much she could carry.

'YYOOWW! . . . AAAHHH! . . . OOOF!' he was going on, face streaming with sweat, fingers white with strain.

'Er . . . Colon . . . nel . . .' she said, finding it difficult to speak with her head pounding into the pillow.

'Yes, my dear . . . OOOH! . . . AAAAH!'

'How . . . much . . . baggage . . . will I . . . be able to . . . t . . .

142

take ... on the ... f ... f ... flight ... OOOHH!'

'Ha! Hurt you ... my dear ... ?' he laughed swinishly. 'Oh, as ... much as you ... AAAH! ... want ... OOOH! ... OHHH! ... Oh my GOD ... !'

'What's the ... m ... m ... matter ... ?'

'Delores ... it's goin' to *happen* ... ! Any ... second ... now!'

'No ... no, you swine ... don't do it!'

'Too ... late! Too ... late ... !'

'Er ... herm!'

Berskin shot round. 'NOOO ...! PEABODYYY ...! NOT NOW, YOU BLACK ... HEARTED ... SWIIINE ...!'

'Er, begging your pardon, sir, but there's a telephone call. It's the police.'

'NO ...! NO ...! NO ...! NO ...! *NO ...!*'

'I regret very much having to disagree, sir – but it *is* the police. A rather urgent matter, I gather – apparently concerning the crew of the launch-flight aeroplane. They would appear to have been arrested.'

'Ohhhhhh ... BUGGERIT!!!'

14

Colonel Godfrey Berskin, consumed by the vilest of rages, swept into his office and threw himself into his chair, fit to burst. Slumping across his desk, head lowered between his shoulders in the stance of a charging bull, he glowered from beneath bristling brows at nothing in particular and swore revenge on the whole damn world.

God ... *dam*, that bloody Peabody! he cursed vehemently, gnashing his teeth. And damn that Rogers ... and that McKenzie ... and that poncey Englishman – Crittal-Paisley – or whatever his poncey name was. And damn that stupid Sergeant Haimaiker and his idiot cops! Five *hours* they'd kept him down there, staking bail for those lunatics – an', by God, if he hadn't needed them for the campaign he'd have let them rot in hell before he pledged one red cent for their release.

Damn ... damn ... damn, he swore again and booted his

waste-paper basket across the room.

But – foul though Berskin's mood was at that moment, as furious as was his fury – it was about to become fouler and furiouser. For just then the intercom buzzed, heralding tidings destined to send him into a rage bordering upon coma.

'Yes?' he barked, bashing down the key.

'The newspapers you asked for are here, Colonel . . .'

'Send 'em in!'

Jerking a cigar from his breast pocket, he ripped off the wrapper, crunched an inch off the end and spat it ragefully towards the ashtray. But even his aim was lousy this morning and it plopped into his coffee.

'Aaaaaaahhhh!' he choked and beat his blotter to a pulp.

The door opened and his second secretary, Miss Emily Leghorn, entered, hiding behind a great mound of papers.

'Drop 'em down there, Horny,' he rapped, 'an' get me another coffee!'

'Y . . . yes, sir,' she quavered, picking up the cup and exiting hurriedly, knowing Berskin's purple rage was about to explode into white-hot frenzy.

Chunnering to himself about idiot pilots, Berskin puffed the cigar into life, showering the desk with angry sparks, and reached for the first paper, noting abstractedly it was the *Hoboken Herald*. With no more than a glance at the headline which read 'HIJACK PUBLICITY STUNT – STARTLING REVELATION BY SENIOR CAPTAIN' he gave a snort of disgust and turned to the first inside page, muttering derisively, 'By God, some guys will do anythin' to hit the headlines.'

Quickly he scanned the first inside double page . . . ripped the page over . . . scanned the next . . . then the next . . . his disappointment mounting with each barren scan. Damn it – could it be possible the Glamour launch had attracted no space at all?

Angrily he threw the paper aside and was reaching for the next when the name 'ROSSITER' leapt out at him from the sub-headline of the *Herald*. He grabbed it up, covered the article in a sweep, eyes bulging with disbelief as he read:

Berskin Building, Central Park West. At a Press reception held here yesterday to announce the launch of Glamour Airlines, America's newest international line, a startling and disturbing revelation was made to me by Captain Alfred Rossiter, Chief Pilot and Senior Captain of Glamour. Rossiter told me in strict confidence that Colonel Godfrey Berskin, chairman and sole owner of Glamour Airlines, was planning to hijack the Boeing 707, nicknamed 'Glamour Puss', due to depart Kennedy Airport in two weeks time on its inaugural flight to points unknown.

Drawing me aside and speaking in hushed, concerned tones, Captain Rossiter confided: 'Overnight, Berskin plans to put Glamour on the lips of the world. The day after the launch flight departs from Kennedy, the newspapers of the world will be full of the hijacking. Make no mistake – Berskin is one smart operator. When it comes to promotion he makes Mike Todd look like a no-hope copy-writer. He is totally ruthless . . .'

Berskin's eyes were now bulging so hard they looked in imminent danger of plopping out on the blotter. Gagging, gasping, choking and grunting, incapable of any coherent speech, he threw the *Herald* aside and reached for the next paper on the pile, his lower lip beginning to quiver apoplectically as his eyes fell upon the headlines of the *Fort Worth Fanfare*:

NEW AIRLINE IS COVER FOR LARGE-SCALE SMUGGLING CLAIMS CHIEF PILOT.

Hurling the *Fanfare* across the desk, he grabbed the next paper . . . and then the next . . . his anguish redoubling as each headline told its terrible tale:

I CAN'T FLY PLANE! – ADMITS CAPTAIN OF GLAMOUR AIRLINES. STEWARDESS IS TRANSVESTITE PILOT!

AIR WORLD SHOCKED BY CHIEF PILOT'S REVELATION! MYSTERY LAUNCH FLIGHT COVERUP FOR DOPE RING ACTIVITIES!

Now Berskin's head was shaking, slowly, its rhythm counter-pointing the waves of disbelief washing through him with each beat of his thundering heart. His cheeks were puce, blown up and out by the pressure of an awesome fury that in the next instant erupted in a demented explosion of crazy sound.

'THEGODDAMSONOFABITCHTHE CRAZYLUNA-TICBASTARDILLHAVEHISBALLSBARBECUEDAND STUFFEDUPHISASSBEFOREHESANHOUROLDER...!'

Crash! He slammed down the intercom switch. 'GET HIMMLER HERE ON THE DOUBLE!'

'M ... Mister H ... Himmler is r ... right here, Colonel ...'

'THEN SEND HIM IN, DAMMIT – YOU WANT ME TO YELL THROUGH THE DOOR!'

The door imploded and in marched Himmler, his arms full of newspapers and his countenance wreathed in smiles.

'Good morning, Colonel, good morning – and my heartiest congratulations! Sir ... *how* can I fully express my admiration for ... well, I suppose it's hardly correct to congratulate genius – but nevertheless I feel compelled to do so. What flair! What style! What *genius* to employ Rossiter in that way. You realize, of course, that there isn't a single newspaper from here to San Francisco that hasn't made this headlines this morning? The agencies must have released it overnight. Colonel ... you are already known all over the country ... !'

Berskin gaped, in shock.

Himmler, shaking his head was saying, 'Boy, you *really* hit it. There were three hundred calls on the recorders when I got here at eight this morning and they're still pouring in. With your permission, sir, I will set up a major Press conference in the Assembly Hall for tomorrow afternoon – at which you will undoubtedly reveal (here a sly smile) that the whole thing was a huge practical joke on Rossiter's part ... ?'

'Er, yes ... naturally,' nodded Berskin, staring wildly.

'Boy, oh *boy*, what flair! To think of using *one* shocker leak-out would have been brilliant enough – but *five*! Hijacking ... smuggling ... dope-ring ... illegal immigrants ... *and* a trans-vestite pilot! Y'know, sir, I think that's my favourite – the transvestite pilot. Tee hee, that is really rich ...'

'Himmler ...'

'Yes, sir?'

'You don't think there could be any ... *legal* repercussions from this? ... nothin' from the F.A.A. for instance ... ?'

Himmler shook his head confidently. 'Not a chance, Colonel. Rossiter was gossiping as a private individual – not as a spokesman for the company. If there *was* any danger of legal action I'd advise you to deny all knowledge of everything at the Press conference tomorrow and if need be throw Rossiter to the wolves – make out he's a nut and get yourself a new chief pilot.'

'O.K.,' Berskin nodded thoughtfully, now seeing that the whole fiasco could, if cleverly handled, be turned to excellent promotional use. 'Just so long as you think the Press will swallow the practical joke angle.'

'Sure they will, Colonel. The American Press hasn't had a good belly laugh on its front page for years. The public will lap it up. Makes a refreshing change from Korea ... Vietnam ... political skullduggery and social mayhem.'

'Yeah, I guess you're right at that, Himmler. And you ... don't reckon the Press will claim we've gone too far – that we're guilty of bad taste? I'd sure hate to tarnish the Glamour image before it's even launched.'

Himmler shrugged. 'There *may* be one or two of the more right-wing sheets that go little pi on us, Colonel, but I reckon the vast majority will not only see the joke but will send up a prayer of thanks to Rossiter for increasing their sales.'

Berskin nodded, his fury long forgotten, a surge of well-being to warm his old opportunist heart. 'Fine ... fine ... well, thanks for the congratulations. Himmler. I ... realized, of course, that I was sailin' a little close to the wind – but faint heart never won fair fortune, as they say. Nothing ventured – nothing gained, eh, Himmler?'

'Indeed not, sir. As brilliant a coup as ever was pulled. Hee hee, that transvestite pilot bit sure slayed me.'

'O.K., well, you'd better nip off and set up that conference for tomorrow. I've gotta have a talk with Rossiter.'

'I, er, sort of anticipated you might, sir, and took the liberty of summoning the good captain to the building. I felt you might like to congratulate him on his performance.'

'Oh, you did? Well, that was smart thinkin', Himmler. O.K. – send him in.'

Himmler exited, happily humming an old Nazi firing-squad song, and no sooner had the door closed when it opened again and in ambled Rossiter, dressed for leisure in his decrepit rabbit-keeping clothes, cigar butt stuck in his face.

'You wanna see me, Colonel?'

'No, Rossiter, I do *not* want to see you ... the vision is distinctly painful. I do, however, wish to speak to you. Sid-down.'

Rossiter sat, crossed one leg over the other, folded his arms across his stomach and gazed at his right shoe, noting that he could see his sock through a hole in the sole.

'Rossiter – how come you're dressed like a Bowery bum? You rehearsin' for a play or somethin'?'

'Nope – the pantomime rehearsal was yesterday, Colonel. You shoulda caught my clown's outfit – nipple pink and silver lamé – you'da died laughin'.'

Berskin slammed the newspapers with his first. 'You seen these, Rossiter?'

'Sure I've seen them.'

'Well?'

'Well, what?'

'Well, what've yuh got to say about it?' demanded Berskin.

'I want a raise in pay, that's what I've got to say about it!' retorted Rossiter.

'A r ... Rossiter, are you completely *nuts*!'

'Sure, I'm nuts – otherwise I'd be flyin' for a sane, respect-able outfit instead of paradin' around like a goddam Christmas tree! Of all the cockamamie ideas ...'

'So *that's* what's buggin' you! *That's* why you did this!'

'Sure, that's why! It was my protest at havin' to wear that fairy suit!'

'Y ... you were tryin' to wreck the whole Glamour project so you wouldn't have to wear that uniform?'

'Sure, I was.'

'Well, I'm sorry to disappoint you, Rossiter, but your mali-cious campaign has had precisely the reverse effect! Your salacious rumours and blatant lies have probably done more to put Glamour on the map than all the advertising I'm planning to do during the whole of next year!'

'I know, dammit – that's why I'm askin' for a raise!'

'You ... !' Berskin stopped, mouth open. 'Rossiter ... you are incorrigible.'

'I know – but do I get the raise?'

'I should really fire you ...'

'So – fire me!'

'But I need you ...'

'So – give me a raise.'

'... I need you tomorrow at the Press conference ...'

'So – fire me!'

'... to corroborate my explanation that the whole thing was *your* practical joke.'

Rossiter released a slow, diabolical smile. 'Well now ... I reckon you'd better make that a *big* raise.'

'How much?'

'Ten thousand.'

'Ha!'

'Five ...'

'Two!'

'Four!'

'Three!'

'Done!' exclaimed Rossiter. '*And* ... I want no more of this "tapes" blackmail – or *I* spill the beans to the Press that it was all your idea.'

'O.K. ... O.K.,' growled Berskin. 'And use the raise to buy some new clothes – you stink of rabbits.'

'Ferrets,' corrected Rossiter. 'Vicious little devils – my landlady's terrified of 'em.'

15

Just once in a while in this quaint life a relatively unextra-ordinary story will rear up and capture the interest of the world's Press in oblique defiance of the story's apparent news-worthiness. Where vicious civil war will fail to draw more than an obligatory journalistic nod, a tug-of-love conflict within an ordinary, unknown surburban family will hit the headlines three days running, setting opinions flying and leader passions burning.

Such a story the launch of Glamour Airlines was turning out to be.

Rossiter's outrageous revelations were, of course, the *prime* cause of the swelling avalanche of interest – and yet there was more to it than that, possibly because so many aspects of this crazy project appealed to so many different factions of the

Press – the business section, the travel section ... social ... fashion ... and pure feature fun. There was, apparently, something in it for everyone – which was probably why, that next afternoon, the huge Assembly Room in Berskin Building was packed to capacity and one hundred additional chairs had to be brought up from the basement than had been allowed for in Himmler's estimate.

'Wonderful ... wonderful!' exclaimed Berskin as he peered through the drapes enclosing the stage from which he would shortly address the gathering. 'There must be over five hundred of them out there, Himmler! Radio ... mobile TV units ... make sure we've got the TV lighting on, Himmler ...'

'It's all been taken care of, Colonel.'

'How about the crew? How're they shaping up?'

'Ready and waiting in the dressing-rooms now, sir.'

'Good ... splendid. Well, I think it's time to bring them on. Go get them and let's get movin'.'

Moments later, led by Rossiter (whose chagrin at having once again to climb into his 'fag suit' was only minimally tempered by his recent raise of three thousand), the crew trooped on to the stage and stood in line before a row of chairs for final Berskin inspection.

'Great ... just great!' he enthused, moving quickly along the line. 'Girls, you look absolutely *ab*solute! Babs, baby, can the heavy breathing, huh – we'll be on TV. Watch the nipples, there's a good girl – or we'll have the League of Decency on our necks quicker than you can say sneeze. O.K. ... er, Rogers – a little less angle on the cap, you look like Errol Flynn in "Wings Over Burma" ...'

'Errol *Flynn*!' gasped Ramjet, cut to the quick.

'The cap, Rogers ... O.K. – everybody ready? You know what to do, Himmler ... hit the fanfare ... make the announcement ... then roll the drapes – O.K.?'

'All ready, sir.'

'Right ... GO!'

Himmler punched the tape recorder button and a moment later the hall resounded to the proud blare of royal trumpets, and as the last blast died away he picked up his own hand-microphone and began his regal declamation.

'Ladies and gentlemen of the Press ... Radio .. and Television ... I give you the Chairman of Glamour Airlines ... Colonel ... Godfrey ... BERSKIN!' and then he thumbed the drape control button.

Nothing happened.

Berskin's head shot round. 'Himmler ... roll the goddam drapes!'

'I'm trying, sir ... they won't work!'

'Oh Christ!'

With enormous presence of mind Berskin stepped on to the low rostrum set at the front of the stage behind the drapes and cleared his throat into his microphone, deafening the audience.

'Ladies and gentlemen of the, er, Press ... Radio ... and TV ...' he began, making furious signals to Himmler in the wing who was pressing, thumping, bashing and banging the offending button. '...in, er, all well-staged musical productions an overture is played to titillate the audience's anticipation of the opening scene ... to whet their appetites for what will be revealed when the drapes are finally drawn...' he switched of the microphone and hissed, 'Himmler! Get the electrician!'

'I've called him, sir!' hoarsed Himmler. 'He's coming right now!'

'Where from – bloody China!'

He clicked on the microphone again. '... so you must forgive us for also using this small dramatic ploy in order to further heighten your interest in what will soon be revealed to you ...'

'Aw, get on with it!' somebody shouted.

'Yeah, we ain't got all day!'

'Himmler ... where's that fucking *electrician*!' gasped Berskin and the hall erupted in gales of laughter because he'd forgotten to switch off the microphone.

As the furore died, a voice called out. 'May we quote you, Berskin?'

'What's he giving us – an illuminated orgy?'

'Come out, come out, wherever you are!'

Berskin was now running up and down the stage, apoplectic. 'We'll have to pull them back by hand! Come on, you guys – get pulling! Rossiter, Rogers, Clifton-Pageant...'

'Crighton-Padgett,' sighed James.

'. . . and you, Wilma – take the far side! McKenzie, Sweet-man, Himmler and you, Babs – take this side. Come on, jump to it!'

The crew ran from their chairs and lined up on either side of Berskin, grabbing handfuls of the heavy drapes.

'Right . . . on three! One . . . two . . . three! PULL!'
CCRRUUNNCCHHHHH!!

Down it came, five hundred square feet of lined silk, smoth-ering the crew, bringing them crashing to the floor, taking Berskin, microphone and lectern with them.

The audience came to its feet, laughing, hooting, cat-call-ing. The radio commentators were commentating and the TV cameras were turning. The vast coverlet of silk was leaping and jumping as the nine stifled souls fought to extricate them-selves from its cloying weight. Finally an arm broke through . . . then a head . . . and one by one they crawled from beneath the heavy canopy, each emergence sending the near-hysterical audience into fresh paroxysms of laughter. Then . . . Babs Buchanan popped out and the audience went potty. Her bra had burst and was hanging round her waist. With a demented cry she flung her arms across her boobs, staggered over the drapes and ran off the stage.

A moment later Wilma Fluck appeared and rocked the hall with a fresh tidal wave of laughter, for she emerged backwards and her knickers had split. A sudden breeze in a sensitive region evoked from her a horror-stricken gasp and with a yelp she was over the drapes and disappearing into the wings after Babs Buchanan.

One by one the crew staggered to their feet, hair awry, uni-forms awry, Himmler's hair-piece hanging over one ear like a muff. Bush McKenzie gave a funny little backward hop to disentangle his foot from a coil of rope and fell off the stage into the front row of the audience.

Ramjet Rogers stood up and immediately fell down again, caught in the back of the knees by Lord Jim as he emerged on hands and knees.

Godfrey Berskin was utterly beside himself, jumping up and down in a lather of fury, screaming abuse at the crew . . . at Himmler . . . at the absent electrician, though nobody could hear a word above the thunder of laughter from the audience.

Then – a stroke of genius from Heinrich Himmler. Staggering over the mound of drapes, he hit the tape recorder button, and the regal fanfare filled the hall, surprising and stilling the crowd. And as the trumpets ended their ringing finale, Himmler stepped to the front of the stage and with a broad, self-conscious grin announced, 'LADIES AND GENTLEMEN OF THE PRESS ... I GIVE YOU THE CHAIRMAN OF *UN*-GLAMOUR AIRLINES ... COLONEL GODFREY ... BERSKIN!'

His humour saved the day, united the audience in a hand of sympathy, drawing from them a storm of spontaneous, sympathetic applause.

Startled by the uncharacteristic levity of Himmler's announcement, delighted by its effect on the audience, and touched by their applause, Berskin's good humour returned instantly. With a huge grin and a fatalistic shrug, he picked up the fallen microphone and held up his hand for silence, getting it immediately.

'Well ...' he grinned, 'you guys were taking notes – what was I saying?'

Someone at the back of the hall shouted, '"Himmler ... where's that **!!**!! electrician!"' and the audience fell apart again.

'O.K. ... O.K.,' laughed Berskin, holding up his hand once more. 'Well, we never *did* find the gentleman in question and it's sure too late now. So if a couple of my stalwarts would kindly come up and remove the Big Top here ... and if what's left of my crew would kindly resume their seats, we'll get on with this disaster of a conference. And first ... let me begin by welcoming you all to this solemn occasion (laughter) and assuring you – *and* the League of Decency – that it is definitely *not* Glamour Airlines policy to employ topless air-stews – with the exception of today!'

More laughter and multiple cries of 'Shame!'

From then on Berskin had them. Inspired by their readiness for humour, he abandoned his planned sober approach and turned the conference into a circus, quickly realizing this opportunity of establishing the image of the airline not only as one of glamour but also of fun.

How often from the ashes of disaster rises the smoke of

inspiration. O.K., he now admitted to himself, even as he addressed the crowd – Rossiter was right. The uniforms *are* a joke ... the *plane* is a joke – so we'll make the whole gold-arned project a joke. Since most people are scared of flying, we'll set ourselves up as the airline that's not only *glamorous* to fly but also *fun* to fly. You just can't feel scared when you're laughing.

This new-found inspiration prompting him to an even greater height of good humour, the conference from then on became a riot.

'O.K. ...' he smiled, as laughter induced by a remark about mink-covered toilet seats died away, 'Well, folks, that's the Glamour launch plan and I certainly hope to see all of you at the launch party a week next Friday night. And now, I guess, one or maybe even *two* of you will have questions to ask – so fire away and I'll do my best to answer them ...'

The hall exploded in a barrage of shouted questions that went on and on, totally unintelligible, until even the audience realized how ridiculous was the wall of noise and the questions finally disintegrated into self-derisive laughter.

'So ... there were *three* of you!' commented Berskin and started them off again. 'O.K. ... I guess I'll have to point to you one by one. You, sir . . in the purple jacket and red tie ... geez, an' I thought *our* uniforms were noisy ...'

The journalist stood up, grinning good-naturedly at the laughter. 'You think *this* outfit is bad, Colonel ... you should see my topless mother-in-law!'

'My pleasure,' laughed Berskin. 'But *after* your question.'

'Well, Colonel ... I think we're all anxious to know why Captain Rossiter slipped some of our colleagues a few outrageous curves at the mini-conference the other day ...'

'YYEEEESSS!!' roared the audience.

Berskin nodded. 'Good question – and who better to answer it than Captain Rossiter himself! Come on, Captain ... come up and face the music.'

Berskin retreated from the front of the stage, meeting Rossiter as he reluctantly shuffled forward.

'Stick to the story or I'll break both yuh legs – here an' now!' muttered Berskin.

'I reckon this is worth more than a lousy three thousand, whadya say, Berskin?'

'I say I'm gonna break both yuh legs here an' now if yuh don't! Here ... !' He thrust the microphone into Rossiter's hand. 'It's all yours.'

Rossiter heaved a weary sigh and shuffled forward, came to a halt, looked out at the audience for a pensive moment, then slowly lowered his head ... lowered his arms to his sides ... and became very still, slumped in an attitude of utter dejection, staring at his feet.

And that was all. Nothing else happened.

Moments ticked by ... and still nothing happened.

The audience, mystified in the extreme by this strange behaviour, were stunned into tense, expectant silence, and for endless moments there wasn't a sound to be heard in the vast hall.

And then ... someone tittered. The titter touched off a chuckle ... which triggered a belly laugh ... which tripped off a guffaw ... which started the entire audience roaring with laughter. Nobody really knew what they were laughing at – except maybe the ludicrous image that Rossiter was presenting up there on the stage – a figure of such forlorn dejection dressed in a preposterous nipple-pink and silver-lamé uniform, his cap pulled too far down so that his ears stuck out at right-angles ... Rossiter ... Chief Pilot and Senior Captain of what was purporting to be the most glamorous airline in the world ... dressed like a clown and behaving like a clown ... now, very slowly, raising his face so the audience could see his contrived hang-dog expression, an expression of blatant dismay and heart-tearing sadness ... now turning his palms outwards in a gesture of utter helplessness ... now breaking into tiny pretended sobs of profound misery ... contorting his face in a grimace of awful anguish ... now jerking his shoulders as though the sobs were ripping out his heart ... and the greater his misery became, the more the audience laughed. They were in pleats, hysterical, helpless ... and then, at the very peak of their hilarity, Rossiter slowly raised the microphone to his lips. glanced down once again at his travesty of a uniform and murmured appealingly, 'I mean ... *really*!'

Moments later, projecting above the continuing maelstrom

of helpless laughter, he said seriously. 'Today, folks, the joke's on me ... the other day it was on you. That's all it was intended to be – just a bit of fun. I hope you won't mind.'

And then, to the accompaniment of thunderous applause, he turned and ambled back to a beaming Berskin.

The Press, by that applause, had forgiven him, had forgiven Berskin, had seen the joke of the whole Glamour promotion and were magnanimous in their coverage.

By noon the following day, as Berskin had dreamed, there wasn't a priest, politician, prostitute or pig-farmer in the entire U.S.A. who had not heard of Glamour Airlines.

And by noon the day after, outstripping even his *headiest* dreams, some four hundred thousand public applications for a place on Glamour's inaugural seven-day, round-the-world flight reposed, figuratively speaking, in Berskin's in-tray.

Yes, there was no doubt about it – Glamour Airlines was already a stupendous success – before even a single aircraft had left the ground! So what, Berskin pondered, would transpire when they actually got Glamour Puss into the air!

Perhaps it was just as well that even Godfrey Berskin's lively imagination could not encompass *that* eventuality!

16

The profusion of compassionate publicity that poured in from the four corners of the nation that next morning precipitated an explosion of boisterous activity and noisy preparation within the Berskin Building that induced one wag to speculate that from now on everyone was being paid by the decibel.

Colonel Godfrey Berskin, as spearhead of the operation, was, of course, one of the chief participants in the furore, spending so much of his time barking orders down the telephone that the lovely Amanda was instructed to enter his office every two hours on the hour and lubricate his bark with a squirt of 'Speke-eezie' throat spray.

But despite this niggling discomfort, Berskin was in his element. Co-ordination his metier, organization his life-blood, he swung from one problem to the next with the agility of a tree ape, solving, succouring, suggesting and inspiring.

And there really was a monumental amount to do – the organization of the Grand Launch Party, the refitting and embellishment of 'Glamour Puss', points of procedure to clear with the F.A.A., the Transport Workers' Union and the Pilots' Association, the intricate planning of the round-the-world flight with its attendant reliance on overseas co-operation (this accomplished by a veritable army of Flight Despatches, Air Traffic Controllers, Flight Engineers and Airport Authorities), and a multitude of other problems to overcome – not the least of which was ensuring absolute secrecy in the matter of the Mystery Flight itself.

In this regard, the dictum had gone out personally and heavily underlined by Berskin himself, accompanied by the threat of instant dismissal for anyone caught divulging any part of the mystery route.

Yes, it was a frantic, hectic two weeks, not only for the vast brigade of behind-the-scenes co-ordinators but also for the stars of the show – the crew.

TV programme producers, fashion houses, radio chat-shows, publishers, journalists and charities clamoured for their appearance. The Berskin office was bombarded with calls from merchandising houses and toy manufacturers requesting licence rights to produce Glamour games, Glamour dolls, Glamour Puss models; for the crew were now known nation-wide, not merely as a group but as individuals, each receiving a public acclaim that was beginning to encroach on adulation.

A chain of supermarkets in the South-West requested Rossiter open their newest store. Women's organizations all over the country begged talks by Lord Jim, Ramjet and Bush McKenzie on their flying experiences; a brassière manufacturer invited Boobs Buchanan to endorse their latest product; and Wilma Fluck received twenty-four offers of immediate matrimony and the lead part in a blue movie.

But – did this deluge of publicity, this overnight exposure to nation-wide fame, this cataract of acclamation and adulation have the slightest effect on these highly responsible, eminently sensible, acutely level-headed souls?

Yes, it most certainly did.

There was not one among them whose posture did not take on that smidgin of aloofness, that mite of regal superiority and condescension so effortlessly acquired by most who soar so quickly to national fame.

And yet – who could truly blame them? Let him without vanity chuck the first brick. Nevertheless, Lord Jim *did* appear to be taking to it all rather *too* well. In fact, were one not privy to his essential niceness, one might have been falsely led to regard him in his new role as just a *teeny* bit insufferable – and therefore to view what happened to him during the course of that two weeks as not altogether undeserved.

It was Wednesday evening of the penultimate week.

James let himself into his Greenwich Village apartment and made straight for the fridge, took out an ice-cold beer and returned to the living-room. there collapsing into an armchair to read with unabashed glee the bundle of fan-mail delivered to Glamour Airlines that day.

With a self-satisfied grin he fingered through the envelopes, counting them and studying the handwriting. There were forty-two – a gratifying ten more than Ramjet Rogers had received, which was precisely as it should be.

He sifted through them again, this time extracting a pale blue envelope addressed in obviously feminine hand. He sniffed at it, wincing at the paucity of its perfume and tore it open. Smilingly, he read:

Dear Mr. Crighton-Padgett … I fell in love with you the moment I saw you on TV. I think you are just wonderful. I pinned your photograph on my pillow and have kissed it so much it got soggy and wore out. I am getting a huge lifesize enlargement done so I can put it in my bed and lie on you and pretend I'm doing you-know-what to you. I think your hair is fabulous. What are your hobbies? Do you like kissing? What size are your shoes? I have a boy-friend who is always trying to do things to me but I won't let him but I will now because I can pretend it's *you* doing them to me. Do you think that's awful? Well, I don't care because I'm in love with you – very desperately! Must go now because my lunch is ready.

Yours for ever and ever, Janice Kent.

161

With a laugh, James set aside the letter and opened another, which read:

> Hello there, you gorgeous brute! If you ever want a real ding-a-ling time with a bunch of real sports – pop round to the above pad any night after ten. No charge – whips supplied.

It was signed 'Willis Hopgarden'.

Jim grinned and stuffed the letter in his inside pocket, reminding himself to pass it on to Sugar.

He was about to open a third envelope when the phone rang. He reached for it.

'Crighton-Padgett,' he announced.

Silence.

'Crighton-Padgett,' he said again.

'I just *had* to hear it again,' she laughed.

Jim's pulse-rate rocketed as the liquid-honey chuckle oozed down his ear. Ah, a man could die happy listening to a voice like that, he mused, realizing at the same time that no bird ever put on a voice like it unless she wanted something – very badly.

'Good evening,' he drawled playfully, employing his beautifully resonant Crighton-Padgett telephone voice. 'Who is this?'

'Oh ... that *voice*!' she sighed. 'So *exquisitely* English. Please say that again.'

'Say what?' he chuckled.

' "Good evening. Who is this." '

'All right. Good evening. Who *is* this? Well, whoever it is, she has a *very* lovely voice herself.'

'Thank you,' she laughed. 'Please forgive the game, but I couldn't resist it. My name is ... Yolande Methewan.'

'Are you ... *fond* of games, Miss Methewan?'

There was a pause. 'Mister Crighton-Padgett ... that is a *very* naughty question.'

'Do you ... object to naughty questions, Miss Methewan?'

Another pause. 'It depends entirely on who is asking them ... and on the point of our relationship. I'm sorry if my voice has in any way given you the wrong impression...'

'The impression it *has* given me, Miss Methewan, is that there is possibly a very lovely, undoubtedly very warm and very friendly young woman on the end of this line who just *conceivably* wishes to interview me. Am I far out?'

'No...' she chuckled. 'As a matter of fact you're right on the button. How did you guess?'

'Well ... since Glamour hit the headlines the other day, requests for interviews have not been *entirely* unknown,' he said with shameless conceit.

'Yes, of course. I'm sure you must be inundated with requests.'

'The price of fame, Miss Methewan,' he replied offhandedly, his mind on the rampage now with thoughts of possible seduction. Who was *she* trying to kid? 'I'm sorry if my voice has in any way given you the wrong impression, Mister Crighton-Padgett...'! Ha! She knew to the last husky syllable *precisely* what her voice did down the phone – they *all* did. 'What publication do you represent, Miss Methewan?' he asked, with considerable indifference.

'*Personalities of the Week* – it's a West Coast publication but I work from an office here in New York.' Her voice softened again. 'Are you saying ... you *agree* to an interview, sir?'

Sir. He liked that. It demonstrated a nice, innate subservience that would come in handy later on.

'Well, of course,' he smiled. 'How could I possibly refuse you anything, Miss Methewan? When did you ... propose ...?'

'Well, any time to suit yourself. I realize how *terribly* busy you must be – all these interviews...'

'Yes, quite.'

'How about ... tomorrow morning?'

He sucked in a breath. 'Ooh, I'm afraid not ... *fright*fully busy all day tomorrow – *and* the next day.'

'I see.' She sounded very disappointed.

'Look – where are you now?'

'Now ...? I'm downtown – at the office ...'

'Well, why not pop up here ... this evening ... right now.'

Another pause ... then more warm, chuckling honey in his ear. '*There*, Mister Crighton-Padgett? To your apartment?'

'Why not? Do you think you won't be safe, Miss Methewan?'

'Perhaps *you* had better answer that. *Will* I be safe?'

He gave a sigh. 'Well now . . . one thing I learned from my great-great-grandfather – an *extremely* wise old man – was "never make a promise you can't keep".'

' "*Can't* keep" – or "have no intention of keeping"?'

He chuckled devilishly. 'Why not live dangerously just this once – and find out, Miss Methewan? You . . . *want* this interview?'

'Very badly.'

'Then come on up.'

Now a much longer pause, ending with an intrigued smile. 'All right . . . I'll just do that.'

'Splendid. See you in . . . fifteen minutes?'

'Fifteen minutes.'

James plonked down the phone, let rip a yahoo and shot out of the chair, then for several minutes, muttering to himself in excited undertones, he flashed around the apartment checking on essential requirements for artful deduction. 'Champagne . . . four bottles . . . should be enough . . . clean glasses . . . clean sheets . . . now! – the paintings . . . !'

He ran to the door, flung it open, raced down one flight of stairs and hammered on the door of the apartment below.

'Come on . . . come on . . . !'

The door opened on a chain and a curtain of lank black hair named Boris Wakachaski muttered, 'Yeah, who is it?'

'Boris, you idiot, it's me – James! Comb your face, for petesake.'

Boris finger-forked a hank of hair from his right eye. 'Yeah, it's James all right. G'bye, James . . .'

Jim stuck his foot in the closing door.

'Boris . . . old chum . . .'

'James, I am *not* your old chum – not any more, not since the last time you borrowed my paintings and returned one with a hole the size of your head in it.'

'Boris . . . *listen* to me!' pleaded Jim. 'This one's a *cert*! So help me, she's so ga-ga she won't even *see* the paintings.'

Boris shrugged. 'So what's the point?'

'I mean ... figuratively speaking. Aw, come on, Boris, she'll be here any minute...'

'Do you solemnly swear to make restitution for any damage inflicted on my life work?'

'Yes, yes ... anything!'

'They're worth fifty bucks apiece.'

'And *extraordinary* good value ...'

'Then I'll make that seventy-five.'

'Don't be ridiculous.'

'O.K., then – just this once. An' maybe one of these days you'll do *me* a favour and seduce an art critic, huh?'

'Anything – just get the paintings.'

'Wait here.'

Boris unlatched the chain and, as he disappeared from view the door swung open a few inches. James could not resist a peek inside. The place was a disaster area – paints, clothing, canvases all over the place.

As he surveyed the debris, a girl appeared in the doorway of an inner room, glanced in his direction and waved.

'Hi.'

'H ... hello,' gulped Jim, recognizing her at once as the statuesque blonde in nearly all of Boris's paintings, his recognition made easy by the fact that she was now, as in the paintings, stark, staring naked, the sight of her tripping his switch, reminding him that he hadn't seduced anyone in almost forty-eight hours and firming his resolve to conquer Yolande Thingummy without delay.

Boris returned at that moment, severing his view of the girl.

'B ... Boris, I have just decided – I am giving up flying and taking up painting and may I please borrow your model?'

'You know your trouble, Crighton-Padgett? – you're oversexed. Here – and don't forget ... fifty bucks apiece.'

'I will guard them with my life. Thanks, Boris...' He ducked to one side, sneaked a last peep at the girl. 'Boris ... how *do* you find time to paint?'

'I don't – I borrow these from a fella downstairs.'

James raced back to his apartment, quickly hung the paintings on the living-room walls, stuck fresh price-tags over

Boris's signature, set up his easel and virgin canvas in the bedroom, then changed out of his Glamour uniform into his artist gear – this time red satin shirt, black trousers and black neckerchief.

He was adjusting his beret when the doorbell rang.

With fluttering heart he hurried to it, paused at the mirror for a final inspection, then opened it.

His heart leapt. She was even more beautiful than her voice had promised – a tall, slender Negress with a stunning figure and devastating eyes that now regarded him with sultry humour from beneath long, dark lashes. Clad in a thin brown silk dress, her stance was a promiscuous pose, an invitation to inspect which he accepted with alacrity, slowly lowering his eyes, devouring her swelling breasts, slender hips and exquisite legs, then just as slowly returning them to her breathtakingly beautiful beige-brown face and playful smile.

'Will I do?' she asked, her voice a lover's touch.

'*Em*inently,' he breathed. 'Please . . . come in.'

She entered, the delicate drift of her perfume drawing from him a muted, light-hearted groan as she passed close to him. He closed the door and turned, watching her enter the living-room, his eyes riveted on her fabulous bottom.

'W . . . would you care for a drink, Miss Methewan?'

'I'd love one.'

'Wonderful . . . please sit down, I'll get it.'

He scuttled into the kitchen, muttering, 'Oh boy . . . oh boy!' nervously blew the cork from a bottle of ice-cold champers, collected two glasses and scuttled back into the living-room, finding her standing at one of Boris's paintings.

'Did *you* do these?' she asked admiringly.

He shrugged modestly. 'Just a hobby.'

'They're *very* good.' She moved on to the next one. 'Now – *that* is sexy. Who's the girl?'

'A model,' he answered evasively, handing her a glass of champers. 'Well . . . cheers.'

She turned and devastated him with a smile over the rim. 'Cheers. You're a *very* talented man, Mister Crighton-Padgett – this will make excellent copy.'

'Please . . . call me Jim. Oh . . . it's not really worth mentioning. I wouldn't bother . . .'

'Nonsense! You're far too modest. I see you've got price-tags on them – do you sell many of them?'

'Er, yes ... a few.'

'Two hundred and fifty dollars ... I'd say that was about right.'

'Oh, you ... know ... something about paintings?'

'A little. It's one of *my* hobbies ... as is silverware ... jewellery ... almost anything of resale value. I, too, run a little business on the side.'

She turned again to the paintings, inspecting them closely, nodding approval and murmuring, 'Hm hm ...' from time to time.

'You ... seem very interested in them,' ventured Jim. 'I ... don't suppose you'd be interested in buying any?'

Well, why not, he thought. Fifty dollars to Boris, two hundred to himself. If it came to a sale he could always say Boris Wakachaski was his pen-name ... brush name.

'I *might* be interested in ... acquiring one or two,' she said off-handedly. 'I'll think about it.'

'Here ... have some more champagne.'

'Trying to lower my sales resistance, Mr. Crighton-Padgett?' she grinned.

'You really think I'd do a thing like that?'

'Without blinking one of those beautiful blue eyes. Cheers.'

'Cheers,' he grinned.

'Tell me ... where do you *do* all this painting?'

He nodded at the bedroom. 'In there.'

'May I see?'

'With ... pleasure.'

He took her to the bedroom door. 'Voilà!'

Her eyes slowly covered the room, taking in the canvas and easel ... then the bed. 'So ... this is where it all takes place?'

'Right here.'

'Yes ...' she nodded, 'I can just see her lying naked there.' She turned to him, smiling sensuously. 'Pleasurable hobby, James.'

Jim cleared his throat. 'Have ... *you* ever been painted, Yolande?'

Her smiled deepened. 'No ... never. It's something every woman would like, of course ...'

167

'Of course.'

'Are you . . . making an offer, James?'

His heart erupted. It was going to happen! His plan was actually working! Soon she would be lying there . . . gloriously naked . . . soft . . . warm . . . it was all too much!

He drained his glass, attempting to regain his composure.

'Of . . . course,' he smiled.

'You mean . . . right now?'

Oh Jeezus.

She laughed. 'James, I do believe you're nervous.'

'N . . . no, not nervous . . . excited.'

She gave a teasing frown. 'You – an experienced artist . . . used to seeing naked women – excited?'

'Of *course* I'm excited . . . you're *very* beautiful, Yolande – the prospect quite overwhelms me.'

'Well, *thank* you.'

'You're welcome.'

'I . . . think, however, that we'd better finish the interview first – otherwise we just *might* not get around to it.'

'M . . . must we?' he pleaded.

'You want me to lose my job?'

'Heaven forbid.'

'And . . . I *think* we'd better go back into the living-room. This "environment" is slightly too distracting. My gosh, that bed looks comfortable . . .'

Quakingly he followed her back into the living-room, unable to believe it was all happening so smoothly. It was like a dream come true – for her to be so beautiful *and* so acquiescent. Well, it *was* happening – so get on with it – and make sure you do a damn good job.

She sat deep in one of the armchairs, shattering Jim, as her little silk dress shot crutchwards, with a knee-to-knickers flash of her fabulous thighs. Seemingly unaware that she was revealing so many goodies, she opened her handbag, took out a pad and pencil, and settled herself for the interview, looking up quickly and catching Jim's gaze riveted on her gams.

Completely unabashed, she released a slow, smouldering smile and said, 'Well, at least *part* of me has your undivided attention.'

He grinned, caught in the act. 'You're . . . not at all easy to talk to. I'm afraid my mind is on other matters.'

'Perhaps a drink might help.'

'Indeed it might. Would you ... care for another?'

'Why not? The night is young.'

'Indeed it is.'

He got up and went into the kitchen, Yolande following his progress until he was out of sight.

Then she moved.

Dropping the pad and pencil on the floor, she opened her handbag, took out a small glass phial, tipped a tiny tablet into the palm of her hand, closed the handbag and came out of the chair.

Plop! Into Jim's half-filled glass it went.

She was settled again in her chair by the time he returned with a fresh, uncorked bottle of champers.

'Here we are – what the doctor orders for nervous disorders.'

She held up her glass and he filled it, the neck of bottle chinking nervously against the crystal. Then he topped up his own drink.

'Well, here's to an ... interesting evening.'

She demurred with a small inclination of her lovely head. 'To an interesting evening.'

Then Jim tipped back his glass and swallowed the lot.

Pouring himself another he looked down at her ... at the blatant sexuality of her partly opened thighs. 'Do we ... really have to bother with the interview? My mind just isn't on it.'

'What ... *is* on your mind, James?'

He plonked down the bottle and his glass and fell on his knees before her, risking his right hand on her knee, his heart leaping because she hadn't flinched, wasn't objecting, was allowing his hand to remain there, was smiling at him, urging him closer ... and in he moved, his hand sliding slowly down the electrifying warmth of her naked thigh ... closer ... closer ... her smouldering smile beckoning him on ... and on ... her legs parting at his hand's approach ... my God, how warm she was in there ... warm as a puppy's mouth ... moist ...'

'Yolande!' he gasped.

Her breasts were heaving ... so close ... so warm ... so waiting to be kissed.

'Yes, James . . . ?' she whispered, her throat constricted.

'I . . . I . . . my God . . . !'

'What is it, James?'

He shook his head. 'I . . . don't know . . . the room . . . your face . . .'

'Poor James.'

'. . . whirling . . . spinning . . .'

'Poor, poor James.'

'. . . spinning . . . whirling . . .'

'You hadn't a chance, had you.'

Slump!

Jim's head flopped face-down in her lap, his cheek at rest, alas uncaring, against her moist, warm thighs; then slowly he slithered out and down and sprawled full-length across the floor, on his back, mouth open, arms akimbo, at peace with the world.

For a moment Yolande looked down upon him, taking in the firm line of his handsome jaw, the strength of his lithe young body, then with a slight, perhaps wistful smile, she shook her head and got up.

Moving to the window she three times drew the curtains and opened them again, finally closing them, and perhaps one minute later the doorbell rang.

She opened it. Two men stood there, one Negro, one white. They entered and she shut the door.

'Any trouble?' asked the white man, whose name was Wallach.

'Is there ever?' she smiled.

He pinched her cheek affectionately. 'Sis, you're wonderful. How fresh did he get?'

'Aw, he was a tiger,' she laughed. 'Wanted to do me in oils.'

'Kinky!' said the Negro, whose name was also Wallach. 'What we got, Sis?'

'More than enough. Come and take a look.'

They moved into the living-room, the men whistling in appreciation at the subject-matter of the paintings, offering no more than a casual glance at the inert, gently snoring form of James DeCourcey Crighton-Padgett.

'Hey, now, just look at these!' grinned the Negro.

170

'This guy paint them?' asked the white Wallach. 'He looks kinda arty.'

'*Claimed* he did,' smiled Yolande. 'Got a sweet little seduction set-up has James – a slight, though interesting, variation on the etchings theme.'

'What do you think these oils will fetch?' asked the white man.

Yolande shrugged. 'Maybe a hundred each, but we'll take 'em. It's the silver in the corner cabinet that makes the trip worth while.'

The men followed her across to the cabinet, the Negro gasping, 'Yeah ... yeah ... *yeah*! Some sweet pieces here, baby – Georgian! Family heirloom stuff.'

'He's the type,' she answered. 'O.K. – turn the place over and let's get out.'

*　　*　　*

James woke an hour later.

He opened his eyes and for quite a while lay there staring at the ceiling, wondering how come he'd fallen asleep in the middle of his living-room floor. Then suddenly he knew why.

He sat up quickly and lay down again even more quickly, blinding pain lanced through his head.

'Ohhh!' he gasped. 'Ooooh! ... Ooooow! ... OHHHH!'

Dammit – the stuff was vintage!

'Yo ... lande!' he croaked to a silent room.

He looked up and around, wincing at the light, certain incongruities in the arrangement of the room slowly penetrating his awareness. The drawers ... the cupboards ... open! He came to his feet and crouched there like a surf-rider until the room steadied, then staggered to the armchair she had occupied and clung to it, squinting with horror at the devastation! The corner cabinet ... bare! The paintings ... gone! Oh my *God* ... !

Now he lurched towards the bedroom, emitting a tortured groan at the sight of more open drawers ... the empty wardrobe! And gaping and utterly woebegone he slithered down the door-jamb and stared at his boots, wondering where his technique had gone so terribly wrong.

It took him half an hour to make an inventory and then he phoned the police, the desk sergeant putting him through to the duty sergeant.

'What ...!' bellowed Haimaiker. 'Not *you* again! Goddam it, Crighton-Padgett, ain't you done enough for one week? O.K., gimme the run-down – what did they get?'

Haimaiker began writing.

'Two hundred bucks in cash ... two *thousand* bucks worth of silver ... Jesus, C-P, they really saw you comin'. Go on ... eight paintings by *who*? Boris Wakachaski? Never heard of him. How much were they worth? Fifty each, huh? Well ... mighta been woise – they coulda bin Van Goghs! Anything else ...? Eight civilian suits an' *what* ...? Your Glamour Airlines uniform! Man, from what I saw in the papers they did you a big favour! Now, why in hell would they pinch that? For kicks, I guess.

'Well, let me tell yuh somethin', C-P – you ain't the foist celebrity t'be hit. This is a sweet racket this gang is workin'. The dame phones for an interview, gives the guy the hot lips down the phone then slips him a Fynn when she gets there. Hard luck, old boy, but there ain't much more we can do than we're doin' already. We'll let you know if anythin' turns up.'

James put down the phone, disconsolate in the extreme. Two hundred dollars in cash ... another four hundred he'd have to pay Boris for his lousy paintings ... eight suits worth a hundred and fifty each ... the silver mater had given him ... *and* his Glamour Uniform. By God, he'd learned his lesson. Never again ... never! Not another dame would cross his threshold ... ever!

Then the phone rang.

He picked it up, switching automatically, despite his dejection, to his Crighton-Padgett telephone voice. Old habits die very hard.

'Crighton-Padgett ...'

'You said that beautifully,' she chuckled, her voice liquid honey in his ear. 'My name is Eloise DeLaney, Mister Crighton-Padgett – I'm a feature writer for *Who's In Town This Week* and I sure would love to do a piece on you ...'

Well, by God – another of 'em!

'You mean ... right now?' he said, playing her along.

172

'Well . . . if you have no objection.'

'Miss DeLaney . . . is it *usual* for you to conduct interviews so late in the evening . . . ?'

'Very. I like to catch my subject relaxing at home, maybe over a drink. I find they're less inhibited . . . talk more easily.'

Boy, I'll just bet they do.

'Miss DeLaney . . . there are a couple of things I'd like you to know first . . .'

'Yes, sir?'

Dammit, he *still* liked that 'sir'.

'I'd like you to know that at this moment of time I am absolutely and stupendously flat broke . . . busted . . . skint . . . cleaned out – do you understand?'

'Er, yes, sir . . . but what . . . ?'

'Furthermore, there is nothing of value whatsoever in my apartment – no silver, no jewellery, no paintings, no clothing . . . nothing! – do you understand that?'

She gave a peculiar laugh. 'Well, yes, but . . .'

'Now, do you *still* want that interview?'

'Well, of course I do . . .'

'All right. Where are you now?'

'I'm . . . at the office.'

'Right – give me the phone number.'

'The n . . . ?'

'The number – let me have it, I'll call you right back.'

She gave it to him.

'Right – stand by.'

He rang off and dialled it. A male operator's voice answered: 'Pipkin Publications.'

'Er, do you have a Miss Eloise DeLaney working for you?'

The guy chuckled, man-to-man. 'Boy, *do* we? Sure we do – she's a feature writer for *Who's In Town This Week*.'

'You sound pleased with the fact,' smiled Jim.

'Mister – I am *pleased,* believe me. When that little lady walks inta the office . . . blonde hair swingin' and that cute ass . . . say, who is this anyway?'

'Never mind – put me through.'

'*Who's In Town This Week*,' she announced.

'I am,' he growled. 'Come on up.'

17

And what, during that two weeks of furious, behind-the-scenes activity, of our other heroes?

Well, Cock-up Rossiter spent some of it searching for a ferret-sitter to take care of the brutes while he was flying round the world, eventually finding a strange kid on the second floor of his own building who was studying to be a vet.

'O.K., kid,' Rossiter finally, and with some reluctance, agreed, grimacing at the specimens of dissected rats, toads and beetles displayed on boards around the child's bedroom walls. 'Only don't get any cute ideas my ferrets would look good up there. I don't need to know what makes 'em tick – just make sure they're still tickin' when I get back.'

'But ... what if one should inadvertently die while you're

away?' the kid asked with infuriating precocity, adjusting his horn-rimmed spectacles.

'*You* will inadvertently follow it,' scowled Rossiter.

Ramjet, of course, was in his element, spending most of his days before a mirror, perfecting the angle of his 'Wings Over Burma' cap, and his evenings in the bars of several Manhattan hotels frequented by visiting air-crews testing the effect of his day's travail.

In that the object of the exercise was to attract female attention he was inordinately successful – and never more so than on the evening of the penultimate Thursday when, seated at the bar of a hotel on Lexington at 42nd, he suddenly discovered Beryl Ormsby at his elbow.

With his sixth-sense radar bleeping 'female', he glanced sideways, seeing a diminutive air-stew wearing short dark hair and that aura of unkempt exhaustion instantly recognized by fellow-flyers as the 'just arrived look'.

She was not pretty, nor ever could be, even after a good night's sleep, yet there was something about her that immediately attracted Ramjet. Her figure was good, slim, full-breasted, yet it wasn't that alone that caused the instant stirring in his loins. It was that indefinable radiation, that transmission of innate wantonness termed, by himself in one of his more erudite moments, as 'Craves-it Waves.'

The bird was a little raver.

'Hi,' he smiled, fixing her with his much-practised V.M. grin and arching brow. 'Just arrived?'

'Yes – on foot.'

'English?'

'Me foot? Yeah, both of them.'

He laughed. 'Which part?'

'All of them.'

He laughed again and decided he liked her. 'May I buy you a drink?'

'Yes – if you can get Flash Harry up this end of the bar. I think he's in love with his sink.'

'I'll get him,' Ramjet threatened.

He slammed his glass down on the counter and the balding barman looked up with a start, shook water from his hands and came up, drying them on a tea-towel. 'You want somethin', mister – a new glass maybe?'

'When you've finished your undies, luv, we'd like a bleedin' drink,' Beryl said scathingly.

Ramjet grinned, 'What would you like?'

'A very large gin.'

'With tonic?'

'If you insist.'

'And a Scotch for me,' ordered Ramjet.

The barman, whose name was Herman Flattery, dispensed the drinks and plonked them down on the counter. 'Should you require any *foither* service, sir – don't bother to call ... just throw your stool at the shelves an' I'll come runnin'.'

'Don't think we won't,' scowled Beryl.

Herman retired to his sink, muttering, 'Goddam air-crew ...'

'Well, cheers,' grinned Ramjet, raising his glass.

'Ta very much,' said Beryl, sinking half her gin. 'Wow, I needed that.'

'Rough trip?'

'Not at all. Just the usual packed-to-capacity, dirt-cheap trans-Atlantic charter flight with nine-tenths turbulence and a five-hundred-foot free-fall smack in the middle of dinner ...'

'Oh.' Ramjet winced. 'What happened?'

'Hardly anything ... eight-nine people sick ... a hundred and four lots of ruined clothes ... an old bird bashed her head on the seat in front ... and a bloke lost his teeth down the loo. Normal sort of flight, really.'

'You poor thing. By the way, what's your name?'

'Weary Beryl Ormsby. Er, pardon for askin', but what's that you're wearin'? You advertising something or something?'

Ramjet frowned, a bit put out. 'You mean you haven't *heard* over in England?'

'Heard what, luv?'

Ramjet leaned closer and pointed to his cap badge.

Beryl's hazel eyes flew wide. 'Glamour Airlines!'

'Ah, you obviously *have* heard,' he grinned, good humour restored.

'*Heard!* You fellas are the talk of every Crew Room in Britain! Well, well, fancy bumpin' into you! Ooh, eh, wait till

I get back home an' tell the girls. They'll be *livid*! Here, which one are you, now ... no, don't tell me ...' she backed off, squinting at him, 'Of *course* – you're Paul Rogers, aren't you – the one that looks like Whatsisname. Don't they call you Fanjet or somethin' ...?'

'Er ... *Ram*jet.' He winced.

'Oh yes ...' She gave a sexy giggle. 'We were talkin' about that. The fellas reckoned it had nuthin' to do with the type of planes you flew and *everythin*' to do with your ... "*sexual pro* ..."' she frowned, 'now what the 'ell was that word?'

Ramjet raised his brow another millimetre, delighted with the course the conversation was taking. 'Proclivity?'

'Yeah, that's it.' She gave a shrug. 'I'd never heard of it. What's it mean?'

'It means ... "inclination",' he grinned.

Her eyes widened again, excitedly. 'Ooh, does it? And ... *does* it – have everything to do with your sexual pro ... thingy?'

'Well ... I'll say *this*, Beryl – it wasn't *me* who gave me the nickname.'

'Oh?' She grinned sideways at him. 'Who was it, then?'

'Oh ... certain friends of mine.'

'Hmm. They wouldn't happen to be *girl*-friends, I suppose?'

He shrugged, modestly.

'You know what I think, Paul Rogers?'

'No, what do you think, Beryl?'

'I think you're a ...' She stopped, her eyes crinkling mischievously. 'Listen ... how'd you like to come to a party?'

'Party? What sort ... where?'

'At a pad up on 90th Street.'

He raised an impressed brow. '90th! Pretty classy, district.'

'It's a classy pad.'

'Whose is it?'

'A real classy fella – a Bolivian bloke ... owns his own airline – among eighteen thousand other things.'

'This I gotta see.'

'You can if you want to.'

'It's that easy?'

'It's open house. Anything we do is all right with the King...'

'The *King*?'

'That's what we call him. His name's really Kingston Something-or-other ... Colchequaca or Colquechacha – something bloody unpronounceable. But can he throw a party! They're the only thing that makes these U.S. trips bearable.'

'Sounds like fun,' grinned Ramjet.

She smiled mysteriously and drained her glass. 'They're fun.'

'Will there be many people there?'

'About a million – mostly fly-types. He's got a thing about air-stews.'

'Can you blame him?' he smiled.

She turned to him. 'Ramjet ... would you do me two favours ... ?'

'Sure, anything.'

'When we get there, will you *try* to remember who brought you? I'd hate to go to all this trouble and have you vanish the moment we get through the door.'

He frowned, suitably appalled. 'Well, of course ...'

She shook her head. 'No, there's no "of course" about it. There'll be some *very* dishy dollies there who are goin' to fancy your Glamour pants like mad and won't lose a second tryin' to get them off ...'

Ramjet's pulse leapt. 'Now, Beryl, you don't think ... ?'

'No, I don't think – I *know*! If a big sexy hunk like you walked in *normally* there'd be a bleedin' great stampede to get at you – but in that Glamour uniform ...!'

'Well ... would you prefer me to change into civvies?' he offered, knowing damn well the suggestion would appal her.

She smiled slyly. 'Like heck, you will. Why d'you think I'm inviting you?'

Ramjet pretended hurt. 'I would like to think for myself alone.'

'That, too – but the uniform comes as well.' She looked at him meaningfully, her eyes softened, becoming sexier. 'You ... won't regret sticking with Beryl, I promise you.'

'Oh ... ?' Her tone set his heart rocking.

'There may be *prettier* birds there, but ... well, looks aren't everything, are they?'

'No,' he gulped. 'No, they're not. And, er, what's the second favour you want from me?'

She grinned and jerked her head. 'Throw your stool at those shelves – I'm dyin' for another drink.'

* * *

Ten o'clock found them half-squiffed in the back of a taxi, heading north to 90th Street.

Beryl had changed from her uniform into a low-cut, red silk, floor-length gown with a naughty split up the side which, in sitting position, exposed her little red knickers – a sight which, in addition to the one of her mostly exposed breasts, had Ramjet's heart in his throat and his fingers itching for action.

'Down boy,' she insisted, pushing him away as he attempted, yet again, to stick his tongue in her ear.

'Aw, come on, baby ...'

'Patience – and get your hand *out* of there! The night is young ...'

'But you're so beautiful!'

'You *must* be pissed.'

She leaned forward and rapped on the protective perspex screen. 'On the right, driver – just here.'

The cabby, in defiance of the closely following traffic, shot across the one-way road and came to a halt outside a tall block of extremely well-to-do apartments.

Ramjet slid two bills into the pay-tray and they got out, weaving nicely, then stood on the pavement, looking up at the block.

'Hey, this is all right,' he said approvingly.

'Well, it's certainly not Scottie Road,' she said, grabbing his arm to prevent him teetering into the gutter.

'Scottie Road? Where's that?'

'Liverpool – one of the slightly less salubrious parts.'

'Is that where you come from – Liverpool?'

'You mean you can't tell? Come on, let's go up ...'

'No – not until you give me a kiss.'

He made a grab for her and she gave a shriek and pretended to struggle. 'Ramjet . . . st*op* it!'

'Give us a kiss . . . !'

'No, you mad fool . . . sto . . .'

Then she was eating him, arms tight around his neck, grinding into him. It lasted a full minute.

'Wow!' she gasped, breaking away. 'Ooh, you randy devil . . . !'

'Well . . . what d'you expect – goin' at me like that?'

'Not here in the *street*!' She gave a giggle and took his arm. 'Come on, you dirty pig. My God, no wonder they call you Ramjet! And you just watch that thing – don't go wavin' it about up there or there'll be a riot. Tie a label marked "Beryl" on it and tuck it away somewhere safe . . . like under your arm or round your waist . . .'

'Flatterer,' he grinned, kissing her on the nose.

Locked together they weaved along the shrub-lined path to a splendid porticoed entrance and rang a button.

'Who is it?' asked a metal grille, set above the button.

'That you, Frenchy? This is the lovely Beryl Ormsby with guest.'

' 'ello, Pussycat! Heh, come on up!'

The heavy glass door buzzed and they pushed through it into a marble-and-gilt hallway bedecked with antiques and gilt mirrors.

'I *say*!' exclaimed Ramjet.

'Huh, you ain't seen nuthin' yet!'

'Er, who's this Frenchy character – and what's with the "Pussycat" bit?'

She smiled at him. 'Frenchy is a one-eyed hump-backed dwarf and he calls every girl Pussycat – O.K.?'

'O.K.'

She hugged his arm. 'And thanks for being jealous.'

'You're welcome,' he grinned.

She pressed the elevator button and the gilt doors opened. They stepped inside and she punched the top button and as the doors closed, Ramjet grabbed her again.

They were still hard at it when the elevator came to rest and the doors opened. A blast of party noise hit them. Ramjet shot round, eyes popping. There was no hallway; the elevator fed

180

straight into the huge living-room, crowded with people.

'My God, I thought you said there'd only be a million here! There must be five!'

'I forgot – it's Thursday. Big night Thursday.'

'Does he throw a party *every* night?'

'More or less. Ah, here comes Frenchy – be nice to him or he may throw you out.'

Ramjet peered around, anticipating the approach of a one-eyed, hump-backed dwarf. What he got was a huge, incredibly handsome guy built like Tarzan.

''ello, Pussycat!' grinned Frenchy, blinding Beryl with about eight hundred snow-white teeth, his dark, flashing eyes frisking Ramjet at the same time, a frown shrivelling his brow at sight of the uniform. 'Hey, hey ... and who do we 'ave 'ere – Captain Marvel?'

'Very funny,' sneered Ramjet, lowering his eye-flaps threateningly. 'How'd you like to be pickin' your teeth off the floor five seconds from now, bub?'

'Now, now, you two,' laughed Beryl. 'Frenchy, you idiot – this is one of the *Glamour Airlines* fellas! This is Paul Rogers! Now, do me a favour and be impressed!'

Frenchy's draw dropped. 'Ramjet Rogers ...! *Sacre bleu!* Aw, Monsieur Rogers, forgive me! I 'ad no idea!' Excitedly he turned towards the crowd and bellowed, 'Hey – boys an' girls – look who's 'ere! Ramjet Rogers of Glamour Airlines ...!'

'Frenchy, you bastard!' snorted Beryl and booted him in the backside.

Two thousand women of all shapes, sizes, colour and aptitude stopped whatever they were doing, let out shrieks of delight and surged across the room, crowding Ramjet unmercifully.

'It's Ramjet Rogers – it really is ... !'

'My *God*, isn't he *gorg*eous ...!'

'Well, hello, big boy ... !'

'Ramjet – may I have your autograph ... on my thigh?'

'Those *shoulders*! Geez, I got *goose*bumps!'

'Boy, he can drop his landing gear on *my* runway *any*day!'

'Ain't that just my luck? Every other dame in the room's got boobs. Me – I got goosebumps!'

Now a tall, wildly curvaceous blonde in a gold see-through dress oozed close and caught Ramjet's hand. 'Hi. You wanna dance, honey? You can bet your sweet wingspan you won't regret it...'

Beryl leapt in, slapped away the blonde's hand. 'Take off, Clara, he's mine!'

'Ha!' Clara laughed cruelly. 'Beryl, baby, go home and play with your pussy – this tiger's mine.'

'Over my dead body he's yours.'

'That can be arranged, sugar...'

'Hey, break it up, girls,' cut in Frenchy. 'Come on, Ramjet, let's get you out of here. Come and meet the King. All right, ladies – back to bed! Go on... mush!'

Forcing a path through the crowd, Frenchy dragged Ramjet, *very* closely followed by Beryl, past a marble fountain playing in the centre of the room to a long, white-leather-fronted bar that occupied the far right corner, and there brought them into the presence of the King himself.

There is no denying vast wealth, Ramjet reflected, as the little fat guy with the chubby olive cheeks and the fierce Hawaiian shirt detached himself from the crowd around the bar and came to meet them. Remove this fella from these luxurious trappings and he'd still look filthy rich. There's something about them, an aura, that lifts them out of the ordinary – or maybe it was the gold that sparkled in his teeth and the million bucks worth of diamonds twinkling on his chubby fingers.

Laughing brown eyes and a cheery wave greeted Beryl as he came towards them.

'Hchello, my leetle pigeon!' he beamed, scraping the 'hch' across the back of his throat. 'So nice to see you again.'

''ello, King, luv, how are you?' she laughed, kissing his cheek.

'Hchal the better for seeing you. Hchey, hchoo you brought this time?'

'This is Ramjet Rogers – of the famous Glamour Airlines.'

'Glamour Hchairlines! Well, we are hchonoured, Senor Rogers! Hchow d'you do?'

He took Ramjet's hand in both of his and shook it heartily, 'Pliss – make yourself at hchome ... drink what you like – eat

182

what you like – stay as long as you like . . .'

'Well, that's very kind of you . . .'

'De nada! You do me a favour – hchelp me spend some of the money. Go on – hchave a good time, I gotta talk some lousy business. Money . . . money . . . money – all the time! Two million dollars I made since breakfast! Hchow can I spend so much!'

With a laugh he wandered back to the bar.

'Isn't he lovely?' smiled Beryl. 'Thanks, Frenchy – see you later.'

' 'ave a ball, Pussycat.'

Frenchy departed and they went to the bar and got drinks.

'Well, well . . .' exclaimed Ramjet, taking an elevated look around the room. 'Quite a place.'

'You should see the bedrooms,' she grinned.

'I should?'

'Later. Come on – let's dance.'

Some time around midnight, now considerably shickered, he lost her, which was not surprising in that crowd and considering the lights were turned down so low he couldn't see his own feet – and considering he wouldn't have been able to see his own feet even in broad daylight.

He was weaving around on the edge of the crowd wondering in which direction the bar lay when a warm, perfumed presence moved close behind him and a low, sultry voice breathed in his ear, 'You wanna dance *now*, honey? You still won't regret it . . .'

His pulse jumped. He turned, Clara's face and frame of blonde hair emerging through the gloom as a vague swirl.

'Clara?' he murmured.

'Well, it ain't Mother Hubbard, honey.'

'Say, have you seen Beryl?'

'Beryl . . . ? Sure – she left half an hour ago.'

'Left . . . ?'

'As in departed . . . scrammed . . . vamoosed.'

'You saw her go?'

'I saw "them" go – she was with some guy.'

'Some *guy*?'

Clara sighed, barely containing her patience. 'Y'know – as

in man ... male ... fella – the kind I'm standin' here waitin'
to dance with ... ?'

'Oh ... I'm sorry.'

Automatically he put out his arms, preoccupied with the
mystery of why Beryl should suddenly take off with another
guy, but then Clara slid home and all thoughts of Beryl disappeared like mist before the morning sun.

The first contact of her warm, supple body made him gasp
which made her chuckle, close, in his ear.

'I told you you wouldn't regret it.'

'So you did ...'

'You're shakin', Ramjet.'

'Yes, ma'm ...'

'Stay close ... this is only the beginning.'

'Yes, *ma'm*.'

Close he stayed, glued to her gently undulating, fiercely
arousing, subtly probing body as his hands slid down the velvet length of her naked spine and came to rest on the voluptuous mounds of her perfect bottom.

'That's nice,' she murmured drowsily, snuggling into his
neck. 'What big ... strong ... hands, you have, Ramjet. I *like*
a man with big ... strong ... hands ...'

'You ... do?'

'Ramjet ... I'm *very* sleepy ...'

'I'm ... kinda bushed myself,' he gulped.

In fact the room was going round something awful. He
didn't know which felt worse, closing his eyes or keeping
them open. Either way, he knew if he didn't lie down pretty
soon he was going to fall down, which was just one reason
why, when she whispered, 'I know a place where we could
grab a little shut-eye' he accepted readily and with downright
relief.

'You do?'

'Hm hm ... come on, this way.'

Taking his hand, she led him through the crowd, out of a
door, along a corridor and into a darkened room, locking the
door behind them.

As his eyes adjusted to the meagre light he barely had time
to locate the bed and then she was in his arms, thrusting her
body into his, her scalding, hungry mouth devouring him.

Passion erupted instantly, engulfing them, carrying them trembling and panting to the bed. Clothing ripped away, they hit the cool silk coverlet in a flurry of kisses, locked together like Siamese twins.

'Oh God ... oh God!' she gasped, kissing, biting, tonguing him tempestuously. 'Oh, you've got me so *excited*! Ramjet ... *darling*! ... I'm *coming* ... !'

'Already!' he gasped.

'Yes ... yes ...! Ohhh ... OHHHH! ... OHHHHH!'

A spasm of ecstasy curled her into an orgasmic huddle, knees high, her cheek against his chest, and there she clung, jerking convulsively, shaking her head as though disbelieving it had happened. Then, suddenly ... she calmed ... and without a word shot down the bed and swallowed him.

Ramjet let out a gasp and really began concentrating on the job at hand. Had he not a reputation to uphold? Then uphold it he would. He had no doubt that this night of wild abandon with the white-hot Clara would quickly and widely be known, and, apart from all other considerations, he must regard this, his debut performance as First Officer of Glamour, as an invaluable investment for the future.

Thus resolved, he set about his duty's execution – and about Clara – in a manner that, some half an hour later, had reduced her to a limp, tousled, sweating, exhausted shadow of her former self.

'Oh ... ohhh ... OHHHH! My God ... *Ram*jet ... !'

'Again?' he chuckled.

She nodded exhaustedly, eyes closed, mouth gaping, 'Again ... my God, what are you *doin'* to me ... ?'

'Don't *you* know?' he grinned.

'Yes ... an' I'm gonna know a week from now. I'm not gonna be able to walk ... ever again ... you beast ... you gorgeous ... horny ... aw, what are you gonna do now ... ?'

'This ...'

'OHHH! Ohhh, that's *fabulous* ... Ramjet ... what *is* a ramjet ... ?'

'A continuous ... *thrust* ... with com ... *pression* by aero-ram ... !'

'My *God*, that's you all right ... oh ... ohh! Ramjet ... you're gonna have to *stop* ... hit me, baby ... please *hit* me!

185

Come in for a landing, you've bin up there long enough ...!'

'On the glide slope now, honey ...' he gasped.

'Oh ... ohhh ... !'

'Passing the outer marker ...'

'Oooh! ... aaahhh!'

'Threshold comin' up ... !'

'Baby ... baby ... !'

'Flaps thirty degrees ... yaw damper OFF ... !'

'My God ... my *God* ... !'

'Hydraulics ... CHECKED ... !'

'Hit me, baby ... *hit* me!'

'And ... TOOUUCCHH DDOOWWNN ... !'

'OOOHHHHHHH !! !'

Laughing convulsively, he collapsed upon her, gasping and chuckling ... replete, drained, bushed and buggered but glowing with pride in a job well done.

'Awwww ... !' she groaned, and 'Ohhhh ... !' she moaned, tossing her head limply, her legs outstretched to the corners of the bed, dead-weight, lifeless, consummately screwed. 'Awww ... ! Ramjet, you terrible man ... what *have* you done to me ...? They'll have to send an ambulance ... a hearse! My God, I pity the women wherever *you* land during that seven days ... but thank heaven you're goin' – it's gonna take me a week to recover ...'

'And ... when I get back?' he chuckled.

She groaned and shook her head. 'No ... no ... never!'

'Never?'

'Gimma a call at the Geisha Massage and Beauty Clinic – it's in the book.'

'O.K. – I'll just do th ...'

A sharp rap on the door and a furious bellow cut him short and dispelled Clara's lassitude instantly. 'Ramjet Rogers ... you in there with that *cow*! Come on – open up!'

Ramjet gasped. 'It's Beryl!'

'Yes!'

'She's back!'

'Ramjet ... I ...'

Now he gaped – at Clara. 'You ... you fibbed! She never left!'

Clara grinned. 'Think what you'd have missed.'

'Rogers ... come on out! I know you're in there with that blonde bag! Open the door ... I'm gonna *shoot* you!'

'Oh Jesus ... Clara – is there another way out?'

'Yes – the fire escape! Outside the window!'

'Come on – before she breaks the door down! Hell hath no fury ...'

BAM! Something slammed into the door – something like a chair.

'Monsieur Rogers ... I must ask you to come out!' shouted Frenchy. 'She is wrecking ze joint!'

They were now out of bed, frantically pulling on their clothes.

'Ramjet Rogers ... you dirty, double-crossing ...' BAM! '...lecherous ... horny ... *louse* ...!' BAM! 'Come out of there!'

'Pussycat ... I *beg* you ...!'

'Outta the way, Frenchy, I'm goin' to *kill* him ...!'

'Ready?' whispered Clara.

Ramjet rammed his cap on his head, heedless of angle, and hurried to the window, took a grip on the aged sash and heaved ... and heaved.

Up it shot with a crash.

'They're gettin' out of the window!' they heard Beryl cry.

'Oh God ...' croaked Ramjet. 'Quick – out you go!'

Clara scrambled over the sill, Ramjet close behind her, and dropped on to the iron platform that ran along for some distance, past several other windows, before beginning its descent.

It was as they passed the next window that a furious fist slammed into it and Ramjet turned to find Beryl's face grimacing at him through the glass.

'Move!' he cried to Clara, and they broke into a run.

As they rattled down the first short flight of iron steps the window above opened with a thud.

'Rogers ... come back here!'

'Like hell,' he muttered.

'RAMJET ...!'

CRASH!

A vase shattered at his feet. He fell against the railings, looked up. It was a terrible mistake.

WWHHOOSSHH!!

A pitcher of ice-water hit him full in the face, ice-cubes and all. He fell back, blinded.

SSLLOPPPP!!

A dish of sauerkraut dropped on his head.

'You won't forget Beryl Ormsby in a hurry, you … lecherous …'

SSPPLLAATT!!

A dish of pickled onion joined the sauerkraut.

'… misbegotten … !'

SSPPLLODDGGEE!!

Strawberry ice-cream with cherry garnish.

'… two-timin' … !'

SSPPLLUUTT!!

Pickled herrings with raw onion rings.

'… skirt-chasin' … !'

WWHHOOFF!!

The contents of a bucket-sized ashtray.

'… PIG!'

CCRRUUMMPP!!

The ashtray.

'*Now* go on an' show your adorin' public what a Glamour boy you are … !'

Ramjet staggered, slipped and slithered down the stairs and fell out on to the pavement, stunned, bewildered, disorientated, and, to his utter dismay, face-to-face with a patrolling cop.

'Good party?' Officer Shulman enquired solicitously, wrinkling his nose. 'Fancy dress, huh? Well, how about steppin' round the corner and tellin' the lads all about it?'

*   *   *

And what, during this fortnight of furious preparation, of the remaining members of our gallant crew?

Well, the girls spent quite a lot of their days getting well and truly 'done' – new hair-do's, manicures, massages and facials – and most of their evenings reading their fan letters and giggling at the contents, Boobs Buchanan leading in the marriage proposal stakes by a short head (142 to 127), but

Wilma way out in front with the blue film and kinky proposition offers, one of which read:

> Dear Wilma ... Seeing yor pikchor in the paper got me all werked up like no pikchor ever did afore, wich tells me yor the gerl for me and if you cud make it down here to Pitchfork, Tennessee, I sure would be a mite oblijed.
>
> It shorely ain't my fault I like doin' it standin in a tub of swine feed an my head-shrinker sez I gotta let my ineebishuns go and do just wot my libeedo diktates. Trubble is ther aint too meny gerls arownd these parts willin to do it standing in a tub of swine feed an it sure gets lonely doin it by yorself.
>
> Ifn you *cud* make it down hear I'd sure make it werth yor wile an who knows you mite get to like it! Let me no by retern an I'll make up a fresh mess a mash.
>
> Yors longingly, Stud Bullrush.

Bush McKenzie, somewhat like-wise, spent most of the two weeks preparing his public image by polishing and pummelling his pecs to the peak of pulchritudinous perfection by pressing pounds and pounds of pre-stressed pig-iron in Pete Pulver's Park Place Palaestra. No kidding.

And on Wednesday night Sugar Sweetman was mugged.

There he was, minding his own business, nattily dressed in *very* sharp civvies, happily strolling along East 43rd Street towards his favourite gay coffee shop in Times Square, when out of the shadows of a doorway popped this terrifying, long blonde-haired creature, dressed in an orange velour shirt, yellow flared hipsters with a just a *teensy* trim of matching orange around the thigh pockets, *gorgeous* tan boots with simply *huge* brass buckles – and a gun.

'Stick 'em up!' he lisped, jerking the gun into Sugar's face.

Sugar let out a yelp and felt for his heart. 'My *God*, you frightened the life out of me! Me poor heart's goin' like clappers. What a stupid thing to do – jumpin' out at people like that, you ought to be ashamed of yourself ...'

'I said – stick 'em up!' insisted the brutal creature.

Sugar peered at him up and down. 'Here – do I know you?'

'Mm . . . ? Er, no . . .'

'Then kindly get out of my way . . . I don't speak to strangers.'

'S . . . stay where you are an' s . . . s . . . stick 'em up!'

Sugar, really a most patient soul, sighed wearily. 'All right – stick *what* up?'

The creature gaped. 'Well . . . your *hands*, silly! Don't tell me you've never heard of "stick 'em up"?'

'No – never,' said Sugar huffily.

'*Never?* But you must have seen cowboy films . . .?'

'Never watch 'em. Got far better things to do with my time, I can tell you.'

'Well, never mind – go on – stick 'em up!'

Sugar tutted. 'Whatever *for*, for heaven's sake? I mean, what good can it possibly do if I stick my hands up in the air?'

'Well . . . er, in case you've got a gun or somethin' . . .'

Sugar sighed again, beginning to like the chap, really. A bit silly but quite personable. 'Look, what's your name?'

The monster's eyes narrowed suspiciously. 'What d'you want to know that for?'

'Well,' shrugged Sugar, 'as long as we're standin' here chatting we may as well know who we're chatting *to*, mayn't we? All right – I'll go first, then. My name's Michael Sweetman – but everybody calls me Sugar. Now, come on . . . what's yours?'

The lad hesitated, but finally murmured, 'Frances – but that's all I'm tellin'.'

'*Well*, suit yourself,' huffed Sugar, tossing his head. 'If you don't want to be friendly . . .'

'Stick 'em up!'

'Oh, don't start that again . . . *really* . . .'

'*Have* you got a gun?'

'No, I have *not* got a gun! Honestly – who d'you think I am – the bleedin' Godfather or somebody? Nor do I have a knife . . . a bomb . . . a sub-machine gun *or* a flamin' catapult. I am *English*, Frances, and we do *not* walk around armed to the teeth!'

'Then what *have* you got?'

190

'I *beg* your pardon!'

'What *have* you got?'

'That's personal.'

'Tell me or I'll shoot!'

'Don't be ridiculous.'

'I will! Turn out your pockets!'

With a disheartened sigh, Sugar began searching through his jacket. 'If you *must* know, Frances, I have upon my person ... a comb ... three snapshots of friends ... a season ticket to the High Queen Massage Parlour ...'

'The High Queen! I go there! Nice crowd...'

'Yes, *aren't* they sweet ... four threepenny English stamps ... a hair grip ... one elastic band ... and a Jews' harp ... a *Jews' harp*! Now, how on earth did *that* get in there ... ?'

'Next pocket!'

'Really, Frances, I'm going to be *terribly* late ...'

'Next pocket!'

'Oh, all right ... one hay-fever tablet ... a paper-clip ... a pen ... a front-door key ... and ... hello, what's this – a pea-nut? Ooooh, no! It's the opal stone I lost from my ring! Now isn't that lucky! I lost that a month ago and I've been looking all over the place for it. Ooh, I'm ever so grateful...'

'How much money have you got?' demanded Frances.

'Hang on, that's the next pocket ... er ... thirteen dollars and forty-two cents ... no, tell a lie – forty-three cents.'

'Hand it over!'

'Eh ... ?'

'Give it to me ... or I'll s ... s ... shoot!'

'Shoot who?'

'You!'

'*Me*? Are you balmy? You'd shoot me for thirteen dollars and forty-two cents?'

'Forty-three cents ... yes, I will.'

'Frances, you must be mad. Anyway, what do you want it for?'

'Er ... coke.'

'Coke? Thirteen dollars and forty-three cents for a *coke*? Huh, you're buyin' in the wrong shop, luv – I can get it for fifteen ce ...'

'Not *a* coke, you silly!' lisped Frances. '*Coke!* "C"! ...'

' "C"?'

'Yes, Charley!'

'Here, who are you calling a Charley...'

Frances tutted and shook his head. 'No, you don't understand ... "C" ... in like "H" ... !'

'Mm?' winced Sugar.

' "H" man ... Horse!'

'Horse?'

'Henry!'

Sugar rolled his eyes exasperatedly. 'Now who in blazes is Henry? Frances, I do wish you'd stop bringing in people I don't know...'

'Cocaine! ... Heroin!' cried the youth in despair.

Sugar's eyes popped. 'Here ... those are *drugs* ... !'

'Oh, save us!'

'*Well* ... you're certainly not getting my money for *those* filthy things ... !'

'Hand it over!'

'I won't! You ought to be ashamed of yourself, smokin' that stuff ... !'

'Smoking?' winced the youth.

'Well, whatever you do with it,' Sugar said loftily, stowing his possessions back into his pockets but pausing to have another peep at the photographs. 'I say ... these really are terribly good. *Don't* we look a smart bunch just?'

'Who's a smart bunch?' enquired Frances, reaching for them.

'Ah-ah! Don't grab! And jolly well say please.'

Frances sighed. '*Please.*'

Sugar took a step to the side. 'Come over here by the light, you can see better. There ... that one of the skipper – Captain Rossiter ... and this one's First Officer Rogers, lovely chap ... absolute sweetie ...'

Frances was peering hard at them, then gave a start. 'Hey – that's ... they're ... they've been on TV ...'

'Of course we've been on TV,' Sugar said aloofly.

'It's Glamour Airlines!'

'Well, we aren't the Grenadier Guards, chicken...'

Frances gaped at him. 'Then *you're* ... !'

'Steward Michael Sweetman,' smirked Sugar. 'Here – that's

192

me in uniform ... *très* chic if I do say so myself. That's me with the girls, lazy slags, but lovely with it ... and this one's the Nav – Jim Crighton-Padgett – and the Engineer – Bush McKenzie. Good, aren't they?'

'Here ... hold this a minute,' said Frances, thrusting the gun into Sugar's hands and taking hold of all the snaps. 'Oooh, I say, fancy meeting you ...'

'Aren't they good?' said Sugar, looking over Frances's shoulder. '*Very* dashing, I think.'

'I'd love to meet them all and get their autographs. I collect autographs, you know. I've got hundreds of them – Bob Hope's ... Paul Newman's ...'

'Well, *I* can get their autographs for you, Frances.'

'*Can* you? I'd be ever so grateful.'

'Here ... here's my pen. Write down your address on the back of one of the snaps and I'll send them to you – I promise.'

'That's very nice of you, Sugar.'

'Not at all.'

Frances wrote the address and handed the pen and snaps back to Sugar. Sugar, in return handed the gun back to Frances, suddenly realizing what he'd been holding.

'Eh? Here, I've been ...'

Frances shrugged. 'Doesn't matter – it's not real, anyway. It's a cigarette lighter.'

He pulled the trigger and a flame shot up from the front end.

Sugar gasped. 'Well, you cheeky ... now *that's* taking money under false pretences!'

Frances grinned. 'But I didn't take any.'

'That's *not* the point. How can I go around tellin' everybody I was mugged by a cigarette lighter?'

'I'm sorry,' said Frances.

'And how many times have you got away with *that* sneaky trick?' demanded Sugar.

'Well, to tell the truth ... this is the first time,' Frances answered sheepishly.

'Yers – I could tell you weren't terribly good at it. A bit nervous, weren't you – not quite *masterful* enough? You've got to be masterful for a thing like this, really.'

193

'Yes, I suppose so,' said Frances.

'Tell me ... did you *really* want the money for drugs, Frances?'

Frances shook his head. 'No ... I'm saving up for a guitar.'

'Yers, well, that sounds more like it. You don't look like one of them ... you're too well dressed for a start. *Fab*ulous gear, Frances – wherever <u>did</u> you get those slacks?'

'These ... ? Oh, I got these from Guys 'n Gals on ...'

With a gasp, Sugar looked suddenly at his watch. 'My *God*, just look at the time! Come on, walk along with me, Frances ... in fact, if you're doing nothing, why not come and have a cup of coffee with the chaps ... ?'

Frances shrugged. 'No, I'm not doin' anything.'

'Lovely. Well, go on ... you were telling me about Guys 'n Gals ...'

'Oh, they've got a *fab* selection of slacks, Sugar. They've got these yellow ones with orange piping ... blue with white piping ... green with brown ... and some others with filigree lace let into the flares as a side-panel. *Very* Spanish, I must say ...'

'How *super*! Oooh, I must have a decko at those ...'

18

And so the two weeks passed and Friday finally dawned. Colonel Godfrey Berskin was out at the airport early, supervising the last-minute touches to the preparation of the vast Glamour hangar.

Theatrical to his hair-roots, he had transformed the stark, towering echoey structure into a pink palace of entertainment, curtaining off Glamour Puss behind a gigantic pink drape which, at a propitious moment during the evening's festivities, would be drawn back to reveal to an astonished audience the newly decorated and shockingly beautiful 707.

In addition, a false ceiling of pink candy-striped material had been erected over the 'party' section of the hangar to introduce a greater feeling of intimacy and colour; a stage had been set up on one side from which the speeches would be made and the entertainment provided, and on which the Grand Draw would take place; and on the opposite side of the hangar innumerable trestle tables, bedecked with flowers and covered with silver-lamé cloths, would at the appropriate time provide more than enough food and drink to satisfy the one thousand chosen guests.

In the matter of parking and routine facilities, the Airport Authority had been most co-operative. A service roadway had been specially provided for direct access to the Glamour hangar and would, come evening, be manned by off-duty Airport Police working bonus overtime – this to prevent the anticipated hoards of sightseers from encroaching on the party.

By mid-afternoon, things, Berskin judged, were going magnificently – every aspect of the organization was under control and he could now concentrate on the entertainment.

He had decided, during the course of the past two weeks, that in addition to treating the crowd to the thrill of guest appearances by his three pop stars – Jimmy Silver, Marc Dart and Wensley Pocket, the musical background for the party would be provided by that up-and-coming aforementioned group 'Skull and Crossbones', and, further, that they should also accompany the guest passengers on the seven-day, round-the-world flight.

Ever the opportunist, he saw no reason why he should not mix business with business and perceived in the tour a first-class opportunity to promote 'Skull and Crossbones' worldwide. Their music, he was fully aware, was quite diabolical but their image was absolutely right – at least the image of their leader, Shag McGee, was absolutely right – particularly since McGee had now been fitted with trousers with a built-in jock-strap to safely contain the four hankies – a measure swiftly taken after a near-riot in the Broken Neck Disco when the hankies had slowly slithered down McGee's leg to form a bulge that had incensed every fella in the room with jealous rage and every bird with a ferocious compulsion to grab it.

And so, with the time now approaching four o'clock, Berskin made his way to the stage where Shag McGee and the other three anaemics had just arrived and were unloading eight million tons of amplifying equipment from a five-ton pick up.

'Everything all right, McGee?' enquired Berskin.

McGee turned, his waist-length orange hair swirling across his face, momentarily blinding him, the movement almost dislodging the parrot.

'Say, how do you take a shower with that thing on yuh head?' asked Berskin, genuinely curious.

McGee shrugged. 'So who takes a shower, man?'

'Yeah,' said Berskin. 'Now, listen, you guys – I want you to realize the importance of this shindig tonight. The eyes of the world's Press will be on you – so play it cool ... I mean hot. But don't go blastin' the roof off with all that equipment. As soon as you're set up I wanna hear a sample of what you're gonna give us tonight – O.K.?'

'Dig,' nodded McGee, and the parrot fell off and hit the floor with a squawk.

Berskin winced. 'Say – doesn't that thing fly?'

'Sure he flies ... but he'd rather walk,' said McGee, picking the parrot up and plonking him back on his head.

'Weird,' muttered Berskin.

At six o'clock the food and booze arrived – acres of it, mountains of it, crates by the score – including enough champagne to give each guest a glass with which to toast the unveiling of Glamour Puss – a typically extravagant Berskin touch, worth its weight in platinum publicity-wise.

By six-fifteen the last of one thousand pink candy-striped balloons bearing the slogan 'Glamour Airlines Love You' had been inflated and were hoisted in their containing net to the ceiling.

At six-thirty precisely three newly painted Glamour buses disgorged an army of serving staff at the hangar doorway – one hundred and fifty waiters, waitresses, barmen and general dogsbodies – all dressed immaculately in new Glamour uniforms.

Six-forty-five – and the Press and TV people began to arrive with their mobile cameras, tape recorders and secretaries.

Seven o'clock. The hangar exploded in excruciating noise as Shag McGee and the idiots hit the opening chords of 'Baby Open Wider – It Won't Hurt A Bit', a tender little ballad based on an old Zulu castration chant.

Seven-fifteen. The crew arrived, absolutely radiant in their ceremonial Glamour uniforms (the product of an eleventh-hour brainstorm by Binky Everard) – the uniforms being essentially the same as their everyday working uniforms but much brighter in colour and with the addition of a pocket power-pack which not only lit up the Glamour slogan, formed in neon across their shoulders, but caused it to flash every two seconds – an unexpected lily-gilder that had plunged Cock-up Rossiter into the most hideous of moods.

'Now, look here, Berskin ... !' he stormed, stamping across the hangar floor, 'so far I've gone along with this ... this *joke* with a willin' heart and a ... goddam it – do these lunatics *have* to make so much racket ...! – but *this* (he jerked his thumb over his shoulder) takes the goddam biscuit! Hell, man, it's bad enough havin' to dress up like a Christmas tree ... but when it comes to imitatin' a Times Square advertisement hoarding ... !'

'Now, Rossiter ...' Berskin pleaded soothingly, 'it's only for tonight. Everard says it'll make more impact on TV ...'

'To hell with TV!'

'All right ... all right – tell you what I'll do! I'll make it worth your while – an Electrification Bonus – one hundred bucks! How about it?'

'Two hundred!'

'One-fifty.'

'O.K.!'

'Right – light up an' let me see it workin'. I'm not payin' a bonus if you're not flashing.'

Rossiter scowlingly turned his back to Berskin and switched on his power pack.

'O.K., you're flashing. Now the rest of you ... about turn! Flash! Great! Wonderful! Make sure you keep your backs to the cameras when they're on you. Right – dismissed! And don't get pissed. Remember – you're flying tomorrow. Girls, you look adorable. Don't catch cold.'

It was now seven-thirty and the guests were beginning to stream in, everyone gowned and tuxedoed for the big Glamour occasion. It was going to be a wonderful night. Berskin predicted ... a *wonderful* night.

* * *

Senator Sam Chortle was the first of the VIP guests to arrive – and he did so with his customary flourish, swirling into the arena, standing in the back of a zebra-striped, open-top convertible, ten-gallon stetson waving to the cameras, Texas-sized cigar clamped in his car-salesman's grin, a latter-day Bodecea come to champion the cause of the masses, heading up a cavalcade of five cars filled with bodyguards, supporters and a general assortment of sycophants.

'Howdy ... ! Howdy ... ! Howdy ... !'

He stepped down from the car, a giant of a man, immaculate in black tuxedo, tooled cowboy-boots and thong tie, and strode across the threshold with the straight-backed magnanimity of DeGaulle liberating Paris.

'Howdy ... ! Howdy ... ! Howdy ... !'

Berskin rushed to meet him, a tiny David overshadowed by a towering Goliath.

'Senator ... an honour indeed. Welcome to Glamour Airlines.'

'Howdy, Berskin – enterprisin' kinda set-up yuh got here. Glamour Airlines ... I like it. It's bold ... imaginative – an' danged if I won't say so in my speech.'

'Your ... speech ... ?'

'Anticipated your wantin' me t'say a few homey words on this auspicious occasion ...'

'Oh well ...'

'Fine, fine – my pleasure.'

A legion of photographers had now surrounded them. 'This way, Senator!' Flash! 'How about the handshake with the Colonel again, Senator ... ?' Pop!

'Ah, sure would like to meet the crew, Berskin,' suggested Chortle, espying Babs and Wilma over by the stage, a good fifty paces away.

'Certainly, Senator, certainly.'

'Here comes Chortle now,' muttered Rossiter. 'Keep your hands on your valuables, girls.'

Berskin and Chortle drew up and Berskin made the introduction.

'Senator, I'd like you meet ... Captain Rossiter – our Chief Pilot and the man who'll be skippering your around-the-world flight.'

'Howdy, Rossiter,' rumbled Chortle, his eyes sliding over the Bab's boobs. 'Mighty glad t'know yuh.'

'Delighted to have you on board, Senator. We'll do our best to see you get a smooth and interesting flight.'

'Oh, it'll be interestin' ... and *smooth*, Ah'm sure,' grinned Chortle, now working on Wilma's legs. 'Yessir, mighty smooth.'

'Er ... this is First Officer Rogers, Senator ...'

'Howdy.'

'Engineer Officer McKenzie ...'

'Likewise.'

'Navigation Officer Crighton-Padgett ...'

'Crighton – how are yuh?'

'Steward Sweetman ...'

'Hi, Stewart.'

'Stewardess Buchanan ...'

'Honey ... Ah thought they'd never get to yuh ...'

Enveloping both her hands in his mighty paws, he drew her close, towered above her, his passion-stoked eyes boring down into hers.

'What's your first name, honey ... ?'

'Boobs ... I mean Babs, sir,' she stammered, his presence overwhelming her.

'Babs ...' he rumbled. 'And you are gonna take care of us for one whole week – right?'

'Y ... yes, sir ... that is – Wilma and I ...'

'Splendid. Well now, we'll jurst have to see whether we can't come up with some li'l ole present at the end of this trip – some li'l ole bauble of some kind – dependin', of course, on jurst how good that service *is* – know what I mean?'

'Well ... that's very kind, Senator, but I'm af ... fraid it's against c ... company rules to ...'

'Nonsense! Ah appreciate company rules, sure nuff – but seein' as how this is a kinda *special* flight, I'm sure Colonel Berskin here will be willin' to close an eye to one li'l teensy rule on this occasion ... ain't that right, Colonel?'

'Oh ... certainly ... surely ... yes, we can forget that one this time ...'

'There, now ...' smiled Chortle, patting her hand. 'Well, it's up to you, now I guess ...'

'Y . . . yes, sir . . .'

He released her hand, winked, and passed on to Wilma who cowed visibly as his rapacious eyes ripped away her see-through skirt and jacket, tore off her tiny pink bikini and gobbled up what lay beneath.

'Well now . . . and who do we have here?'

'Stewardess Wilma Fluck, Senator,' announced Berskin, delighted with the interest the randy old sod was taking in the girls. A complimentary statement by Chortle on his return would do more to promote business than a year's national advertising, so go to it, Sam, they're all yours.

'What grace . . . what beauty,' Chortle was saying, his gaze flicking between Wilma's bosom and Bab's, trying them for size. 'Well, my dear . . . what I said to your lovely friend here surely goes for you, too. You look after old Sam Chortle and he'll sure nuff look after you, yessiree.'

'Gee whizz, thanks a lot, Senator . . .'

'Think nuthin' of it, child . . .'

At that moment a commotion at the door, loud enough to be heard even over the tumultuous din Skull and Crossbones were making, heralded the arrival of Gloriana Fullbrush and her circus of three husky lovers.

Breathtaking in a skin-tight sheath of glittering black sequins, a black mink stole draped about her naked shoulders, her jet hair tumbling over the fur and dark, languorous eyes bewitching the pressing crowd, she posed aloof, while a battery of photographers captured the moment for posterity and the front pages of a hundred newspapers, then, accompanied by her young bulls, stepped regally down from the white Cadillac convertible and trod the red carpet to the stage like unavenging Angel of Death.

'Miss Fullbrush . . . !' gushed Berskin, 'what a delight and an honour . . .'

'Aw, cut the crap, Berskin,' she side-mouthed, 'an' get me a goddam drink, I'm famished. Hello, Chortle – kinda figured you'd be along.'

Sam smiled coldly at his ancient enemy. 'You did? Now, whatever made you figure that . . . Gladys.'

Gloriana's eyes flashed murderously at the threatened exposure of her real name – which was not surprising since her real name was Gladys Makewater – a secret she had so far kept hidden from the Press.

'Better be nice to old Sam, Gloriana,' he murmured. 'You scratch my back an' I'll scratch yours . . .'

'What a *revolting* thought,' she seethed.

They stood there, locked in mutual hatred, until a rousing cheer from the door broke the tension.

It was Delicious O'Hara, extravagantly beautiful, wildly sensual in a tighter-than-skin gown of green satin that managed to reveal more of her lush, huge-breasted body than if she'd been standing there naked – almost.

With a careless toss of her flame-red hair and a sensual, open-mouthed pucker to a hundred cameras, she stepped down from her gold Cadillac convertible and swung her beautiful butt to the stage.

'Miss O'Hara . . . Miss O'Hara . . .' enthused Berskin, taking her proffered finger-tips, 'what a pleasure and a privilege . . .'

'Hello, Shorty,' she drawled, 'how's tricks? *H*ello, Sam . . . yuh don't have t'tell me how *your* tricks are, I've seen 'em on TV. Well, well, if it ain't Gloriana Fullbutt . . .'

'Full*brush*, you cow . . .'

'Honey, you ain't standin' where I'm standin' . . . and just who've we got lined up here, Colonel . . . ?'

Berskin leapt in, anxious to ease the snapping tension. 'Er . . . Miss O'Hara . . . Miss Fullbrush . . . may I present the crew. This is Captain Rossiter . . .'

'*H*ello, sugar . . .' said Delicious with a come-on smile. 'Say, you're kinda cute. Just lo*ve* that uniform. Where d'ya get it – Barnham and Bailey . . . ?'

'No – Warner Brothers,' growled Rossiter. 'Flash Gordon wore it in, "There Are Fairies at the Bottom of My Spaceship".'

Delicious threw back her head and guffawed a laugh. 'Oh, I'm gonna *love* you. I just *adore* grouchy old men.'

And I'm gonna hate you, sister, thought Rossiter, who was now fast approaching the end of his tether. In the past two weeks insult had piled upon injury had heaped upon more insult and he had accepted it stoically, largely through blackmail, but suddenly, with the gathering together of these ... these *nuts*, the prospect of seven days incarceration with them in the close confines of a 707 rose up before him as a horrifying spectre ... a looming nightmare of fighting, squabbling and capital T trouble, and now he wanted out!

'Say, now ...' Delicious was drawling, coming up close to Ramjet and twining her finger round one of his buttons. 'And who's this big, handsome hunk ... ?'

'Er, this is First Officer Rogers, Miss O'Hara ... and, er, Miss Fullbrush ...'

But Gloriana had long ago lost interest and was now gazing around the room with an expression plainly pronouncing insurmountable boredom with the whole affair.

'What's your first name, Big Boy?' enquired Delicious.

Ramjet half closed one eye and raised his brow so high it tilted his cap. 'My name's Paul, Miss O'Hara ... but they call me ... Ramjet.'

'You *naughty* man,' she laughed, poking him in the navel. 'An' you're flyin' all the way with us?'

'All the way,' drawled Ramjet, regretting he couldn't add 'baby'. But never mind – the way things were shaping that would come.

'I like you ... you've got style,' she smiled, then moved on to James, her big green eyes flaring with fresh interest, 'My God ... another of 'em! Berskin, baby, you sure can pick 'em. And what's your name, honey ... ?'

'Er, this is Navigation Officer James Crighton-Padgett,' said Berskin, glancing concernedly at Gloriana, afraid that she might suddenly take off in high dudgeon and devastate his plans.

'Navigation Officer, huh?' Delicious was saying, eyeing James up and down. 'But I'll bet you don't need no maps to find yuh way around, honey. Berskin, I gotta hand it to ya, you sure can pick 'em. Stick around, Jim – fun is on its way.'

She gave him a tweak in the ribs and moved on to Bush McKenzie, but this time was interrupted in mid-gasp by another outburst of cheering from the door.

'It's Vince Martino!' some female squealed.

An open-topped bronze Cadillac convertible had drawn up,

and standing in the back, trying to find the door handle, was the great star himself, handsome as ever and twice as smashed, the inevitable cigarette burning between his fingers, the inevitable happy-go-bourbon grin splitting his tanned, craggy countenance.

'Hi, everybody ... !' he waved. 'Say, would someone tell me how ta open this tin-can?'

Somebody did and he fell out.

'Ho ho ... !' he laughed, clutching at a cop for support. 'Thank you, my good man – now just point me to where I'm supposed to go an' give me a little shove ... thank you, that's beautiful.'

Hemmed in by an escort of adoring females, he managed to remain upright all the way to the stage.

'Thank you, girls, thank you ... hi, everybody!'

Berskin rushed forward, greeting him effusively yet with some consternation, calculating the odds on Martino being on his feet by the Grand Draw ten-to-one against in his present condition.

'Mister Martino, I can't tell you what a pleasure it gives me ...'

'Me, too, Berskin, ole buddy,' grinned Martino, throwing an arm around Godfrey's neck. 'That an' boozin' are the only two things worth fightin' for. Hello, Gloriana ... now, who knitted *your* face an' dropped a stitch? Always laughin', is our Gloriana ... beats me what she finds to be so goddam happy about all the time ... oh, hi, Delicious! I almost didn't recognize you with yuh clothes on ... well, hello, Sam ... free-loadin' again, huh? ... hi, fellas! Well, Berksi, ole kid, that's got the social niceties out of the way – where's the bar?'

'Weirder ... and weirder ...' murmured Rossiter. 'An I used to think *Berskin* was nuts! Man, oh, man what a week this is gonna be!'

Craven Snipe arrived, naturally, in an open-topped convertible landau drawn by four black horses.

Sporting a top-hat, silver cane and swirling opera cape, he advanced into the hangar with slow, imperious gait, acknowledging the tittering amusement of the crowd with the sneering contempt it deserved.

'Mister Snipe ... I'm ... Ross Parks of CKWT ... may I have a word from you, sir ...'

'Certainly, Mister Parks – which word would you like? I have a great many of them. How about "radio", for instance ... ? or "commentator" ... ? Or perhaps a synonym of those, such as ... "unmitigated" ... "ass" ... "nuisance" ... "pest" ... "odious" ... "invidious" ... "obnoxious" ... "abhorrent" ... "loathsome" ... "execrable" ... "abominable" ... "repulsive" ... "repellent" ... "nauseating" ... "revolting" ... or just plain "NO!" Goodbye, Mister Parks ... hello, Berskin.'

'Mister Snipe, what a great pleasure ...'

'I know.'

Snipe joined the happy gathering.

'Gloriana, my dear, how absolutely *ravenous* you look.'

'You mean ravishing, Craven.'

'No, I mean ravenous.' His mean, piggy eyes swept over her three muscular studs. 'And who have we brought with us this time – the Three Stooges? I could have sworn they were dead. Delicious O'Hara, dear heart, how nice to see you ... practically *all* of you ... and Vincent, dear boy – caught your latest epic only last night. Really most enjoyable – *and* most comfortable ... I had the cinema practically all to myself. And Senator ... how well you look. Is that sun-tan or scorch from TV lights ... ?'

'Oh brother ...' groaned Rossiter.

Snipe now transferred his venom to the crew. 'And whom do we have here ... the Folies Bergère in drag? Colonel, *do* please introduce me ...'

'Er, certainly ... this is Captain Rossiter ...'

'Captain ... Rossiter,' Snipe repeated slowly. 'Of the good ship "Lollipop", no doubt.'

'And who might you be, buster?' growled Rossiter. 'The Phantom of the Opera or Mandrake the Magician?'

'How *very* droll, Captain. I can see we're going to get on famously.'

'And ... this is First Officer Rogers,' cut in Berskin, glowering at Rossiter.

'Overwhelmed, I'm sure,' drawled Snipe, stuffing a pinch of snuff up his nose and sneezing over everybody.

'And ... Navigation Officer Crighton-Padgett...'

Snipe's brow rose with interest. 'Of the ... *Boston* Crighton-Padgetts ...?'

James smiled cruelly. 'No, the Berkshire ones – the originals,' and Rossiter guffawed.

'Er ... Engineer Officer McKenzie...' seethed Berskin.

'Hello, cock, how're yuh goin'?' grinned Bush, not giving a stuff.

'Er, how am I going *where*, precisely?' enquired Snipe, intrigued by the accent.

Bush shrugged. 'I don't know. Don't you know, mate?'

Snipe winced, shook his head and passed on to Sugar.

'And this is Steward Sweetman ... who will be looking after your comforts during the flight.'

Sugar beamed. 'Ooh, I say, what *super* gear, Mister Snipe ... just *look* at the lining on that cape ... Rosebud Red, my favourite colour...'

'Indeed?' sniffed Snipe, moving on quickly, pausing merely to nod to the girls, shudder at their costumes, then turned quickly away as though anxious to find the nearest exit.

'Well ...' Berskin said jovially, now aware that he had selected a bunch of VIPs hell-bent on mutual destruction and savaged by the premonition that he'd be lucky to get them on *board* Glamour Puss never mind complete an entire week close-closeted in each other's company, 'it, er looks as though everybody of importance is here ... so I'll get things under way. I'm ... just going to say a few introductory words...'

'Oh, splendid,' said Sam Chortle, 'I'll join yuh, Berkskin.'

'Er, perhaps a little later, Senator...?' suggested Berskin. 'This won't take a minute.'

Berskin scuttled off and mounted the steps to the stage where Shag McGee and the lads were hacking their way through one of their own nightmares, entitled 'Pink Leather Onion Rings and Spotted Dick with Custard'.

'Hold it ... hold it!' bellowed Berskin.

Only the parrot appeared to take any notice.

'HHOOLLDD IITT!!' yelled Berskin, right down Shag McGee's ear, and the parrot shot three feet in the air and came down again with a plonk.

This time Shag looked round. 'Hm? Oh, hi, Colonel...'

'Cut the racket!' bawled Berskin.

'Oh ... sure.'

Shag turned and slit his throat with a forefinger, bringing the group to a slithering halt – all except the drummer who, head down and lost to this world, couldn't see a thing. So the Bass Guitarist threw an ashtray at him, catching him a thump on top of the head.

'Uh?' He looked up. 'Whasamarrer?'

'We stopped, man,' said McGee.

'Oh.'

Berskin approached the microphone.

'Ladies ... and gentlemen ...' he announced, wincing at the noise which was terrific – one thousand free-loaders going at the booze and the bites like there was no midnight. 'Ladies ... and GENTLEMEN ... !' he tried again. 'Settle down, now ... please, can we have a little quiet for just a ... ladies and ...' In exasperation he turned to McGee who was feeding peanuts to the parrot, whose name incidentally was Marlon.

'McGee – give me a roll, for Crissake!'

McGee looked up. 'Uh? Oh, sure – ham or cheese ... ?'

'A *drum* roll, you fucking idiot!'

'Oh.' He turned to the drummer who was picking his nose with his stick. 'Stanley – a roll for the Colonel.'

'A what?'

'A roll ... you know – brrrrrrrrrr.'

'Oh, sure. Brrrrrrrrrrrr.'

'No, with the sticks, Stanley ...'

'Oh ...'

Stanley did a beautiful roll.

'O.K. – that's enough,' nodded Berskin. 'Stanley ... THAT'S ENOUGH!'

This time the Bass Guitarist hurled a plastic cup.

'Hey, man, that hurt,' complained Stanley.

'O.K., Colonel,' said Shag authoritatively. 'It's all yours.'

'Ladies and Gentlemen ...' Godfrey announced to a much more receptive audience, 'my name is Berskin ...'

'Oooh ... rude!' laughed a drunk.

'... and I welcome you all to this launch party commemorating the inauguration of Glamour Airlines. We are indeed

honoured tonight to have with us sebral celivr ... several celi-
brated...'

'He's pissed!' commented the same drunk.

'...public personalities who, with the greatest personal
pleasure, I now introduce to you. Firstly, ladies and gentlemen
... star of stage, screen and radio ... and mistress of the famous and fabulous Madonna Moonstone ... Miss ... Gloriana
... Bullfrush...! Oh Jesus ... FULLBRUSH!'

The Skull and Crossbones hit a nicely discordant fanfare,
gradually slithering into tune, huge spotlights blasted down on
Gloriana, still cameras flashed and TV cameras churned and
as the crowd erupted in thunderous applause, Gloriana
mounted the steps and queened it across the stage to the
microphone, waving, blowing kisses, tears touchingly misting
her big brown eyes.

As the applause died, she stepped to the microphone, gazed
out over her horde of admirers, bathed them with her famous,
self-effacing, bitter-sweet smile and began pouring it on.

'Ladies and gentlemen ... *friends* ... how kind of so many
of you to come ... and how fortunate for me that I have just
finished my latest film – a stirring adventure story entitled
"The White Hell of Eskimo Nell", which will be at your local
cinemas very shortly and which I *know* you will enjoy immensely. Apart from being a *thrilling* adventure, it also has, of
course, a strong love interest with me, naturally, playing the
romantic lead – the part of the bewitching Amoralia Lud-
chenko, exotically beautiful Russian counter-intelligence
agent, crack shot and superb horsewoman, who ventures alone
into the hell of the Arctic to...'

Berskin glanced at his watch. Dammit, he hadn't invited the
bitch to make a speech. Now, they'd *all* want to make one.
Well, just let 'em try!

'And now...' Gloriana was declaiming, 'the moment you
have all been waiting for! No doubt you have been wondering
whether I would bring the famous Madonna Moonstone with
me tonight and were disappointed not to see it on my finger.
Well, I have a wonderful surprise for you...' she glanced
down below to where her three stallions were standing like
stuffed mummies. 'Gerald ... let's give the folks a thrill!
Bring up the Moonstone!'

Shag McGee, sensing the need, hit another fanfare, this time creditably in tune, and Gerald marched up the steps with the aplomb of an Oscar winner, strode across the stage and presented Gloriana with a black suede jewellery box.

'Cameras ready ...?' she teased. 'Holding on zoom ... ! Then – here it is!'

A great gasp went up as she opened the lid, revealing the fabulous, walnut-sized stone.

Berskin plucked his lip thoughtfully, wondering how could he so easily have lost control of the situation. This wasn't the Glamour Airlines launch – it was the goddam Gloriana Fullbrush Show!

'Er ... herm,' he coughed.

'Over here, Miss Fullbrush ... !'

Flash!

'Wave it around, Gloriana – let's see it sparkle!'

Plop!

'Er ... herm ... ladies and gentlemen...' Berskin slid between Gloriana and the microphone. '... a round of applause, please, for Miss Gloriana ... Fullbrush ... !' he announced, slipped her an insipid smile and caught her firmly under the elbow, easing her towards the stairs. 'Thank you, Gloriana, thank you ...'

'Yuh crumb, I was only half-way through ...'

'Time *is* pressing, Gloriana ...'

Mopping perspiration from his brow, he returned to the microphone, determined none of the others was going to do that to him.

'Ladies and gentlemen ... and now the *second* of our Glamorous stars present here tonight ...'

Down below he could see Delicious O'Hara straining at the leash, her skin-tight gown hitched to the knees in preparation for the ascent. Oh no you bloody don't, he determined, The crowd, he could sense, were getting restless, were anxious to get on with the boozing and the dancing. Three more speeches and the room would be empty.

'... and the *third* and the *fourth* ...' he continued hurriedly. 'Light ... cameras ... and applause, please, for ... Miss ... Delicious O'Hara ... ! ... Mister Vincent ... Martino ... ! ... and your favourite TV politician ... Senator ... Sam ...

Chortle . . .! Stay right where you are, *if* you please, folks, the cameras are on you now . . . er, Mister Martino . . . sir . . . would you mind staying right th . . . Mister Mart*ino* . . .!'

But the old Irresistible Force wasn't having any. Up the steps he swayed, glass in one hand, fag in the other, smiling beatifically, smashed to the gills.

Berskin uttered an agonized groan and, wilting, surrendered to the inevitable, throwing in an automatic though hopeless plea as Lush Martino hit the stage.

'Mister Martino . . . *please* . . . I'd be most appreciative if you'd keep it kinda short . . . we have so much to get in and . . .'

'Well, *hello* there, Berskin, ole buddy – here, have a li'l drink . . .'

'Er, no . . . thank you, Mister Mart . . .'

'Hi, fellas!' he waved to the group. 'Say, that's a cute eagle you got there, Slim . . . maybe *he'd* like a li'l drink . . .?'

'Sure,' shrugged Shag. 'He drinks anythin'.'

'We gotta lot in common. C'mon, birdie, have a slug.'

The parrot cocked its eye at the glass, popped in its beak and gulped a couple of good ones.

'Hey, that's enough,' said Lush, 'you've gotta sing.'

The crowd were in an uproar of laughter – everyone except Berskin who was fuming to himself. 'Now it's the bloody Lush Mart*ino* Show!'

Lush had now located the microphone and had draped himself around it, holding on for dear life. 'Say, talkin' of parrots . . . I heard the craziest story the other day . . . a *true* story, mind you . . . about a rabbit, a lizard and a turtle . . . you wanna hear it?'

'YYEESS!!' roared the crowd.

'Oh . . . *no*!' groaned Berskin.

'O.K. . . . well, this rabbit, lizard and turtle were *city* guys . . . lived in Brooklyn, no kiddin' . . . but one day they decided they'd had enough of city livin' and reckoned they'd move out to the country . . . hey, you heard this before . . .?'

'NNNOOO!' laughed the crowd.

'O.K. – this is a good one . . . worth an hour an' a half of anybody's time. *So* . . . these three fellas hit the road – and about three months later they come across a *beautiful* valley

210

with a mountain on the left ... an' a forest on the right. Got that? Kindly remember that 'cos it's important ...'

'Oh, my sufferin' mother!' groaned Berskin.

Lush threw back his head, drained his glass and continued. 'You still out there ... ? O.K. ... well, now, this rabbit, lizard and turtle decided this valley was the place for them ... but when they inspected the soil they found it needed fertilizing ... and s-o-o ... they drew straws to decide who should go all the way back to civilization for the fertilizer ... O.K.? And the poor old rabbit lost! Say, has anyone got a drink down there for a thirsty star – anythin' 'll do just so long as it's damp ...'

Ten glasses were held up to him and he accepted the lot, lining nine up at his feet and swallowing the tenth.

'Ah, that was beautiful ... gin an' boot polish. Now, where was I ... oh, yeah – the poor old rabbit lost ... s-o-o, he waved goodbye to his pals an' off he went – all the way back to Brooklyn for this load of fertilizer. Well, he picked it up and off he set again for the valley ... and he'd been travellin' for about four months ... he was slower this time, y'see, because of the load he was carryin' ... an' then one day ... ONE DAY ... he was hoppin' along an' suddenly he came upon the valley. "This is it!" he said to himself. "There's the" ... altogether, now! ... "the mountain ..."'

'THE MOUNTAIN ON THE LEFT ... AND THE FOREST ON THE RIGHT!' roared the crowd.

'Aw, that was too beautiful ... too beautiful. "*But*," said the rabbit ... "what's this!" And there right in front of him was the most magnificent colonial mansion ... marble columnade an' everythin'. So up he hopped to the front door and knocked on it with his paw ... an' a moment later it was opened by a *very* snooty English butler ...'

Lush came erect and raised his nose snootily in the air. '"Yers?" enquired the butler. "What do you want?"

'"Er, does Mister Lizard live here?" asked the rabbit.

'And the butler replied, "Mister Liz-*ard* ... is out in the yard."'

The crowd roared at Lush's plummy English impersonation.

'"And ... does Mister *Turtle* live here?" asked the rabbit.

'And the butler replied, "Mister Tur*tel* . . . is down at the well."

' "I see," said the rabbit. "Well, would you mind tellin' Mister Liz-*ard*, who is out in the yard . . . and Mister Tur-*tel* who is down at the well . . . that Mister Rab-*bit* is back with the . . . fertilizer?" ' '

As the hangar shook with a great roar of laughter, the microphone stand collapsed under Lush's weight and he fell arse-over-elbow off the stage into Cock-up Rossiter's arms who staggered backwards, bringing down Ramjet Rogers, Delicious O'Hara, Craven Snipe and three members of the public.

Appalled at this development but delighted that Lush Martino was off the stage, Berskin made a dive for the microphone, bawled at Shag McGee, 'Well, don't just stand there – destroy something!' and announced breathlessly to a falling-about audience, 'One thing about Vincent Martino, ladies and gentlemen, he really throws himself into his work. And now . . . on with the party! A little later on we'll be holding the Grand Draw to see which members of the Press and public will be accompanying the stars on Glamour Airlines' seven-day, round-the-world Mystery Flight . . . and immediately *after* the draw will come yet another highlight of the evening . . . the unveiling of Glamour's glamorous new baby . . . "Glamour Puss" – and *your* chance to climb aboard and walk right through her! So now . . . ON WITH THE PARTY!'

'An' a one . . . two . . . three!' Shag McGee stamped on the stage with his right heel and it fell off his boot.

Regardless, the lads exploded into 'Kumma-Ki-Yi-Yippy – My Mother Is A Hippy' and the party really took off.

Berskin staggered down the stairs, wiping copious sweat from his brow, and ran into Heinrich Himmler who had just rushed up, very flustered.

'Himmler, where in *hell* have *you* been for the last two hours! Goddam it, you shoulda been here!'

'Colonel . . . I've been locked in one of the Glamour Puss lavatories! I went in to make sure everything was satisfactory for the public tour and the door jammed! I've been in there for over an hour – shouting myself hoarse!'

'O.K. ... O.K. Well, is everything ready for the Grand Draws?'

'Yes, Colonel – the drums are ready to bring on stage.'

'Good. Now, let me see that list of Press names again – I wanna make sure all my babies are on it. This is gold in the bank, Himmler ... or rather – between the sheets, an' I don't want anythin' goin' wrong ...'

Explanation:

Berskin's wild adventure with Delores Delores having opened his eyes to the possibility of mixing business with a great deal of personal sexual satisfaction, he had, during the preceding week, scoured the Press applications for not only the best-looking dolly journalists but those who were also 'most likely to' in exchange for a free seven-day, round-the-world flight – and he had come up with a list of some twenty highly probables, the fact that one or two represented publications so highly irrelevant to Glamour promotion as *Knitting for Pleasure and Profit* and *The Tortoise Lover's Weekly* being neither here nor there. If they 'did' – they were in, and as Berskin had already personally conducted interviews with the little darlings and established faith, no fewer than fifteen of the twenty were in.

'Now, let's see ...' said Berskin, scanning the list, 'Billy Jo Labinovitch ... hoo hoo, a right little screamer ... yes, I've got her. Sandy Mann ... by God, Himmler ... yes, she's in. Tricia Pell ... oh, man oh, man ... yes, she's O.K....'

'But, sir ... isn't it going to look just a *weeny* bit suspicious when you call out the names and *every* Press winner is a stupendous piece of crumble ...?'

'Don't worry, Himmler, I've thought of that one – that's why I'm including five *male* journalists – to throw the sceptics off the scent.'

'Good thinking, sir.'

'Yeah, ain't it? O.K. – get the drums set up on the stage now. We'll give this shower one hour's boozin', then announce the draw. And make sure those cops are at the bottom of the entrance stairs when we open Glamour Puss for viewing. We don't want any fall-down drunks bein' sick all over the upholstery.'

'Right, sir.'

'Good man. It's goin' just fine – but, by God, I'll breath a sigh of relief that that thing takes off at nine tomorrow night. With maniacs, like Martino around anythin' can happen. Huh! Mister Rab-*bit* is back with the fertilizer. It doesn't even rhyme!'

'Sir?'

'Skip it, Himmler – you were locked in the can.'

*　　*　　*

'Well, Skip, what d'you think?' asked Ramjet, throwing a treble Scotch into the back of his neck.

'What do I think?' scowled Rossiter. 'I think I must be outta my head even contemplatin' this flight, that's what I think. Did you see those two fruity bitches, O'Hara and Fullbrush, strainin' to gouge each other's eyes out – that's trouble! That Martino guy is gonna be motherless from the time they throw him on board to the time he falls down the steps a week from now – that's more trouble! That pain-in-the-ass Snipe is gonna be stirrin' up eighteen kinds of mischief every mile of the way – even more trouble! An' that boring old cunt, Chortle, is gonna be shootin' off his lip forty-two hours a day – an' when he's not in the galley fingerin' the girls he'll be up in the cockpit tellin' us how to fly the goddam plane – *more* trouble! You wanna know what I think, Rogers – I think we got trouble – T for Terrible, R for Rotten, O for Awful, U for Unbelievable, B for Bloody, L for ...'

'Liquor,' cut in Lord Jim, handing Cock-up a glass. 'Drink up, Skip, you'll feel better. Personally, I'm rather looking forward to it ...'

'Yeah, you would, you dick-happy twit! You can see no further than O'Hara's boobs! Well, if she gets to you, God help us all – we'll be damn lucky to hit the right *continent* never mind city.'

'I wonder where they will send us, Skip?' remarked Bush. 'I hope it's Aussie. Wouldn't mind a lay-over in Sydney for a night.'

'A lay over *who* in Sydney, McKenzie?' cracked Rossiter. 'Well, I reckon the chances are pretty good we'll get there. If it really is a "round-the-world" jaunt we'll have to drop down there for juice if nothin' else.'

214

'Good-o. I'd like to show you fellas round a bit.'

'You're on,' winked Jim. 'And if we hit London...'

'Which we're bound to do,' interjected Cock-up.

'... then the show's on me.'

'Listen...' said Rossiter, 'what the hell you guys reckon this is – a night-spot tour for crew? I'll make a bet right now with you – that after a day's flyin' with that maniac bunch, you'll slump over the controls an' scream to be left alone – you'll have nothin' left for birds an' booze!'

James winked at Ramjet who in turn winked at Bush.

'We'll take that bet,' grinned James.

'Set your mind at rest, Captain mine,' said Sugar with determination. 'Any trouble from *them* in *my* cabin and they'll have me to deal with. Any interferin' with the girls or drunken rowdyism and they'll get such a mouthful of Sugar their ears'll drop off, I can promise you.'

'Gee, that makes me feel so much better, Sweetman,' drawled Rossiter.

'Now, don't you underestimate Sugar,' Babs squeaked defensively. 'We've seen him put some very awkward customers in their place, haven't we, Marilyn?'

'Gee, he's got a *terrible* temper when he gets riled,' breathed Wilma. 'Quite frightening, really!'

'I can imagine,' said Rossiter. 'Well, it's good to know everything is gonna be kept in check back there. We're gonna be busy enough in the cockpit tryin' to figure out where we're heading without being lumbered with cabin bother.'

'Just leave everything to me,' Sugar promised vehemently. 'At the first sign of trouble I'll call for the "seat belts" sign and strap the lot of them in!'

'Hope springs eternal,' sighed Rossiter, signalling a passing waiter for another drink.

* * *

The hour was up and not, reflected Berskin, before time. The booze was flowing over the bars like Niagara Falls in high flood, and out of the thousand people there only about six were still sober – and they were A.A. members.

With a nod to Himmler he collected the Press file and

mounted the steps to the stage. Shag McGee was still hard at it but the parrot had fallen asleep.

'O.K., McGee, bury it an' gimme a roll!'

Shag stopped gyrating so suddenly the parrot loosened its grip with surprise and took another header into the deck.

'What's the matter with that thing?' demanded Berskin, watching Marlon staggering around the stage.

'He's pissed,' exclaimed McGee, replacing the cross-eyed Marlon.

Stanley, the drummer, came up with a beaut of a roll and Berskin stepped to the microphone, holding up his arms for hush.

'Ladies ... and ... gentlemen ... and now ... the moment you have all been waiting for ... the GRAND DRAW!'

Thunderous applause and drunken cheering.

'Thank you ... thank you. Now ... as you know ... tomorrow night at nine o'clock, fifty very lucky people will take off from Kennedy here aboard the luxuriously transformed 707 "Glamour Puss" ... on a seven-day ... round-the-world adventure – destination unknown! Yes – unknown even to the crew! (Great gasp of surprise.)

'And if you want to know how that is possible ... and I'm certain there are at least fifty of you very *anxious* to know how it's possible ... (Laughter) ... I can tell you that all the routes have already been planned by an expert back-up team – and that all Captain Rossiter has to do is sit up there in the cockpit and change direction when instructed to do so from the ground. (Much murmuring and chatter.)

'Nothing, of course, has been left to chance and all eventualities have been guarded against. "Glamour Puss" is fitted with the very latest radio and radar equipment ... but in the highly unlikely event that all communication with the ground should fail – there will be navigation maps aboard giving Captain Rossiter complete independence of movement.'

'Good ole Rossiter!' someone shouted.

'Your father?' James murmured to Cock-up.

'My mother,' scowled Rossiter.

Berskin continued.

'Now ... who will those fifty fortunate passengers be – and why only fifty? Well, as you will see when you view "Glamour

Puss", radical changes have been made to her interior ...
many seats have been removed for the greater comfort and
entertainment of the guests on this long flight, so her capacity
on this trip is essentially limited.

'Now – who will those fifty passengers be? Well, *ten* of
them will comprise our guests of honour here tonight ... Miss
Gloriana Fullbrush and her three ... advisers ...'

'Ha!' snorted Craven Snipe.

'... Miss Delicious O'Hara ... Mr Vincent Martino ...
Senator Sam Chortle ... and special guest, Mr. Craven
Snipe ...'

'Tha's on'y eight!' shouted the same drunk.

'Ha ha – give that man a kewpie doll!' laughed Berskin,
muttering 'Smart-ass' beneath his breath. 'Yes, sir, as you so
rightly say – that is indeed only eight ... the other two guests,
who could not be with us this evening, being an airline doctor
... *and* a French chef de cuisine – the one, one might say, to
attend to the requirements of the "body" – and the other of
the ... "sole" of our passengers. (Heavy groans all round.)

'Of the remaining forty places ... twenty have been allocated to members of the Press – and twenty to members of
the public, who, during the past few weeks, have sent into
Glamour their applications for a place on the flight. Now ...
since the applications received have reached an astonishing
half a million ...! (Gasp of astonishment) ... obviously
many, many of you are going to be disappointed. And so it will
be with many members of the Press. However – somewhere
out there ... quite possibly in this *very* room – forty of you are
soon going to be very, very happy. And so – with no more
delay ...'

'Hear hear!' cheered the drunk.

'... on with the DRAW! And we'll take the members of the
Press first. McGee – a fanfare – if you please!'

Shag thumped the stage with his remaining heel and the
group blasted the room with a rip-snorter.

Berskin unhooked the microphone from its stand and
crossed the stage to where Miss Destry was standing, adjacent
to two huge metal drums, with a clip-board and pen.

'Ready, Miss Destry?'

'Ready, sir.'

Berskin gave Himmler the nod and the Press drum began to turn, its action having not the slightest effect on the outcome of the draw since the names of the winners reposed not inside the drum but safe and warm in Berskin's right-hand coat pocket.

'Right ... here we go, ladies and gentlemen ... the draw for the twenty lucky members of the Press who will accompany the stars on the Glamour inaugural flight. Silence ... please, for the first name! All right, Himmler, stop the drum!'

The drum came slowly to a halt and Himmler opened the little trap-door. Silence, except for the steady gulping of free booze, gripped the room. Berskin stepped forward, withdrew his hand from his right-hand pocket and plunged into the drum.

A quick convincing grope, as though thoroughly mixing the slips of paper, then out it came.

Berskin cleared his throat. 'The first lucky winner ... Miss ... Billy ... Jo ... Labinovitch ... of the ... *Tennessee Tatler*! Is Miss Billy Jo Labinovitch by any chance in the room?'

'*Is* she?' gasped Ramjet, digging James in the ribs. 'Jim – just getta load of that dame!'

Miss Billy Jo Labinovitch, a strapping, long-legged Amazon with a mane of glorious brown hair, squeezed out of the crowd and strode full-breasted across the open floor towards the stage, grinning with delight both at the selection of her name and at the flurry of cat-calls and wolf-whistles received from four hundred drunks.

'Ho ho ho!' chuckled Ramjet, rubbing his hands together in fiendish anticipation. 'She'll be on board for a whole week! James, I've just decided – you can run through the check-list with Cock-up, I have a little pre-start preparation to do in the cabin.'

James unpolitely told him what he could do with his check-list, adding, 'Ah, the joys of being a navigator on a plane that needs no navigator. Ramjet, old son, this is going to be a *very* strenuous flight.'

'But you've already got Delicious O'Hara!' protested Ramjet.

'Oh, I can find something for them both to do,' Jim assured him.

218

'Hey, you fellas, what about me?' pleaded Bush McKenzie.

'Sorry, Bush,' said James, 'I can*not* find anything for you to do.'

To enthusiastic applause, Billy Jo Labinovitch, a very popular winner, mounted the steps to the stage, slipped Berskin a cute, secret wink, and took her place behind him, wreathed in smiles.

Miss Destry entered her name on her board and gave Berskin the nod.

'Right ... number two coming up!' he announced and in went his hand, cunningly concealing the name of ...

'Miss ... Patricia ... Bell ... no, it's Pell!' announced Berskin, playing it very cool. 'Miss Patricia Pell of ... *Healthy Mind – Body Beautiful*! Is Miss Pell by any chance among us?'

Miss Pell was among them, though certainly not by chance. Tall, straight-backed, lithe and blonde, epitomizing the very title of the magazine she represented, she covered the floor with a zestful stride, beaming a radiant smile to the cheering and whistling of a delighted crowd.

'Holy *Boeing*, I don't believe it!' gasped Ramjet.

'*Two* of them!' exclaimed Bush McKenzie.

'Is there to be *no* peace in this life?' groaned James, adding 'Hee hee!'

Miss Patricia Pell mounted the rostrum, slid a nose-wrinkled at Berskin, and took her place beside the ravishing Labinovitch, as fine a pair of grumble-bugs as ever seen.

'Number three!' called Berskin, inwardly beside himself thinking about the future. 'And the lucky winner is ... Mister Jonas P. Hickory of the *Pennsylvania Post* ... !'

Yes, Berskin was now implementing his plan to thwart suspicion, for not only had he chosen five middle-aged and highly professional male journalists from leading dailies (thus ensuring an abundance of coverage of the flight), but he also proceeded to call out the names of several 'married' female journalists (having previously ensured they would not attend the party), the title 'Mrs.' further allaying suspicion.

And so some fifteen minutes later there were arrayed behind him *all* of the five male journalists but no more than seven of the fifteen selected dolly birds.

Yet seven was more than enough to transport Ramjet, Lord Jim and Bush into paroxysms of sexual enchantment and even Cock-up appeared to have cheered up at the prospect of living cheek to cheek with such a bundle of titillating charms for one whole week.

'Well, mate,' sighed Bush McKenzie, slapping Ramjet on the back, 'things are certainly lookin' up. That's two each and shares in the seventh. I ... think I'll start with ... Billy Jo Whatsername – just about my weight.'

'That Sandy Mann's for me,' leered Ramjet. 'I like the coltish type ... they usually enjoy horsin' around. James – what do you fancy for starts?'

'The filly with the long blonde mane and the superb fetlocks,' grinned Jim.

'Ah, you guys disgust me,' growled Cock-up. 'Don't you ever think of anything else?'

'No,' they said.

'Well, it's all right for you fellas,' complained Babs, pouting a bit. 'Look what *we've* got – Sam Chortle, Craven Snipe and five rickety pen-pushers!'

'How about the group – Skull and Crossbones?' Ramjet reminded her.

'Them! Not even if they were sheep-dipped,' she scowled.

Meanwhile, Berskin was getting nicely through the public draw (this one fair and square since there was no percentage in doing otherwise). And as was to be expected, since the odds against winning were very long indeed, not one of the winners was present at the party.

Their absence, however, did in no way detract from the excitement of the occasion since all those present were fervently hoping to be among the winners, and every name drawn was greeted with generous applause.

At last the final name was drawn and Shag McGee and his stalwarts hit a resounding fanfare as Berskin once again took the microphone.

'Well, ladies and gentlemen, there it is. The winners will be notified by telephone immediately and all the guests embarking on the seven-day flight will assemble for a mini pre-take-off celebration in the VIP lounge tomorrow evening at seven-thirty. Congratulations again to all the winners – your troubles are over for the next seven days. I can promise you sight-seeing in some of the most thrilling capitals of the world ... accommodation in the most luxurious hotels in those cities ... and the very best of food, wines and entertainment – in short ... the Glamour flight of a lifetime!'

Resounding applause.

'And now ... to yet *another* highlight of your evening. I have been assured that all of you now have a glass of champagne with which to raise a toast ... and so I give you ...'

Another superb fanfare from the lads, and as it died ...

'Ladies and gentlemen ... I give you ... GLAMOUR PUSS!'

Himmler hit a switch and this time there was no foul-up. To the whirring of electric motors the winches turned and the immense floor-to-ceiling curtains began to part.

The very first glimpse of the nipple-pink nose of the gigantic 707 evoked a stupendous gasp from a thousand upturned faces ... and as more and more of the towering, exotically beautiful mastodon was revealed the gasps came again and again.

Now the crowd began surging forward, drawn by the plane's startling flamboyance, stunned by the glittering beauty of its four mother-of-pearl encrusted engines, its soaring candy-striped tail section, dainty heart-shaped windows and bold heart-shaped doors.

Now the hesitant surge became a precipitated rush, an excited urgency to explore the promise of delight that lay within ... to feel, to touch, to smell, to sensuously feed upon. The crowd divided – some running for the forward stairs leading up into the open heart-shaped door; others ducking beneath the fuselage, running beneath the wings, laughing, pointing, as each surprising innovation was revealed to them – the candy-striped underwings, the sequin-encrusted engine cowlings, and the slogan 'GLAMOUR AIRLINES LOVE YOU' blazing in brilliant day-glo puce along the entire length of its underbelly.

And inside the cabin – the parade had now begun, the first people through the door so overwhelmed by the colour, the beauty, the radicality of design, that for many stunned moments no one made to move. Then, propelled by a barrage of invective from behind, they began to pass slowly down the centre aisle, open-eyed in wonderment at the galleys – designed in stainless steel and equipped with infra-red and microwave appliances – at the candy-striped walls of the fuselage, the dainty heart-and-flowers curtains framing the heart-shaped windows, the petite, grey-silk-shaded lamps replacing the normal, austere aircraft lighting.

Immediately inside the cabin, on the left – a tiny stage ... and on the right, a little way down – a gazebo-styled bar, ornate, colourful and cutely-canopied.

But it was, perhaps, the sixty specially made, deeply luxurious, white-fur-covered, armchair-snug seats with their humorous cupid-motifed safety belts that evoked most exclamations of delight. Nestling cosily, two-by-two, each pair thoughtfully separated from the next to provide not only an extravagance of leg-room but an abundance of privacy, they simply begged to be sat in, wriggled in, snuggled into – an invitation eagerly accepted by the first sixty sightseers on board.

And that was what caused the riot.

'Come on – move along, folks, you've had your turn!'

'Drop dead, Charlie.'

'Hey – you two! Come on – break it up! This ain't no hippy love-in!'

'Wanna bet, mac?'

'What's the hold-up in there? There're a thousand people back here waitin' to come through!'

'It's the bums up front – they've settled down in the seats for the night.'

'Oh, is that right – well, now we'll just see about that!'

'Come on, you people – move out an' let the others through!'

'You talkin' to me, Baldy?'

'Yeah, I'm talkin' to you!'

'Go find your own plane.'

'Listen – are you comin' outta that seat peaceful or wid a broken head?'

'I'll come out when I wanna come out – push off!'

'O.K., buddy – a broken head it is!'

Thump! Thwack! Sock! Thuck!

Screams and shouts, bellows and yells.

Intrigued by the uproar another hundred people shoved inside. And now the cops moved in. Twenty of them clattered up the exit stairs at the rear of the plane and as soon as the last one had disappeared inside, the first evicted sightseer came hurtling out, tumbled in a graceless heap down the stairs and landed with a thump at the bottom.

Only it wasn't a sightseer, it was poor old Himmler, who, having drawn back the drapes, had quickly taken up his position by the rear exit door in order to supervise the tour.

Jacket ripped and hair-piece awry, he staggered to his feet and wobbled over to meet Berskin who had heard the racket and run from the stage.

'Himmler – what the hell is goin' *on* in there?'

'Oh, it's awful, sir ... they're fighting ... fighting for the seats ... !'

'The seats? You mean they're ripping them out?'

'No – squatting, sir. The seats are so comfortable the first sixty people on board won't budge ... !'

'Bloody ridiculous! Well, what are the cops doin' about it?'

In answer, four more people came flying out of the rear door and hurtled down the stairs.

'Quick!' said Berskin, ever a man of quick decision. 'Get one of my lads up on the stage ... no! – get all *three* of 'em up there – Silver, Dart and Pocket – give this lot something else to think about ... and draw the drapes! Glamour Puss is drivin' them crazy!'

As Himmler shot off, Berskin ran to the entrance steps where ten cops were holding back a desperate crowd, clammering to get in. There were sightseers and souvenir-hunters everywhere – swarming like voracious ants over the wings, the roof, the tail section ... unscrewing screws ... chipping sequins off the engine cowlings ... carving their names on the fuselage ...

'Oh no ... no ... no!' wailed Berskin, covering his eyes in despair. 'No ... no ... not this!'

Up on stage, totally oblivious to the furore going on around Glamour Puss, Shag McGee and his merry buccaneers were thrashing themselves into a froth on the eighty-third chorus of

223

'Bilge', one of their own compositions based on an ancient Egyptian clitoral circumcision chant, and the parrot was hanging on for dear life, somewhere around Shag's left ear.

Then, suddenly – adding to this horrendous, ear-bashing cacophony (though not necessarily detracting from its entertainment value) – the hangar resounded to the shattering whoop of police sirens as into the arena swirled six car-loads of reinforcements.

And did those stalwart boys in blue have everything back to normal in ten minutes flat?

No, they did not.

It was twenty of the most horrifying minutes of Berskin's life before Glamour Puss was finally cleaned of the last of the rabble and everyone was safely back behind the closed drapes, now enraptured anew by the stultifying idiocy of that trio of boffo super-stars – Jimmy Silver, Marc Dart and Wensley Pocket.

But inside Glamour Puss – quite another story. Seats ripped ... lamps broken ... shades missing ... curtains missing ... under-seat life-jackets missing ...

'The ... misbegotten ... bastards!' seethed Berskin, fists clenched in fury and bitter disappointment. 'Ravishers ...! Rapists ... ! Despoilers of beauty ... !'

'Thank God we screwed down the floor,' observed Rossiter.

'Oh ... Colonel ... just *look* at it!' wailed Sugar. 'My beautiful cabin!'

Berskin jerked round, his mouth a thin, grim, determined slash. 'Yes, and it'll be beautiful again, Sweetman, or my name's not God Berskin! You think I'm gonna let this spoil my plans for tomorrow night – no, siree! Himmler – get Engineering over here – on the double! Check for external damage! And get on to Service – tell them I'll pay the painters, electricians and chippies *six times overtime* – but I want them here NOW! I want this baby put back in *exactly* its original condition and I want it done by six tomorrow night – got it?'

'Certainly, Colonel.'

'Right, I'll come over with you in case you get any grief.'

Exit Himmler and Berskin, leaving the crew, on board together for the first time, to cast an eye over their new home for the next seven days.

'D'you think he'll do it?' Ramjet asked Rossiter, falling into one of the new armchair seats with an expression of delight. 'Hey ... these are terrific!'

'He'll do it,' replied Rossiter, popping his head into the forward galley. 'I'll take a bet she'll be gleamin' like a new pin long before six tomorrow night. Say, he really has gone to town on this bucket. Come and take a squint at this, girls...' he said, entering the galley.

Babs and Wilma joined him at the door.

'Ohh!' squealed Babs, 'it's *enormous*!'

'That's what all the girls say,' cracked Rossiter.

'Hey – what you showin' them in there, you dirty old bugger!' called Bush.

'Ooh, it'll be a real pleasure to sweat in here, Marilyn,' enthused Babs.

'You'll sweat all right when Sam Chortle gets you in the corner with your ass up against the infra grill,' grinned Rossiter.

'*Ooh*, I say ...!' exclaimed Sugar, joining the girls. 'Isn't it *super*!'

'Come in and play with your gadgets,' said Rossiter, leaving the galley and heading for the cockpit, followed by Ramjet, James and Bush.

He pushed open the door, let out a groan and stood rooted. 'Oh my God...'

'What is it, Skip?' asked Ramjet, craning over Rossiter's shoulder.

'Let's have a decko, Skip!' pleaded Bush.

Rossiter moved into the tiny cockpit, swung a leg over the centre console and dropped into the left-hand seat, the position a captain always takes.

'My my... !' exclaimed Ramjet, following him in, squeezing himself into the right-hand seat and stretching out his long legs to the rudder pedals. 'A complete face-lift! Nipple-pink seats and cupid safety harness!'

'Yeah,' gruffed Rossiter. 'And what's the bettin' we pick up Snow-White on radar!'

225

Bush McKenzie took his Engineer's seat, immediately behind Ramjet, and cast an eye over the vast array of familiar dials and switches on the panel in front of him, feeling instantly at home, his fingers itching to move, to flick and turn. It didn't matter a damn what they did to the upholstery and seat-belts, dials would always be dials and these they wouldn't dare muck about with.

Now James took his seat – at the Navigator's table immediately behind Rossiter – and the crew was complete.

'Well, lads...' said Rossiter, giving the stabilizer fly-wheel a thump, 'here we are and here ... for seven long, completely bewildering days ... we will stay. Christ only knows where we'll end up ... Hong Kong ... Hawaii ... Honolulu ...'

'Hog's Back, Idaho...' suggested Ramjet.

'Hampstead Heath,' suggested James.

'Maybe even Hermannsburg,' put in Bush with a shudder.

'But ... wherever it may be,' continued Rossiter, his voice acquiring a noble ring, 'yes, wherever the four winds and fickle fate elect to plot our course ... let all men be assured that, come what may, we will do our duty. Come hell or high water ... tempest or storm ... epidemic or war ...'

'Coffee or tea?'

'We ... hm?' Rossiter spun round. Babs was in the doorway, holding two pots and smile of radiant accomplishment. 'Look what I've got! Coffee and tea – made in ten seconds on that new fast thingummy!'

'Splendid girl!' applauded Rossiter. 'Just what we need right now. Make mine coffee, Babs.'

'Tea, luv,' said Bush.

'Coffee, angel,' ordered Ramjet.

'Tea would be quite divine,' grinned Jim.

She ducked back into the galley and a moment later entered with four bone-china cups on a silver tray.

'My God – just look!' gasped Rossiter. 'China cups ... in a cockpit! A milestone in aviation history – I'll mark it in the log. Thank you, Scrumptious, that's just beautiful.'

The men took their cups and Babs departed.

'Well, now, things may not be so bad after all,' grinned Rossiter, preparing to sip. 'If the worst comes to the worst out there, we will lock ourselves in here, get out the cards, and luxuriate in endless cups of Boob's delicious coffee...' and then he took a sip.

Ramjet sipped.

James and Bush sipped.

And all let out a howl of dismay.

'Jeeezus ... KRIST!' bellowed Rossiter. 'What in hell is *this* ... elephant piss!'

'Can't be,' said James, shaking his head. 'That's what I've got.'

Rossiter slumped. 'Gentlemen ... how *could* I have forgotten? In Boobs and Wilma we happen to have chosen two of the worst tea an' coffee brewers in civil aviation today.'

Bush McKenzie groaned. 'Seven days of ... *this*!'

Rossiter nodded, filled with gloom. 'Seven days of this ... plus ... Gloriana Fullbrush ... Delicious O'Hara ... Lush Martino ... Sam Chortle ... and Craven Snipe ...'

'But ... also one or two others,' added James, slipping a wink to Ramjet.

'Yeah...' grinned Ramjet, tipping his cap over one eye, 'let us by no means forget the one or two others.'

Bush raised his cup with a mischievous grin. 'Gentlemen ... to the one or two others,' then he drained it, pulling an anguished face. 'Gawd, that is *awful*!'

Then all three exploded in laughter, leaving Rossiter to wonder what was so goddam funny about a lousy cup of tea.

19

Time: 7 p.m. the following evening.

Place: the VIP Lounge, Kennedy Airport.

Occasion: The pre-flight booze-up of the Glamour Airlines seven-day, round-the-world tour.

Those in attendance: Colonel Godfrey Berskin, Heinrich Himmler, the Crew, Very Important Guests, twenty representatives of the Press, twenty bewildered and extremely excited winning members of the public, Shag McGee and the group – and, of course, Marlon, the parrot.

Atmosphere: Sheer Mardi Gras – excited, boisterous, noisy and promisingly lecherous.

'I tell yuh . . .' chuckled chubby little Karl Makepiece, a pork butcher from Minnesota, addressing fluttery Miss Minnie

Wattle, a retired librarian from Boston, 'when that telephone call came through last night I just couldn't believe my luck. I thought maybe it was my neighbour, Jake Spender, playin' one of his infernal practical jokes.'

'Neither could *I*, Mister Makepiece!' fluttered Miss Wattle. 'This is the very first thing I've ever won in my life ... no, I tell a lie – I once won a book prize at school for elocution – though I don't suppose that really counts, does it ... hic! Oh, I *do* beg your pardon ... I'm afraid it's this gin – it always gives me hiccups.'

'Aw, what's a little hiccup between friends. Drink up an' have another one. Relax, Miss Wattle – you're on vacation! We're *all* on vacation! Seven beautiful days of doin' absolutely nuthin' but enjoy ourselves – an' *I* fully intend to enjoy myself. I'm just gonna sit back an' let Glamour Airlines fly me wher*ever* they want ... North Pole ... South Pole I just don't care. This is the first vacation I've had in ten years an' I'm gonna get stinko every single day!'

'Oh, Mister Makepiece,' giggled Miss Wattle.

'Say, lissen ... how about you an' me sittin' next to one another on the plane, hm? I *like* you, Miss Wattle ... you're very nice – an' I think you an' me could have a lot of fun together, whadya say?'

'I ... think I'd like that, Mister Makepiece,' she smiled coyly.

'Karl ... make it Karl, hm? We're gonna be together for a whole week an' it seems kinda crazy to go on callin' each other "Mister Makepiece" and "Miss Wattle" the whole time, whadya say? How about tellin' me your first name?'

'It's ... Minnie ... Karl.'

'Minnie ... what a lovely name. Now, whadya say to another little drink, Minnie ... ? Here – let me have your glass, I'll get it for you ...'

'Well, perhaps just a *teeny* one, Karl ... I'm afraid I'm feeling a tiny bit whoozy already ...'

'Good – it's the only way to fly.'

While in another part of the room:

'Hi.'

James turned. 'Well, hell*o* ...'

229

'I'm Billy Jo Labinovitch of the . . .'

'*Tennessee Tatler*, yes, I know.'

She raised a cute, surprised brow. 'You have an excellent memory.'

'For the things I want to remember.'

'Hm hm,' she grinned. 'Now – which one are you?'

'Navigation Officer Crighton-Padgett – at your service, ma'm . . .'

'How utterly adorable.'

'. . . but if you find that too much of a mouthful – Jim will do.'

'Jim. I like that much better. So you're the Navigation Officer . . . sounds *terribly* responsible. I suppose that means you'll be locked away in the cockpit all the time – working out where we're going and how to get there.'

James smiled disarmingly. 'Fortunately it means nothing of the kind. In fact there'll almost be nothing for me to do on this trip.'

'Oh, come on,' she laughed. 'I know Englishmen are prone to understatement but that's taking it a *bit* far . . .'

'No, truly. With the navigation equipment we've got on board these days there's really no need for a Nav any more. It's all done with mirrors – well, with radio and radar.'

Her pretty brow furrowed. 'Then . . . why are you . . . ?'

'Regulations. We must carry a Nav when we fly over big water.'

'I see. So we *will* be flying over big water?'

'I would presume so.'

'But you don't know for sure?'

'I really haven't a clue where we're heading – nobody does. At least nobody on board.'

'But . . . how will you know . . .'

'By radioed instructions,' he grinned. 'We'll be given a heading and an altitude to start off with, then new headings as the fancy takes them. Fun, hm?'

'Terrific!' she laughed. 'So . . . by tomorrow morning we could . . . anywhere!'

He nodded. 'Anywhere. Europe . . . South America . . . over the Pacific. I haven't heard what our fuel load is yet, but I imagine it'll be capacity . . .'

'What does that mean?'

'Full tanks means around 70,000 kilos – about 70 tons.'

'Seventy *tons*!' she laughed. 'Gee, an' I thought my Mustang used gas. So – how far would that take us?'

'Oh ... that's about twelve hours flying ... say ... six thousand miles.'

'Six *thousand*! So we could fly to Europe and back non-stop!'

'Yes, practically.'

'F'heaven's sakes! Well, now ... that *is* interesting.' She tilted her head and smiled coquettishly at him. 'And ... you'll be spending very little of the time in the cockpit ...?'

'Not ... overly much,' he smiled.

'Now, that's even *more* interesting ...'

'Oh? And why is that, Miss Labinovitch?'

'Oh ... I thought you might like to pay a visit to the cabin at some time and give some background about yourself ... for the paper, of course ...'

'Of course. I should be only too delighted.'

'How splendid.'

And simultaneously:

'Would you like another drink, Miss Pell?'

'Er, not just yet, Mister McKenzie. I don't drink all that much. I try to keep in good shape, you know.'

'Oh, I do know ... and I can see you succeed admirably. If I may say so, you have a bod ... I mean, a figure in a million, Miss Pell.'

Her clear blue eyes crinkled mischievously. 'Well, you're not exactly going to seed yourself, Mr. McKenzie. I ... noticed your ... physique the moment I arrived, as a matter of fact ...'

'You ... did?'

'Of course. To walk into a room and catch sight of such outstanding muscle development is a rare thing .. a rare event these days. Your *superb* deltoids quite ... took my breath away.'

'They ... did? Well, I do try, Miss Pell ...'

'And likewise all too obviously succeed, Mister McKenzie. You've no idea how delighted I am to find a man like you as

231

part of the Glamour Crew...'

'Oh?' Bush gulped.

'Oh, indeed. To be frank, I was doubtful I would find anything connected with this tour to interest my *Healthy Mind – Body Beautiful* readers – but here *you* are ... the epitome of all we stand for. Mister McKenzie ... I would very much like to concentrate on *you* during the next seven days ... get to know your habits intimately.'

'H ... habits, Miss Pell?'

'Yes – how you exercise ... what you eat ...'

'Oh ... those habits.'

'Perhaps ... even watch you work out during one of our stopovers?'

'Well, certainly. I usually try to get in an hour or two wherever we land – a bit of weight-lifting ... a sauna ... rub-down ... shower. You'd be more than welcome to join me.'

'That's very kind, Mister McKenzie ...'

'Er ... Bush.'

'Hm?'

' "Bush" – it's my nickname – on account of I used to spend all my time in the outback.'

' "Bush",' she repeated. 'I like it. It sounds so ... *virile.*'

'It does?'

'And for once what a joy it is to find the virility to match the name. Bush ... I shall look forward immensely to our ... liaison.'

And me bleedin' too, he thought.

Meanwhile:

'Ramjet ... I'm sorry, I really am. You know I wouldn't have stood you up if I could *possibly* have got away.' She raised huge, imploring eyes, begging forgiveness. And looking and smelling as wonderful as she did, what else could he possibly do but give in to her.

'Well, it's going to cost you, Delores Delores,' he grinned wickedly, arching a devilish brow.

'Cost me?' she repeated innocently. 'Cost me what, Ramjet?'

'At least one night out during the tour.'

'*One* night out? That's *terribly* lenient.'

232

'I'll think about it. It really was a very bad thing you did.'

'Awful,' she admitted, lowering her eyes contritely. 'And . . . I'm ready to take my punishment.'

'You are? No . . . matter what?'

'No matter what, Ramjet . . . I deserve *all* I'm going to get – and I leave the details *entirely* to you.'

Oh, brother . . .

While over in the corner:

'Now, don't tell me – you're Wilma, aren't you, my dear?'

'Gee, that's right, Senator . . . how nice of you to remember.'

'Nonsense,' chortled Chortle. 'Easiest thing in the world to remember the name of a pretty girl . . . an' by golly you are a pretty girl. You know, you remind me of someone an' danged if Ah can put mah finger on who.'

'A . . . film star or somebody?' she suggested, wiggling her lips magnificently.

'Well, of course, a film star!' he chuckled. 'Who *else* would a lovely creature like you remind me of?' He moved closer, driving her deeper into the corner. 'Well, now it sure pleases old Sam no end t'know you'll be lookin' after his comforts on board during this flight. Y'know, when a fella gets to be a certain age, he kinda likes a li'l fuss . . . sorta likes bein' tucked up in bed an' kissed goodnight when he gets his head down – metaphorically speakin', of *course* . . .'

'Of c . . . course,' stammered Wilma. 'Well, I'll certainly do my best to make you comfortable, Senator . . .'

'Ah'm sure you will, my dear . . . an' make no mistake about it – old Sam Chortle is not an ungenerous man. If he thinks someone has done him a big favour – why, there's no *limit* to what he can come up with in the way of a big thank you, no siree. Now, you jurst remember that, hm?'

'Yes, Senator, I certainly will.'

'Good girl. Ah just *know* Ah'm in for a mighty pleasin' trip,' he chortled. 'Yes, siree.'

And at the bar:

'Well, *hello*, sugar . . . say, you're kinda cute.'

Sweetman turned, agog. 'Why, Miss O'Hara, however did

you know my nickname?'

'Hm? Whatya mean, you're nickname, honey . . .?'

'We – ll, that's what they call me – Sugar Sweetman. My name's Michael really but all my friends call me "Sugar".'

'Oh?' Delicious's brow rose suspiciously. 'What . . . *kinda* friends, baby . . .?'

'Ooh, all sorts, Miss O'Hara . . . poets . . . dress designers . . .'

'Sugar, honey, I'll see yuh around, huh?'

'Huh,' muttered Sugar. 'What's up with *her*, then?'

*   *   *

Time: 7.30 p.m.

Place: The same.

Atmosphere: Highly cordial – pun intended.

Captain Alfred Rossiter looked at his watch and gave the nod to Ramjet who reluctantly terminated his discussion with Delores Delores regarding the gruesome details of her punishment and ambled over.

'Better get the layabouts together, Rogers and get down to Briefing.'

'*What* briefing?' Ramjet asked cynically.

Rossiter shrugged. 'Yeah. We'll let's see what they've got to say.'

Ramjet circled the room, gathering James, Bush, Sugar and the girls.

'Well, see you on board,' winked James.

'You'll see me,' promised Billy Jo.

'Well, ta-ta, luv,' said Bush, bracing his starboard biceps one last time.

'Don't stiffen up before I get there,' Tricia Pell grinned.

'Well, bye-bye, Cyril,' Sugar bade the barman. 'Take care.'

'Have a good trip, angel, see you when you get back. And *do* watch your step if you set down in Arabia.'

'Wilma, what *was* Sam Chortle saying to you?' squeaked Babs.

'Gee, Babs, I dunno about that guy . . . I think we're gonna have trouble.'

'Well, if he tries anything in the galley with *me* . . . I'll just let him have it.'

234

As the crew vacated the lounge and headed towards Briefing, Lush Martino climbed on to a table and began to croon 'Swanee', Senator Sam Chortle slid into a chair next to Delicious O'Hara and slid his hand on to her knee, Craven Snipe was scouring the room for his next insult victim, Gloriana was deciding which of her three bulls would share her first night favours, Karl Makepiece was handing Miss Wattle her third gin-and-gin of the evening, and *everyone* was having a truly lovely time.

Time: 8 p.m.

With Captain Alfred Rossiter proudly in the lead, the crew exited the Departure building and crossed the short expanse of tarmac to where the once-more-beautiful Glamour Puss stood tall and powerful in the airfield lights.

Mounting the forward stairs and entering the cabin, Rossiter walked slowly down the centre aisle, followed by the others, marvelling at the magnificent job of renovation accomplished throughout the day by the army of painters, electricians and chippies on six times overtime.

'Great ... just great,' enthused Rossiter. 'Ain't it amazing what money can do. O.K. Sweetman ... girls, she's all yours. We're starting the pre-start check right away – take-off at nine. Come on, you guys. Bush – go walk around outside.'

'Right-ho, Skip.'

While Rossiter, Ramjet and James settled themselves in the cockpit, Bush, as Engineer, had an external check of the plane to make. And so, collecting his check-list from the cockpit, he descended the forward stairs to the apron and began his 'walk around', starting with the forward fuselage.

'Pitot mast ... OK. – cover removed,' he muttered to himself, thinking a little bit about the pitot cover but mostly about Miss Tricia Pell. 'Radome ... O.K. Nose gear and ground lock ... O.K. – cover removed ...'

Ho ho, Miss Pell ... you're in for hell ... if I ever get you naked in the sau ... na!

'Steering disconnect pin and cable ... connected. Torque links, strut inflation ... O.K. Nose wheels and tyres ... inflation O.K....'

235

'Pssssst!'

'Eh...? Now where did that come from ... we've got a leak somewhere...'

'PSSSSSSTTTT!!'

'Jesus, now ain't *that* a bitch – we gotta leak!'

'Bush McKenzie...!'

Bush shot round, peered beyond the nose-gear. It was a mechanic, dressed in white overalls, beckoning to him. Bush moved round the gear and approached him. 'What's up, mate, I'm on pre-flight...'

'Hi.'

Bush staggered back against the gear. Blimey ... it was a sheila ... a bird ... a girl! And a real good-looker – despite the dirty overlarge overalls.

'Who are you!' he gaped. 'What you doin' out here?'

'Ssssh!' she chuckled. 'I've come to see you.'

'Me? Are you crazy? How'd you get past Security?'

'My father's a mechanic ... I borrowed his overalls.'

'Well, I'll be buggered. But ... what do you want with *me?*'

She smiled impishly. 'I saw your picture in the papers and ... thought you were really something. I just had to come out and say hello – or rather goodbye. You'll be off in an hour, hm?'

'Yes! Look ... luv. I'm supposed to be doin' my pre-flight now – not talkin' to you ...'

She shrugged. 'Go ahead, do it – I'll walk around with you.'

'You'll ... look, sweetheart...'

'Beth. Beth Chantry.'

'Look, Beth, it's very nice of you to pop out and say goodbye but I can't have you walkin' around with me while I'm doin' the...'

'Why not? I'll help.'

'Help! Good God, the skipper would have my throttle for a thrust lever...'

'He won't know, will he? If anyone comes down, I'll slope off like I was a mechanic.'

'Aw, Beth...!'

'Come on – where were you up to?'

'Er ... I ... I'd just checked the nose wheel and tyres ...'

'Right.' She ducked her head under the fuselage. 'Next ... nose gear inspection window ... clean. Nose wheel brake pads ... O.K. ...'

'Here ...!' Bush gaped. 'How the 'ell do you know what's ...'

'I told you – my father's a mechanic. Right ... nose gear drag brace ... removed. Ground pressurization cap and test points ... secure and wire locked.'

'All right ... all right,' laughed Bush. 'You probably know more than I do. O.K., you can stick around but *I'm* doin' the checks.'

'O.K.' She shrugged. 'Carry on ... nose gear doors ...'

'I *know* what's next,' he grinned. 'By golly, I've never met a bird like you before ...'

'Would you ... like to meet one again? Say – when you get back?'

'I'd love to,' he laughed, 'providing we ever get away! Now, will you just keep quiet and let me get on with this?'

'Sure. Who's stopping you?'.

Meanwhile, upstairs in the cockpit, Cock-up and Ramjet were beginning their own engine pre-start check, while James was messing about with charts and things trying to look busy, his mind fully occupied with thoughts of Billy Jo Labinovich.

'O.K., here we go,' said Rossiter, 'Radio buses ...'

Ramjet reached up into the roof and flicked on the master switches. 'One and two ON, Skip.'

'Flight recorder ...'

'Tested ... guard closed.'

'Anti-skid ...'

'Off – four black tabs showing.'

'Spoiler bypasses ...'

'Guard closed.'

'Doppler ...'

And so on and so on ...

There are twenty-nine such points to be checked between captain and co-pilot before the Engineer is required on board; without his presence the checking of the remaining twenty-eight points of the 'Engine Pre-start check' cannot be accomplished.

Some fifteen minutes passed and Rossiter and Ramjet were nearing the end of their duet.

'Warning horn . . .' recited Rossiter.

A-HOOOO-HAAAA

'Checked,' said Ramjet, somewhat unnecessarily.

'Stabilizer trim . . .'

Ramjet ran through the test. 'Checked, Cutout normal. Brake off.'

'Aileron Trim . . .' Rossiter turned and glanced back through the open cockpit door. 'No sign of Bush yet?'

'Er, no, Skip . . .' replied James, jerking out of disgusting reverie. 'Still walking around.'

'O.K. . . . Aileron trim . . .'

'Checked and set.'

'And . . . Flap indicator . . .'

'Zero. Pre-flight check completed.'

'O.K., you guys, relax.'

Jim relaxed.

Meanwhile . . . down below:

'Wow . . . !' she gasped, breaking away. 'My God, Bush McKenzie . . .'

'What's the matter, pigeon?'

'What's the *matter*! Geez, you've gotta kiss like a fuel pump!'

'You complainin'?' he grinned.

'Complainin'? Come here . . . I'll show you what a *boost* pump feels like!'

While over in the terminal:

'Aw, come on, Colonel . . . open those doors an' let's get on board . . . !'

Berskin held up his hands, 'Please . . . bear with us for just a few minutes longer. I realize you're all terribly anxious to get out there and begin your flight but the crew aren't quite ready to receive you yet. Rest assured, we'll get you aboard just as soon as we can.' Side-mouthed to Himmler he muttered, 'What's holdin' them up out there? If we don't open these doors soon we'll have a riot on our hands. What's the time, Himmler...?'

'Er ... eight-twenty-five, sir.'

'Aw, hell they must be finished with the checks by now. Hell, I'm gonna let them go.'

'Yes, sir.'

'Open the doors, Himmler...'

Himmler did so. 'Ladies and gentlemen ... this way if you please...!'

'YYYIIIPPPEEEEEE!!' yipped Lush Martino. – 'All aboard Glamour Booze...!'

And simultaneously, out on the tarmac:

'Beth, will you cut that *out*! I'm not half-way through the check-list yet...'

'Screw the check-list, I *want* you, McKenzie!'

'Beth ... get your hand *out* of there! Oh, Jesus ... ACU ram air inlets ... clear. ACU access doors secure. ACU turbo fan exits ... cl ... ear! Beth, let *go* of me! ACU ram air exit doors closed. Now ... the right wing ... Beth, will you please go home! We're takin' off in thirty minutes and ... oh! ... Oh, that's beautiful...! but, Beth ... oh, Lord luv us, that is fantastic...!'

And up above:

'Where in hell is that bloody McKenzie!' bellowed Rossiter. 'Jesus wept, he's had enough time to change a bloody engine!'

And in the cabin:

'I'm ... for ever ... blowing ... bubbles ...' sang Babs, going cheerfully about her tasks.

'Coo ... lucky old Bubbles,' teased Sugar, taking a glance out of a port window and coming to an abrupt, horror-stricken halt. 'Oh my God...! Girls...! Here come the passengers! Now, who let them out without tellin' us? Oh, they all look as pissed as a-holes! All right, loves, well do your best. I've got vibrations about this lot, I can tell you, and they're not at all pretty ... Babs, angel – take the forward door ... Wilma – get the back end – and may the Lord have mercy on our poor old souls. Oh, Gawd, just look at them . . . !'

While down below:

Bush stopped, rigid, at the 'Q' inlet duct and let out an appalled, 'Oh Jesus . . .'

'What's the matter?'

'Beth . . . it's the bleedin' passengers! They're comin' aboard!'

'Oh, Bush . . .'

'Go on, beat it! Scram! Hell's bells, I'm late! The skipper will be goin' potty!'

'Goodbye, lover . . .'

'Goodbye . . . go . . . quick!'

'One last kiss . . .'

'BETH!!'

'See you when you get back?'

'Yes . . . yes . . . but go . . . GO!'

She went.

'Oh, bloody hell . . . navigation lights . . . O.K. Now – left wing . . .' He raced under the fuselage, groaning, 'Women . . . why do they have to show up at the wrong bloody time . . . hydraulic oil tank . . . sight glass covered, cap secure. Main gear and ground lock . . . O.K. . . . lock removed. Torque links . . . strut inflation . . . of all the bloody times . . . a mechanic's daughter! Snubber and levelling cylinder . . . O.K. pressure normal. Jesus, I wish mine was . . .'

Cockpit:

'This is bloody *ridiculous*!' stormed Rossiter, peering at the clock. 'Hell, I'm going to find him!'

Leaping over the centre console, he barged through the cockpit door, turned right and came to an astounded halt at the external door. 'Oh . . . NO!'

'What's the matter, Skip?' called James.

'They've let the bloody passengers loose! They're *here* – coming up the stairs!'

'Hi, there, Captain!' Karl Makepiece called up, helping a weaving Miss Wattle up the steps.

'Wh . . . who said you could come on board!' demanded

Rossiter. 'Jesus *Christ*, what's goin' on around here . . . ?'

'Tt-tt, Captain,' admonished Miss Wattle, wagging an unstable finger at him. 'Watch your language, please . . . and kindly excuse me . . .'

She pushed past him, flattening him against the wall, then spotted James and Ramjet in the cockpit and gave them a little wave. 'Good evening, gentlemen . . . lovely night for flying, isn't it?'

'Lovely,' they agreed.

'An' you oughta know,' growled Rossiter.

Stymied by the ascending crush of passengers, he had no alternative but to fight his way back into the cockpit, which he did, slamming the door.

'What in holy hell is goin' *on* around here! My engineer is missing . . . the passengers come aboard without my say-so! Has everybody gone stark, raving mad . . . !'

'Er, without appearing unduly pessimistic, Skip,' offered James, 'does anyone else get the feeling that this could well be the harbinger of things to come . . . ?'

'Oh . . . shut up!' rapped Rossiter – and opened the door again. 'Bedlam! One hundred per cent, unadulterated, five-star CHAOS!'

He was not wrong.

The cabin was a nightmare of clutter and noises. To Rossiter's mind it was totally unreasonable that only fifty people could *make* so much racket. Sam Chortle was chortling, Lush Martino was crooning, Babs Buchanan was squeaking and everybody was shouting something to somebody – and Sugar was having a quiet nervous breakdown.

'Madam . . . do you *mind*! Now, you can't *possibly* get that hatbox in the luggage rack, it really should have gone in the hold, you know . . . sir . . . sir! watch that umbrella, for heaven's sake – you nearly did Miss Buchanan a mischief! . . . no, madam, the bar *isn't* open – not until we're airborne . . . now can we have you *all* seated, *please*! Ooh, honestly, you may as well talk to yourself . . sir – no smoking, you can see the sign's on, can't you . . . no, madam, I *don't* know if we touch Iceland . . . we certainly won't if I've got anythin' to bleedin' do with it, I'll tell you . . . now, where's *she* goin'!'

Clamping his hands over his ears, Rossiter once more

braved the outside world and headed for the external door –
only to be driven back yet again by Shag McGee and the group
thumping up the stairs with a thousand kilos of equipment.

'Oh ... NO! !' whimpered Rossiter, backing into the forward galley.

'OUT! !' commanded a voice behind him.

Rossiter shot round, coming face-to-face with a little fat,
moustachioed chef brandishing a cleaver.

'Eh?'

'OUT! – of my kitchen!'

'I ... wh ...' spluttered Rossiter. 'I'm the BLOODY
CAPTAIN!'

'I don't care if you are ze Sultan of Baghdad! Zis is *my*
kitchen – OUT!'

'AAAAAAAAHHHHH! !' wailed Rossiter, stepping backwards through the curtain and smashing into Shag McGee.

'Hey, easy, man – watch the parrot, huh? Stanley, push the
drums through ... right, now jiggle that amp round here...'

While somewhere underneath:

'Crew oxygen blow-out disc ... intact. Holy Cow, he'll be
havin' a flamin' baby! Static vents ... clear. Toilet service
panel ... cover closed. Well, thank God for that. Now ... to
get on board!'

Bush ran round to the forward stairs and raced up them,
meeting Rossiter racing down.

'McKenzie ... !'

'Oh, hi there, Skip ...'

'Where the fucking hell have you been – Tasmania!'

'Er, no, Skip ... I, er, had a bit of trouble with the ...
thingy ...'

'The ... thingy,' nodded Rossiter. 'Strangely, McKenzie, I
do not recall a "thingy" on the check-list.'

'I mean the er ... rear toilet service panel ... the cover
wouldn't close properly ...'

'I see ... but you managed to get it closed?'

'Oh yes – eventually, Skip.'

'Splendid! We wouldn't want any *more* shit flyin' around
here than there already is, would we? Now, McKenzie ...

would you *kindly* get on board so we can get this fucking ill-fated heap off the *ground*!'

'Yes, Skip ... certainly, Skip ...'

They ran back up the stairs and fought their way over a mountain of guitar cases, amplifiers, drums and cymbals to the cockpit passageway.

'Holy ... mayhem!' gasped McKenzie, glancing down the aisle.

'And they say music hath charms to sooth the savage breast!' seethed Rossiter, booting a cymbal out of the way.

'Oh, Captain ... excuse me, Captain ...!' Sugar came panting through the crowd.

'Yes, Sweetman, what is it?'

'They're all asking me what time we'll be taking off. When shall I tell them?'

'Tell them, Sweetman, that the way things are goin' we'll be calling for taxi clearance just before Labour Day week-end!'

'But ... that's a month from now ...'

'Right!' bellowed Rossiter and slammed into the cockpit. Bush followed and closed the door, exchanging raised brows with James and Ramjet, and slid sheepishly into his seat.

'*Now*, gentlemen ...' snapped Rossiter, in a tone of barely concealed dimentia. 'Now that Mister McKenzie has finally decided to favour us with his presence – may we proceed with the check-list? Gear locks and covers ...!'

'Aboard,' gulped Bush.

'Hydraulics ...' he rapped into his boom-mike.

Ground control answered in Rossiter's earphones. 'Clearance to pressurize!' and Bush went into action.

'Library and cert. file ...'

'Checked and stowed,' chorused Ramjet and Bush.

'Oxygen ...'

Everyone had a go this time. 'On. Checked and a hundred per cent. Goggles checked.'

'All C/Bs ...'

'In.' Bush's voice cracked.

'Fire shut-off's ...'

'Full forward,' Bush replied.

'Fire test ...'

BRRRRRRRNNNNGGGG!! went the bell and the cockpit door flew open. A bald head with a happy, motherless face peered in. 'Shomebody rang . . . ?'

'*Jesus*!' screamed Rossiter. 'McKenzie – shut that bloody door and lock it!'

'Hi, fellas,' grinned the little guy. 'Now, don't you mind me – you just go ahead an' wind this thing up. Shay, where d'you put the key in . . .'

'Sir . . .' pleaded McKenzie, closing the door on the guy's head. 'Sir, would you mind takin' your head outta the . . .'

'Jumpin' Jupiter – jus' *look* at all them clocks . . .'

Then another face appeared in the crack, mean, pinch-nosed. 'What you found in there, Clem . . . is somethin' goin' on?'

'No, they're just sittin' here, Ella . . .'

'Lemme in there, Clem – I wanna take a snapshot!'

'AAAAAAAHHHHHH!!!' Rossiter flew out of his seat, leaped over the console, caught his toe on the aileron trim and crashed to the floor at Clem's feet.

'What's goin' on . . . what's happenin', Clem?' demanded Ella.

'The captain's fallen down, Ella.'

'Why – is he drunk or somethin'?'

'Looks kinda like it . . .'

'I AM NOT DRUNK!' howled Rossiter, beating his fist on the floor. 'I . . . AM . . . NOT . . . DRUNK!'

'Ye Gods, he's goin' crazy!' gasped Clem – and Ella was away down the aisle like a shot.

'Hey, everybody . . . the captain's goin' crazy in there! He's lyin' on the floor, beatin' at it with his fists! Clem reckons he's *loaded* . . . !'

'Oh Christ!' gasped McKenzie, his head round the door. 'Skip . . . she's runnin' through the plane tellin' everybody you're pissed!'

'WWWHHHAAATTT!!'

Rossiter shot to his feet, wrenched the door open, hurled Clem to one side and stormed down the aisle. 'Now, listen to me, everybody . . .'

'My God, he *is* crazy . . . !'

'He's shickered all right – just look at his eyes!'

'Everybody . . . QUIET!'

Everything stopped.

'Now, will everybody *please* take their seats and maintain a semblance of good order until we take off! The crew and I are *trying* to get this plane ready for flight and we're gettin' nowhere very fast – what with people bargin' into the cockpit an' makin' so much noise we can't think straight! Now, there'll be plenty of time for jollies once we get up aloft, but until we do – please settle down and let us get on with our job!'

'Hear hear!' responded Lush Martino who was esconced behind the bar, waiting for the off.

'What a *nice* man,' commented Miss Wattle, breaking into applause.

'Three cheers for the captain!' called someone else and those assembled cheered him to the echo.

'Thank you,' said Rossiter stiffly and turned quickly, trampling Shag McGee into the ground.

'*Hey*, man . . . that's number two! You tryin' to kill me?'

Astute, reflected Rossiter.

'Listen, you fellas,' he said to the group, 'make sure all that equipment is good an' secure. I don't want those ten-ton amplifiers flyin' around the cabin if we hit turbulence.'

'You gotta safety belt for Marlon,' enquired McGee.

'Stick him in the bass drum,' suggested Rossiter.

'Hey, that's not a bad idea.'

Rossiter pushed past McGee and strode back up the aisle, slowing as he reached the forward galley.

'Chef . . . get everything secure for take-off.'

'Keptain – please do not give me orders in *my* kitchen! Do I tell you how to fly zis airplane?'

'Chef – if you don't do as you're damned well told, you'll be wavin' us goodbye from the tarmac! Now – batten down and belt up!'

Rossiter flung out of the galley and slammed into the cockpit, firmly locking the door behind him.

'Maniacs – every goddam one of them! And watch out for that Bolshie chef – he's a mite too quick on the draw with that cleaver to suit me.'

He flopped down once more into his seat and crammed the earphones over his head, weary unto death.

'O.K. . . . now, where in hell were we . . . ?'

245

'Fire test, Skip,' answered Bush.

'Well, don't ring that bloody bell again, f'Crissake! O.K. – PSU fan...'

'As required.'

'Flowmeter Power...'

'Normal.'

'Electrical panel...'

'Checked. Battery on.'

'Wing anti-ice...'

'Off. Lights checked.'

'Engine anti-ice...'

And so on ... and so on.

While in the cabin:

'Look, *will* you chaps stop fooling around with that equipment and take your *seats*!' demanded Sugar, really getting his paddy up. 'I've got work to do, you know, and I can't get on with it until you're all strapped in!'

'Just give us five, man,' begged Shag. 'We gotta get it hooked up an' tested.'

'Well, just five minutes and not a second more. And, listen – keep that parrot under control. I don't want that thing flyin' around *my* cabin an' poopin' all over the place.'

'He can't help it,' protested McGee, feeding Marlon a grape. 'It's natural.'

'It's bleedin' filthy – you ought to fit him with trousers or something...'

As if in protest – or maybe he'd get the grape stuck in his throat – Marlon let out a hideous squawk and struck at Sugar's pointing finger.

'OW! Here – that thing's *vicious*! Right – that does it, McGee. If it so much as sets a foot off this stage, I'll flush the bloody thing down the loo, I promise you! Now, hurry up and plug that lot in and get sat down. Honestly...!'

And over in the terminal:

'Just look at that crowd up on the waving bay, Himmler. By... golly, what a turn-out! Must be five thousand people up there. Well, no doubt about it – the launch has been a super-boffo success.'

'Indeed it has, sir ... indeed it has.'

'Yes, sir ... by the time Glamour Puss gets back a week tonight we'll have more bookings than PanAm and TWA ever dreamed of. The next step is to enlarge the fleet, Himmler. I want to see *forty* of those beauties sittin' out there ... hey! – they're pulling the steps away and closing the doors now! Guess it won't be long, huh? Everything ready up top ... the band, TV cameras ... ?'

'Everything is ready, sir.'

'Great. Well, let's go on up. This is a moment to be proud of, Himmler ... any time now that beautiful bird out there will go thundering down the runway and lift gracefully into the air, proclaiming to the world that GLAMOUR AIR-LINES is launched. Who knows how many people ... how many potential *customers*, coast-to-coast ... will see the lift-off? By heaven, Himmler, I'm beginnin' to wonder if forty 707s is gonna be enough ...'

Cockpit:

The engine pre-start check was now complete and start clearance had been obtained from the tower.

At this point, Rossiter anticipated information that would give them a clue as to their destination, but none was forth-coming. All that he'd been given were bare essentials for take-off – weather conditions, wind velocity, temperature, the num-ber of the departure runway, a heading of zero degrees, and had been told to attain a height of five thousand feet, expect-ing thirty-five thousand.

'Zero heading!' exclaimed James. 'They're sending us to Baffin Island!'

'How's the night-life on Baffin?' enquired Ramjet.

'Plenty of birds,' answered Bush. 'Penguins ... seagulls ...'

'You fellas mind if we start the engines?' asked Rossiter.

'Not at all – go right ahead,' said Jim.

Rossiter curled his lip. 'Hello, Ground ... the doors were shut at nine-ten ... we would like ground clearance, please.'

Ground responded, 'Chocks in position, fire guards posted ... all engines clear ... gear locks and covers aboard. Clear to start 3.4.2.1 ... pressurizing the manifold now. Beacon rotat-ing.'

'Thank you, Ground. Aux pumps ...'

'Both on,' replied Bush.

'Thrust levers are ... idle. Door-warning lights ... out. Starting three, Ground ...'

'Clear three ... rotating.'

'Green light,' said Bush.

Distantly they heard the slow building whine of number three engine, the whine becoming a rumbling roar as the colossal Rolls-Royce power unit expoded into life.

'Three alight,' announced Rossiter. 'Stand-by four ...'

Now with the four engines alight and ground vehicles removed, Rossiter call up Sugar on the P.A. for his pre-taxi cabin check.

Sugar came on. 'Cabin pre-taxi check complete, Captain, but heaven *knows* how we've got it done! Ooh, we are goin' to have some trouble with this lot. I've been *mauled* by that parrot and I've only just got that McGee creature into his seat.'

'I told him to stick that goddam parrot in the bass drum!' snapped Rossiter.

'Yes, he's done that – but my finger's *ever* so sore. Well, never mind, we'll cope somehow – off you go.'

'Thanks a lot, Sweetman,' growled Rossiter.

He cut into the tower, requesting taxi clearance and got it.

And at last Glamour Puss began to roll.

20

And high up on the waving bay:

'There she goes, Himmler ... by God, what a wonderful sight. Is the band ready for the take-off?'

'All set to go the moment it starts down the runway, sir.'

'Splendid ... splendid. Just *look* at the TV coverage we're getting, Himmler. How many viewers would you say ... fifty million ... a hundred million ... ?'

'Nearer a hundred I'd say, sir.'

'A hundred ... million ... people ... about to see history made. By heaven, Himmler ... I feel quite choked.'

'Sir ... ! Glamour Puss has reached the beginning of the runway ... ! It's ... any moment now, sir ...'

'Oh, the excitement of it ... the excitement!'

'The thrill of a lifetime, Colonel.'

Cockpit:

Rossiter looked round. 'Everybody set?'

'All set, Skip.'

Rossiter's horny hand reached out to the console and gripped the four throttle controls. 'Well, here we go ... it's too damn late to get off now.' And he began to ease the throttle levers forward.

Slowly the monster jet began to move ... inching forwards ... now beginning to pick up speed ... ten knots ... twenty ... thirty ... and Glamour Puss was on her way.

Waving Bay:

'There she goes!' cried Berskin. 'My *God*, what a beautiful sight! Go on, baby ... do your stuff! Carry the glad tidings that Glamour is launched to the far ends of the...'

The bandleader lowered her baton and Berskin's words were lost as the Weehawken Women's Brass Ensemble crashed into a gay selection from 'Glamorous Nights'.

The huge crowd erupted in a heartfelt cheer ... the cameras turned ... and a tear of joy trickled down Berskin's cheek and dribbled down his tie.

'Oh, Himmler...!' he cried, 'I'm so happy... so *happy* ...!'

Cockpit:

Fifty knots ... sixty ... seventy ... and nothing could stop them now. The runway hurtled beneath them as fast as the adrenaline coursing through their veins. Up ... up ... and away ... only ten more seconds to V-One and then they were committed to the air.

Nine ... eight ... seven ... six ... five ... four ...

And with three seconds to go it happened.

THUMP...! THUMP ...! THUMP...! on the cockpit door and Sugar's demented wail over the P.A.

'Captain ... Captain! The cabin's full of smoke! We're on fire ... we're on FIRE!'

Even before the final words of Sugar's awful warning were spoken, Rossiter's command was on his lips.

'ABANDON ... ABANDON!'

'SPOILERS ...!'

250

'FULL REVERSE ... !'

'WHEEL BRAKES ... !'

The monstrous, hurtling mammoth roared and snarled in protest as every available braking aid was hurled against its thundering thrust. But now the gargantuan power of the four great engines was blasting in reverse, lopping off the knots, choking down the behemoth's onward rush, and with precious little runway left, Glamour Puss came to a shuddering, swerving stop, surrounded by a legion of howling fire-tenders.

Sweat streaming from his face from the exertion of standing on the brakes, Rossiter leapt from his seat and yanked open the cockpit door, finding Sugar on the threshold, white and trembling, the cabin beyond breathtakingly clear of smoke.

Rossiter gaped – at the cabin ... at Sugar. 'W ... wh ... wha ... well, where's the fire?'

Sugar's face creased in anguish. 'Captain ... you're going to *hate* me ...'

'I'm ... I ...' Rossiter swallowed hard. 'Sweetman ... where ... *is* ... the goddam *smoke*!'

Sugar gulped. 'It's ... gone.'

'Gone! Gone *where*?'

'Out ... through the air conditioning.'

Rossiter opened and shut his mouth three times. 'But ... wh ... what ... how ...'

'Captain, I thought the entire *cabin* was on fire. The smoke ... *honestly* ... it was *awful* ... I couldn't see ...'

'But what *caused* it, Sweetman! A galley fire ... *what*, man?'

Sweetman was shaking his head, very miserably. 'No ... it was ... one of the group's amplifiers ... they'd connected it up all wrong.'

'Th ... they ... *them*!' howled Rossiter. 'That ... Godal-bloody-*mighty*!' He flung out an arm. 'Just listen to those sirens, Sweetman ... eight hundred bloody fire-trucks out there ... the *whole* of Kennedy on full emergency stand-by ... *we've* abandoned take-off, Sweetman, and are fouling up one entire international runway ... and up on the waving bay the TV cameras are turning ... millions and millions of people are watching this fiasco, Sweetman ... have just seen the Grand Launch of Glamour Airlines take a nose-dive into ignominy!

251

And now we've got to crawl back to the beginning of the runway with our tail between our legs and start all over again! What *fun*! Sweetman ... get those bloody amplifiers disconnected and *keep* them disconnected until McKenzie can get back there and hook them up properly! And keep that goddam group strapped in their seats until we are at thirty-thousand feet – *got it*?'

'Y ... yes, Skip,' whimpered Sugar.

'Jesus ... *Christ*, what a bloody fiasco!'

Beside himself with rage, he turned into the tiny passageway leading to the external door and pushed the door open. Down below, the tarmac was a miasma of flashing lights, wailing sirens and frenzied coming and going.

Rossiter threw up his hand as a blinding spotlight struck him in the face, and in the next instant something else struck him.

Over-excited and temporarily unhinged by this, his very first real emergency, Fireman (Junior Grade) Willis P. Friendly opened the nozzle of a high-powered foam hose and let Rossiter have it, plumb in the heart.

'AAAAAHHHHHHHH!!' yelled Cock-up, driven back inside the plane, drenched, covered ... now buried in the stuff – and still it poured in ... blossoming ... ballooning ... now changing direction and moving into the aisle.

'GEMME OUT ... ! GEMME OUT ... !' Rossiter was yelling, coughing, spitting, choking. 'SOMEBODY STOP THAT BLOODY IDIOT! ROGERS ...! MCKENZIE...! STOP THAT FOAM...!

James and Bush ran from the cockpit, straight into the jet of foam still pouring through the open doorway. By now it was shoulder high and filling the tiny aisle. While Jim took a header down below to find Rossiter, McKenzie fought his way to the door and bellowed, TURN IT OFF, YOU FUCKING GREAT IDIOT! TURN IT OFF! ... STOP! ... DESIST!' and finally whipped off his boot and hurled it with all his might at the frozen, mortified, gaping figure of Willis P. Friendly.

While on the waving bay:
'Colonel ... Colonel ... speak to me ... speak to me!'

But Godfrey Berskin, head-down over the handrail, merely continued to mutter incoherently ... babble insanely while staring into nothingness, shaking his head like a broken doll.

'No, it didn't ... it couldn't ... he wouldn't ... they can't ... here, Glamour Pussy ... there's a good pussy ... wanna fly, pussy ... off you go, pussy ... pussies don't fly ... pussies stay on the ground ... right here on the ground ... pussy's never gonna fly ...'

'Colonel ... *please* – it's me, Himmler ... speak to me! Will someone get a doctor ... will someone *please* get a doctor!'

'... here, pussy pussy – you lousy, stinkin' fat-assed, club-footed bitch! Oh why, oh why didn't you fly, oh, fly ...? All those people ... all those millions ... and millions ... and millions ...'

'Colonel – *listen* to me! This could have worked out for the best! Think of the *publicity* ... think of how much more *attention* this is gonna get than an ordinary, routine take-off ...'

'Here, pussy pussy ... come to Uncle Godfrey. Here, pussy pussy ... pissy pussy ... pasty pansy ... potty putty ... cosy posy ... shitty kitty ... you rat-faced bag! Oh, Himmler ... *Himm*ler ... !'

Poor, poor Berskin.

But he was wrong. Pussies do fly; and pussy did fly.

An hour later:

Cleared of foam and cleared by tower, she thundered down the runway in a spirit of regenerated pride, as though determined to eradicate the ignominy of her shameful debut and restore the faith of her countless well-wishers.

Into the air she rose, wings back, chest out, a thing of beauty, power and grace, climbing with careless ease to five thousand feet, her pretty pink nose pointing towards the northern pole.

'Well ... we made it,' sighed Rossiter, flicking off the 'seat belts' and 'no smoking' signs and relaxing in his seat. 'Though where in hell we're headin' Berskin-only knows. O.K., Jim – take a look at the cabin an' see what's goin' on.'

'Roger, Skip.'

James unshackled his straps and opened the door, grinning at the sight confronting him, observing: Lush Martino (who had charge of the bar) dispensing drinks faster than a 747 dumps fuel; Gloriana Fullbrush playing eenie-meenie-mynee-mo with her three young studs; Senator Sam Chortle peering cross-eyed with delight down Bab's boobs as she bent to serve him; a *laughing* Craven Snipe – settling down to intimately interview Delicious O'Hara; Karl Makepiece – jigging around with little Minnie Wattle to the taped cabin music; Stanley, the drummer – thumping the bass drum into tune and the forgotten Marlon staggering from the drum like a hung-over drunk; Shag McGee – picking at his guitar and his nose simultaneously; Sugar Sweetman – receiving a sly but not unwelcome goose from the passing chef ... and *everybody* – nose-down on the starting blocks, preparing for a thorough going, ten-star, no-holds-barred, inaugural rave-up.

James turned to Rossiter and yelled, 'Well, Skip, they're ...'

'Yuh don't have to tell me, Crighton-Padgett – I can hear it!' bellowed Rossiter. 'Holy ... *doppler*, what a racket! Shut the door, Jim!'

James did so, plunging the cockpit into comparative silence, then disconsolately resumed his seat, exchanging a forlorn grimace with Bush McKenzie who responded with a despondent shrug.

'Thirty-five thousand, Skip,' Ramjet announced, turning his head to catch the exchange between Jim and Bush, and contributing to it with his own 'what-the-hell-are-we-doin'-in-here-when-all-the-action's-out-there' grimace.

'Thirty-five thousand,' acknowledged Rossiter ... and the cockpit sank into dismal, droning gloom.

On ... and on ... and on ... into the clear, cold nothingness of night. For more than thirty long minutes not a word was spoken, each man lost in his own thoughts, frustrations, desires – tantalized by the faint sounds of unbridled hilarity seeping now and then from beyond the cockpit door.

And then ...

Rossiter suddenly jerked forward in his seat and sat hunched in listening attitude ... and a moment later, in a tone of cheerful relief, he replied, 'Roger, Boston ... this is GA 427. We are turning right to oh ... six ... four degrees and maintaining three-five thousand...'

Now the cockpit came excitedly alive.

Ramjet turned to Rossiter. 'Oh-six-four! Skip – we're headin' for Europe!'

Rossiter nodded. 'Looks kinda like it.'

'London!' exclaimed Jim.

'Paris!' laughed Bush.

'Rome!' grinned Ramjet.

'Could be ... could be,' smiled Rossiter, relieved at last to be heading *some*where. 'O.K., Ramjet – let's put her in auto an' let someone else take care of baby.'

'Ro-*ger*, Skip!'

'Auto ... on,' announced Rossiter.

And then ... silence.

James shot a glance at Bush; Ramjet slipped a frown to Jim; then with a mischievous grin Rossiter spun round on them. 'Well, what in hell are you guys sittin' *there* for? You think you're bein' hired to *fly* this crate? Get back to that cabin an' start doin' what you're bein' paid to do – be Glamorous! An' tell the folks we're headin' for Europe while you're at it ...'

There was a stampede through the door, James beating the others by a short head, Ramjet slamming the door closed behind him, leaving Rossiter muttering to himself. 'Well ... it sure beats the heck out of boring old know-where-you're-goin' flying. Boy ... oh boy, what a cockamamie week this is gonna be ...'

Suddenly the door burst open and Sugar popped his head through. 'Aah, shame – all by yourself, Skip?'

'No, Sweetman – as you can plainly see, I'm sittin' here with the New York Philharmonic orchestra. How're things goin' back there?'

'Oh, they're having an absolute *ball*, Captain. Can't you put this into auto-thingy and join us?'

'It is *in* auto-thingy, Sweetman and, yes, I may slip back later on an' join in a chorus or two, but not just yet.'

'Oh, *su*-per! Anything I can get you in the meantime – a nice cup of tea, perhaps?'

'Sweetman, you are kindness itself.'

'Think nothing of it. We must all abide by our new motto, mustn't we?'

'And what motto is that, Sweetman?'

'Why – Glamour Airlines Love You!'

'Oh ... yeah,' winced Rossiter. 'Sweetman ... go get the tea ...'

'No sooner said than done, my Captain. One hot, strong cup of Rosie Lee coming up – just the way you like it – with two super big lumps of ... EEEEEEEKKKKKK!!'

Something shot over Sugar's head and smashed into the windscreen, clattered all over the controls, took off into Rossiter's face, flew three times round the cockpit and finally came to wobbly rest, standing on one leg on the centre console.

'SSWWEETTMMAANNNN!!' roared Rossiter. 'GET THIS BLOODY PARROT OUTTA MY *COCKPIT*! JESUSKRIST – HAVE I GOTTA PUT UP WITH THIS GODDAM BIRD FOR A WHOLE GODDAM WEEK!!'

The parrot cocked its head on one side, stared Rossiter straight in the eye ... and crapped all over the radar screen.

'AAAAAHHHH!!' seethed Rossiter, leaping out of his seat, 'Right – that *does* it! Sweetman ... *you* stay in here an' fly this bloody thing ... I'*m* gonna get drunk!'

Sweetman gaped at the slamming door, then rounded on the parrot. '*Now* see what you've done! And what have you got to say about *that*, you cross-eyed mess?'

'Shag McGee ... Shag McGee!' squawked the parrot – and bit him on the thumb.